# PRAISE FOR THE NOVELS
## OF PATRICIA SPRINKLE

### *Friday's Daughter*

"*Friday's Daughter* is a vibrant and l... ...t sometimes strangle but are also cord... ...o wounded souls use their gift of healing to heal not only others, but themselves as well. I fell in love with Tobias and Teensie in this beautiful story of their journey toward forgiveness and self-discovery."

—Karen White, author of *On Folly Beach* and *Beach Trees*

"Patricia Sprinkle has captured the spirit of the Smoky Mountains with tenderness and warmth in this charming Cinderella story. I was sorry to put this book down at night and looked forward to picking it up the next day; is there any higher praise for a novel? These endearingly crafted characters—Wonder, Teensie, Tobias, Monique, Gage—will linger in my imagination for a long, long time. I just adored this book."

—Donna Ball, author of the Ladybug Farm series
and *Keys to the Castle*

"With a fine eye for detail, Patricia Sprinkle has created a heartfelt love story set against the Great Smoky Mountains and laced with Cherokee lore. You will find yourself rooting for Teensie MacAllester, the spunky, generous heroine, always eager to help others, and nearly forgetting herself as she strives to do what is right. *Friday's Daughter* is a truly warm and captivating novel."     —Katharine Davis, author of *A Slender Thread* and *East Hope*

*continued . . .*

Written by today's freshest new talents and selected by New American Library, NAL Accent novels touch on subjects close to a woman's heart, from friendship to family to finding our place in the world. The Conversation Guides included in each book are intended to enrich the individual reading experience, as well as encourage us to explore these topics together—because books, and life, are meant for sharing.

Visit us online at www.penguin.com.

## Hold Up the Sky

"Sprinkle brings these women's lives together in a portrait of friendship, love, and Southern gumption as they help each other face their challenges." —*Birmingham* magazine

"Particularly satisfying." —*Atlanta* magazine

"Deftly handled by a writer who understands the secrets we keep and the truths we discover as women, *Hold Up the Sky* is a heartfelt story of losing the things that only seem to matter and finding the ones that truly do."
—Lisa Wingate, national bestselling author of *Beyond Summer*

"Touching." —*Southern Seasons Magazine*

"Patricia Sprinkle takes us deep into the thoughts and feelings of four women who realize the only way to true strength is to share their faith, their hearts, and each other's lives. A beautiful and thoroughly Southern story of the enduring bond of women's friendships through the seasons of the year and the seasons of life. Sprinkle knows this world and we are lucky that in her lyrical language she shares it with us!"
—Patti Callahan Henry, national bestselling author of *Driftwood Summer*

"Sprinkle has a gift for developing a full, rich world."
—*Publishers Weekly*

# Friday's Daughter

## PATRICIA SPRINKLE

NAL
ACCENT

NAL ACCENT
Published by New American Library, a division of
Penguin Group (USA) Inc., 375 Hudson Street,
New York, New York 10014, USA
Penguin Group (Canada), 90 Eglinton Avenue East, Suite 700, Toronto,
Ontario M4P 2Y3, Canada (a division of Pearson Penguin Canada Inc.)
Penguin Books Ltd., 80 Strand, London WC2R 0RL, England
Penguin Ireland, 25 St. Stephen's Green, Dublin 2,
Ireland (a division of Penguin Books Ltd.)
Penguin Group (Australia), 250 Camberwell Road, Camberwell, Victoria 3124,
Australia (a division of Pearson Australia Group Pty. Ltd.)
Penguin Books India Pvt. Ltd., 11 Community Centre, Panchsheel Park,
New Delhi - 110 017, India
Penguin Group (NZ), 67 Apollo Drive, Rosedale, North Shore 0632,
New Zealand (a division of Pearson New Zealand Ltd.)
Penguin Books (South Africa) (Pty.) Ltd., 24 Sturdee Avenue,
Rosebank, Johannesburg 2196, South Africa

Penguin Books Ltd., Registered Offices:
80 Strand, London WC2R 0RL, England

First published by NAL Accent, an imprint of New American Library,
a division of Penguin Group (USA) Inc.

First Printing, March 2011
10  9  8  7  6  5  4  3  2  1

Copyright © Patricia Sprinkle, 2011
Conversation Guide copyright © Penguin Group (USA) Inc., 2011
All rights reserved

 REGISTERED TRADEMARK—MARCA REGISTRADA

LIBRARY OF CONGRESS CATALOGING-IN-PUBLICATION DATA:
Sprinkle, Patricia Houck.
    Friday's daughter/Patricia Sprinkle.
      p. cm.
    ISBN 978-0-451-23219-9
    1. Fathers and daughters—Fiction. 2. Sisters—Fiction. 3. Inheritance and succession—Fiction.
4. Families—Southern States—Fiction. 5. Domestic fiction. I. Title.
    PS3569.P687F75 2011
    813'.54—dc22    2010039718

Set in Granjon
Designed by Alissa Amell

Printed in the United States of America

Without limiting the rights under copyright reserved above, no part of this publication may be reproduced, stored in or introduced into a retrieval system, or transmitted, in any form, or by any means (electronic, mechanical, photocopying, recording, or otherwise), without the prior written permission of both the copyright owner and the above publisher of this book.

PUBLISHER'S NOTE
This is a work of fiction. Names, characters, places, and incidents either are the product of the author's imagination or are used fictitiously, and any resemblance to actual persons, living or dead, business establishments, events, or locales is entirely coincidental.
    The publisher does not have any control over and does not assume any responsibility for author or third-party Web sites or their content.

The scanning, uploading, and distribution of this book via the Internet or via any other means without the permission of the publisher is illegal and punishable by law. Please purchase only authorized electronic editions, and do not participate in or encourage electronic piracy of copyrighted materials. Your support of the author's rights is appreciated.

*To Bob, who for forty years has remained faithful*
*to his wedding vow to enable my mission as his own.*
*He never imagined how many meals*
*he'd have to miss or eat out.*

*Monday's child is fair of face,*
*Tuesday's child is full of grace,*
*Wednesday's child is full of woe,*
*Thursday's child has far to go,*
*Friday's child is loving and giving,*
*Saturday's child works hard for a living,*
*But the child that is born on the Sabbath day,*
*Is fair and wise and good and gay.*

—MOTHER GOOSE

# PART ONE

# The Marble House

# One

We buried our father on an October Friday with the ceremony due a former college president and Georgia senator. Since my sisters had planned the funeral, it would have been perfect if lamenting geese hadn't flown in bewildered circles overhead during the committal service, drowning out the voice of the college chaplain.

"What was with the geese?" asked my brother-in-law Holcomb, fumbling in his pocket for a cigar as soon as the service was over.

"They're probably looking for that pond the college filled in for our new athletic field," said my other brother-in-law, Albert, who was the current president of Unizilla College.

Susan's strong voice floated over the crowd as she led our family from the grave to waiting limousines. "I may write a poem about those dratted geese—cries of the old order making way for the new."

Regan shaded her eyes to look up. "Or about silly geese who think the whole world ought to revolve around them." She minced across the grass in expensive heels.

I let them go ahead while I took a moment to thank the chaplain. I had to clear my throat of tears before I spoke, for while King had not been an affectionate father, seeing his coffin poised over his grave saddened me more than I had expected. "Thank you. It was a lovely service." I felt a teardrop trickle down one cheek. Having given Regan my last tissue, I swiped the tear away with my fingers.

The chaplain patted my arm. "King MacAllester was a fine man, admired by many." He glanced up at the still-circling flock. "Too bad about the geese."

That made me smile. "I figure that's King in the lead, wanting the last word as usual."

His eyes twinkled. "The thought did occur."

Philip Potts, a music professor who often escorted me to college functions, stepped up. "Would you like a lift, Teensie? Your family has left without you."

King's will was read in his own living room on the Monday after his funeral. Judge Elmer Brantley—King's executor and oldest friend—set the meeting for four o'clock.

The afternoon was so balmy that I shoved up all the windows before the rest of the family arrived. A moist breeze carried the scent of apples being harvested in the valley below. As the breeze riffled music on the piano, I hoped North Georgia wouldn't get a storm until the judge returned safely home.

My sisters were early, of course. One of King's maxims had been *Always arrive early to an important meeting. It gives you the edge over those who come later.*

Regan strolled in with Holcomb, talking to Susan over one shoulder. "I want Mother's china, crystal, and silver. You don't care about things like that and Teensie won't need them."

"I want the rugs," said Susan, two paces behind with Albert.

"Not all the rugs," Regan objected. "I want the Aubusson in the living room."

"All the rugs. You wouldn't believe the carpets in our house. I think the last president's dog squatted in every room. I want the piano, too."

"You don't play."

"Neither do you, but you already have a Steinway. I need this one for parties."

"If you get the piano, I want Mother's jewelry." As if Regan didn't have more jewelry than Tiffany's.

"I don't care about the jewelry. I want King's Mercedes. We need a third car now that Monique has come back home to stay."

They bargained their way across the hall.

My sisters had little in common except both were tall, dark, and carried themselves like King's daughters. Susan, forty-eight, was large and confident, like her voice. She had inherited our father's brilliant mind, large bones, and strong jaw. Like him, she had a strong personality that dominated any gathering she attended. An English professor and poet of modest renown, she inhabited a plane above women's fashion. Her hair—raw umber with a touch of gray—was caught up at the back in a wooden clip. She wore what she had probably thrown on that morning to teach medieval literature: a beige linen tunic over a long brown skirt.

Regan, two years younger, was the beauty of our family, with a Southern drawl you could spread like honey. She had Mother's delicate features, willowy figure, and hair as soft and dark as mink, which she wore in a twist that would have looked old-fashioned on most women. On Regan it looked elegant. I suspected the tawny pantsuit she wore had cost more than my whole autumn wardrobe.

At the double sliding doors to the living room, Regan and Holcomb stepped back as a matter of course to let Susan and Albert precede them.

Susan's daughter brought up the rear. Twenty-one, Monique

was tall and dark like the others and would have outclassed Regan as the family beauty if she hadn't applied makeup with a lavish hand, adorned each earlobe with five silver studs, and styled her hair to resemble a cave woman's after a strenuous night on the furs. She sauntered in wearing tight black pants, a tight red sweater, and high-heeled boots. With a casual flick of one wrist, she said, "Hey, Teensie."

At least she greeted me. My sisters had paid me no more attention than they did the life-sized marble nymph by our front door. From the time I was born—six years after Regan and eight after Susan—they had made it clear that I was an insignificant appendage to the royal family. I was certain that when Regan made up holiday dinner lists or Susan chose whom to invite to college faculty events, they each said, when they got to the bottom of the list, "Oh, and Teensie."

Since childhood I had kept sketchbooks the way other women keep journals, recording happy, sad, or humorous events in caricatures. My earliest drawings showed two large princesses playing various games while a small princess watched.

That afternoon I glanced in the hall mirror to reassure myself that I wasn't invisible. In another family I might have been considered decently attractive. I had a pleasant enough face and what my mother used to call "honest" eyes, but some rogue ancestor had made them hazel instead of dark and bequeathed me flyaway auburn hair, a light dusting of freckles, and a soft voice that could never match my sisters' decibels. For a middle school art project I once drew a comic strip in which a redheaded Highlander sailed down the west coast of Scotland, serenaded the MacAlister castle, and captured the heart of a proud, dark MacAlister daughter long enough to give her a son. At the end she sent the Highlander away and named her son Ian MacAlister—which was the name of the earliest ancestor King had been able to trace.

I wished the Highlander had been taller. I stood five-two in heels.

Before I joined my family, my reflection and I exchanged a nervous smile. Susan and Regan might consider me beneath their notice while they wrangled over who got what, but Judge Brantley would have the last word. I knew what it would be.

When I entered the living room, Regan was asking Albert, "Have you found a dean of students yet?" Regan was the newest member of the Unizilla College board of trustees.

Albert toyed with his Princeton ring. "Yes, you should get a letter tomorrow. We've hired Stacey Childers. She arrives next week."

He and Susan occupied the dark green leather chairs flanking the fireplace where King and his honored guests used to sit. Regan was enthroned on Mother's pale green brocade sofa, a good background for her ensemble. Holcomb sat beside her, while Monique sprawled in the floral wing chair. Her perfume and Regan's met in a strong, wild clash that marked the territory as belonging to the women in the room.

I wished Susan and Albert had left Judge Brantley one of the leather chairs. He was eighty-eight, as our father had been, and an armchair was easier to get out of. I moved a small straight chair with arms into a more prominent position. Nobody noticed.

"You hired a woman dean?" Regan's perfect eyebrows rose. "What does her husband do?"

Albert shifted uneasily. "Ms. Childers is not married." He sounded defensive, as if he were in some way responsible.

Regan frowned. "King always said married faculty and staff are more apt to put down roots in the community."

"King is dead," Susan reminded her, "and Dr. Griffin has retired. Albert is the president now. He is perfectly capable—"

"Ooooh!" A moan at the side window stopped her in mid-sentence. The face pressed against the screen was distorted and hideous.

Susan gasped. Monique started to rise. I waved her back. "I'll go."

A wide front porch was one of the glories of our big marble house. Yes, marble, for we were near the North Georgia quarries and the house had been built as the president's house when Unizilla College was founded a century before.

I skirted four rockers and rounded the corner. "Wonder?" I called.

The face rearranged itself into the delicate features of my four-year-old great-niece. She bounced on her toes, dark eyes dancing. "Was I fee-ro-cious?"

She was an elf of insatiable curiosity, with the light caramel skin of a biracial child and a cloud of soft dark hair. I had known her less than a week and already I adored her.

"Simply terrifying," I assured her. "However, your nana was not pleased."

She lifted thin shoulders and lowered them with a sigh of weariness much older than her years. "Nana is de most un-pleased woman I know."

I managed not to smile. "Would you like to come help get refreshments ready? I need to wipe dust off your nose, too." Her mama would have to wash her pink ruffled dress when they got home. In the convoluted relationship that exists between mothers and daughters, Susan had dressed Monique in corduroy and cable-knit sweaters when the child wanted pink ruffles; Monique dressed Wonder in pink ruffles when the child preferred T-shirts and jeans.

She pranced over to join me. "Is Jester in de kitchen?"

"No, I've put him in the backyard for the afternoon. Your granddaddy doesn't like dogs in the house."

Wonder heaved another sigh at the failings of her relatives. "Poor Jester." She slipped an endearingly fragile hand into mine. "Let's don't go in yet, Teensie. Look at dose mountains over yonder. Aren't dey simply bee-*you*-ti-ful?"

Silent, we contemplated the view. The small town of Unizilla—a corruption of the Cherokee word for "cloud"—sat high in the North Georgia mountains. Some days we were covered with clouds that brushed our cheeks with cold, damp kisses. That afternoon the air was so clear we could see workers in the valley orchards. Beyond the orchards, ridges ascended in violet and blue until they blended with the sky.

Those who love the Rockies sometimes deride the Appalachians as mere hills, but that's the brashness of youth failing to appreciate the beauty of age. Geologists claim the Appalachians are the oldest mountains on earth, once higher than the Himalayas. If the Rockies last so long, they should hope to look so lovely. Our ancient crests have been reduced by aeons of wind and rain to gentle mounds that flow like waves toward the horizon. Nearer flanks display a cover of dark green pines interspersed with hardwoods. On that October afternoon the mountains sported early autumn outfits of pink, tangerine, dark green, and gold. I had lived most of my life in Unizilla, but sometimes the beauty of those mountains still stopped the breath in my throat.

To Wonder, who had come the week before from the Georgia coast, the mountains were a perpetual delight—but many things delighted Wonder: bugs, shapes in clouds, quirks in her newfound family. Had she developed her keen sense of pleasure because of her name, or had Monique seen something in her newborn's eyes that made her name the child?

"Look!" she cried. "Dere's de veg'table man!" She darted to the wide marble balustrade to yell at a dusty black pickup climbing the hill. "Hey, Mr. Veg'table Man! It's Wonder!" An arm in a blue work shirt waved out the open window as the truck passed.

"Who's the vegetable man?"

"He bwings healthy veg'tables to de college. He's one of my bestest fwiends. Let's go fix de 'freshments." She tugged me toward the big, dim hall. All the rooms were spacious—the living room and kitchen to the left, King's study and the dining room to the right, a powder room and a butler's pantry tucked behind the wide marble staircase that curved to the upper floor.

As we passed the marble nymph, she gave it a pat. "Hey, Muriel."

"Muriel?"

"Dat's her name, like my best fwiend in Savannah." She gave the statue a reproving look. "*My* Muriel wore clothes."

"Hey, Alice," she greeted my cook when the kitchen door swung shut behind us. "We're here to help." Alice—tall and rawboned—stood at the round oak kitchen table, assembling crystal goblets on a large silver tray. She gave us a dour nod.

A woman of the mountains, Alice used few words. I knew nothing about her except she had little schooling, cooked like an angel, cleaned indifferently, lived with her mother up a valley, and had a brother called Red who spent a good bit of time downstate. Alice had been with us ten years before I learned from Coco Ihle—Judge Brantley's daughter and what Wonder would call "my bestest fwiend"—that Red was partial to strong drink and brawling, and "downstate" was a euphemism for the state prison. Red must have inherited all the fire and ginger their family had to offer. Alice's blue eyes and orange hair were so pale they looked like they had been washed too many times.

Wonder perched on the edge of a kitchen chair with her elbows on the table. "When will dat judge get here?"

"He said he'd come at four. That's a few more minutes."

"Tell me de story, den. I habbent heard it for a long time."

Not for twenty-four hours.

I had made up the story the week before, when Monique

showed up at my house after five absent years to announce, "This is my little girl, Wonder. Wonder, this is Teensie. She'll take care of you while I go talk to my parents." She had left without giving me time to object.

I had fed Wonder milk and cookies and racked my brain to think how I could entertain a four-year-old. Wonder had pinned me with coal black eyes. "Tell me a story 'bout pwincesses." I had been so startled to see my father's eyes in that small tan face that I couldn't remember a single fairy tale. The best I could do was make one up.

During their week in town Monique had left the child with me several times while she ran errands. Every time, Wonder had demanded the story, requesting new details and expecting them in future editions. Since Alice had never heard the story, I began with trepidation.

"Once upon a time there was a king with three daughters. The oldest was brilliant. The second was beautiful. And the third—"

"—was not bwilliant or beautiful, but she liked to help people."

"No point in helping other folks," Alice declared. "They'll suck the life out of you. Take care of number one. That's my motto."

"Who is number one?" asked Wonder.

"Myself. Yourself," said Alice. "If everybody would take care of number one, the world would be a better place. That's what I always say." While she spoke, Alice was filling the goblets with ice. I added a purple plastic cup of milk to the tray. She set out teaspoons and forks. I arranged a small crystal bowl of lemon slices and mint leaves. We had performed this ritual so often that we needed no words.

"You're not a pwincess," Wonder pointed out.

I hastily continued. "A brilliant prince came to the castle

one day. He married the brilliant princess and took her to his kingdom—"

"—where eb'ryone was bwilliant."

Wonder settled herself more comfortably on her chair. I set dessert plates on the tray. In honor of the occasion, I was using Mother's Royal Doulton china with the blue and gold rim.

"Right. Soon after that, a rich and handsome prince came to the castle and married the beautiful princess. He took her to his kingdom—"

"—where eb'ryone was wich and beautiful. But de t'ird pwincess neber got a pwince." Wonder's face drooped, as mournful as her voice.

I laughed as I placed snowy white napkins in a small silver basket. "The youngest princess didn't need a prince, remember? She liked to help people, so she became a nurse."

I took the foil off a pan of brownies Coco had brought that morning with a twinkle in her eyes. "They're laced with rum. I suspect you're going to need rum this afternoon."

Alice—a staunch Primitive Baptist—had repudiated the rum by whipping up a lemon pound cake. She gave a satisfied toss of her head as she sliced pound cake onto Mother's cut-glass cake plate and set it in the center of the tray, leaving no room for brownies. Ignoring her theatrics, I began arranging brownies in concentric circles on a small silver tray.

"Go on wit' de story!" Wonder waved one hand in an imperious gesture.

"I swan!" Alice exclaimed. My sentiments exactly. How could King's ponderous blood run so thick in the veins of that quicksilver child?

"The third princess became a nurse," I repeated, "and she worked for four years in a large hospital in a faraway city. She was very happy."

"Eben if dere weren't any pwinces?"

"She didn't need princes."

Before Wonder could object, I hurried on. "One day the king's sister, Princess Teddy, got sick. He asked his youngest daughter to leave the hospital to care for her aunt. The princess agreed, because she loved her aunt very much. They lived together until Princess Teddy died. By then the king's wife—"

"—de queen—"

"Yes—Queen Regina—was ill. So the king asked the youngest princess to move back to the castle to look after her mother."

"And de pwincess agreed because she loved her mudder vewy much."

"Right. The princess cared for her mother until she died. Afterward, the princess wanted to return to her hospital . . ."

". . . but de king said, 'P'ease stay wif me,' for he did not know how to take care of himself."

"Kings got servants to take care of them," said Alice tartly as she poured iced tea into a silver pitcher.

"Yes, but dis king only had one servant to cook his dinner," Wonder explained. "He needed somebody to cook his bweffast and supper." We had clarified that the day before.

"Yeah, the king needed that, for sure." Alice gave me a wink. I didn't know whether I was more astonished by the wink or by her entering into the spirit of the story. "The king needed somebody to help with his parties, too," she added, tossing her head. "That king plumb loved parties." I had always suspected Alice stayed after Mother died only because of the important people who ate at King's table.

"Before we came to Nana's, I fixed bweffast," Wonder informed us. "Mama put a little pitcher of milk in de fwigerator and she put Fwuit Loops and a bowl and a spoon on de table, and den she went to work. I fixed my bweffast so I didn't have to wake up . . ." A stricken look froze her face.

"Your daddy?" I suggested.

She traced circles on the tablecloth with one small finger. "We aren't 'posed to talk about him." Her shoulders slumped like the wings of a grieving angel.

I gave Alice a warning look. We would not quiz Wonder about forbidden subjects. "Where were we in the story?" I asked.

The child's voice was listless. "So de youngest pwincess stayed with de king in his castle and dey lived happily togedder. De end." She traced a couple more circles on the tablecloth. I was glad when she puckered her forehead with a new question— until I heard it. "Did she stay with de king because she loved him vewy much?"

With Alice's ears perked, that required careful answering. "The king was a stern man, hard to love, but the princess respected and admired him."

Alice carried the tray from the kitchen with a disapproving sniff. I had skated too close to the edge of the commandment "Honor thy father."

Made reckless by anticipation, I added a bit more to the story as soon as the door swung shut behind Alice. "The princess also stayed because the king made her a promise. He promised that if she took care of him for the rest of his life, when he died he would leave her the castle, his furniture, and money enough to invite old people to live with her, so she could take care of them. Wasn't that a nice promise?"

"Yeah!" Wonder's eyes shone. "Den her pwince could come!"

"I told you, she didn't need a prince. She needed to help people."

Wonder gave me a mutinous frown. "Pwinces are 'posed to come."

"Not always. Some princesses don't need a prince."

"Yes, dey *do*, Teensie. Maybe he will come in de foreseeable future."

"Where on earth did you hear about the foreseeable future?"

"Granddaddy said we can live with dem wight now but Mama has to make important decisions in de foreseeable future." She slid down from her chair. "Can I fix de bwownies prettier?"

"If you wash your hands real good."

With hands like deft little crabs she rearranged the brownies into a tower. "Dat's better." She steadied the top brownie to keep it from falling. I hoped I could get the plate into the living room without toppling half its contents.

"Will you carry the napkins for me?" I handed her the silver basket filled with Mother's snowy luncheon napkins. Bearing the brownies, I followed her down the hall.

My hall in my house. I inhaled pure happiness. My heart quaked, though, as I pictured how my sisters would take the news.

Wonder stopped in the door and waited until every eye was on her. "De king is dead!" she announced. My topmost brownie toppled to the floor.

I retrieved the brownie and tucked it behind a vase for later retrieval while, in the living room, Wonder passed napkins and Alice started pouring iced tea.

Regan gave a regal wave. "You don't have to stay, Alice. Teensie can finish serving."

Alice departed with a sniff. Unaware—or uncaring—that she had offended, Regan gave the china a proprietary look. "One brownie and no lemon for me, and Holcomb won't want cake or a brownie. He's on a diet." Holcomb might have been ten years older than she, but she bossed him like a child.

He gave me such a glum look that I suggested, "This is a special occasion. Can't he diet tomorrow?"

He brightened. "That would be great."

I handed him a plate with both a brownie and a slice of cake. He wolfed down his brownie in three bites.

I had always wondered whether Regan married Holcomb for his blond good looks or his money. Either way, she had been fortunate. Though he was bulkier than when they had met, he was still handsome, and he had built up his father's poultry business into a brand recognized across the South. She had certainly not chosen him for his scintillating conversation. His world was limited to business and sports. King—who never thought looks or wealth compensated for a sluggish intellect—privately called him the Chicken Czar. Mother used to chide him, "Regan needs a rich, adoring husband more than she needs a brilliant one."

Even so, Regan's life wasn't idyllic. I saw the hungry way her eyes followed Wonder. She had never had a child.

Susan had both a child and a grandchild, but neither was permitted to interfere with her dedication to poetry. The way she referred to "we poets" made me think she expected that one day she, Sidney Lanier, and James Dickey would form the Southern poets' triumvirate in high school literature.

"I'll take some pound cake and extra lemon in my tea." She held out a big hand for me to bring them to her.

Albert frowned as he gave the tray a failing grade. "I'll just have water, Teensie. Sugar is so bad for the human body."

Albert's appearance had improved with age; his disposition had not. He had been a scrawny young medieval historian when Susan met him in Paris, where they were both finishing doctoral dissertations. The summer night Susan brought him home, our father declared, "That young man has a mind like a rapier and a tongue like a sword."

King was one of the few people who saw those qualities as virtues.

I was nineteen at the time, sentimental enough to wonder how Susan could stand that argumentative, sharp-tongued scarecrow with stringy black hair to his shoulders. I also could not understand why within the month Mother had arranged a lovely wedding while King took Albert to his own barber and tailor and found him a place on the history faculty. Susan, of course, had been headed for a slot in the English department since she could form sentences.

Monique had been born six months later.

Albert had benefited from good tailoring and expert barbering. In middle age he looked like a president any college could be proud of: prematurely white hair above an austere face, his body slender and fit in a navy blazer and gray flannels. Rumor was, though, that stouthearted seniors shuddered when summoned to his office. I suspected he'd been elected college president because only one member of the board dared to vote against him. Regan now sat in that member's seat.

I went to the kitchen to fetch him a goblet of water and returned to find Wonder flinging herself where others feared to tiptoe. She said, through a full mouth of chocolate, "Dese brownies is *good*, Granddaddy. You ought to twy one."

"It's 'try,' not 'twy,'" said Susan, expert at diversion. "And look! You are dropping crumbs on the rug!"

Monique beckoned. "Come sit with me. I've got a plate you can share." As Wonder tucked herself under her mother's arm, Monique deliberately brushed a few crumbs from her pants onto the rug. Susan gave a familiar "How could we have produced this child?" sigh.

Their daughter (named for their French period?) had grown up in an intellectual household with two work-obsessed scholars, yet from her toddler days Monique had liked princesses, parties, and pink. Susan and Albert had taken her to museums and chamber music concerts to improve her mind, only to be baffled when she developed into a rebellious teen. In her freshman year in high school, she dated Junior Walters, a swaggering redneck senior who thought he was God's gift to the world. "He's sweet when you get to know him," Monique insisted, adding the boast she knew would best get her father's elitist goat: "He's real smart, too." We had all breathed a sigh of relief when Junior graduated and went into the army.

After Junior, Monique had dated a string of boyfriends her parents deplored until at sixteen she dared the ultimate rebellion: she pursued Benny Yancey, a college sophomore and the only black male on campus. Anybody who knew Monique had to know she was the aggressor, but Albert told Benny to either leave the college or be prosecuted for contributing to the delinquency of a minor. Benny chose to leave. Monique went after him.

I had liked Benny. He was a gentle, serious boy who came to college with the dream of becoming a doctor. He had done yard work for us to supplement his scholarship. After he finished the yard, we used to discuss his plans. I was as sad as Wonder that we couldn't talk about her daddy.

"Here." I handed Wonder the purple cup of milk. "Would you like another brownie?" When she nodded, I reached for a plate.

Regan's perfect eyebrows rose in horror. "Don't give that child Royal Doulton! Get her a plastic plate."

"I don't own one. I just bought the plastic cup yesterday."

"Wait a minute." With a huff for my deficient skills as a housekeeper, Susan strode to the kitchen. I carried my own plate to the straight chair beside Mother's drum table in the corner. Susan brought back the scratched top of an old Tupperware container. "Here, Wonder. Use this and come sit on the leather ottoman by me. You don't want to spill on the upholstery."

Wonder's brows met in mutiny. "I doesn't want a ugly plate. I wants a pretty plate like eb'rybody else and I wants to sit by Teensie." She wiggled down from her mother's chair, scooted the ottoman over beside me, and plumped down with her own chin high.

I balanced a plate of dessert on her small lap. "Be very careful," I whispered.

"Okay." The sunny smile Wonder gave me was exactly like her father's. Did any of the rest of my family see Benny Yancey in his child? Would they admit it if they did?

On the dot of four the doorbell rang.

"De judge!" Wonder clasped her hands under her chin with a delighted shiver. "I nebber saw a judge in my whole life!"

When nobody else moved, I went to answer the door.

I suspected Wonder was going to be disappointed. Judge Brantley was a small, slender man whose only outstanding feature was an overabundance of white hair. I drew him as an elderly cockatoo with bushy white eyebrows and little tufts sprouting from his ears. A widower, he lived with Coco in an antebellum house down the hill from ours.

I was surprised when he walked past me with only a brusque "Hello, Teensie." As he set his black fedora on the hall table, I concluded he didn't want an unguarded look to give away our secret. I was embarrassed to see his grandson, Gage, behind him. Gage was a personable young man of twenty-nine with red curls, a deep voice, and his granddaddy's fine mind. As a child he had run in and out of our house, and I had been delighted when he returned to Unizilla to practice after law school. He was now our family lawyer, but his arrival presented me with a hostess's dilemma: I was one chair and a place setting short.

I hurried to the dining room to fetch a chair, but Gage was too much of a gentleman to let me carry it. "I'll get that, Teensie. You go on in and sit down."

His step checked when he saw Monique. I doubted if he

recognized her. He'd gone to Yale the year she'd entered middle school and she had left town before he graduated from law school. I left them to reintroduce themselves while I fetched another plate, goblet, and fork.

On the kitchen table I noticed a note I had overlooked while getting Albert's water: *I no when Im not wanted. I took sum cake to mama.*

I sighed. Alice in a snit would take a good bit of placating, but I couldn't worry about that at the moment.

Wonder was waiting for me in the hall, holding her plate at such a tilt that her brownie was in peril. I steadied the plate with a free finger. She spoke in a whisper as loud as a teakettle. "I didn't know judges was such hairy men. Dat's de hairiest man I eber did see!"

I heard Gage choke back a laugh.

"Shhh," I cautioned. "Come eat your brownie. Carry the plate carefully."

We entered to an uneasy silence. My sisters were watching the judge like cats under a bird feeder. The judge was in no hurry. He ate his cake like he was counting chews and accepted a second piece with a refill of tea. When Gage reached for the briefcase beside his chair, his grandfather waved him back. "We'll get around to business in a minute, boy."

Wonder squirmed. Albert frowned. Susan called softly, "Come sit with me, honey." Wonder obeyed. As they whispered in the big leather chair, I caught an unguarded smile on Susan's lips. Was that crusty college professor turning into a doting grandmother?

It seemed an eternity before the judge set down his plate. "Very well, Gage."

Gage pulled out the expected document. "Since Mrs. Mac-Allester predeceased Dr. MacAllester, the will is straightforward." He began reading the legalese that always precedes the gist. I trembled as he approached the important sentence: "I leave everything of which I die possessed to all my children in equal shares."


"Noooo!"

That couldn't be me. I was too numb to wail. I felt like I had walked into a familiar room only to step into an unexpected hole that plummeted me to a dark, chill basement. I swayed and had to put a hand on Mother's drum table to steady myself.

Nobody noticed.

Wonder voiced the protest I could not. "No, no, no!" She flew across the room to pound Gage's knee with fists like small mallets. "De king pwomised his house to de t'ird pwincess so she could take care of people in it!"

"Hey! Hold on!" With a laugh, he caught her wrists to keep her from hitting him again.

Wonder tugged to get free. "De youngest pwincess gets de castle!"

"Wonder!" Susan rebuked her.

Gage kept Wonder's wrists but held them loosely. "I'm sorry, sweetie. That's not what Dr. MacAllester's will says."

Wonder set her jaw. "De youngest pwincess is 'posed to get it."

Gage looked to his grandfather for reinforcement.

With an unerring instinct for where the power lay, Wonder moved to stand in front of the judge. Hands clasped behind her, she explained in an earnest voice, "Mr. Hairy Judge, de youngest pwincess is 'posed to get *eb'ryt'ing* because she took care of de old pwincess and de queen when dey was sick and she took care of de king eben if she didn't love him, dist wespected and admired him."

Albert choked on his water.

"Wonder!" Susan rebuked her again.

Wonder paid them no attention. She was intent on her mission. "So you has to gib de castle and eb'ryt'ing to Teensie. She is not bwilliant or beautiful, but she likes to help people and she wants to help dem in dis house."

"Go outside and play," Albert commanded.

Wonder didn't move.

Monique shoved her toward the door. "Go swing, honey. The grown-ups need to talk."

"I'll go play with Jester." She threw her grandfather a glower. "He's lonesome out dere all by himself." At the double doors to the hall she stopped with one hand on her hip. "Don't you forget to gib Teensie dis house, Mr. Hairy Judge."

When the door closed behind her, Judge Brantley spoke to my sisters. "While the child's argument is a bit unorthodox, her verdict is sound. King did intend to leave the house to Teensie for all she has done for this family. This will was last revised when Regan was six months old. Like so many men, King developed a superstitious fear as he aged that revising his will would hasten his death. When I reminded him from time to time, he'd say, 'Trying to bundle me off already, Elmer? I'll get around to it one day.' Last week after his stroke, when he could not speak, he tried desperately to tell me something. I think he wanted to make things right. You two older girls are comfortably placed. Why not let Teensie have King's estate?"

Regan's hands tightened on her plate. "Not the china, silver, or crystal. She won't have any use for those. She shouldn't get all the money, either."

"I need the piano and the rugs—all of them." Susan's nostrils flared as she dared Regan to object. "And I agree that Teensie shouldn't get all the money."

"Teensie's the only one who plays the piano," said Holcomb. The others ignored him.

"In all fairness," Albert said, in the tone of one pointing out the obvious if only others would think rationally, "the house should revert to the college. It's on campus property, one of two original buildings erected by the college founder with marble from his own quarry. We sorely need it for small guest lectures, dinner parties, and community education classes. I'm certain the trustees will name it the King MacAllester Center. Don't you agree, Regan?"

Before Regan could answer, Monique asked Gage, "So how much do *I* get?"

He shook his head. "The will stipulates that King's *children* inherit in equal shares."

"I'm his granddaughter. Don't I get anything?"

"Your mother inherits a third. You will eventually inherit her estate."

"That sucks! She'll spend her share long before I see a penny of it." She jumped up and strode out.

Before the screened door slammed behind Monique, Regan and Susan were divvying up furnishings again while Albert mustered additional uses for the house. Gage and the judge pointed out that King hadn't left the house to the college. I said nothing. I was cold as marble.

In a lull in the chaos Holcomb lifted his bass rumble. "I think you ought to consider King's intentions. If the judge knows King meant for Teensie to have the house and its contents, let her use her third of the estate to buy you girls out." With the air of a reasonable man who has settled a foolish argument, he lumbered out of the room. In another moment the scent of his cigar wafted through the windows facing the front porch.

Every eye in the room turned to me. "King did promise it to me." I wished my voice were stronger. In the big room it sounded like that of a child. "After Mother died, he promised that if I'd stay with him, he would leave me the house, the furniture, and enough money to open a small nursing home for people who can't afford to go anywhere else. I don't think a third of the estate would pay for all that."

"A nursing home? In the old president's house?" Albert couldn't have sounded more scandalized if I had proposed opening a brothel.

My sisters murmured in unison, "A little dim." They had taunted me with those three words since childhood because my full name was Deborah Ingram MacAllester.

Had King also opposed my nursing home idea? Was that why he'd put off revising his will? Like a lot of successful politicians, the old scoundrel was a master at passive aggression.

"You can work in a nursing home." Susan spoke as if that would settle all our problems.

Anger gave me a spurt of bravado. "I don't want to work in a nursing home! I want to run a small place of my own—and I've earned it. For fifteen years I took care of Teddy and both our parents while you all—and King—did whatever you pleased. It ought to be my turn." Could they hear my heart agitating like an unbalanced washing machine? I pressed my lips together, afraid the pounding would dislodge the brownie in my stomach.

"You got free room and board all these years," Susan reminded me, "plus a couple of trucks over the years. King never bought me anything to drive."

"I had to have transportation when I moved back up here."

"You didn't have to do much for King," Regan argued. "You had time to work."

Unizilla was twenty miles from the nearest hospital, but we had a small medical clinic that provided local services for our far-flung rural community. It was perpetually short-staffed and underfunded, but the director managed to keep it afloat with part-time nurses and volunteers. After Mother's death I had started working there on Wednesdays and Fridays, doing home visitations. Did my sisters have no idea of how much I'd done for King? Or that driving into the mountains to visit patients offered a few precious hours of escape from his demands?

Because my dreams were so big, so important, I dared to try again. "King *promised* that if I'd stay with him—" I hated that I sounded petulant. Standing up to my sisters, I always felt four years old.

Susan interrupted with an impatient shrug. "You could have left."

Knowing it was futile, I still tried to reason with them. "Who would have taken care of him? His vision was too bad for him to drive, read, or answer mail. He couldn't choose his own clothes, and you know he always wanted to look nice."

Regan waved a hand with nails as red as blood. "We were here."

She and Susan might have driven him around town when it was convenient, but King could never have attended political meetings all over the state. They might have lamented that their once-proud father wore mismatched clothes, but they would never have taken the trouble to help him dress with his customary elegance. How could I have left King to them?

"King did intend to leave the house, furniture, and most of his money to Teensie," the judge told them again, "for all she did for your family."

Regan recrossed her beautiful legs. "We never asked her to come back from Atlanta."

Susan nodded in agreement. "She chose to come."

"I didn't," I protested. "King ordered me home. You know what he was like."

Everybody in that room knew what King MacAllester was like: generous with cronies, severe with subordinates. He wasn't a hereditary ruler, of course—his mother had simply given him her maiden name, as many Southern mothers do—but his name shaped the way he saw himself: the ruler of Unizilla College, his private realm. He came in his late twenties to teach political science and by thirty-six was the college's youngest president, a position he held for thirty-four years. At thirty-eight he had married Regina Ingram, only child of the town's oldest family—if you didn't count the Cherokees, which people seldom did. Mother had been a tall, regal woman twelve years younger than King and devoted to him.

By the time I was born, King was beginning to be active in state politics. After he retired from the college, he served in the Georgia Senate. I was in nursing school then, and saw my parents occasionally when they were in Atlanta. Mother's deteriorating health made King turn down a call to run for governor, but after her death, he and his cronies were, in King's own words, "the invisible hands on the tiller of the Georgia ship of state." He was at a political fund-raising dinner when he collapsed with the stroke that killed him.

King had strong opinions on the place of women. They should either be gracious wives who served on boards and hosted elite dinners to boost their husbands' careers or be at the top of some profession. He was proud of Susan's Ph.D. He would gladly have sent me to medical school. He let me become a nurse, though, only because his sister, Teddy, insisted that I be permitted to see if I liked it. Four years after I got my first nursing job, he summoned me home. Poor Teddy's mind had weakened too much for her to protest, and to King my return was logical: why hire somebody to care for his sister when he had an unmarried daughter trained as a nurse?

Regan lifted her perfect chin. "What I know is that his will says we are to split the estate three ways. If you want to use your third to buy my share of the house, that's fine with me."

"Fine with me, too," Susan said—then caught Albert's eye. "If the college also gets a chance to bid on it. After all, the house once belonged to the college, and you don't really need this huge place." She addressed Judge Brantley. "How much money is there?"

The old judge waved a hand at Gage, disclaiming all responsibility for the answer. Gage pulled another sheet of paper from his briefcase. "I spoke with King's broker this morning. Dr. MacAllester's investments suffered like everybody else's in the last economic downturn, but they have made some recovery. At this point his total cash assets amount to two hundred thousand dollars. However—"

My dreams evaporated like August rain on a Georgia sidewalk.

"That's it?" Regan's dismay echoed my own. "There has to be more than that! King lived like a millionaire. He must have money hidden somewhere."

Gage ran a finger around his collar as if it had grown too tight. "The broker said King had been living on his capital for years, and last spring—"

She turned on me. "Why didn't you stop him?"

I recoiled at the unfair charge. "He never discussed money with me."

"The kind thing to do would be to give everything to Teensie," the judge said, trying again. "That was what King intended. I think Teensie would be glad to let each of you take mementos from the house."

"Mementos? I don't want mementos!" Susan waved her arms like King used to do. "I want to start a poetry journal that will put Unizilla College on the map. I can't do that with mementos."

"I want more than that, too," said Regan. "Sorry, Teensie, but you'll have to share." She started putting dishes on the tray. Was she planning to take them home with her that afternoon?

"Do you have any idea what the house is worth?" Albert looked around, probably envisioning lecturers standing by the fireplace.

"Can't you do *anything?*" I implored the judge.

"Not a dad-blamed thing except forbid anybody to remove anything. Listen to me, Regan and Susan." He wagged a forefinger at them as if they were children. "Do not remove *anything* from this house until you have called in experts to valuate the furnishings so they can be distributed equitably. Also call in an appraiser to set a fair market price for the house."

"I'm sure Sam Tolbert's firm will help us there." Albert's voice was confident. Sam, one of the largest Realtors in North Georgia, was a college trustee.

The judge's voice was testy. "Conflict of interest. Get an independent Realtor."

"I need this rug by Sunday," Susan told him in the voice of one accustomed to getting anything she needed. "This is Parents' Weekend and we're having a reception. Our living room carpet is awful."

"Not one rug or fork is to leave this house until appropriate values have been placed on everything and an agreement has been reached about equal distribution." If the judge had had a gavel, he would have banged it.

Susan frowned. Regan traced figures with one forefinger on her green linen lap. "So we each get sixty-six thousand plus a third of the house."

She hadn't made it a question, but Gage answered anyway. "Not exactly. You see—"

Nobody paid attention. Susan and Albert were talking together in low voices while Regan made calculations on her lap. What could she possibly want that Holcomb wouldn't give her?


After everyone left, I contemplated the shambles of my— correction, Albert's—living room. For years I had pictured the gracious parlor full of elderly people on modest incomes enjoying their final years in pleasant comfort. At the moment it was full of smeared plates and its carpet was sprinkled with crumbs. Alice might sulk for days, so I would have to deal with the mess in order to turn the dishes and rug over to my sisters and the house over to my brother-in-law. Why not do as Alice did? Why not close the double doors to the living room, pack my clothes, and leave everything as it stood? Let them wash the dishes, vacuum the rug, sort King's things, take whatever they wanted, and give me my share in cash. At the moment there wasn't a thing in that house I wanted.

I picked up a plate and frowned at it.

"Don't smash the Royal Doulton, Teensie!" Monique's imitation of Regan was so perfect, I jumped.

She held up a handful of stones. "Wonder made me come get a rock collection she left on the back steps. Did Mother and Regan let you have the house?"

"No. Your dad wants to buy it for the college."

"I could kill him! I could just kill him!" Her fists clenched around the rocks.

"Your father?" I was touched by her unexpected support.

"No, Grandfather King. He promised he'd take care of us! If he wasn't already dead, I could kill him."

"He promised? When?"

Monique hadn't come home until King's stroke had been aired by media across the state, and he had died without ever regaining his ability to speak.

"When did he promise?" I repeated when she didn't answer.

She bit her lip. "I don't remember. I've gotta go. I've got a date tonight."


Dusk was closing in. As I moved around the downstairs turning on lights, I found myself listening for King's call, "Ready for our game, Teensie?" When he was alive, that was the signal for me to join him at the mahogany game table in his study.

King loved chess. Along with the marble house he had bought a marble chess set that had been a gift from the founder to the first president of the college, and he had tried to teach Susan and Regan to play. Regan found the game too slow and Susan considered it too structured. "It has no poetry," she said once in scorn. King never invited her to play again.

I had watched when he played with friends and I had no trouble learning the moves. The chess pieces were like my family. The queen was Mother, willing and able to go any lengths in any direction to support her king. The bishops were Susan, moving obliquely to achieve their aims. The rooks were Regan, moving ahead in a straight line to capture anything in their path. I knew the family saw me as a pawn—helpful yet expendable—but in my heart I was a knight, leaping from nowhere to save the king or queen. By middle school I had gotten good enough for King to invite me to an occasional game. In high school I started a chess team that went to state finals my senior year. Chess was the one thing I excelled at that King respected. After I returned home to care for Mother, we played most evenings. I cherished my father's honest praise when I managed to win.

Fury at him rose like a red tide. "How could you betray me?" I flung the white king across the room, then collapsed into King's chair at the table and wept. I wept for broken promises and wasted years, and I wept because in spite of my anger at him, I missed King. Without him to take care of—and without him as the anchor of my days—what would I do?

The first thing I had to do was clean up after the family, even though I felt as lifeless as Styrofoam. I cleared the living room, washed the dishes by hand, ate a scrambled egg with toast, and took some of Coco's brownies with milk to my upstairs sitting room. From habit I closed the door. For seven years that room had been my sanctuary.

Unlike the rest of the house—which Mother had decorated with mahogany furniture, Oriental rugs, and velvet or damask drapery—that room was filled with light Mission-style furniture, Navajo rugs and pottery, and watercolors of the Southwestern desert. Teddy had married an artist from Santa Fe and had brought part of the Southwest to Unizilla when she came east after her husband died. She was forty-five and I was three, but we were soon great friends. Teddy was as quiet as King was flamboyant, as loving as Mother was distant. A third-grade teacher, she often took me to her house in the afternoon to draw, stir up child-sized cupcakes, or snuggle under a quilt and read. I loved going to her little house.

Teddy left no will. When King inherited everything as her next of kin, he told me with a careless wave, "Call in somebody to buy it all, lock, stock, and barrel."

"Could I put some of her furniture in Susan's old bedroom for a sitting room?" I had asked as I prepared to move back home. I had suspected that if I didn't carve myself out a private nook in the house, I'd suffocate.

Mother had wrinkled her nose. "We have nicer things in the attic."

"If you don't mind, I'd rather have Teddy's."

Mother gave an elegant shrug. "Take anything you want."

I chose two oak end tables, a coffee table, three bookshelves, Teddy's desk, and a sofa and matching chairs upholstered in soft caramel leather. I also took the Navajo rugs and the watercolors Teddy's husband had painted.

I did a little painting of my own: birdhouses that Coco designed from real homes or historical buildings in Georgia. "High school shop class benefited me as much as my years at Berkeley," she claimed. We sold the birdhouses in gift shops and the campus bookstore to earn what Coco called our "mad money." Occasionally we donated one to a charity auction.

At the moment I had four on my painting table with their undercoat dry, ready for detailing. The red one would become the brick governor's mansion with ostentatious white columns. Two creamy white ones would become replicas of Main—the other original marble building on the Unizilla College campus, which for years had housed administrative offices. Main and college chapel birdhouses sold well to students looking for gifts for their mothers. The fourth birdhouse was small, with a pointed roof. Coco had said when she dropped it off, "Paint it cute and we'll donate it to the clinic fund-raiser." I had given it a coat of yellow paint but had gotten no other inspiration for "cute."

Stripped of my own home, I was in no mood to work on anybody else's—not even a home for birds. Where would I go? What would I do? I could return to Atlanta to find a nursing job, but that big of a move would take more energy than I had at the moment. I had not kept up with anyone there. I would have to begin life again as raw as a newborn. Could I do that? Could I leave the mountains a second time? How could I leave Wonder so soon after I'd gotten to know her?

I took my sketchbook from its drawer, as I did at the end of most days. I never thought while I sketched, just let my feelings flow through my fingers while the room worked peace in my soul. When I finished, I looked at what I had drawn.

Usually I drew in colored pencils. That night I had chosen charcoal—the color of ashes. I had drawn a small princess up to her chin in a lake of tears.

# Two

Susan showed up Tuesday morning while I was drinking my first cup of coffee.

I was in a dreadful mood. I had cried myself to sleep, slept fitfully, and wakened to hear water thundering down the drain spouts. A mournful howl rose from the yard. Jester! He was old, with arthritic hips, and his house let rain blow in. I stumbled downstairs to find him crouched against the screen, trying to escape the downpour. He limped in, leaving muddy paw prints all over the floor. With a reproachful look he shook himself, soaking me. I dried him off while he deposited as much moisture on me in wet kisses as I rubbed out of his coat.

I poured his breakfast, hiding a pain pill in his food. While he wolfed it down, I called Alice. Before the appraisers came, the house needed a better cleaning than we generally gave it.

I was prepared to grovel. "I am real sorry Regan hurt your feelings yesterday."

"She didn't hurt my feelings none. My stomach was feeling poorly, so smelling all that liquor in them brownies got me dizzy. I been in bed since I got home and I don't feel a speck better. I doubt I'll be able to come back until next week."

"I really need you." I didn't bother to hide my desperation.

"Sorry. I might be better by Monday."

Which meant I'd have to spend the day cleaning house.

I donned jeans with a shapeless green sweatshirt and pulled my hair back with a rubber band. If I had to play Cinderella, I would dress the part. Besides, I wouldn't be seeing a soul. Who would come out in all that rain?

When I returned to the kitchen, Jester nudged his bowl toward me for a refill. The bowl had been one of Monique's eighth-grade art projects: purple pottery with his name incised around the rim. The name jarred me like an electric shock.

"Do you realize you own a bowl with your name on it while I don't own one blessed thing except a little furniture and a truck? Not one plate, fork, knife, or glass, not a sheet or pillowcase, not one pot or pan to keep house with?"

Jester paid my lament no more attention than King would have. He just nudged the bowl closer to my feet. I refilled it, then put on coffee. While it brewed I roamed the kitchen, taking inventory of essentials I would need. Who would care if I had to take blackened muffin tins while Susan got an Aubusson rug? Who would notice if I had to choose Tupperware while Regan chose Royal Doulton? By the time the coffee was ready, I was feeling so ornery that it was a wonder I didn't take a meat cleaver to Susan when she marched into the house without ringing the bell. She had always had a key and it was certainly her right as a one-third owner of the house to walk in whenever she chose, but for a second I felt a wild impulse to mark off my third of the kitchen like children do in shared bedrooms.

My mood didn't improve when she greeted me. "You look a mess. This place smells like wet dog, too, and look at those prints all over the floor! You haven't let that animal run around on Mother's rugs, have you?"

"Of course not." I flung a bowl of Cheerios on the table and said, none too cordially, "If you came to hassle me about that rug, you need to talk to Judge Brantley." I plopped the jug of milk beside the cereal, feeling as defiant as a teenager sneaking a smoke. Our family never put a plastic milk jug on the table or drank from mugs. We used cups and saucers. We never ate in the kitchen, either. Perhaps that's why I grew up thinking the pinnacle of coziness was eating at a kitchen table with food spread out around me.

Susan cocked an eyebrow. "A bit grumpy this morning, aren't we? And not exactly well dressed."

"I've got to clean house, since Regan drove Alice off. Do you want some coffee?"

"Yes, please. But I didn't come to discuss the rug. I came to discuss you." When I joined her at the table, she regarded me over the rim of her cup for a long moment, exactly like King used to regard somebody he wanted to persuade to his way of thinking. "Albert and I want you to come live with us. We have two unused bedrooms, so you can have one for a sitting room, like you do here. You'll have to share a bath with Wonder, but you can use the piano whenever you like unless we have something going on in the living room. Everybody benefits. You get a place to live. You're a better cook than I am, so you can take that on, and you can watch Wonder while Monique preps for her SAT in December. Hopefully she can start classes next semester."

I was momentarily distracted from my pity party. "Has she finished high school?"

"She got her GED down in Savannah, thank heavens."

"Where will she go?" Unizilla College didn't admit students who hadn't gotten a regular high school diploma, and never let freshmen enter in the spring semester. Maybe Monique could go down to Atlanta to one of the many colleges there. Maybe we could live together.

I came out of my daydream to realize Susan was still talking. ". . . get the admissions office to make an exception." Susan was our father's daughter, all right—make strict rules to control the masses but consider the rules mere technicalities when they aren't convenient for you. Of course Monique wasn't going to Atlanta. She would matriculate at Unizilla in January.

"Why don't you put Wonder in the college preschool?" I asked.

One of Unizilla College's best departments was early childhood education. An award-winning preschool was connected to the program.

"I don't want Wonder mingling with children at preschool. She'd bring home germs."

Susan wasn't worried about germs. We both knew that. I felt ornery enough to needle her a bit. "Wonder was in day care in Savannah without catching anything fatal."

She cradled her cup between her hands. "Children can be cruel."

I didn't say a word, just looked at her.

She set her cup in her saucer with an irritated *click*. "Look, if we lived down in Atlanta, none of this would matter, but you know how people can be up here."

"Preschoolers don't have much prejudice," I pointed out.

"Their parents do, and children parrot what they hear. I don't want Wonder hurt. Besides, I think she may be ahead of the other children. She needs one-on-one attention, somebody who will stretch her mind, teach her our values, provide some culture, and work on her diction. You can do all that. She already adores you." I forgave Susan the vinegar in that last sentence. If my grandchild had preferred her to me, I'd have wanted to scratch her eyes out.

Considering what Susan was offering, I already wanted to smack her. "Let me get this straight. I move in with you, do the cooking, keep Wonder while Monique goes to college, and I get what?"

Susan wasn't used to my challenging her decisions—or asking anything for myself. "Free room and board. Monique will pay you, too. Not a lot, but she can get a part-time job to pay you something."

"I work full-time for Monique's unskilled half-time pay? What happens in four years when she graduates? Do I stay on to take care of you and Albert in your dotage?"

"Don't be sarcastic. I am trying to help. I know you won't have enough to live on forever, and since you aren't married . . ."

"Is my feminist sister suggesting I find a husband to support me?"

Susan grimaced. "Don't be silly." But color rose in her cheeks.

All of us occasionally betray our proclaimed values. I said, to make up for embarrassing her, "You are the silly one. I am a trained nurse. I can get a job—a good-paying job—anywhere in the world. I'll have to brush up, but I've kept up my license."

"But if you leave town, you'll break Wonder's heart. Come live with us. You can work evenings at the hospital if you want to."

I stared. "You think I could keep up with Wonder all day, then drive forty miles round-trip to work evenings? It may have escaped you, but I am not Superwoman."

She stood with a huff. "I'm trying to help, Teensie. I know you were disappointed by King's will. I'd like to make it up to you. Think it over, okay? In the meantime, please vacuum the living room rug. It's covered with crumbs, and I'm certain Judge Brantley will see reason and give it to me in time for our Parents' Weekend reception."

I wanted to say, "The vacuum is in the utility room. If it's your rug, you clean it." Instead, I felt my head give its habitual nod.

After the front door latched behind her I hurled my saucer across the room. It shattered in the sink with a satisfying crash.


As I dusted and vacuumed the downstairs, I found myself considering Susan's offer. The notion of spending a year or two with

Wonder had a certain appeal, and Monique would need help if she went to college full-time. In another year Wonder would be ready for kindergarten. Why not defer looking for a job in Atlanta until then?

I hadn't reached any conclusion when the doorbell rang. I opened the door to find Regan propping an emerald umbrella against the outside wall. She also had a key to the house, but she always rang.

She, too, gave my outfit a glance of surprise. "I'm cleaning house," I explained.

"Oh." She startled me by giving me a hug. "Are you all right? I hated to think of you all by yourself in this big house during that awful storm."

"I was all right. I've stayed here alone lots of times."

"Yes, but the place feels—I don't know—emptier now that King isn't coming back."

That was unusually perceptive of her. I had not slept well since King's death. His protective mantle over the house seemed to have departed with his final breath.

I gave in to a sisterly impulse before it died. "Would you like some coffee?"

I watched her lips shape themselves to say "No" but she changed her mind. "Sure."

"Shall we have it in the kitchen? It's warmer in there." That was a lie—I had lit the gas logs in the living room while I cleaned it. However, Jester was dozing on Susan's rug behind the closed double doors and I had a keen sense of self-preservation where my sisters were concerned.

When we sat at the table with coffee and slices of Alice's pound cake on Mother's second-best china, Regan said, "Sweetie, I want you to come over to our house for a few nights."

Whenever Regan rolled out a drawl so thick you could cross

a river on it, she was after something. "Why? I've never stayed at your house before." She lived only sixteen miles away.

"It was Holcomb's idea, really. On the way home yesterday he said, 'Poor little Teensie must be plumb worn out after taking care of your folks all those years, not to mention dealing with the funeral and everything. She ought to get a nice little vacation.' Now, we know you won't let us send you anywhere—"

I pictured a tropical beach, a drink with a little umbrella in the glass. "I'd be glad—"

"— but if you come to our place, you'll have privacy in our little guest suite."

I returned to rainy Unizilla with a mental thud. "I've got privacy here."

"You don't have Lynyetta to do your cooking, and we could go down to Atlanta one day to buy clothes for Wonder. Wouldn't that be fun?"

I took a sip of coffee while I thought that over. A few days at Regan's would be more luxurious than any resort I'd ever stayed in. Her "little guest suite" included an enormous sitting room with a wide-screen television and a rack of movies, and a huge bathroom with a Jacuzzi. She had a horse, a heated indoor pool, and a superb cook. Shopping for Wonder could be fun, too. I had never been on a shopping spree with either of my sisters.

On the other hand, Regan was up to something. She and Holcomb were not selfish—they gave away more money than I ever hoped to have—but their gifts were tied with strings. The new building at their church was the Harris Family Life Center. The new burn center over at the hospital was the Harris Burn Center. Since it was unlikely that Regan expected me to change my name, I asked, "Is there something you want me to do for you?"

"We-ell." She dragged the word out so far I wasn't sure she

could get it back, then spoke in a rush. "Holcomb had a brilliant idea. Ginny Linn is getting the teeniest bit forgetful."

Ginny Linn was Holcomb's mother. She used to run a stud farm over near Dalton and still lived in the beautiful house that went with the farm. She had a double portion of Southern charm and wicked wit in public, and an accent you could spread like butter, but at home she had one of the meanest dispositions I'd ever met in a woman. The only servant she had managed to keep for long was Julia, her cook, because Julia was deaf. She let Ginny Linn rant all she wanted, then did as she pleased. Ginny Linn forgave her because she was the best cook in Dalton.

"It's nothing serious, of course." Regan gave a careless little laugh. "Certainly not Alzheimer's, like her doctor thinks. She just does dumb things like forget she's turned on the stove. Julia has found it burning several mornings when she arrived. Ginny Linn puts things in strange places, too. I found unpaid bills under a sofa cushion last week. And she's fallen a few times. Holcomb is afraid she'll fall some evening when she's alone in the house. She's got tons of room. You could have the whole up-stairs to yourself and pretty much do anything you wanted dur-ing the day. All you'd need to do would be drive her when she needs to go somewhere and be there in the evening after Julia leaves."

Ginny Linn was the kind of woman who thought a day wasted unless she went out to lunch or a bridge party. Add in her weekly beauty appointments, shopping trips, and doctors' visits for a long list of minor ailments, and any nurse who lived with her would be a chauffeur by day, a prisoner by night.

Regan didn't give me a chance to point out any of that. "Hol-comb is willing to pay—handsomely, I might add. You'll make more than you would in any other job around here, for a lot less work. So what do you say?" She gave me the smile that had won her two homecoming crowns. "Is it a deal?"

I'd had years to develop immunity to Regan's smile. "I need to call in people to appraise the furniture and the house."

"That's all taken care of, hon. They're coming Thursday morning."

"Are these independent appraisers, like the judge requested?"

"Don't be silly. We need people we can trust."

"I wish you hadn't made that decision without asking me."

"I talked it over with Susan. We figured you wouldn't want to be bothered with all this." She laid her hands over mine, dwarfing them. "We care about you, Teensie. We really do. I am brokenhearted you are having to leave your home, and I know you hoped for more from King's estate. I would like to try to make it up to you."

Twenty-four hours earlier, I would have basked in having Regan tell me how much she cared for me. That afternoon I took my hands back and went to fetch more coffee. At that distance, I could be brave. "Give me your share, then. You can afford it, and with two-thirds of the house plus two-thirds of the money, maybe I can buy Susan out."

She bit her lower lip. "I can't."

"Why not? You've got more money than Susan and me put together."

"Holcomb has money. I only have what he gives me." She gave me a considering look. "Can you keep a secret?" Her dark eyes sparkled like a child's on Christmas Eve.

I gave her a cautious nod.

Although we were alone in the house except for Jester, Regan lowered her voice to an excited whisper. "God has promised to give me a baby, like he did those women in the Bible. He is going to open my womb!"

I must have sat there a full thirty seconds with my mouth hanging open. Could Regan be serious? Granted she was only forty-six, a lot younger than some of the barren women in the

Bible, but the sons of those biblical women were all destined for great roles in Israel's story. Did Regan believe God would contradict the natural order of things to provide an heir for a chicken empire?

"How did God make this promise?" I asked. "A voice from the clouds? A visiting angel?"

I believed in God. I sometimes got what I believed were messages from God. However, my messages tended to come in three forms: verses that appeared in my Bible where I'd never noticed them before; wise counsel from friends who weren't generally that smart; or a strong push to do something for somebody else—often something I'd rather not do. Regan and Holcomb had left the college chapel several years before for what Teddy used to call "an undenominational church." After that, Regan started talking about what God said to her as casually as she reported what Susan said. If God really said all that she claimed, her frequency of hearing from him was greater than that of Abraham, Moses, David, and the Virgin Mary combined. Also, while I was willing to get down on my knees and repent if I was doubting an authentic divine utterance, I had noticed that unlike God's dealings with me—and with people in the Bible— Regan's words from God seldom involved discomfort, inconvenience, or sacrifice.

Regan gave me a look I had no trouble reading: *You don't know God like I do. I'm not even sure you are saved.*

"Don't be silly," she said. "God's been speaking to me in *many* ways. Our preacher is doing a series on how much God loves us and wants us to be truly happy. All I need to be truly happy is a baby. And did you read in the paper recently about that woman who had twins at sixty? Her name was Megan. How significant is that? And last week I was down in Atlanta at the mall and a little girl came running up to me crying, 'Mama! Mama!'"

"Did you look like her mother?"

"No, except we both had on red jackets. That same day, on my way home, my hand accidentally hit the radio scan button on my steering wheel. Next thing I knew, somebody was singing, 'Unto us a child is born, unto us a son is given.' Isn't that amazing?"

"You probably got the classical station playing portions of Handel's *Messiah*."

"I don't know what station it was, but there are no coincidences, Teensie."

As her sister, I wanted to ask, "Are you flat-out crazy?" As a nurse, I was concerned for her mental state. I said in a neutral voice, "I agree there are no coincidences. I agree that God speaks to us. However, it's not always easy to read the signs. It's also easy to see things as signs when we want them to be."

"God is going to give me a child. He would not deny me the one thing I need to be happy. We have a right to happiness. The Bible says so."

"That's not the Bible—it's the Declaration of Independence, and even the Declaration doesn't say we have a right to happiness, only the right to pursue it."

"Whatever." She dismissed my argument with a graceful gesture. "You don't believe God wants people to be miserable, do you?"

"You aren't miserable."

"I'd be happier if I had a baby."

We weren't going to come to a theological meeting of the minds anytime soon. I might as well verify what I was beginning to suspect. "So you are going to use King's money to adopt?"

"Oh, no. Holcomb would never adopt. He's gotten interested in genealogy lately, what he calls 'our bloodline.' You'd think we were Ginny Linn's horses, the way he talks. I need money for fertility treatments. God uses medicine as well as miracles."

"Medicine *is* a miracle."

"Of course it is, but Holcomb says if God wants to give us a child, we don't need 'all that folderol.' I'm going to get the treatments without his knowing anything about it."

That was the most intimate conversation Regan and I had ever had. It certainly gave me new insights into her marriage. However, as a nurse I felt compelled to point out one slight flaw in her plan. "Unless you plan on artificial insemination, which would violate his precious bloodline, Holcomb will have to be part of the process."

"Oh, he will be, he just won't know it." Regan took out her mirror to repair her flawless makeup with a confidence I envied.

"Won't he think something's fishy if you get pregnant with quintuplets?"

She closed her purse with a snap. "Five new branches on his family tree? He'd be ecstatic. So you do see why I have to have money, don't you? You won't need to worry about money if you're living with Ginny Linn, though. You won't have any expenses and Holcomb will pay you well. She can be real sweet when she wants to."

"Ginny Linn raged at me like a banshee the year I called to tell her King wanted everybody to eat Christmas dinner here instead of at your house because Mother was too sick to travel."

Regan smiled rueful agreement. "She has her moments, but you're good with people."

"Let me think about it."

Regan's exasperation came out in an impatient breath. "The trouble with you, Teensie, is that you are a drifter. You drift through life letting other people decide what you ought to do. It's time to decide for yourself. Moving in to help Ginny Linn through her final years would be a thoughtful—and lucrative— thing to do."

"I said I'd think about it." While I didn't want to move in with Ginny Linn, it was true that I managed her better than some nurses would. After a few years of caring for her, I might save enough to revive my dream.

"We need you, Teensie, and you need us. Pray about it, okay?"

"I'll let you know. I'll take a rain check on coming to your place, though. I've got a lot to do around here."

As Regan stood to leave, I decided to take advantage of her mellow mood. "Will you and Susan let me take basic things from this house to furnish a place without counting them as part of my inheritance? Nothing valuable   everyday dishes, pots and pans, sheets, towels, and blankets. I'd have all that already if I had a place of my own."

"It sounds like stuff we'd give to a thrift store."

"It probably is. Oh—you all also need to know that the furniture in my bedroom and sitting room is already mine."

"I didn't know you had a sitting room. Where is it?" She looked around like she wondered if I'd added a room to the house.

"Susan's old bedroom."

"Oh. What do you have up there?"

"Furniture from Teddy's. Mother told me to take anything I wanted, so I did."

Regan wrinkled her nose. "That Mission stuff? I certainly don't want it."

I should never have added, "And Teddy's bedroom set."

Back when I was choosing furniture to fix up my sitting room, Mother—in a rare maternal gesture—had suggested I take the bedroom furniture. "It was Mary Bird's wedding present from John, you know. I think Teddy would want you to have it."

I had been so overwhelmed by Mother's offer, I had flung my arms around her. She was sick enough to permit the hug.

Although Mother and King spoke of Mary Bird and John

MacAllester as if they were relatives living across a distant mountain, the fact was that Mary had married John in North Carolina in 1805. I had loved Mary Bird's name so much as a child that I gave it to my favorite doll. I was delighted to replace my old scratched bedroom furniture—which I had inherited from Susan when she got new furniture in high school—for Mary Bird MacAllester's simple walnut chest, nightstand, dresser, and a four-poster bed so high that it came with a little set of steps.

In my kitchen on that rainy Tuesday, I watched Regan process data to generate the right conclusion. "The set that belonged to Mary Bird?"

"Yes. King and Teddy's mother gave it to *Teddy*." I knew that wouldn't cut any ice with Regan. It didn't.

She said, like a mother to a obstinate child, "Those are family heirlooms."

I was swamped by the same sense of doom I'd felt one Christmas when Regan had wanted the red-haired doll Santa brought me instead of the brunette he had brought her. "I'm the biggest," she had argued. "I get to choose first." Desolate, I had handed it over.

I was no longer four, I reminded myself. I stood up so I was closer to her height, resisting an impulse to climb on my chair so I could look down on her like she was looking down at me. "That furniture belonged to *Teddy*," I repeated.

"King inherited everything as Teddy's next of kin, so the furniture is part of his estate. Susan can't use it in the president's house, so it comes to me."

"King didn't want it. He'd have sold it with the rest of her things. Mother gave it to me because I was still using Susan's old furniture."

"To *use*, Teensie, not to *keep*. Mother had no right to give that set away. *King* didn't give it to you."

"King never gave me *anything*," I said with heavy emphasis, "but he didn't want it. If Mother hadn't given it to me, he would have sold it in the estate sale."

"Do you have anything in writing to prove it's yours?"

My stomach twisted, as it always did when I tried to stand up to my sisters. "You got a fat check when you got married. Susan got a check plus her bedroom furniture. Do you have anything in writing to prove they were yours?"

"Neither of us got family heirlooms."

"It's mine," I insisted as I followed her through the hall. "King would have sold it."

"Prove it." Regan opened the front door. As I followed her onto the porch, a gust of wind billowed the rain like silver sheets on a line. With a swish of wet tires, a black truck drove downhill toward the campus kitchen carrying a load of fresh greens. If it was Wonder's vegetable man, he would get soaked unloading, but his collards would be thoroughly washed.

From her raincoat pocket Regan pulled out a scarf the same green as her umbrella. "You won't ever have a house nice enough to put that furniture in." Her careless assurance stung worse than deliberate cruelty would have.

My stomach churned as I watched her Lexus descend the hill. I had lost Teddy, my parents, my house, and my dreams. Would I lose my bedroom furniture as well?

As I went back inside, the phone rang. "You doing all right up there?" The deep voice was as rough as the granite chips around our flower beds.

I smiled for the first time in so many hours that my face had almost forgotten how. "Hey, Coco." We were the sort of friends who didn't have to start a conversation with greetings.

From her voice, strangers might think Coco had spent a lifetime guzzling whiskey between cigarettes. Perhaps she had, during her college years at Berkeley and what the judge always referred to as "that disastrous marriage." Coco never referred to her marriage except to mention once that she had been lucky to get out with a suitcase.

I was fifteen when she returned to care for her mother during her last illness. Since then she had kept house for her father and volunteered with almost every charity in the county. As a teenager I was fascinated by Coco because she was an exotic flower in our midst. She wore her long red hair hanging down her back and peasant blouses with skirts in electric colors that brushed her sandaled feet. She smoked and didn't hide it like my mother did. She had a laugh that gurgled like a stream when she got tickled.

As an adult, I loved her because she was smart, kind, and quirky.

"Daddy, Gage, and I are all sick about this mess," she said. "I've been thinking about you all day long. I had to call to ask what you plan to do."

My sisters' offers perched like vultures on each shoulder. "I'm not sure yet. Susan wants me to move in with them to take care of Wonder so Monique can go to college. Regan came by offering a handsome salary if I'll move in with Holcomb's mother, who is in the early stages of Alzheimer's."

"Don't you dare take your sisters up on their unholy offers!" Coco had the temper that went with her red hair.

"I ought to consider them for what Wonder calls 'the foreseeable future.' They need me. They really do."

"Don't you make me come over there to give you a good shaking! Your family will always need you. You are what some folks call 'the designated daughter.' It's time you let them take care of their own problems. Get on with your own life!"

I hung up feeling energized, but in spite of Coco's good advice, I felt I ought to at least consider my sisters' offers. I carried a legal pad to the kitchen table to list pros and cons of moving in with Susan or taking care of Ginny Linn. On the pro side were questions like "How can I turn them down when they need me?" and reminders like "It would be some income," and "They are all the family I have." On the con side I scrawled, "How long, O Lord?" I was still writing when the phone rang.

"Have you seen Wonder?" asked Susan without preamble. "Is she there with you?" She sounded more annoyed than alarmed.

"No. Has she wandered off?"

Faculty children roamed the campus freely. Students and staff watched out for them. I hoped Wonder had the sense not to cross the road at the front gate, though. It was a federal highway, and cars seldom slowed to the posted speed limit.

"Yes. Monique took her for a walk—"

I looked outside. Rain was still falling by the bucketful. "In this weather?"

Susan exhaled exasperation. "Yes. Regan brought her a yellow raincoat and boots a little while ago, and nothing would do but for Wonder to try them out. Monique stopped near the cafeteria to chat with somebody and when she looked around, Wonder was gone."

"How long ago was that?"

"Fifteen minutes, maybe? Monique glanced in the cafeteria and a couple of other buildings before she called me. I've alerted campus security to look for her, but I thought maybe she had come up to see you."

"No." I remembered something. "Did Monique check the college kitchen?"

"Why would Wonder go back there?"

"There's a man who delivers vegetables who is, Wonder informs me, one of her bestest friends. I saw him driving down the hill to make a delivery a little while ago. She might have—"

"Oh, dear God. If he has taken that child . . . I'll call security again."

"I think he's harmless. Let me go to the kitchen to see if she's there. It won't take a minute." The college cafeteria was right downhill from our house. "I'll call you back."

I stuck my cell phone in my poncho pocket and ran as fast as I could. I didn't want one of the campus security guards reaching Wonder before I did. Given Albert's predilection for law and order, they tended to be selected more for brawn than brains. By the time I reached the loading dock, my bangs were plastered to my forehead, wisps of hair were glued to my cheek, and my loafers were squishing.

The black truck was backed to the dock, its bed empty. Under the dock's narrow roof, Wonder—bright in her new raincoat and boots—perched on an upturned wooden box. Humidity had turned her hair into an electric frizz above her head but she didn't care. She was listening intently to the man who sat on another box beside her. His voice—deep and husky—was in the middle of a story.

He wore jeans, a gray sweatshirt with the hood up, and muddy boots. The hands clasped between his knees were raw—probably from cutting greens in the rain. His profile was sharp, as if carved from rust-stained granite. What little I could see of his hair under the hood was as black as the thick brows over his eyes. I could see why Wonder, to whom all things unusual were delightful, would find him attractive, but in spite of my assurances to Susan, I hoped he wasn't a child molester who had fixated on the child. He had certainly discovered the way to her heart.

Neither he nor Wonder paid me any attention as I sloshed up the steps at the end of the dock. I waited until I was near them to call, "Wonder? Did you know people are looking everywhere for you?" My voice came out sharper than I intended.

The man flicked me a look as he finished what he'd been saying. ". . . and that, or so they say, is how we got the Milky Way."

Wonder ran to tug me toward him. "Hey, Teensie! Yuck! Your hand is cold." She began to rub it between her two warm ones.

"I had to come from my house in the rain. Your mother doesn't know where you are."

The drama queen heaved a mighty sigh. "I told her where I was going, she dist didn't listen. I came to get a glass of milk, den I found de veg'table man. Mr. Veg'table Man, dis is Teensie. She tells stories, too. Teensie, dis is de veg'table man."

He gave me a curt nod, probably thinking I looked like a drowned rat.

Wonder went on without pausing for breath. "He was telling me about de Milky Way. Did you ever see—"

A security car screeched to a halt next to the black truck. A stocky guard jumped out, gun drawn. "Freeze, mister!"

"No!" I cried. "Be careful!" The guard looked like a man with more belly than sense.

"Get the child out of the way," he ordered.

The way he was waving that gun around, I obeyed. My knees felt like jelly as I dragged Wonder down the dock. He pointed the gun in the vegetable man's direction. "What were you doing with that child?"

I was close enough to read his name in red script above the pocket of his gray shirt: JAY.

"Telling her a story." The vegetable man's voice was level as he looked at the gun with eyes that did not blink, an eagle regarding a bulldog.

I wasn't dumb enough to step between them, so I spoke loud enough to get the guard's attention. "It's okay, Jay. The child is fine. Put away your gun. It was a false alarm."

"The president's wife said . . ." His voice was truculent.

I would gloat later over Susan's demotion from Dr. MacAllester-Madison to "the president's wife." At the moment . . . "I'm Teensie MacAllester. Susan is my sister. She occasionally makes mistakes and this is one of them. Wonder wandered off on her own, didn't you, sweetie?" I hoped she didn't feel me shaking.

Wonder took her cue like a rising starlet. "Yes, ma'am. Mama was talking and talking, so I came to get milk, den I asked de veg'table man to tell me a story. He dist finished."

"I'll call Susan to tell her the child is found." I pulled my cell phone from my pocket.

"If you are sure . . ." Jay holstered his gun with obvious reluctance. He had probably never had an opportunity to draw it before. "You watch your step now," he growled at the vegetable man as he climbed back into his car.

Hoping again that the vegetable man wasn't a molester with his eye on Wonder, I punched in Susan's number.

I heard him say, "When you get home, tell your mother you're sorry you ran away."

Wonder's voice quivered with indignation. "I did not wun away. I told her—"

Susan answered, so agitated that I didn't get any words in except, "She's found."

While Susan poured out all her worry, I heard the vegetable man say in the background, "When we are right, we can afford to apologize. When we are wrong, we can't afford not to."

Wonder scuffed one boot on the floor. "I guess so."

"Some night when there isn't much moon, ask her to take you outside. If you look up, you will see what looks like a smeared cloud across the sky. That's the Milky Way."

"Made out of cornmeal?"

"So the story says."

She heaved a tremendous sigh. "Mama doesn't take me out at night. I has to go to bed. I guess I'll nebber see it in de foreseeable future." She sighed again.

Amusement flitted across his wide mouth. "You will grow up soon enough."

She put out her hand as formally as a queen. "Good-bye, Mr. Veg'table Man. T'ank you for de story. It was as good as Teensie's."

I meant to tell him how sorry I was for the trouble we'd caused, but by the time I had hung up he had leaped down from the dock as if it were two feet high, not four. He drove away without saying a word to me.

Wonder pulled up her hood as we stepped into the rain. "Don't I look bee-*you*-ti-ful in my new wain clothes? I even got boots." She stuck out a foot to demonstrate.

"They're lovely. I wish I had yellow."

"Green is pretty," she said generously. "It looks good wif your freckles."

The whole time we squished across campus, Wonder told me about a "Cherky" farmer whose cornmeal was eaten every night. "Dey didn't know who was taking it, but it was a great big dog dat came down from de heavens in de northern sky. Did you know dogs lived in de sky, Teensie? Dat one did. So de family hid one night and came out to beat de dog with sticks. Wasn't dat mean? He shoulda eaten dem up, but he didn't. He flew up to de sky wif his mouf full of cornmeal and all de cornmeal fell out of his mouf and made the Milky Way. Dat's what the Cherkys say. Did you know dat?"

I needed a minute to translate what she was saying. "It's Cher-o-kee, not Cherky. The Cherokee are a tribe of"—I hesitated, uncertain what the recent preferred term was—"of people who used to live around here and the Milky Way is really a galaxy made up of thousands of stars. Our sun and all the planets are part of it."

"Nope. You learned it wong. Now you know de weal truth—

it's made out of cornmeal. Dat's what the *Cherkys* say." She emphatically rejected my pronunciation.

We walked several more yards. "What is cornmeal?" she asked.

"The yellow meal your mother makes corn bread out of."

"My mama makes corn bread out of a little blue box. We put in a egg and a little bit of milk and give it a stir and dat's all dere is to it. You ought to try it, Teensie. It's easy."

As we started up Susan's drive, I warned, "You'd better stay with your mother from now on when you are out of the house, or she and your nana are going to be unhappy."

That got a mutinous expression. "None of dis would have happened 'cept for dat man. I told Mama where I was going, but she was too busy talking to listen."

"What man?"

Wonder shrugged. "Dist some man with no hair. I don't like him, not one bit. He better stay away from my mama, dat's all I got to say."

I waited until Susan took Wonder up for her nap before I asked Monique, "Who were you talking to when Wonder disappeared?"

Monique wore jeans so tight I wondered how she could breathe, a blue sweater that showed off every curve, and her high-heeled boots. She patted her carefully tangled hair. "Somebody I used to know."

"Not Junior Walters, I hope."

Three years before, Monique's former boyfriend had been given a medical discharge from the army. He had come back to Unizilla and applied to the college under his legal name, Herbert. Because he had a decent high school record and impressive test scores, and because the admissions director was new and not privy to Junior's former connection to Albert's family, he was admitted. Albert suspected Junior had been responsible for several unpleasant incidents involving coeds, but none of them would name him. Junior maintained such an excellent academic record that Albert could find no other reason to expel him.

Monique tilted her chin. "Who I see is nobody's business except mine."

"If you've got Wonder in tow, you'd better pay attention to what she says."

"I can't listen to her all the time. I have to have a life, too, you know. Did Mama ask if you can watch Wonder while I cram for the SAT?"

"She said something about that, but we didn't come to any agreement. I'll have to let you know."

"Okay." She snatched up her raincoat. "Gotta go—I'm late for a date. Don't tell Mama." It wasn't a request; it was a command.

I went home to make myself a pot of tea. By then the rain had parted its western curtains to reveal a gorgeous sunset: lavish streaks of red, coral, and lavender. I carried my tea onto the front porch and stood at the railing, taking deep breaths of freshly washed air. Dark clouds were still hurtling across the Smoky Mountains to the northeast while the sun bid the day farewell.

" 'I will lift up mine eyes unto the hills, whence cometh my help,' " Coco intoned from the bottom of my front steps.

Now fifty-five, Coco had given up smoking and cropped her hair, but she kept it the same shade of red it was when she was a girl. She still favored exotic skirts and shawls, too, but over the years she had become as good a Bible scholar as Teddy.

She and Teddy had been great friends. Coco had continued to drop in for afternoon tea even after Teddy no longer remembered who any of us were.

She kept talking as she climbed the steps. "That was one of

Teddy's favorite Psalms, remember? Newer translations render the verses 'I lift up my eyes to the hills. Where does my help come from? It comes from God,' which may be more accurate theologically, but it will never rival the other for poetic beauty." She pressed her hand to her heart and a dozen silver bangles caught the evening sun. "Whew! You need an elevator. Those steps are killers."

"The old version is equally true," I said, picking up her original conversation. "If we look at the mountains long enough, they usually remind us that our troubles are small in the general scheme of things."

"Oh, honey!" She gave me a squeeze. Coco was one of few women in town as short as I was. I did not trust myself to speak. Together we stood looking at the hills.

She gave a little sigh. "Those mountains have known a lot of sorrow over the centuries, haven't they? Cherokee women setting out on the Trail of Tears, pioneer women clasping dead babies to their breasts before burying them, wives and mothers watching for the return of their men from what they call down in Charleston 'the Late, Great Unpleasantness.' Yet the mountains never change."

Until a couple of years before, Coco had taught American history at the high school. One student told me, "Miz Ihle makes history seem like real life."

Real life was too real at the moment. I reached over the railing to strip the nearest boxwood of its uppermost leaves. Not until a twig sliced my palm did I notice what I was doing. I brought the stinging hand to my mouth to suck the small drops of blood. The odor of boxwood used to mean home. Now it was the scent of betrayal.

"Ouch!" Coco exclaimed as she saw the blood. "That hurts."

I lifted one shoulder and let it drop. "It's a reminder I'm still alive."

Coco gave me another squeeze. "Of course you are. Listen, don't worry about getting those birdhouses painted, with everything else you have on your plate right now. And you call if there is anything I can do—you hear me? Anything at all."

Her friendship was so precious, I had to swallow a lump in my throat before I could speak. "No, I'll get to the birdhouses pretty soon. Painting will take my mind off things."

Fire flashed in her eyes. "What your father did was utterly despicable. If it were up to me, King MacAllester would burn in hell a hundred years. You gave him everything. Your youth, your career, even—what was the name of that man who came to see you once up here?"

"Michael?" I smiled, but it wobbled.

"Yes, Michael. I wish I'd met him. I know Teddy said he wasn't any loss, but . . ." She broke off and veered in another direction. "You and I have something in common, you know. We each had a brief taste of freedom, then we deferred our lives for other people, thinking we could pick them up where we left off. I've found that life doesn't wait around. Have the gumption I didn't, you hear me? Run after life! Catch it while you can!"

As I watched her go down the hill, I wasn't thinking of Coco. I was remembering Michael. How many years since I'd thought of him?

He had not been a prince, only an intern in the hospital where I worked. His brown hair was unruly, his clothes untidy even when he hadn't slept in them, his face strained from exhaustion the whole time I knew him. We had met over the bed of a dying man—Michael's first. He was so shaken that I took him to the nurses' station and gave him coffee. After that we exchanged tentative smiles when we met in the hall. A week later he carried his tray to my table in the hospital cafeteria. We began to meet for meals when our schedules permitted. One weekend he asked me to a free afternoon concert at Emory. On our way we drove through a community of large brick homes. Michael pointed to a Georgian house up an ivy-covered hill. "I want to live in a house like that one day. Can you imagine what it would be like?"

I didn't mention that I'd grown up in a house far grander than that. "I like that one." I pointed to a modest home tucked among the big ones. "It looks cozier."

"Too small. I want something a family can spread out in."

After the concert we spent half an hour driving through winding streets comparing houses we liked. He teased me that I knew nothing about "living the good life." Later he took me to his apartment, which was as untidy as his clothes. Ours had been a fumbling, awkward relationship—neither of us had had much experience with the opposite sex—but I had hoped our little bud might blossom if we gave it time.

We didn't have time. Three weeks later King had phoned. "Teddy is getting forgetful. She drove to Canton this morning and got lost on the way back. Lost, when she's lived up here twenty years. She can't stay alone any longer. You need to come on home."

He tried to pretend it was temporary, of course. "Just for a while, shug, until we can decide what else to do. I'm taking over her checking account, so I'll pay you. Not as much as you make at the hospital, but you'll get free room and board—and it's just for a time."

Was he trying to convince me or himself?

I did not go easily. I suggested several alternatives. King demolished each of them, heaping guilt on my small spurts of rebellion. "Teddy would hate living in a home. She'd hate worse having strangers in her house. Your sisters can't take this on— they've got husbands and homes to look after. We can't have her here. Your mother doesn't have time to look after her—she has enough to do looking after me, this house, and all her committees, and I've got an election coming up this year. Besides, Teddy loves you best. She always has."

"Only for a few weeks," I vowed as I packed my things. Still, I told my housemates to find a new tenant for the third bedroom. Life has a tendency to run along in ruts unless we take the initiative to steer out of them, and I knew I would never steer a course contrary to King's wishes. Sure enough, weeks had blurred into months, months into years. By the time Teddy died I had been back in Unizilla for eight years and Mother had been diagnosed with the cancer that would kill her three years later. After she died there was King, sad and surprisingly humble as he asked me to stay.

Michael had come to Unizilla once, a few weeks after I left Atlanta. The day was not a success. Both of us were exhausted. Teddy insisted I take him to meet my parents, and she became so agitated when I resisted that I agreed. Michael was awed by the marble house. Mother was kind to the young man in scuffed shoes, but when she served us iced tea and cake, she made him so nervous he spilled tea on her rug. King was too hearty, asking questions that mortified me: "I don't guess interns make much, do they?" "How many years before you'll make enough to support a family?"

Once we were alone, there was nowhere private to go. Sitting on a bench on campus we found little to talk about except the hospital. When he took me back to Teddy's, he gave me a quick kiss. "I'll be seeing you," he said. We both knew he wouldn't. Anything that had germinated in Atlanta had withered in Unizilla.

I didn't weep as I watched his car disappear down the mountain. Away from the hospital, which conferred godlike status to interns, Michael was boring. At twenty-four I had told myself I had years ahead in which my prince could come.

At forty I backed into a rocker and, while night settled down on the hills, I grieved Michael, my lukewarm love, as if he had been a grand passion.

"Is this a bad time for a visit?" Phil Potts, the music professor who had given me a lift home from the cemetery after King's funeral, stood on my front walk.

I brushed tears from my cheek. "No, this is fine."

I must not have sounded hospitable, for he said, "I saw you on your porch, so I thought it was okay to come." Phil lived on campus in college housing for single faculty and his back windows faced our house. In Unizilla, if you were on your porch, you were open to company.

He held up a music case. "I have a new transcription of Bach's *Air on a G String*."

I mustered what enthusiasm I could. "I'd love to hear it. Can you see to play?"

"I don't need to see."

I settled into a rocker while he took out his instrument.

Phil stood only a couple of inches taller than me, and looked like Prince Charming in miniature: golden curls, skin as white as porcelain, and a handsome face with a dimple in his chin. Female students constantly developed crushes on him. A freshman once asked me with a giggle, "Don't you want to cuddle him?"

No, I didn't. Students presumed we were romantically involved because we showed up together at college functions. Their soppy little minds never imagined we were simply dates of convenience: he the only single man on the faculty and I the only single woman in town who shared his love of music. Because students came and went, they didn't know Phil and I had been "dating" for seven years. Our evenings out were pleasant enough, for we agreed on music, plays, and lectures and we never discussed what we didn't agree on. However, in all that time he had never kissed me except for a perfunctory peck on the cheek when he brought me home. His passion went into his music.

Sometimes during college breaks he invited me to drive down to Atlanta for a weekend. We saw a play, attended the symphony, and ate a couple of elegant dinners. I loved those escapes, but I always paid for my own meals and tickets and we had separate rooms in separate hotels. King reserved my rooms himself and put them on his credit card "for the public record." I had never been tempted not to use my room. After a companionable evening I found it a relief to close my door, climb into pajamas, and read for an hour before I went to sleep. One night as I drifted off, I reflected that going out with Phil was like sitting on ice while wrapped in a blanket: bits of you were warm, but you were always aware of a chill underneath.

I had no idea how Phil felt about me. My own feelings were simple: he was a personable partner for events where it was awkward to show up alone. He was also a marvelous musician. On the saxophone he moved with equal skill from classical to jazz to rock, and I was flattered that he liked to try out new arrangements on me before performing them in public. In the past fifteen years I had perfected the art of living in the moment and putting off consideration of my future.

Which had risen up that week to stare me in the face. Determined to put off thinking about the future for a little while longer, I let the sweetness of Phil's music carry me over the dusk-kissed mountains, high above the marble house filled with disappointment. When he finished, he let the silence speak before he did. "You like it?"

I drifted to earth. "Wonderful. Nobody brings me closer to heaven than Bach."

"And the arrangement?" His voice was anxious.

"Perfectly lovely. I keep telling you, you ought to record some of your stuff."

"Maybe I will one day." I wondered if he knew how much yearning he put into that sentence. "Would you like to hear what I've done with one of Scott Joplin's pieces?" He began to play without waiting for my reply.

Bach had suited my mood. Joplin jarred.

To make it worse, when he played jazz, Phil writhed like a cobra following a flute. I sometimes wondered if jazz was as close as he ever got to sex. It clearly exalted—and exhausted—him. With his eyes closed he played in such tremendously long phrases that if I watched, I found myself holding my breath with him. Only when his face was bright pink did he take a desperate gasp. If he ever did record his arrangements, he'd need to edit out the gasps.

I closed my eyes to avoid looking at him and found myself thinking a startling thought: *Phil and I are exactly alike. We are middle-aged people still standing on the threshold of life, waiting for happily-ever-after to come riding out of the mist.*

I caught a ragged breath. What had come out of the mist for me was not happy-ever-after; it was bleak, empty, and terrifying. Would Phil ever find happy-ever-after? Or would he go on teaching at Unizilla, yearning to record his music until he became an old might-have-been?

When he brought the Joplin to a triumphant finish, I gave him light applause.

He dropped a red scarf with a weight on one end down his instrument and pulled it through to dry the interior. "Would you like to go to dinner?" He shoved a cleaner through the mouthpiece to complete the drying process.

"To dinner?" I gave him what must have been a blank look.

Phil and I never went out in Unizilla except to college events. Aside from the fact that I didn't relish fueling student rumors, there wasn't anywhere to go except the college cafeteria, a student-ridden pizza parlor, or Danny's Diner, which specialized in grease.

He nodded. "We could drive to that seafood place in Blue Ridge."

It was tempting. Phil loved sports cars. At the moment he drove a red Miata convertible, and the weather was still warm enough to have the top down. I would love to ride fast and feel the tug of the wind in my hair.

On the other hand, my spirits were as raw as if they had been rubbed with coarse sandpaper. I would be terrible company. I stood to let him know the visit was over. "Thanks, but not tonight. Can we make it another time?"

"Of course." He didn't pick up his case to leave.

I touched his hand. "You were kind to come."

"Not kind." Those spatulate fingers that were clever on the saxophone closed around mine. He drew me so close, I had the feeling I was about to vanish inside him.

"I couldn't speak while your father needed you." His breath was hot on my forehead. "Now that you are free . . ." He dropped my hands to wrap me in his arms.

Kissing Phil was like being attached to him by a glue gun. His lips were hard against mine but utterly static. As the kiss went on and on I began to feel claustrophobic. Over his shoulder I saw lightning dance in the eastern sky.

I pulled my head so far back I nearly dislocated my neck. "Please, Phil. No."

He released me, stepped back, and looked into my eyes. My honest eyes. I wondered what he was seeing there. Confusion? Astonishment? Afraid it might be dismay, I looked away. Lightning flickered again, too far away to hear the thunder.

He caught both my hands in his again. "I'm sorry, Teensie. I know I was precipitate, but I wanted you to know how I feel." Before I could step away, he pressed his lips to mine again.

I knew how I felt: embarrassed to be standing on my front porch in the arms of a faculty member. I detected no desire in his kiss. He simply pressed his lips to mine and left them there, like the adolescent exercise of kissing a mirror. Waiting for the kiss to end, I considered the pros and cons of marrying him.

We would not be passionate, obviously, but he was kind and respectful. In a few years he would probably chair the music department—especially if he was married to Albert's sister-in-law. We would have a ready-made circle of friends among faculty couples. While we would never be wealthy, we would have enough for concerts, plays, and trips during college breaks. I wouldn't have the marble house or my nursing home, but we could lease one of the attractive faculty houses that surrounded the campus. My life would not be exciting, but I would still be able to work at the clinic, sing in the chapel choir, and continue the quiet process of keeping house for two. My sisters would respect me, since I would have taken vows to enter the Order of Married Women. Wonder would be ecstatic that the third princess had found her prince and she would make a darling flower girl. Best of all, every evening I could curl into the corner of our couch and listen to Phil play.

*Do I want to spend my life sitting on ice while wrapped in a blanket? Shouldn't there be a few tingles?*

I felt nothing but dizzy, and that wasn't passion. Playing the saxophone had given Phil more lung capacity than I had. Had I deferred passion, as well as life, until it was too late?

Disappointment gnawed my bones.

I pulled away to breathe. "I'm sorry. I'm too exhausted right now to be good company."

Courteous to his core, Phil stepped back immediately. "Of course. You've worn yourself out these past two weeks."

"A bit. I'll be all right after a few more days. Thanks for

coming. I was feeling sad and you've cheered me up. The Bach was beautiful."

"I'm glad. We'll talk later. For now, get some rest." He gave me a swift, gentle kiss on the cheek. "I'll be seeing you." His farewell words—Michael's farewell words—remained in my ears long after he was gone.

I couldn't get to sleep that night for competing voices in my head: *You like and respect Phil*, said Reason. *Maybe you will learn to love him.*

*You don't love him*, retorted Romance. *Not the way you ought to love somebody you marry.*

*He may be your last chance*, countered Reason. *Why not settle for this decent, kind man who offers security and music?*

*Don't settle for anything!* cried Romance. *Without love, you are better off as you are.*

I twisted and turned until my gown felt like a straitjacket. As I got out of bed to resettle it, I wished I could settle the debate in my head that easily. I gave my bed a nurse's rigorous remake and climbed back in. Sleep wouldn't come.

*Maybe I don't know how to love.* That thought spiraled up from the hellish pit that cracks open near anyone who worries in the middle of the night.

*Of course I do!* I retorted bravely. I was a Friday's child, loving and giving. I enjoyed helping others.

*Who have you ever really loved?*

The weight of that question perched on my chest as I sought an answer. For King I had felt awe, fear, and—in his last years—the pity one feels at watching an old lion grow helpless. Was that love? I had yearned for touches or words of affection from Mother that rarely came, and I had cared for her tenderly her last three years. Was that love? Was it love for my sisters that made me wish we three could be like sisters in books who laughed together and shared insider jokes? I had not loved Michael and I had never loved Phil.

*I'm an iceberg.* Tears slid from the corners of my eyes. *I'm just like Phil. Maybe I ought to marry him. Women marry all over the world without being madly in love with their husbands.*

My fingers plucked restlessly at my spread, seeking a pencil.

To still them, I turned on the light and pulled a sketch pad from my nightstand drawer. My pencil sketched a long shelf of miniature clay vessels. Beneath them appeared the words DO YOU REALLY WANT TO BE TEENSIE POTTS?

I laughed aloud. Of course I had loved. I loved Teddy. I loved Monique. I loved Wonder. I loved Coco, and the judge, and Gage. I wasn't incapable of love; I simply didn't love Phil Potts. Reassured, I went to sleep.

# *Three*

Regan's crew arrived Thursday before I finished my breakfast. "My name's Raymond," the head appraiser said in a brisk manner. "This is Mary and that's George."

Raymond strolled around the house cocking his head at furniture like he was asking it to give him its history, then wrote busily. Mary went over china, silver, crystal, and bric-a-brac like a detective looking for clues. George spent a lot of time on his knees examining the backs of Mother's rugs, making little sounds of pleasure deep in his throat. Once in a while I noticed Raymond consult a sheet at the back of his clipboard and silently point out something to one of the others. When he left the clipboard on the hall table while he stepped out on the porch to make a call, I peeked. As I had expected, the list included the Royal Doulton china.

When I went upstairs later to paint birdhouses, I saw Raymond in my bedroom running his fingers over my dresser. "That's not part of the estate," I told him.

"I was told . . ."

"Nothing in this room," I said firmly. "See the sign on the door?" I waited until he left.

When the Realtor arrived, she announced, "I'm from Sam Tolbert's office."

"Judge Brantley insisted that an independent Realtor should appraise the house."

"I don't work for Sam. I work out of his office."

How dumb did she think I was? The only thing that kept me from asking her to leave was the scene I'd have with my sisters if I did. The Realtor examined the hall and King's study without comment, but in the dining room she exclaimed, "I do like this. Very English."

"Oh, yes." I found the walnut paneling gloomy and the six oil paintings that adorned it more suitable for a museum, but she didn't need to know that. "King loved this room."

She dismissed me with a wave. "You can go. I'll have a look around."

I went to King's study, wrote my name on two of his business cards, and went out on the porch to wait for my visitors to finish. As they left, I handed the Realtor and the head appraiser a card. "Please send me a copy of your appraisal. I am as interested in this as my sisters are." The surprise in their eyes confirmed my suspicion: they had thought I was the housekeeper.

I wondered why I felt happy when I wakened on Friday, until I realized I would be working at the clinic all day. I wouldn't have to spend long hours in a house that was dying. I wouldn't have to deal with any of my family. Between King's illness and death, I had been away from work for two weeks. I looked forward to getting back.

Susan phoned before I left. "Are you going to be home this morning?"

"No, it's my day at the clinic." I waited for her to ask me to keep Wonder instead.

"All right. I'll talk to you later." She hung up without saying good-bye.

I received a hug from Dr. Mimi Starnes, the clinic's founding director. "Welcome back. We've missed you." Mimi was a dedicated internist whose husband was chief of surgery at our nearest hospital. Whenever anyone praised Mimi for the work she did, she said, "Give the praise to Larry. He puts food on our table so I can do this."

We only had a few people needing visits that day, so I finished early. Normally I would have stayed to help in the clinic. That morning Mimi told me, "Go on home. You've done enough for your first day back."

I picked up a few things from the grocery store and drove up the alley to our garage.

When I reached the house, I was puzzled to see the back gate ajar and a large white truck pulled up to the back stoop. My kitchen door stood open, too, and the screen door was propped back by a chair. I cautiously approached the steps. As I passed the truck I saw a red logo on the door: HARRIS POULTRY. From inside the house, I heard a familiar voice. "Careful! Careful!"

I dashed up the steps to collide with two burly men carrying my chest of drawers. "What is going on?" My heart pounded like a jackhammer as I blocked the door.

"Moving a few things," said one of the men gruffly. "Let us by, please."

"That is my chest. Put it down!"

"You'll have to discuss that with her." He jerked a thumb behind him.

"Regan?" I tried unsuccessfully to peer around them. "What are you doing here?"

She appeared from behind the men. "I talked to Susan. We don't think you ought to get Mary Bird's bedroom furniture. By rights it should go to her as the oldest daughter, but since she can't use it, I'm taking it as the next oldest. When I die, I'll leave it to Monique."

I had caved in all my life whenever Regan had wanted my new barrettes, lollipop, or doll. *Not this time*, I vowed. *Not this furniture.* For once Regan wanted something I was willing to fight for. "You're going to be dying sooner than you think if you try to take that chest out of this house. Put it back!" I waved to the men. "Now!"

They backed up a step.

"Ignore her," Regan commanded. "She is clearly hysterical."

"I'll show you hysterical." I pelted down the steps and through the gate, slammed it shut behind me, and climbed into my truck. Shaking with fury, I positioned my truck to block the gate, then called Judge Brantley on my cell phone. "Regan is over here trying to take my bedroom furniture. I told her Tuesday that furniture was Teddy's and that Mother gave it to me after Teddy died. She came to take it while I was at the clinic. If I hadn't come home early, she'd have been gone before I got back."

"Put her on," ordered the judge.

"Judge Brantley wants to talk to you," I yelled, holding the phone out my open window.

"I have nothing to say to him," she shouted.

"I heard that," said the judge. "Tell her not to leave with that furniture. I'll be right up."

"She's not going anywhere," I promised.

Regan glared at me. "Move your truck!"

I locked the doors, closed the windows, and stuck out my tongue.

"Teensie! This is ridiculous."

I cracked my window one inch. "Theft is never ridiculous."

"Put it in the kitchen," Regan called to the men. "We'll have to do this another way."

"Like over my dead body," I called, "or over yours. Tell them to carry it back upstairs while they're at it. You aren't taking it anywhere."

The men carried the chest back inside while Regan stood on the back stoop tapping an impatient toe, her arms akimbo. In a few minutes the men came back out. The bigger one motioned for me to move. I shook my head. "Judge Brantley is coming," I called through the crack in my window. "I'll sit here until then."

"Hey, lady, have a heart. We were following orders."

"That's what Hitler's storm troopers said. The judge is on his way."

They stood beside the truck with glum faces.

I presumed Regan had left her Lexus on campus so I wouldn't see it. I didn't know what I'd do if she decided to abandon her troops before the judge arrived.

Before she thought of that, Judge Brantley's white Cadillac pulled in behind me. Since he lived less than a short block downhill from us, he usually walked. I wondered whether he'd brought his car to hurry or to make a more impressive entrance. His Caddy was built in the era when size proclaimed them the aristocrats of the American car industry. It would probably outlast us all, the way the judge kept it up. "What is going on here?" he demanded.

"Ask her." I jerked a thumb toward Regan.

She came down the steps with perfect poise, every hair and her smile in place. "Hello, Judge. Teensie and I have had a little misunderstanding about a set of bedroom furniture that has been passed down to the oldest daughter in our family for several generations. It isn't part of King's estate, it belongs to Susan. Since she doesn't need it at the moment, I'm taking it home until Monique wants it."

I felt at a disadvantage sitting in the truck, so I climbed down. "It was Teddy's, Judge, and as I told you—and told Regan earlier this week—Mother gave it to me when Teddy died. Even if she hadn't, Susan got her bedroom furniture when she got married and Regan got a check instead of hers when she married, so I would deserve that furniture if it weren't already mine."

"Did King and Regina offer you bedroom furniture when you married?" Judge Brantley asked Regan.

"Yes, but we didn't take it. It had twin beds and Holcomb's parents gave us a check to furnish our house. My old furniture wasn't anything like these family heirlooms, though."

"Did Susan get bedroom furniture when she married?"

"Yes—"

"Why didn't either of you ask for these *heirlooms*"—he bore down on the word—"back then? When you got married would have been the logical time to get them."

"They were Teddy's at the time."

"So they weren't your father's to give." He turned to me. "If I remember correctly, Teddy died without making a will, so King inherited. He let an agent sell everything in her house."

"Except for what they gave me to furnish a sitting room and my bedroom."

"That was when you were moving back to this house to take care of Regina?"

"Yes. Susan and Regan both got new furniture in high school, but my bedroom still had Susan's old furniture in it, so Mother told me to take Teddy's."

"Don't bother me with this foolishness," the judge snapped at Regan. "Obviously the things are Teensie's. I don't want to hear another word about it." He slid under his steering wheel. Before he slammed the door he warned, "If I catch you taking one more thing from this house before the contents have been properly valuated, I am going to charge you with theft and use what influence I have to see that you get a hefty fine."

"Everything was valuated yesterday," Regan told him.

"By people she and Susan called." I hated to sound like a tattling little sister, but if little sisters don't tattle, who ever knows the mischief big sisters are up to? "The Realtor came from Sam Tolbert's office and the appraiser had a list of everything Regan wants—I saw it. He was pointing out her items to the people who work for him."

Regan glowered at me. The judge frowned at Regan. "I told you to get independent people in here from another town. I'll have Gage call somebody for another appraisal."

"I already did," I told him. "Yesterday after the others left. She's coming next week."

The judge gave a nod of approval. "Good. Call a Realtor, too. By gum, if King could see the way his girls are carrying on over his bits and pieces, he'd take a cane to all of you. I've half a mind to do it myself. I don't want any more squabbles and no more thievery until those reports are in. Do you understand me?"

Regan nodded with obvious reluctance. The look she shot me would have melted the Wicked Witch of the West.

"Please tell your men to carry my chest back upstairs," I told her with dignity.

When she said nothing, the judge gestured. "You men— move that furniture back where you got it from. Right now!" The men ambled back into the house.

When the judge drove away, Regan narrowed her eyes at me. "You needn't think this is going to end here, baby sister. I'll take you to court over Mary Bird's furniture and we'll do it in a county where you don't have a judge in your pocket. Do you know how much it costs to go to court? By the time I'm finished with you, you won't have a penny to your saintly name."

When I got up to my room, I found my chest there, but everything that used to be in the drawers was piled haphazardly on two chairs. I shuddered to think of those men handling my underwear. My mattress and box springs leaned against the wall and the bed was dismantled on the floor. In the past I would have called maintenance men from campus to set it up. Whom could I call now? I could call Gage when he left his office, but I hated to impose on him. What did women do who didn't have an entire college staff to wait on their family? I would have to learn.

The problem wasn't critical. I had beds in two more bedrooms. I could sleep in one of them until I could ask somebody to help me with the furniture. For the time being, I would play the piano until I calmed down.

I couldn't. When I returned downstairs, I discovered that the piano and the rug were gone. Susan had propped a note on the mantelpiece:

*Now that we know how much the things are worth, I've gone ahead and taken what I need for Sunday's reception. I'll get the rest of my stuff next week.*

For the second time that day I called Judge Brantley. "Don't worry," he snapped. "I'll take care of this."

I rocked restlessly on the porch while I waited to see what would happen. The mountains failed to soothe me. I had crossed not only Regan and Susan that afternoon, I had crossed a Rubicon. It would take more than a king's horses to put our Humpty Dumpty family back together again.

After the piano and the living room rug were returned, I couldn't bear to stay in the house. The air felt charged, as before an electrical storm—or was that just me? The day was lovely. I pulled on jeans and a long cotton sweater and walked to the river.

Our backyard sloped down through a hardwood forest. At the bottom of the forest tumbled the Unizilla, birthed by mountain springs. At that altitude the river was little more than a wide creek, the center barely deep enough for kids on tubes to float a mile to the nearest rapids. On the bank nearest our house was a broad, flat rock where I went when I needed to vent.

I settled myself on its rough surface and peered up and down the water. Not a soul was in sight except a fisherman on the other bank, far downstream. Knowing he could not hear me above the gurgling water, I poured out to naiads and dryads what I had not said to a human being. "It's not fair! King promised me the house and money, and he let me take care of him all those years knowing he hadn't rewritten his will. My sisters have husbands, nice houses, enough money to buy anything they want. It wouldn't hurt them to let me have King's house and what money is left. I'm going to be the poor little sister the rest of my life, and I hate it! I hate it! Why should they get everything they want all the time?"

"Hey, Teensie! Who you talking to?"

Wonder skipped down the path, a streak of energy in jeans and a green polo shirt with an orange bug embroidered on the pocket. She kept talking as she and her mother approached my rock. "We dist had to get out of dat house. Nana's pitching a fit! De hairy judge and a p'liceman came wit' two big men and took Nana's new wug and piano! De judge said if she takes anyt'ing else from her daddy's house wit'out permission, she will go to jail. I didn't know nanas went to jail, did you? I didn't know dey cried, neither, but she did."

Monique gave me a wry smile. "So now you know all our family's business—and so does that man downstream." She climbed onto the rock.

I sent up an apology to heaven. My sisters did not get everything they wanted. I felt a twinge of sympathy for Susan. Should I have let her keep the piano and rug until her party was over, then asked her to bring them back Monday? What harm would that have done?

"Can I wade?" Wonder broke into my reflections. She was already pulling off her shoes.

"The water's ice-cold," I warned.

"I don't care."

"Let me roll up your pants," her mother told her, "and stay by the bank."

As Wonder waded out to perch on a small boulder, I asked Monique, "Remember how you used to wade here?"

"Yeah, and sunbathe naked on the rock as a teenager. Did you know that?"

"Thankfully, no."

I banished my sisters from my mind. Nobody should quarrel on such a gorgeous day. The warm air was musky with damp leaves, the sky so clear it stretched to eternity. The trees overhead were lively with migrating birds comparing journeys like RV enthusiasts in a campground. Beyond our rock the water gurgled in its stony bed.

"Hey, y'all!" Wonder teetered on her boulder like a stork. "I'm looking for tadpoles."

I nearly called, "It's the wrong season for tadpoles," but why spoil her fun? "Okay, but don't go far from the edge," I called back. "With all the rain we've been having, there's a strong current just now."

"Okay." As Wonder squatted to peer at the surface of the water, her seat skimmed the water. Since her mother didn't mention it, neither did I. I lay flat to enjoy the warmth of the rock on my back.

"When did King promise to take care of you?" I asked when we'd basked awhile.

Monique gave the shrug of somebody pretending something isn't important when they know good and well it is. "Last summer."

"Last summer? He found you?"

She gave me a sour smile. "He hired a detective who found us almost immediately, and King called right after that. He said he was coming to Savannah on business and wanted to take me to lunch to 'discuss my situation.'" Her fingers sketched quotes.

I knew exactly when that trip had been. King had informed me he had hired a driver so I wouldn't have to miss my days at the clinic. I had thought he was being thoughtful because I was so worried about Monique that I was not sleeping well. I had even thanked him. After that, he had always hired a driver to go to Savannah.

"Did you go to lunch?" I asked.

"Sure. He was taking me to Paula Deen's. Benny and I couldn't afford to go there."

"Why didn't he bring you home?"

"At first he was all 'Come on home, Monique. Everything will be fine.' He changed his tune when I told him I was pregnant. Then it was 'Okay, let me help you get rid of your little mistake.' I told him what I thought of that idea and stomped out."

The rock was getting hard. I sat up. "Why didn't you write after that? Send us pictures of Wonder?"

"King told me not to. He said nobody here wanted to see my half-breed baby's pictures."

"You believed him?" Of course she did. The hurt in her voice showed that. I covered her large hand with my smaller one. "Didn't you know I was frantic?"

I saw a glitter of tears in her eyes. "No. I thought he'd told you he'd found me. When you didn't write, I figured you were furious."

I hugged my knees to my chest. "I'll bet he told your parents. Not long after that your mother stopped bugging the police and your father started telling people who asked about you, 'When she gets hungry enough, she'll come home.' I thought they were callous. Instead, they were probably better informed. Why didn't you trust me, Monique? Why didn't you call?" My voice rose on each question.

"I had problems of my own, okay?" she shouted. "So drop it. I don't need this from you."

"Hey!" Wonder yelled. "Are you grown-ups fussing?"

Monique might seem like a grown-up to her daughter, but she had been little more than a child when she left, and she was still young. If I wanted to hear what she'd been through, one of us needed to be the grown-up. "No," I called to Wonder. "We're exercising our lungs. It's good for you once in a while." Monique gave me an embarrassed smile.

"Mama!" called Monique's "little mistake." "I saw a fish this big!" She held her hands wide. Unbalanced, she slipped on wet moss, teetered with her arms held out, and slid in to her knees. She giggled as she splashed back up onto the rock, her pants soaked above the knees.

"That's great, honey. Maybe we can come up someday and catch him for our lunch."

"No, Mama. He has a wife and children at home."

"Okay. Send them my love."

"You're a good mother," I said softly.

"Wonder's the best thing that ever happened to me. If I don't give her anything else in life, I want her to know she was loved."

All parents want their children to have what they themselves did not get.

Wonder bent over the water to scream, "Go home, Mr. Fish! Tell your wife my mama loves her!"

"Do you have to be so loud?" Monique called.

"Yes, Mama. I'm exercising my lungs."

Our last traces of anger dissolved in laughter.

Wonder jumped off her rock to continue her exploration of the water. I continued my exploration of King's treachery.

"So when you insisted on having your baby, King offered to take care of the two of you? Kind, generous, and forgiving weren't traits usually mentioned in King MacAllester eulogies."

"He said if I'd leave Benny, move into a home for unwed mothers, and put the baby up for adoption, he'd pay my bills. He also said it was best if I stayed downstate and used an assumed name. We both knew who that would have been best for."

"You obviously declined."

"Of course—and told him what he could do with his money."

"I'm impressed. None of King's daughters ever succeeded in defying him."

Although Monique gave a little shrug as if it were nothing, I could tell she was pleased as she said, "Benny and I both had jobs at a grocery store, and we were paying our bills. After Wonder was born, I worked the first shift and Benny worked evenings, so one of us was with her all the time. The next year he started back to college. A neighbor watched Wonder while he was in class."

The two of them had earned the right to the pride I heard in her voice. "It doesn't sound like Benny got much sleep. Wonder said she fixed her breakfast so she wouldn't wake him up."

"She did that maybe three times, when Benny was so zonked I told him to sleep in. He was a good daddy. He really was."

"You keep using the past tense. Have you all split up?"

Monique didn't answer for so long, I feared I had hit an invisible boundary. When she spoke, her voice was so low I could hardly hear above the river. "He got killed last winter."

"Oh, no!" I felt my shoulder blades sag like Wonder's had when she'd been talking about her dad.

"Yeah. He was about to finish college and he'd gone to the post office to mail applications to med school. We lived in a pretty rough neighborhood—it was all we could afford—and two rival gangs started shooting at each other. He got caught in the cross fire."

"Had you all ever gotten married?"

"No. Neither of us wanted to. We didn't have much in common except Wonder. He said, though, that if I'd help put him through med school, he'd put me through college. After that, we planned to go our separate ways but live close enough for Wonder to see us both."

"I always thought he'd make a good doctor."

"He would have. He deserved more out of life than to be gunned down in a gang fight."

He had deserved more than to be chased by a silly girl and saddled with a child to derail his dreams, too—or to be forgotten by his only child. "Why have you told Wonder not to talk about him?"

"Why do you think? Nobody in this family wants to hear about Benny."

"I do. I liked Benny."

"Me, too." Her voice was soft.

"Then let's talk about him to Wonder. She needs to know her daddy was a special man."

We rested on the warm rock while the river worked sibilant peace within us.

"Did King ever meet Wonder?" I hoped he had and had loved her as I did.

"Oh, no. Whenever he invited me to dinner, he made it clear it was for me only. I wouldn't have gone, except I wanted to know what my parents were up to. And you."

"I was never up to much."

"More than Grandfather King believed, I'll bet. He'd say, 'Oh, you know Teensie. Works over at the clinic on Wednesdays and Fridays and goes to choir practice once a week. Has a book group, too, I believe. Otherwise, she putters around the house and paints those birdhouses.'"

"Putters! He said 'putters'?" I felt like I'd been slapped in the face with a wet fish. "I waited on that man, planned his dinner parties, entertained his guests, fetched his prescriptions, took his clothes to the cleaners, laid out what he should wear, packed for his trips, kept track of his appointments, drove him to doctors *and* all over the state to political meetings, picked up everything he left lying around, answered his mail, typed up speech notes because he never did learn to use a computer or to type so anybody could read it—" I ran out of breath before I ran out of tirade.

Some folks might have backpedaled and assured me that King did appreciate me. Not Monique. "He could be a real jerk, all right. Every time we got together, he handed me an envelope with a hundred-dollar bill in it. When I told him I was putting it all into Wonder's college fund, he had the nerve to say"—her voice deepened to a mockery of King's—"'That's great, shug, but do me a favor. Don't send her to Unizilla.' And he laughed! But then he said, 'If you ever need more money, let me know,' so after Benny died, I called him."

"You called the house?" King had never mentioned that, either. If he hadn't been dead, I might have throttled him.

"Yeah. I picked a Wednesday when I knew you'd be at the clinic. I told him about Benny, and that day care cost as much as I made. He said he was coming to Savannah the next week, so we could talk then. Over dinner he started by saying he'd been thinking about my predicament—his word, not mine—and he had decided that the best thing would be to put Wonder up for adoption. When I told him what I thought about that, he said he hadn't thought I'd accept it, that I had never been able to see beyond the end of my nose, but that if I was determined to raise her, I wasn't to worry—he'd take care of us so long as I didn't bring 'that child' to Unizilla. I was so furious I wanted to refuse his money, but I couldn't afford to. His checks made it possible for me to work. The last time I saw him, back in August, he said, 'I'm not as young as I used to be, shug, but I'm gonna take care of you. When I'm gone, you'll be sitting pretty.'" She sounded as bitter as I felt.

"Instead of which, we are sitting on a rock."

"You get a third of the house and all that money."

"There's not much money—he spent most of it before he died. And we can be sure your father is going to pay a rock-bottom price for the house, so my share of that won't be a fortune, either. I'm going to have to find a job pretty fast."

"You'll stay in Unizilla, won't you?"

I was touched that she sounded anxious, but I had to be realistic. "And do what? The clinic can't afford to hire me full-time. What else could I do here?"

"Oh, Teensie! You can't leave! This place would be unbearable without you!" Monique gave me a fierce, awkward hug, her cheek wet against mine. "Looks like my child is not the only bastard in our—"

Wonder screamed.

By the time we looked around, she had disappeared.

I scanned the water. "There!" Wonder flailed her arms as she tumbled toward us.

"Swim, baby!" Monique leaped from the rock. "I'm coming!"

The water normally didn't come to her waist in the center. That autumn the river was high from record rainfalls. As the water rose to her chest, Monique lost her footing. She was carried several yards underwater before she came up, swiping hair from her eyes. "Where is she? I can't see her!"

"Over yonder." I pointed to Wonder, valiantly dog-paddling. As Monique struggled toward her, my hands clutched each other so tightly they shook—or was I shaking and my hands the only thing holding me together? *Please, God, please, God, please!*

Monique grabbed for her but missed. Wonder swept past her crying, "Mama! Mama!"

"Dear God!" Monique swam with frantic strokes while Wonder, light as a cork, bobbed faster. I was not a strong swimmer and the deepest water was probably higher than my chin, but I couldn't let her drown without trying to save her. I ran downstream trying to calculate where she would be by the time I could reach her. At the most likely spot I dropped my jeans and sweater on the bank, kicked off my shoes, and ran into the water. I winced as sharp stones cut my arches.

Wonder screamed again as she scraped a large rock. Panicked, she began to flail her arms. She went under, only to pop up like a little windmill a second later. I heard her gasp for breath as she went under a second time. Could I reach her? I plunged ahead, gasping as icy water reached tender skin.

"Stay there! I'll get her." Downstream the fisherman churned into the river from the other bank. Although the water came to his waist, he moved with sure, easy strides. Long black hair swung below his shoulders. With a muscular arm he grabbed Wonder as she passed and lifted her head to his shoulder, safe above the swift-moving stream. Wonder struggled in his arms. "I wants my muvver! I wants my muvver!"

His voice carried over the water in a husky rasp. "You'll be all right. I've got you."

I backed into shallow water to get a surer footing while he carried her toward me. As he climbed the sloping riverbed, water flowed from his jeans and blue work shirt, sculpting a sturdy body. The sun was on his face, which was swarthy with a touch of cinnamon. His features could have been carved from granite. Although he looked familiar, I couldn't put a name to his face.

He towered over me, the child in his arms. "Thank you. Oh, thank you," I managed between chattering teeth. I clutched her to my chest. She sobbed. I felt tears on my own cheeks.

The stranger didn't seem moved by our tears. His eyes, the color of burnt cork, held no expression whatsoever. "Beat her," he commanded. When I looked startled, he added, "Get the water out of her."

"I'm a nurse," I snapped, stung because I'd needed reminding. I pounded Wonder's back and she threw up half the river.

"Is she all right? Dear God, is she all right?" Monique yelled.

"She's fine, just a little waterlogged," I called back.

Wonder struggled to leave my arms. "Mama! I wants my muvver!"

I held her tight. "She's coming, baby."

Intent on warming the child, I ran up the bank for my sweater and wrapped her in it like a pig in a blanket. I didn't notice the man had left until I heard Monique call, "Thank you so much. I don't know how to thank you," and his reassuring "She'll be all right. Get her warm and dry." Only then did I realize I stood there wearing only wet underpants and my bra.

Wonder called in a reedy little voice, "T'ank you, Mr. Veg'table Man." Startled, I looked after him. He had looked smaller in his gray hooded sweatshirt, sitting on a box.

Without turning around, he lifted one hand in a wave.

I pulled on my jeans, too late for modesty. I let Wonder keep my sweater. The path to our house was private.

A bedraggled band, we limped up the path. The white house towered above us like a castle of safety. How long would that last?

My teeth still chattered, both from the chill and from shock. While Monique and Wonder took a shower, I pulled on a sweater and corduroy slacks, shoved my feet into shearling slippers, and turned on the heat. Then I found a white sweatshirt Wonder could wear. Nothing of mine would fit Monique, so I hurried to King's room for his old wool bathrobe. As I inhaled the scent of him lingering in its weave, I knew I had loved him.

"You won't be stylish, but you'll be warm," I called through the bathroom door.

I had milk heating on the stove when Gage arrived with potato soup. "Granddaddy told us what happened this morning, so Aunt Coco made you some soup. And I have something to tell—" His jaw went slack.

I looked over my shoulder. Wonder pranced like a lively angel down the stairs, my sweatshirt hanging down past her knees. Monique followed, King's bathrobe belted tightly around her. With her face bare of makeup and her hair in damp curls on her shoulders, she was beautiful enough to stop any man's mouth.

Wonder frowned. "You're de man who didn't give Teensie dis house."

Gage nodded. "But it wasn't my fault. I just read what her father said. I'm sorry."

She heaved a big sigh. "Okay. I forgive you." She flapped the sleeve extensions of her arms. "But don't look at me. I doesn't have any underpants."

"We can't see a thing," he assured her.

"Come to de kitchen." She tugged Gage toward the back of the house like he was her new bestest friend. "Teensie is making hot chocolate."

"Oh, no. I can't stay."

I didn't take his protest seriously. "I have plenty." As Wonder led Gage down the hall, I whispered to Monique, "Do you want some underpants? I could lend you a pair."

"Don't bother. Gage doesn't look like a man with much imagination."

When we got to the kitchen, Wonder was reciting the day's adventures and displaying the granite scrapes on her calves. She seemed not to remember her terror until her mother sat down; then she climbed onto Monique's lap and leaned back with one thumb in her mouth.

"As you've heard, Wonder had a little accident," I said as I handed Gage a steaming cup of cocoa.

Wonder took her thumb out long enough to correct me. "A big accident."

"A big accident," I conceded, pouring chocolate for her and her mother. "She fell into the current. Monique jumped in to pull her out—"

"—and de veg'table man saved me," Wonder finished for me. "Do you know de veg'table man?" She addressed the question to Gage.

"I can't say that I do. Is he related to the muffin man on Drury Lane?"

Wonder giggled.

"I'm thinking we don't want to mention this to Susan or Albert," I told Monique.

"You've got that right. I'd never live it down. Don't tell Nana or Granddaddy you went swimming today," she ordered Wonder. "And stop sucking your thumb. You're too big for that." Monique gave her daughter a squeeze to take the sharpness out of the command.

Wonder's lower lip trembled. "I did not go swimming. I nearly drownded. Why can't I tell Nana and Granddaddy?"

"Because they'd never let me forget I'm such an irresponsible mother that I let my child fall in the river in front of my very eyes."

"You didn't let me fall in. I did it all by myself." She hung her head. "I'm sorry I disobeyed, Teensie." Her contriteness lasted half a second before she explained to Gage, "Teensie said, 'Stay near de bank,' but I saw a little frog and I wanted to see him good, so I stepped across de tops of de rocks. All of a sudden I fell in and dere wasn't any bottom! And de tide was going out weal fast. . . ."

"A river doesn't have tides. It has a current that always goes the same way," Monique interrupted her recital. "And you know how the ocean bottom goes like this?" She held one hand at a slant. "In a river, it does this." She brought her two hands together in a V. "It's shallow on both sides and deep in the middle."

"I didn't know dat." Wonder made her own hands into a V and studied it. "Now I do."

"And the current can carry you right down to a waterfall," I warned. "Don't ever go into that river without grown-ups with you."

"All wight, I won't."

While we were talking, Gage had been taking surreptitious glances at Monique with the expression of a man trying to decide whether the snake in his path was harmless or deadly.

Wonder gulped down her cocoa—which I'd cooled with extra milk—and slid down, holding the bottom of her sweatshirt to preserve her modesty. "I wants to watch a movie."

"Teensie doesn't have any children's movies," said Monique.

"She does, too. She's got five."

Monique looked at me in surprise.

"I picked them up at a garage sale," I admitted. "Would you like *Finding Nemo*?"

Wonder shuddered. "No water, Teensie."

"How about *Aladdin*? It takes place in a desert."

I took her up to my sitting room to watch it. She flapped a hand at me as the music started. "You can go now. I doesn't need a grown-up when I watch a movie."

Dismissed, I returned to the kitchen in time to hear Gage say, ". . . mess yourself up like that for?"

"Like what?" Monique stood at the stove pouring another cup of chocolate. She tilted her chin, ready for a fight.

"You know, all that"—Gage fiddled his fingers over his head—"poufy hair, too much makeup, those clothes . . ."

"This isn't my robe. I'm borrowing it while my clothes dry.

I thought it looked pretty good." She stroked the robe over her hips in a provocative way.

Gage flushed. "Not the robe, the trashy things you wore earlier this week."

"I like them. And what right do you have—?"

I decided to intervene before war broke out. "I was about to wash our wet clothes when you came, Gage. I forgot to turn on the washer." I started toward the utility room behind the kitchen. "Which reminds me—you said you came because you had something to tell me?" I paused at the door for his answer.

"Oh, yeah, it's something that concerns both of you, actually, about Dr. MacAllester's investments." On the familiar ground of law, he was comfortable again. "Like I said, his brokerage account has two hundred thousand dollars in it, but last February he put a hundred thousand of that into an education fund for Wonder."

The air went out of me. I had half the investments I'd thought I had?

"The angel! You're an angel, too." Monique flung her arms around him. "I knew Grandfather King wouldn't let us down!" She planted a kiss on his cheek.

Gage leaned back like he'd identified a rat snake only to discover it was a copperhead. "The fund is not for you. The money is for Wonder's college."

"I can save for her college later. Right now we need money to live on." She did a little jig.

"You can't use this. The account is designated for Wonder's education, with the stipulation that she can attend any college of her choice except Unizilla."

Monique waved her arms—exactly like her grandfather used to do. "So I have money for my child's college education but nothing to support her until she's ready for college? What happens to the money if she dies of starvation before she's old enough for college?"

"Look, I didn't write the will or manage the investments. Granddaddy is still upset about what Dr. MacAllester did to Teensie, and as for her sisters this morning . . ." He stopped, perhaps remembering one of those sisters was Monique's mother.

Her lip curled. "So upset he's home having a brandy while you run his errands for him?"

"No, he's—he had something else to do." Gage pushed back his chair. "I've said what I had to say. I'm sorry, Teensie. You know I'd make things right if I could."

"I know you would." I tucked my arm through his and walked him to the door.

"I didn't want to say so in front of *her*," he said in the front hall. "Granddaddy and Coco had to go out to Lena's. Kaitlin called. Lena's drunk again." He shook his head in sorrow. "It's such a tragedy when somebody from a fine family turns out like that, isn't it?"

The quick look he gave the back of my house left no doubt whom he meant.

"Monique's not like Lena," I assured him. "She just likes to look odd."

He gave me a look full of pity. "The family is often the last to know."


"Was Gage talking about Lena Thompson?" Monique must have sneaked into the butler's pantry to hear what he said.

"Do you know her? I wouldn't have thought your paths had ever crossed."

"I know who she is—the town drunk, with two little kids whose daddy ran off with another woman."

"You've got most of the story straight, but there are three kids now: Eric, Kaitlin, and Carrie. She had Carrie after you went away."

"Why does that *person*"—Monique's voice rose an octave as she pointed at the door Gage had gone through—"think I'm like *her*?"

"Shhh." I motioned toward the stairwell. "I left my sitting room door open." I had a sudden inspiration. "Would you help me put my bed back together? Regan tried to steal it this morning, and her men left it in pieces on the floor. We can talk in my room."

Upstairs, Monique closed my bedroom door behind us with a furious *thunk*. "Why does Gage Brantley think I'm a drunk?"

"I told him you aren't." I started putting underwear in drawers.

"You told him I like to look odd."

"Should I have said 'exotic'? You have to admit you are a bit unusual for Unizilla."

"Hick town." She stewed in silence until curiosity got the better of her. "Is Lena related to Gage? Was that what he meant by people turning out like that in fine families?"

I folded pajamas and put them in their drawer. "No, but Lena was in Gage's class at school and the Brantley law firm administers a trust Lena's daddy left for Lena and her kids, so Gage knows her pretty well. Help me with the bed, will you?"

As we slid side rails into the old wooden headboard, Monique said, "I'd have thought Lena was years older than Gage."

"Hard living ages people."

"So does raising kids alone. Some days I feel a hundred. How does she support her kids?"

"The trust fund. Can you get that footboard?"

Monique set it in place. "Why does Gage think I'm like her?"

"Maybe because she ran away with a man and had his child?" I started putting slats between the rails. "That was a dreadful month."

I didn't realize I had spoken aloud until Monique asked, "Why?"

"Lena took off not long after you did. Abandoned her two older children and called Gage to pick them up after school. Kaitlin was just five, and Gage and Coco had to take care of those kids for over two weeks. Alice went around our house muttering, 'Two down and one to go. Troubles always come in threes.' When Holcomb's little brother got killed over near Dalton—"

"Uncle Carleton?" Monique's eyes widened in shock. "He died? He was such a *sweetie*."

I was sorry to have broken it to her so bluntly. I had forgotten how fond she had been of Carleton, and that she might not know. Since Carleton wasn't married and he and Ginny Linn had no other family, they always joined ours for Thanksgiving and Christmas at Regan's. Carleton had dubbed Monique "my favorite niece" and brought her extravagant presents.

I shook the bed frame to be sure it was secure. "I thought he was a sweetie, too, but don't tell Regan."

"I won't. Remember how mad she got when Carleton inherited half the company after their daddy died? Mama said Regan might never get over that."

"Regan had good reason to resent it. Carleton was a playboy with expensive habits and he never helped Holcomb run the company."

"Uncle Carleton was a lot of fun, though. I'm sorry he's dead. What happened to him?"

"He wrapped his Porsche around a tree one night when he was too drunk to drive."

"Ouch!" She pressed one hand to her mouth. When she spoke, her voice was bitter. "Regan probably considered that divine justice. Did Holcomb get the company?"

"Of course. After Carleton died, Alice said, 'That's that, then. Our third disaster, like I said.' I pointed out that Carleton died over in Dalton, so he didn't count unless she included all of North Georgia in her trouble circle, but she wasn't convinced—

until Lena came home and turned out to be pregnant. That satisfied her rule of three. It's hard to believe now that so much happened within a few weeks." I gestured toward the box spring. "Think we can lift it?"

"Sure." Monique took one end. "Do you reckon Lena went off with her ex-husband?"

We walked the springs to the side of the bed and let them fall. "Doubtful. Her last little girl—who is about Wonder's age—doesn't look like the other two. They are skinny with dark hair and eyes. The little one is chubby with brown hair and lovely blue-gray eyes."

Monique set my reading lamp on the nightstand with special care. "So Gage thinks I'm like Lena because I left town and had a baby without getting married." Her voice was flat. She slammed my clock radio down beside the lamp in a way guaranteed to stop time. "Not everybody who has a baby and isn't married is a tramp!"

"Lena's not a tramp. She's had some hard times and made some poor choices. When she was fourteen, her mother died. A year later her dad married a woman Lena couldn't stand. She started running with a wild crowd and met her future husband, who introduced her to alcohol. Unfortunately, Lena discovered she couldn't control it."

Monique lifted a corner of the mattress. "I can feel sorry for her, but I'm not at all like her. Let's get this thing in place."

While we maneuvered the heavy mattress onto the bed, she asked, "Has Lena been drunk ever since she went on that bender and got pregnant?"

"Off and on, although I begged her to stay sober while she *was* pregnant and she did. The damage alcohol does to a fetus is irreversible, in case you didn't know. As soon as her baby was born, Lena started drinking again. Since then, she's been off the wagon as much as she's been on it. The judge sent her to a couple of rehab sessions, but when she got caught sneaking liquor into the rehab center the last time, he stopped paying for it. He says the children will need that money for their education."

"How old are the older kids now?"

"Twelve and ten. Coco says Kaitlin, who is ten, holds the family together." I gave the mattress one last nudge. "We're through here. I can make the bed later. Your clothes must be finished washing."

Monique frowned. "They aren't going to be dry for ages. I'm going to call Daddy to come get us."

Before I could offer to drive them, she had gone to the phone. "Hey, Daddy, could you pick us up? We're at Teensie's. . . . We *can't* walk home. Wonder and I, uh, spilled stuff on us and Teensie is washing our clothes. I've got on Grandfather King's bathrobe and Wonder is wearing one of Teensie's sweatshirts— and like she told somebody a little while ago, we doesn't have any underpants. Of course, if you *want* me to cross the campus wearing nothing but a bathrobe, I guess I could. . . . Okay, we'll be on the porch."

As she left, Monique said in a soft, intense voice, "I am not having two more kids anytime soon and I don't drink too much or *like to look odd*. You tell that to Mr. High-and-Mighty the next time you see him."

That night I took a glass of King's scotch out on the porch. I didn't turn on the light. I didn't want to invite company. Autumn had sent a forerunner: a sharp wind that blew over the hill, but I sat wrapped in a warm throw while I considered my future. I did not want to look after Wonder full-time, or Ginny Linn Harris, but with half the money I'd thought I had, how long could I afford to stay in Unizilla? I still had money in the household account King had put my name on when I moved in to care for Mother. I had a small savings account from the sale of birdhouses—I hadn't had many occasions in the past few years to spend mad money. But how long would the pittance I earned at the clinic, what I had in the bank, plus King's bequest support me? Not for long, and it certainly wouldn't add anything to a retirement account. I needed to find a nursing job pretty soon.

The idea did not excite me as much as it had the first time I moved down to Atlanta. Back then I had been eager to leave Unizilla. I had seen myself as setting off on a grand life's journey to improve the world. In the past fifteen years I had learned how precious lifelong friends are, and I had come to appreciate how deep my roots were planted in mountain soil. I had grown accustomed to frequent contact with my family, although at the moment my sensibilities were flayed by King's betrayal and by my sisters' high-handed removal of what they wanted and their presumption that I had done little of value since I'd come home. The thought of finding work, finding a place to live, making new friends, and dealing with a city commute filled me with dread.

*You must be getting old*, I told myself as I went upstairs to start the tedious process of drawing bricks on the governor's mansion birdhouse. I wished I were laying real brick to build a small house for myself somewhere near all the people I loved.

When we are quiet, peace has a chance to creep in unannounced. Before I slept, I took out my sketch pad and thought I would draw Regan and Susan stealing my furniture, Monique and Gage shouting at each other from opposite pedestals, and myself sitting on a pile of money that was blowing away. Instead I drew Wonder being lifted from the river in an eagle's claws.

# *Four*

O n Saturday Phil came back. I was standing at the porch railing with my second cup of coffee, still trying to get my head around the fact that I had half the investments I'd thought I had, when his Miata pulled up at the sidewalk. "Hello, Juliet! Waiting for Romeo? Will I do instead?" He ran up all eleven front steps without panting.

"Show off," I teased. "I'm having coffee. Would you like some?"

"In a minute." He kissed me as if it were his right.

I didn't have time to shut my eyes. Over his shoulder I saw Lena Thompson's two older children trudging down the sidewalk, each carrying a sagging plastic bag.

What Phil lacked in passion he made up for in duration. As his kiss went on and on, I wondered whether the college kitchen staff was sending food home with the children. I hoped so.

Phil lifted his lips from mine. "I care for you, Teensie. I hope you know that." His voice carried in the silent morning air. The boy below us gave a hoarse laugh. I grew hot with shame to think he found our performance amusing. When I still didn't speak, Phil elaborated, "I care for you very much."

"Phil, I . . . I'm about to spill my coffee." *Brilliant, Teensie!* But I had no idea what else to say. As soon as I'd seen him get out of the car, I knew I did not want to be Teensie Potts. However, neither did I want to hurt him. He had been a pleasant escort.

I moved down the porch railing a few feet. He followed, and put his hand over mine in a gesture so possessive that I instinctively pulled away. "Let me get your coffee."

When I returned, he was leaning against the porch railing with both arms folded over his chest, looking at the facade of the house. "This is such a beautiful place you have here."

I handed him his cup. "Except I don't have it."

He puckered his forehead. "What do you mean? Your dad left it to you, right?"

I had confided King's promise to Phil one night after a little too much wine, a slip I had immediately regretted. Since I had shared that much, though, I might as well confide the outcome. It would be all over campus soon enough anyway.

"King never got around to writing a new will, so my sisters and I inherit equally. Since I won't have enough to buy them out, Albert will probably buy the house for the college."

He stared at me. "Dr. MacAllester promised you—isn't that what you said? He promised?" His voice rang out in indignation.

I nodded, not trusting my voice. If I'd had Phil's indignation beside me the day the will was read, might I have fought more boldly?

"Oh, Teensie!"

The despair in his voice buckled my knees. Sorrow shared wasn't divided; it was multiplied. I backed into the nearest rocker.

If Phil had taken me in his arms at that moment to console me, I might have married him. Instead, he paced the porch, looking now at the house, then at the mountains—which were spectacular that morning, gilded by slanting rays of the morning sun. His face was as mournful as Jester's when I put him out for the night.

I found myself wanting to reassure him. "I'll be okay. I'm considering several options."

He walked over to my chair and placed one hand on each of my shoulders. "Of course you will be okay. You are a marvelous woman and you are going to be fine." He exhaled as if he'd been holding his breath during a performance. "I'd better go. I have some work to do. I'll call you." He gave the house one last mournful look as he galloped down my walk like a horse heading for the stable. In another second his car roared down the hill, a streak of red retreat.

I watched him go with my mouth wide open. Even though I didn't want to marry him, I felt like shrieking after him, "How dare you kiss and cuddle me to get my house?" I didn't, of course. Nothing restricts self-expression like good breeding.

The next exciting event of Saturday was the locksmith's visit. While he was working, I called Gage and asked him to stop by at his convenience to pick up the only set of spare keys.

Around three that afternoon Susan brought over a couple of husky students. She rang the bell impatiently. "My key doesn't work," she complained through the big beveled-glass pane in the oak front door.

"New locks," I called back. "What do you want?"

"Let me in and I'll tell you."

"If this is about the living room rug and the piano, we have nothing to say."

"Forget the piano for now. All I want is to borrow the rug for a couple of days. You'll have it back tomorrow evening. Nobody need know except you and me."

I eyed the two students through the glass. "Plus the whole

student body and their parents. Besides, you heard what the judge said: nothing is to leave this house until we've made our lists and met to talk about them." I left her fuming on the front porch and went up to my sitting room to watch *Aladdin*. It was reassuring to know that some princesses go through trials and still live happily ever after.

Alice returned Monday, but her dusting and vacuuming were more halfhearted than usual. When I made a mild complaint about her lackadaisical swipe at dust on the hall mirror, she tossed her head. "If those sisters of yours want their stuff any cleaner, they can clean it when they get it home."

I saw no point in arguing, since I agreed. "I'm going to buy something for our lunch."

Ahead of me in the grocery line was a man in a denim jacket. I recognized the eagle profile and that long, dark hair, caught back with a leather thong. "Mr.—um . . .?" I didn't know his name and didn't want to call, "Hey! Mr. Vegetable Man!"

"Sir?"

When he didn't respond to my voice, I maneuvered awkwardly around my grocery cart to touch his arm. It was hard as granite under my fingers.

He looked over my head. "Down here," I said. His face was impassive as he looked at me. I smiled and stuck out my hand. "I am Teensie MacAllester. I want to thank you for saving Wonder on Friday. If you hadn't been there—"

"It's okay." He took his change from the clerk, picked up his bag, and strode out.

The clerk shook her head as she watched him go. "Them Indians never got much to say, do they?"

I was startled. I hadn't known the vegetable man was Cherokee.

I was filling my front yard bird feeders that afternoon when Wonder showed up. She looked like a woodland sprite in a tan sweater with leaves appliquéd on the front. Her expression, however, was more dragon than sprite. Before I could say hello, she propped one hand on her hip and announced, "I am mad at you, Teensie."

"How did you get here?" I asked. Monique was nowhere in sight.

"Mama has to go study, so she told me to come to your house, but I am mad at you, so I am not coming inside." She plopped down on my bottom step, her lower lip stuck out a mile.

I was baffled. We had parted on the best of terms Friday afternoon. While I finished filling the sunflower feeder, I asked, "Why?"

"You made my veg'table man go away and nebber come back no more."

"I did no such thing." I sat down beside her, clasping my hands around my knees. She might be warm enough in corduroy and a sweater, but I was chilly in jeans and a cotton turtleneck. I hadn't intended to stay out long. "This marble is cold. Could we talk inside?"

"No. I do not want to go inside your house. I am mad at you."

"What is it you think I did?"

She slid me a sideways glare. "You told Granddaddy de veg'table man was bad. Now he ain't nebber coming back no more."

"I haven't talked to your granddaddy for a week and we've never talked about the vegetable man. What makes you think he isn't coming back? Maybe he hasn't had another delivery since you saw him last."

"Nope. He's gone. I went to de kitchen on my way here to ask when he was coming back and my friend Millie said he ain't nebber coming back no more."

"He isn't coming back *anymore*," I corrected her. "That's what you should say."

Wonder gave one of her famous huffs. "Dat's what I would say, but Millie said, 'He ain't nebber coming back no more.' She said de president—dat's Granddaddy, you know—de president found out de veg'table man has been hanging awound me so he ain't nebber coming back no more."

She was obviously fond of the phrase. I let it pass. I was remembering the man's behavior when I tried to speak with him in the grocery store. Losing the college order would have been a blow. Did he, like Wonder, blame me?

"Teensie! You aren't listening!" Wonder pounded my thigh. "I said, what does 'hanging awound' mean? When he told me de Cherky story he was sitting, not hanging. De next time, he was saving me from drowning."

"'Hanging around' means being with somebody. Your granddaddy doesn't know the man saved you from the river, does he?"

She hung her head and rubbed a tiny hangnail. "Yeah. I told him. On our way home Granddaddy was fussing at Mama for spilling on herself so she had to wear de dead king's bafrobe, so I said, 'She didn't spill, she jumped in de wivver 'cause I fell in, but she couldn't catch me, so de veg'table man saved me.'" Wonder heaved a sigh bigger than she was. "I didn't mean to tell, Teensie. De words dist popped out of my mouth." Never one to remain contrite for long, she remembered her earlier question. "Is hanging awound with people bad? I'm hanging awound wif you wight now. Will Granddaddy tell you to get out of your house and not come back no more?" She cast an anxious look over one shoulder toward my door.

I was tempted to tell her Albert was trying his dead level best to do exactly that, but I squelched the impulse. "Of course not. He must have thought the vegetable man was doing bad things to you." Or maybe her grandfather was a paranoid, prejudiced fool.

"Like what?"

How could I alert the child to the possibility of dangerous strangers without killing her easy friendliness? "Oh, like take you home with him."

I had forgotten where Wonder had spent her first four years. She probably knew more about dangerous strangers than I did. "Kidnap me?" Her voice dripped scorn. "He wouldn't do dat. Besides, I'da screamed bloody murder."

"Well, whatever your granddaddy has done, I didn't tell him a thing."

Her eyes narrowed. "I'll bet it was dat bad man with de gun."

"There is a good chance you are right."

She stood, a small pillar of purpose. "I'm gonna tell Granddaddy dat he has to let him come back. I hasn't heard all de Cherky stories yet."

"Aren't you supposed to be staying with me while your mother studies?"

"Yes, so you have to come with me. You can get your jacket." Her tone was exactly like King's when he used to issue an edict, then follow it up with what he presumed was a magnanimous gesture.

I fetched my jacket and we walked down the hill. At least, I walked. Wonder stomped. She stomped all the way to Main. At its marble steps, she held up a peremptory hand. "I'll dist be a minute. You wait wight here." She stomped up the front steps.

I sat on a nearby bench to enjoy the day. Towering oaks strewed golden leaves on campus paths where squirrels competed for acorns. Crape myrtles blazed along the drives. Birds chattered about their upcoming migrations. Bradford pears splashed the landscape with pink, gold, and green—as if an artist had come by with a brush and given each of them a casual flick of a different color. I took deep breaths of air as heady as brandy, but kept one worried eye on the administrative building. I hoped Albert wouldn't be too curt with the child. I was relieved to see her skipping down the steps.

"Okay, I am not mad at you anymore." She tucked her hand into mine. "Granddaddy says it wasn't because of me dat de veg'table man ain't never coming back no more. De college can't 'ford spensive vegetables. Dey doesn't have dat kind of money. I said dey could have all of mine—I have four dollars and twenty cents—but Granddaddy said it's not quite enough."

I fumed. Unizilla College's former president had been a dedicated ecologist who had instituted recycling programs and urged the college food service to buy local, organic foods whenever possible. I had no doubt that Albert—who considered penny-pinching an art form and was a master at killing as many birds with as few stones as possible—had used the incident with Wonder as a justification to reduce campus food costs. What did it matter that he had dismissed the farmer who had saved his granddaughter's life?

That was the kind of person who wanted my house? I was too angry to speak.

Wonder seemed mollified. She chattered beside me. "Tomorrow Granddaddy is going to town. While he's dere, he said he'll go to a bookstore and buy me a book of Cherky stories."

I thought that over. "Was anybody in your Granddaddy's office when you went in?"

"Yeah. Aunt Regan."

I'd figured Albert must have had somebody in there he'd wanted to impress.

We settled down to play Chutes and Ladders, which I'd found at another garage sale. Wonder was beating me for the second time when Gage stopped by. "I came for those keys." He picked up an extra marker and set it back down. "I never could win at that."

"Maybe you learned how by now," Wonder encouraged him. "We'll let you play."

To my surprise, he pulled up a chair. When Wonder beat us both, she crowed. Then we moved on to Old Maid.

Monique arrived an hour later with Junior Walters in tow. He had exchanged the long hair he'd worn in high school for the skinhead look and had added a few tattoos of snakes, but his swagger was unchanged.

Monique introduced the men casually. "This is our lawyer, Gage. This is Junior."

Junior jutted his pelvis out. "Pleased to meet you." His tone implied the honor was ours.

"He's been helping me study," Monique explained. "Can you keep Wonder again tomorrow? I've got a lot to learn before the test." As usual her hair was a mass of messy curls, her lipstick bright red, and her sweater tight. When Junior put a possessive hand at her waist, Wonder gave him a look that ought to have laid him out cold.

"What test?" Gage ignored Junior and spoke to Monique.

"The SAT. I'm taking it in December and I think I've forgotten everything I ever knew. Junior's helping me remember."

Gage and I remained on the porch as Monique, Wonder, and Junior headed down the hill. At one point Junior tugged Monique back to him to give her a long kiss. Gage grunted. "I'd be willing to bet he's teaching her things the SAT never asked."


My appraiser came Tuesday morning. "My assistant ought to be along in a little while," she said. I asked her to set a value for my bedroom furniture along with the rest, because I was curious whether it was sentiment or something else that made

Regan want that set so badly. The appraiser ran her hand over the footboard with obvious pleasure. "This is amazing—early nineteenth century and in excellent condition. I'll have to do a bit of research when I get back to the office, but I think you are going to be pleasantly surprised."

So much for Regan wanting the set for sentimental reasons.

For a few minutes I stood watching the woman work, wondering how you learned to set a value on other people's belongings. She was still upstairs when a young man rang the bell. "I've come to look at the paintings," he said.

He had pale blue eyes behind round horn-rimmed glasses and a nervous habit of twitching his head to one side. He wasn't dressed very professionally—his brown corduroys were rumpled, his tan shirt looked like he'd slept in it, and he had on scuffed loafers without socks although the day was cold. He made me so uneasy that I followed him around as he strolled through the downstairs peering at pictures like he was in a gallery. He had no clipboard, simply jotted a few notes on the back of a crumpled envelope.

When he started upstairs, I said, "None of the pictures up there are worth your time." He ignored me. When I reached the upper landing, he was opening the door to my sitting room.

"Not there!" I called, running up the stairs. "Nothing in there is part of the estate."

He paused at my birdhouse table to say in a disdainful voice, "Tourist schlock," then crossed to Teddy's husband's watercolors. "Very nice." He seemed especially taken with a sunset over the desert seen through a saguaro cactus. That was the only enthusiasm I detected the whole morning. I could have been the nymph in the front hall for all the attention he paid me.

He didn't speak when he'd finished, simply walked out the door and got into a small gray car down the block. In a few minutes his partner followed. "I'm finished. I'll send you a report as soon as I can get it typed up."

"Great. Your helper already left."

She wrinkled her forehead. "My helper called while I was upstairs and said she couldn't come. One of her children is sick. I thought that man was somebody you had called." We stared at each other in dismay. She chewed her lip. "Oh, my. Sometimes an undesirable element . . . I would lock my doors carefully, if I were you, especially since you are alone in the house. And when you go out, try not to be gone for too long at a time."

That night I not only locked my doors, I put chairs under all the knobs and let Jester sleep in my room. Even so, the house developed new creaks in the darkness and the vast, empty rooms seemed full of a breathing presence I could not see. I could picture it, though: a man with round glasses who had not been my appraiser's helper.

After Gage sent the new appraisals to my sisters, both of them called me to insist that "your people were working in your best interests." I called Gage and asked him to bring in a third set of appraisers and another Realtor of his choosing. "Otherwise, my sisters may kill me. And stop laughing. I'm dead serious."

When Gage's appraisers agreed with mine, my sisters' dispositions grew as sharp as homemade pepper sauce.

Albert showed his displeasure in a particularly nasty way. When I went to exchange books at the campus library—we didn't have a public library for twenty miles—I was informed by an embarrassed librarian that the president had revoked privileges I'd had since I was six.

I called him to protest.

"I'm sorry, Teensie," he said, "but you aren't really part of the campus community. I don't feel we can justify giving you check-out privileges." That from the man who was willing to bend two college policies to enroll his daughter?

He had the nerve to continue. "I have been wanting to talk to you, though. We still have not found a donor to help us buy the house, but I've been talking to Susan. She is willing to donate her interest in the house to the college if we can get a grant to start the literary magazine she wants. Would you donate your third as well? It would be a great kindness."

Albert had made a tactical error by asking me on the tele-phone instead of face-to-face. I was bolder when I didn't have to look at him. "I'm going to need every cent I can get from this house, but while we're discussing kindness, I believe Wonder told you about falling in the river and a man pulling her out?"

"She mentioned it, yes."

"That man literally saved her life. He used to have a contract with the college for vegetables, but you canceled it. Out of grati-tude for what he did for Wonder, as well as the excellent quality of his produce, it would be a *kindness* to restore his contract."

"We can get produce at lower prices through one of our wholesalers."

"Not the same quality," I pointed out.

"It is adequate. Now about my suggestion. If you donate your share of the house to the college, you can deduct it as a charitable donation."

"I'd be deducting more than I am likely to earn in several years. Sorry, Albert, your offer is *not* adequate. If you want the house you must buy it." I hung up without saying good-bye.


Judge Brantley climbed my front steps one frosty morning to chide, "Gage has lists from your sisters stating what they want from the house. He hasn't heard from you."

"I don't want any of it except the things in my bedroom and sitting room, which you've agreed are already mine. Mother's style is too elegant for me. Besides, I'm going to need cash more than furniture."

"Choose some things you plan to sell, then. Your sisters aren't going to willingly hand over wads of money to you."

"I think Susan and Regan between them have chosen all the valuable things."

"That doesn't keep you from putting them on your list."

"I don't want to fight over furniture I don't care a thing about. Let them—"

He fixed me with a stern look. "Girl, you have a giving heart and that's a good thing, but you've got to learn to discriminate. Help those who truly need it, not those who think they are entitled to take anything they want in this world and who expect you to be content with their leavings. Loving people is not synonymous with being a doormat. Your sisters need your charity like Georgia needs more granite. For once you must stand up to them. You are entitled to one-third of the furnishings of this house. Do you hear me?"

"I hear you."

"Then let's put our heads together to make certain you come out with a few things you'd like to have." He pulled a pen from his breast pocket. "Fetch some paper and let's walk through the house. Tell me which things have special meaning for you."

*All of them,* I wanted to cry as I followed him into the front hall. *I want this house to stay exactly like it is.* I had been truthful, though, when I said Mother's style was too elegant for me. I had wanted her things only for the people I had hoped would live in the house and enjoy it. As I looked around the front hall and into the living room I wanted none of it. Except . . .

"I'd love to have the piano, but Susan isn't going to give it up."

"Miracles do happen. All you need is the right persuader. Let's put it down. What else?"

I looked around the living room again and shook my head. "Nothing else in here."

I followed him across the hall to King's study. "I'd like those two watercolors. I painted them from our front steps. If I have them, wherever I live I'll still have my favorite view."

"They ought to be yours by right, but for the sake of peace in the family, we'll put them down. What else?"

"Nothing in here."

"Not the chess set?"

"Of course the chess set. My sisters don't play, so I presumed—"

"You can't presume anything. You need to request anything you want. Otherwise it will go to one of your sisters or into the estate sale. I definitely think you want the chess set on your list. The game table and chairs, as well?"

"Oh, yes, and the floor lamp beside them."

As I followed him toward the dining room, it took my breath away to realize how easily I could have lost the chess set without that smart old judge.

He put one gnarled forefinger on Mother's long mahogany table. "You'll need a table and chairs to eat on. What about taking this?"

"I'll never have a dining room big enough to hold it, much less the sideboard and china cabinet. I would like the oak table and chairs in the kitchen, though, and the matching hutch."

I must have shown more enthusiasm than before, because he gave a little smile. "Good."

He rested his pad on the table to add them to the list. "What about the paintings in here?"

They were lovely, depictions of rivers and hills painted with glowing light. "I love them, but they'd never feel at home in any house I'm likely to have. Let Regan hang them in her mansion, or let Susan display them in the new president's house."

"Very well." He pushed opened the swinging door to the butler's pantry. "Anything in here? You'll need dishes."

I peered through the glass-fronted cupboard doors. "I've always liked Grandmother MacAllester's china. Teddy used to have it. It's not as fine as the Royal Doulton, but I prefer it. I would like to have that."

"And the crystal?"

"Regan has it on her list."

"Doesn't she have a complete set of Waterford? I seem to remember giving her a couple of glasses for a wedding present. And what do you plan to eat with, your fingers?"

I opened a felt-lined drawer. Remembering my early threats, I might have taken the best silver if it hadn't been so heavy and ornate. "I'll take the second-best silver, too."

"You don't have to take the second-best of everything, you know."

"I know, but the silver, like the china, belonged to Grandmother MacAllester and Teddy, and I like them better."

"Second-best silver and china, then, and I'm putting down the crystal."

Until that moment I had thought only in terms of practical furnishings for a dreary place to live. As he scrawled the words, I saw myself setting the oak table with my own beautiful things. Instead of a house full of Mother's belongings, the marble house changed into a treasure trove from which I could select things that pleased me—not only because of memories they evoked but because I would enjoy living with them. Was that what my sisters had already seen?

"Let's go back to the living room," I said. "There are some lamps there I would like."

Upstairs Judge Brantley paused for a moment in the doorway to King's bedroom before he stepped inside. "I miss the old scoundrel, you know. Why don't you take his furniture? I don't remember either of the other girls listing it. You could use it in your guest room."

"I doubt I'll need a guest room. I don't expect overnight guests."

"Wonder might stay over occasionally, mightn't she? And I'd hate for this set to be sold out of the family."

He had a point. It was an attractive set, and I had probably been conceived in that bed.

"Put it on my list, then, although heaven only knows where I'll store it if I start out in a one-bedroom apartment—which I'll need to until I find a job."

"You can rent a storage unit. That's what they're for." As we descended the stairs, he asked over his shoulder, "How are you fixed for cash? Do you have enough for groceries?"

"I'm fine for now. King gave me an allowance, you know, and put my name on the household account when I came home to help with Mother. There's still quite a bit in it—unless that's part of the estate."

"Absolutely not. If the account has your name on it and King designated it for household expenses, use it for that. Now let's get back to this list. This still isn't enough. The things Susan has selected are worth a good bit more than this, and Regan's choices are far more valuable. Select some more things."

"I really don't want anything else."

He tapped his pen against the paper while he looked around the downstairs. He ambled into the dining room again. "Go ahead and take these paintings."

"I'd never have anywhere to hang them, nor would I want to. While they are beautiful, they have no meaning for me."

"They would beef up your list, though, and some of them might fetch something at auction. Paintings have an advantage over furniture, too—they are easier to store. You could probably fit most of them in one closet and sell them at your leisure."

I gave him a rueful smile. "I may be living in one closet and I know nothing about selling paintings. I truly don't want them, Judge."

He huffed. "Teensie, let me put it as plainly as I can. Your father's will stipulates that you girls are to share equally, so Gage will have to make sure that happens. You can't simply give everything to your sisters. However, they are taking many valuable things out of this house and will use every subterfuge in the book to keep from handing over cash to make up your share. For pity's sake—or out of pity for Gage—take the damned pictures."

To please him and avoid a series of family fights, I agreed to put the paintings on my list. Even so, my list scarcely came to half a page.

Gentle rain fell the afternoon I met my sisters in Gage's office to settle the matter of furnishings. As I shook out my umbrella in his foyer, I had the fanciful impression that Mother was weeping in heaven for the breakup of her home.

Gage ushered me into his small conference room with such professional suavity that nobody would have guessed he had been playing Old Maid at my kitchen table the previous afternoon and had chortled like a kid when he bluffed Wonder into choosing the old maid. Regan and Susan already sat on the far side of the glossy table, for another of King's maxims had been, *If you cannot sit at the head of a table, always sit facing the door. It gives you an edge over those who have to sit with their backs to it.* Gage waved me to a seat across from my sisters and took his seat at the end. "I believe you have something to say as we begin, Teensie?" he said when I was seated.

I nodded. "I've got a list here of ordinary things I need."

I handed the list to Regan, who barely scanned it before she handed it to Susan.

Susan perused it for less than five seconds, then looked at Regan. In unison they murmured, "Still a little dim."

Indignant that they would think I was silly enough to ask for only mundane things, I said, "Gage has the list of things I want from the estate. These are just things I need to set up housekeeping, since I never got a chance to have my own place until now."

Susan shrugged. "Take them. We'd probably give them to charity anyway."

In some things, my sisters were eerily alike.

They must have consulted on what they wanted from the house, too, because when Gage distributed copies of all three lists, theirs contained no duplicates. Regan, however, had put my bedroom set at the top of hers while Susan wanted the dining room paintings, the piano, and King's chess set and table. Each of their lists ran to several pages. As they scanned my list, their eyes narrowed.

"Not the bedroom furniture," Regan vowed.

"And not the piano, paintings, or chess set," Susan added. "Albert wants the chess set."

Pleasing Albert was not on my list. "Albert doesn't play chess."

"That set was made for the college founder. It ought to be in the president's office."

Gage held up a hand to ask for silence. "Obviously we have a few points of difference here. Regan, Granddaddy tells me the bedroom furniture already belongs to Teensie. You'll need to take it off your list."

Regan uncapped an expensive fountain pen and struck through it with one firm stroke. "Until I see her in court."

Gage went on as if she had not spoken. "Susan, you and Teensie need to negotiate the piano, the dining room pictures, the chess set, and the game table."

Susan cleared her throat as she always did before she made an important statement, a professor's trick to get everyone's attention. "Since those pictures were bought specifically for the dining room, Albert says they should go with the house—like lighting fixtures or kitchen appliances. He wants the chess set and I need the piano." She addressed the last sentence to me as if that settled the matter.

"The paintings do not go with the house," Gage informed her. "You and Teensie can negotiate which of you gets them, but if you get them, you must add their value to your list."

"I'm not getting them. They will stay in the house when the college buys it."

"You may donate them to the college for a tax deduction, but for the purposes of distributing your father's estate equitably"—he stressed the word— "they must go on your list."

"That's fine with me," I agreed. "I only want them to sell. If you want to keep them on your list, I'll be glad to take cash. I do want the piano and the chess set."

Susan and Regan exchanged a frown. The judge was right— they did feel entitled to take what they wanted and expected me to be content with what they chose to leave.

Gage shuffled papers to find the one he wanted. "Before we begin these discussions, we have a couple of preliminaries to go through. As I understand it, all three of you agree to the appraisals of the furnishings by the independent firm I called in and to the asking price for the house that my Realtor has set. That's what this document states." He laid it on the table.

"The house?" Susan said uncertainly. "I'm not sure—"

"Get over it," said Regan. "Both Gage's Realtor and Teensie's appraised the house higher than Sam's woman did. Albert's not getting my share for a bargain price. Did your appraiser put a value on the heirloom bedroom set, Gage?" She scanned the page before her.

"He did not. As I said, that already belongs to Teensie."

"For the time being." Regan uncapped her pen again.

Gage held up one hand. "Before you sign, let me call in my assistant, who is a notary."

When she glided in, Gage held up his copies of our lists. "Are you also agreed that anything not on one of these lists will be sold, and if there is a discrepancy between what the three of you take in furnishings, anyone getting furnishings of a lesser value will receive more cash from the sale of other furnishings and, if necessary, a greater portion of King's investment portfolio to make up differences between you?"

"The stocks and bonds?" Regan objected. "I don't think—"

"Dr. MacAllester stipulated that his estate is to be divided equally among you. Therefore, you must each get exactly one-third of the whole estate." Gage sounded like he was giving a lesson in third-grade arithmetic.

My sisters looked at me as if I were there for the sole purpose of defrauding them.

Gage passed around another sheet. "Please sign above your names. Jardine, will you notarize these two documents for me, please?"

When his assistant had affixed her seal and left, Gage reached for a calculator. "Okay. If Susan gets everything on her list and Regan gets everything except that bedroom set, which Granddaddy has stipulated belongs to Teensie and wasn't appraised anyway—"

"See you in court, sweetie," Regan muttered under her breath.

"—and if Teensie gets everything on her list except the dining room pictures, the piano, the chess set, and the table it sits on, she will need to receive a good bit of compensation from the sale of the other furnishings and the investment portfolio."

"How much?" Regan asked.

"Here's what I come up with." He handed her a legal pad. Susan choked as she read it. "That can't be right."

"Teensie is getting very few things, none of which is particularly valuable. The Mercedes alone is worth as much."

"I don't think the car ought to be counted. It's old, and we only want it so I can let Monique have mine. If King had known she was coming home—"

"We cannot base our decisions on conjecture or Teensie might get it all," Gage reminded her. "Monique was not mentioned in the will."

"Teensie needs to choose more things," Regan declared, "and she needs to pay for all that household stuff she's taking. Your appraiser didn't set a value on it, I notice."

Gage found another sheet in his file. "I thought you might ask about that, so last week while Teensie was out looking for a place to live, I went over to the house with a secondhand dealer and Teensie's list. He said he'd give you a hundred and fifty dollars for the lot. Shall I add that to your list, Teensie?"

I nodded. "Fine with me."

"That scarcely makes a dent in her total," Regan argued.

"True," Gage said. He folded his hands across his stomach. "How do you want to reconcile this?"

I watched raindrops slide down the window while my sisters reexamined the lists. When they began to whisper together, I produced what the judge had called "the aces up your sleeve."

"If you like, Regan, I'll put my bedroom furniture on my list. I know the judge said I could have it, but I don't want to fight about it."

"Oh, we're going to fight about it, baby sister. I already told you, when we're through with this stuff, I'm taking you to court for that furniture."

"I hope you won't. I had my appraiser valuate it. It would bring my total up quite a bit."

I expected her to gasp when she saw the valuation. When she didn't, I knew she'd had a shrewd idea of its value all along.

With eyes narrowed, she weighed giving me cash from the estate plus the cost of taking me to court against giving me the furniture. "Take it," she said with an impatient wave. "I don't have a vacant bedroom anyway."

The judge had been right. "Regan was born greedy," he had said. "Offer a deal that saves her money and she'll take it and run."

That wasn't why I offered to buy the furniture. *So far as it depends upon you, live peaceably with all* was a Bible verse Teddy used to quote when I came to her house raging against my sisters. That afternoon, since it was within my power, I preferred to add the bedroom furniture to my list rather than live with Regan's hostility for the rest of my life.

I took a deep breath as I looked at Susan, for she was less predictable than Regan. "I'd like to have the piano, the chess set, and the game table. I've played on them all my life, so they mean more to me than they do to you—or to Albert. I'll take the dining room pictures, too, if you like, to beef up my list."

"But—" Susan began.

"Let her have the piano," Regan advised. "She plays. You don't. You can buy a piano good enough to use at parties for a lot less than that one's worth, and don't clutter your list with things Albert wants. As for those pictures, ask alums to donate pictures for that room."

"Take them all, then," Susan said with little grace. "How would that make the totals come out, Gage?"

While Gage punched in more numbers I sent up a quick prayer of thanks for the judge's experience in dealing with our family. "Start with Regan," he had advised. "Make her happy and she'll convince Susan."

"Although Teensie still gets more cash than the two of you

when the rest of the furniture sells," Gage reported, "it's a lot less than she did at first."

When they saw the figures, they wore the smug look of women who have gotten the best of a deal.

The judge must have alerted Gage to possible future repercussions, because he produced a third sheet of paper for us to sign. "This stipulates that once you have agreed on who gets what, there will be no later protests about this decision either privately or in a court of law."

Regan grimaced as she scrawled her name. For once, my signature was as bold as hers. I was elated to have gotten the three things I wanted most. Taking six paintings I neither wanted nor needed was a cheap price to pay for peace in the family.

As they gathered up their purses Gage held up a hand. "One more thing. Since the house hasn't sold"—I appreciated his tact. What he meant was, "Since Albert hasn't come up with money to buy the house"—"I suggest that Teensie remain in it until it sells. I won't hold an estate sale until we have a buyer, and you won't want the place vacant with all that good furniture in it."

I was too surprised to speak. I had never imagined anyone would expect me to move before the house was sold.

"Very well." Susan had a class and was eager to be off.

Regan bit her lower lip and narrowed her eyes at me. "Will she pay rent?"

"I will not," I said. "If that's the deal, I'll leave the place by the end of the week." Although heaven only knew where I'd go.

"If you expect Teensie to serve as curator," Gage said in a tone designed to pacify, "she should get paid. I suggest—" He named a figure that would keep me from having to look for work until the estate was settled and I had moved. I sent up another prayer of thanksgiving for the old judge and his grandson.

"She gets free housing," Regan pointed out.

"That places her under no obligation to stay. If you want

to leave that furniture in an empty house . . ." From his grave expression, a stranger would think Unizilla was riddled with crime.

Susan stood with an impatient wave. "If you pay her to stay, it has to be taken from the estate." That made sure I paid one-third of my own stipend.

Gage stood and held out a hand to each of my sisters. They were already heading for the door when he reached for mine. When we shook, he gave me a wink. I left grateful that even if my family regarded me as negligible, I had protectors in Unizilla.

The next day Regan, Susan, and Albert came with men and trucks to remove what they were taking. Gage stood in the front door and checked off each item as it was carried out. When Regan told her men to take a pair of marble lamps that were not on her list, Gage sent them back. "You can buy them from the estate if you like," he offered.

She gave a disgusted huff. "Never mind. I didn't really want them."

The only notice any of them took of me was when Susan pointed to a thick layer of dust on the floor where Mother's china cabinet had sat before Regan's men removed it. "I trust you'll give this place a good cleaning before you leave."

"My people will do that," Gage informed her.

I gave him a grateful smile and went upstairs. In my sitting room—an island of sanity in the chaos—I painted houses for birds while my sisters dismantled mine.


Susan and Regan took valuables. They left me with the detritus of years.

For the next few days, I wandered through decimated rooms, grieving for their departed beauty. Every closet I opened was full of things I had no idea what to do with: luggage, boxes of photos, Christmas decorations, King's collection of hats. He was a fervent believer in hats, wearing felt in winter and straw in summer. "Makes sense with all this skin cancer about," he used to boom. "Dumbest fashion decision men ever made was to give up dress hats."

I secretly suspected he wore them in lieu of a crown.

On Sunday, Coco stopped me after chapel. "Are you still up for painting birdhouses? The college bookstore says they can use ten each of Main and the chapel before Christmas. I've got five of each built."

"Bring them over," I said. "I've almost finished the last ones you brought, and now that King is gone, my evenings are free."

"I'll bring them tomorrow afternoon," she promised.

Before Coco arrived, Wonder rang my bell. As soon as I opened the door she announced, "I am not taking a nap and dat is final." Susan had finally gotten her granddaughter to pronounce "r," but "th" still eluded her.

Bewildered at the greeting, I said, "Fine. Where's your mother?" I didn't like the habit Monique was developing of sending the child rather than bringing her to me. What if Wonder started chasing a butterfly one day and wandered off?

She heaved one of her famous sighs. "She's with dat Junior again. I told her I do not like dat man and I do not like my mama hanging around wif him, and she said I must be tired to be so fussy. I am not tired, I am mad, so I am not going to take a nap."

"I'm fixing to clean out the utility room. You can help."

She was a good little helper, happily climbing into lower cabinets to drag things out. At one point she backed out to inform me, "I forgot to tell you. Dat Cherky book Granddaddy bought me is a baby book, not stories at all. He must not know I'm growed up."

Around three, Coco arrived with ten unpainted birdhouses. When we took them up to my sitting room, she frowned at the bluebird house, which I had moved from my painting table to my desk. It still had no paint except the yellow undercoat. "I thought you'd do something cute with that—the witch's gingerbread house, maybe, or an English cottage."

I touched its gray shingled roof. "I think it's cute as it is. I wouldn't mind living in it. I might even keep it and give a donation to the clinic. Who knows? Maybe I'll have a house one day with a yard full of bluebirds."

"It would have been mighty cute as an English cottage, but suit yourself. Let me take the three you've finished to my car and bring in some lemon tea cakes I baked for you."

"Great. I'll put on coffee."

When Coco joined me in the kitchen, she nodded toward a jumble of boxes and half-full bottles of cleaning supplies beside the sink. "What on earth is all that mess?"

"We're cleaning the you-lity room," Wonder called. Her voice was so muffled, I figured she was inside the cabinet. "We doesn't t'ink Alice used up a whole bottle of anyt'ing de whole time she's worked here."

Coco chuckled. I blushed. "I'll have to be more careful what I mutter in the future," I said softly before asking in a normal voice, "What am I supposed to do with that kind of stuff?"

"Leave it for Gage's estate sale, except for what you can use in your new place."

"Just sorting the useful from trash could take months. King lived in this house over fifty years and neither he nor Mother ever got rid of anything. Sorting his papers will take weeks."

"That's not your job. They should go to the college."

"Can I send them King's clothes and five half-full bottles of aftershave? Or the half-used box of Mother's bath powder I found in his bathroom? It's too good to toss, but I don't use it."

"I likes baf powder," called Wonder. "I will take it home wif me. Right now I gots to finish my cleaning."

Coco mimicked large ears on each side of her head. I nodded. "Ready for coffee? I was needing a break."

"Do you still have a cup to put it in?"

"I certainly do. In fact, thanks to your daddy, I have a china one." I fetched two and Wonder's purple cup.

Coco raised her cup to look at the light through its delicate porcelain. "China and silver are not essential to daily life, but I find a little elegance does wonders to lift the spirits."

Wonder appeared in the doorway, cobwebs clinging to her hair. "I'm done dusting."

"Then come have some refreshments with Coco and me," I replied. "But first, wash your hands good."

When we were all settled at the table, Wonder commanded with a wave, "Tell Miss Coco de story." She had not made that request since King's will was read.

I was embarrassed. "Coco doesn't need to hear that story."

"What story?" asked Coco.

"Something I made up for Wonder."

Wonder shot me a defiant glare. "It's about princesses and a bad king. De youngest princess was 'posed to get de castle, but de bad king didn't keep his promise."

One of the curses of being fair with auburn hair is that you blush easily. I felt a tide of red rise from my neck to the roots of my hair. To keep from looking at Coco, I bent close to give Wonder the benefit of my frown. "That was not the story I told you. It was about a princess who liked to help people."

Wonder arranged her face into Mournful Minnie. "She had to leave de castle, and she didn't get a prince in de foreseeable future."

"That wasn't in the story, either, and you know it. She didn't need a prince."

"She did, Teensie!"

Coco licked lemon frosting off her tea cake. "Princes are vastly overrated, you know."

Wonder was distracted at once. "What's fastly over-ated? Does dat mean dey eat too much too fast?"

"No, it means not all of them are as wonderful as people think. Princesses are better off without some of them."

Wonder's eyes were round with concern. "Did you get a bad prince, Miss Coco?"

Knowing Coco's reluctance to talk about her marriage, I said quickly, "Miss Coco lives with Judge Brantley."

"Dat hairy judge is not a prince! He is a very old man."

"Wonder!"

Coco gurgled with laughter. "You are right. He is also my daddy. But I did have a handsome prince once." She leaned close to Wonder to confide, "He was not a nice prince, though. I never wanted another one."

What had she wanted instead? I remembered her impassioned *Run after life! Catch it while you can!* What would Coco have done with her life if she had not stayed with her father all those years? Perhaps someday I would find the right moment to ask her.

Now was not the time. She was still talking to Wonder. "Besides, it's not always a prince who wins a princess. In some stories, a lot of princes try to win a princess by killing a dragon or climbing a tall mountain to reach a treasure, but they all fail because they are proud and foolish. It's an ordinary man who is brave and kind who accomplishes the job and wins the princess. Those stories teach us it is better for a princess to have a man who is kind and brave than to have some princes."

Wonder puckered her forehead while she thought that over. "Okay." She gave me a sunny grin. "Maybe de t'ird princess will get a man who is not brilliant or rich, but who is brave and kind and likes to help people." Having settled my future, she finished her milk in one long swallow. "May I watch *Finding Nemo?*"

"It's got lots of water," I reminded her.

"Nemo lives in a nocean, not a river, and fishes can't drown." She had obviously been giving that matter some thought.

After I settled her upstairs I came back with trepidation, expecting Coco to ask about the story. Instead, she sat drinking her coffee with a bemused expression. "Have you ever noticed how much Wonder resembles King? When she ordered you to tell me that story, she was his spitting image."

"Hush your mouth! We don't want him whirling in his grave."

She laughed. "Nevertheless, you'd better warn Monique what she's got on her hands."

"What I've got on my hands right now is a royal mess." I went to pour us more coffee.

Coco joined me at the counter and looked over the assortment of supplies we'd unearthed in the utility room. She picked up a box of cleanser. "I think this belongs in the Smithsonian. I haven't seen that brand since I was a child." She set it back on the counter and crossed her arms over her chest. "You don't have to deal with anything here except what is yours, you know. Pack what was on your list and carry it up to your sitting room, put a Private sign on the door, and have Gage deal with the rest. But before he holds the estate sale, you have earned the right to go through the house for incidentals you will need to start your own home—cleaning supplies, food in the pantry, things like that."

"What do I do with family photos and Christmas ornaments?"

"Call in your sisters to divvy those up, or they're sure to yell bloody murder later." She opened a cupboard door and shook her head at the vast array of dishes. "Don't bother yourself about stuff you don't want. You'll be amazed at what people will buy at an estate sale, and when that's over, Gage will send the rest to charity or toss it. Then he'll hire somebody for the final cleaning. Would Alice be up to that?"

"Cleaning isn't Alice's forte. Here's a good example of her style." I opened the cabinet under the sink to reveal an unholy jumble.

Coco looked from the mess to me. "So you cleaned this place all these years?"

"I went behind her a bit."

Coco pressed her lips together. "God had better redeem those years," she said. "The Bible promises that all things work together for good to those who love the Lord. I want to see King's betrayal work something good in your life."

I heaved a sigh I could have learned from Wonder. "I do, too, but let's not hold our breath."

We drifted back to the table to finish our snack. "Where are you going when you move out?" she asked.

"I have no idea. I haven't found anything yet."

"What about apartments?"

"None of them will let me bring Jester."

Hearing his name, the big dog rose and crossed the kitchen with a scratch of toenails on the vinyl floor. He pressed his head against my knee and I rubbed the hard skull between his ears. "As Wonder would say, he's one of my bestest friends."

"I hope Daddy, Gage, and I are on that list."

I felt a frog fill up my throat. "Most definitely."

"I'd better be going." Coco fetched a plate from the cupboard and slid the rest of the tea cakes on it. "Keep these to nibble while you work."

"Thanks for bringing them. They are delicious."

"Of course they are. I used Teddy's recipe."

We shared a moment of silent remembering.

*     *     *

King used to say that most people wait until they are leaving to bring up the most important thing they have to say. I was about to open the front door when Coco put up a hand to stop me. "Don't let the cold in yet. I want to talk to you about a possible job. Lena Thompson is getting worse and can't give her kids the care they need. Lena does what she can when she is able, but a lot of the time it's Kaitlin who cooks and does laundry. She's only ten. A child should not have to run a house at that age. Before somebody reports Lena for neglect and the county takes the children away, Daddy is looking for somebody to move in with them to be sure those children eat right and have some supervision. I wondered, since you are a nurse— There's money to pay you, of course. Daddy pays their bills and keeps charge accounts for them at several stores, and he'd pay you a fair wage."

"They don't need a nurse—they need a cook and a nursemaid," I protested. "Why don't you ask Alice? I've already cut her back to mornings, and I can do what needs to be done here until the house sells."

"That's an idea. Neither Lena or the kids would care if she's a sloppy housekeeper, and she can certainly cook. I'll suggest it to Daddy and see what he thinks."

I stood in the door to watch her down the steps. When she reached the bottom, I heard her mutter, "Being alone in this big empty house would give me the willies."

# Five

November marched in through pounding rain. Clouds settled on the mountains like they planned to stay and the Unizilla River boiled over its banks. Its thunder played along my nerves like fine rage.

The marble house was always bleak in the rain, and that autumn my future seemed as bleak as the house. Some days I was tempted to abandon the house to Albert and flee to Belize. I had heard living was cheap down there, they spoke English, and they probably needed nurses. If Wonder had never come to Unizilla, I might have boarded a plane in a flash. Instead, I lit the living room gas logs and pounded out fugues and études on the piano with a fervor that would have surprised their composers.

I began to pack my possessions, although I had no idea where I would take them. Regretfully I decided to put the little yellow birdhouse in storage until I had a yard of my own. I called a professional packer to crate the dining room pictures—they deserved to be treated well—but when I saw how bulky they were in crates, I knew I would probably have to rent a place to store them. Storage fees could cost more than I would get for them.

I cleaned out closets and drawers, although Coco continued

to insist I leave all that to Gage's people. I could bear for others to paw over my parents' decent possessions, but I could not bear for anybody to see the rubbish their deaths had left behind.

Jester padded along with me as I trundled between the kitchen, the butler's pantry, and the upstairs. We needed each other in those high, chilly rooms.

Each evening I painted birdhouses, for Coco was building them at a prodigious rate. I told her one evening when she dropped off five more, "If the rest of construction in Unizilla kept pace with you, I wouldn't have a problem finding somewhere to live."

When I wasn't packing, painting, or clearing out the house, my days were spent entertaining Wonder and looking for a place to rent. I had to find a job, too, but housing was my most pressing need. I knew that as soon as Albert found a donor, he would have no compunction about putting me on the street—or sending Susan to pressure me to move in with them "for the time being."

Looking at rental houses and apartments was a depressing exercise, though. After the large rooms I was used to, other rooms seemed as cramped as Jester's kennel. I told myself they would look better on sunny days, but I could not picture Teddy's furniture in any of them.

As rain poured down for days and days, the marble house grew gloomier and chillier. When I went out on my porch to look at the mountains, the valleys were full of dark, foreboding clouds as if the mountains wore shrouds.

One evening, though, when I put Jester out for a run around the yard, I was surprised to see that the sky was clear. Hundreds of stars pricked the sky. I stood and marveled at them until the phone called me back indoors.

"Teensie!" Wonder shrieked in my ear. "You know what Granddaddy showed me? De Milky Way! I told him de Milky

Way story, but he musta read de same book you did, 'cause he said it was dist lots of stars and he'd show me one night. Tonight, when I was fast asleep, he woke me up and he wrapped me in a quilt so I wouldn't get cold. Den he carried me outside and I saw it! I did! I can't talk much, 'cause I have to go back to bed, but I told Mama I haf to tell you somefing first." Her voice dropped to a husky whisper. "It really is cornmeal on de sky."

The next morning the world was as crisp as Rome apples. The mountains blazed with so much color that the air wore a burgundy tinge. The autumn sun slanted sharply across the valley, gilding all the edges. My spirits rose with a flock of birds that took to the sky. My life was not over; I was entering a new season. I felt a tingle of anticipation. As a stiff breeze waltzed down the valley, I lifted my face to it and felt it carry away my past.

That afternoon Wonder and I walked down to the river. "Look, Teensie!" She pointed to long white lines across the blue sky. "God is writing a letter!"

"Those are contrails," I explained. "Places where warm airplanes went through a cold sky. How many can you see?"

". . . eight, nine, ten," she counted. She peered up with concentration. "I t'ink dey *could* be God writing. I don't see any planes, do you?" Susan might be reshaping Wonder's diction but she could not curb the child's imagination.

I could imagine the beginnings of enormous letters in those lines. Three lines there might be an "A." Two nearby could be a couple of "L's." Into my mind flashed the comforting message given by God to Julian of Norwich centuries before: *All will be well and all will be well and all manner of things will be well.*

Unpredictable as lightning, Wonder hopped onto the large rock and changed the subject. "Mama's gone to 'lanta to get a dress for de harbest ball. Isn't dat a funny name? It's not a ball you can frow—it's dist a dance, and dey don't even have corn and stuff. Are you going, or can I stay with you?"

How could I have forgotten the Harvest Ball? It was the biggest autumn event on campus, held the weekend before Thanksgiving and attended by students, faculty, and administrators. Mother and King had introduced ballroom dancing to the curriculum years before, and it remained a popular elective. The ball gave students a chance to use what they had learned and faculty a chance to dress up. The Harvest Ball seven years before had been my first date with Phil. We had attended together ever since. Although he played in the band, he came down to the dance floor now and then to dance with me, and the rest of the time I danced with married faculty and administrators. King always gave me a couple of waltzes.

I hadn't heard from Phil since his nonproposal, and had not given the ball a thought. For a couple of seconds I regretted that he and I were no longer—what? Friends? Insignificant others? Was there a category called "acquaintances of convenience"?

"Stay with me," I told Wonder. "Maybe your mother will let you spend the night."

Monique was delighted with the idea of a weekend to herself. She brought Wonder over Saturday afternoon and promised to pick her up late Sunday.

We dragged boxes of Christmas ornaments and photo albums into Regan's old bedroom to go through them. While I separated tatty Christmas things from good ones, Wonder wound tinsel around her arms and put big red bows in her hair. When I lifted out one of Mother's glass snowflakes from the studio of Hans Godo Fräbel, she gasped. "Dat is bee-*you*-ti-ful!"

King had bought Mother a limited-edition snowflake every Christmas for many years. I was surprised Regan hadn't claimed them. "Let's take them downstairs. I'll show you where they used to go."

The living room was dim. I lifted out the snowflakes, which were mounted on bases, and stood them in a row on the living room mantelpiece. When I turned on the crystal chandelier, the snowflakes sent the light back in tiny sparkles. The effect used to be more spectacular before Regan took the big mirror over the fireplace, but Wonder was delighted. Her mother used to look at those snowflakes with exactly that awe.

"Do you think your mother would like to have them?" I asked on impulse. None of us had asked Monique what memento she would like from the house. "You couldn't touch them until you grow up, but one day they would be yours."

"Mine? Oh, Teensie! Dose are the prettiest t'ings I eber did see!"

As I tucked her into King's bed and kissed her good night, she asked sleepily, "Are you sorry you didn't go to de ball? Dere mighta been a pwince dere."

"No princes," I assured her. "Only trolls."


After lunch on Sunday, Wonder took a nap while I read. Gage arrived around three, his face too grim for him to be simply stopping by. All sorts of scenarios flitted through my mind: Coco was sick, the judge had had a fall. "What's the matter?" I asked.

Gage rubbed his hand over his mouth like he wished he didn't have to speak. "I came to tell you something I didn't want to say over the phone. Albert called a few minutes ago. He has an anonymous donor who is going to buy the house, and he wants to close as soon as possible." Before I had assimilated that, he added, "I need to hold the estate sale next weekend. Can you move out before then?"

"But that's Thanksgiving!"

"I know, and I hate like the dickens to interfere with your

holiday, but I've got to have time to get things organized here."
When I didn't say anything, he asked, "Could you move by the
following Tuesday? And put everything that's yours in one of
your two rooms or put a not-for-sale sign on it?"

He looked so embarrassed, I felt sorry for him. "I'll try, but I
have to find a place that will take Jester."

Gage scratched the dog's wide head. "I could take him for a
while. He's no trouble, and I have a fenced backyard." Gage had
bought a bungalow three doors down from his grandfather and
Coco. With all the work he was doing on it, it would be easy to
sell or rent when he inherited the big house. I wished it were for
rent right then.

"Teensie is 'posed to get dis house," Wonder announced from
the staircase. I wondered how long she'd been there.

"I didn't get it," I reminded her, "so I have to leave. I won't go
far, though. You can still come see me."

Her skeptical little face reminded me she had lost her daddy,
her first home, and all her friends in the past year, and didn't
need more change in her life. "You can help me fix up my new
place," I offered, mustering enthusiasm.

With the lightning change of mood she excelled at, she
bounded down the stairs. "Okay! Do you want hot chocolate,
Gage? Teensie can make us some, can't you, Teensie? And she
still has cookies Miss Coco brought."

The three of us drank hot chocolate and ate the rest of Coco's
tea cakes while we played Uno all afternoon. Gage was such a skill-
ful player that Wonder managed to win our first two games. I gave
a crow as I tossed my next-to-last card in the third game. "Uno!"

The doorbell rang. Monique had come to fetch her daughter.
Her hair was wilder than usual and her lips had a bruised look.

"How was the dance?" I asked as we walked back to the
kitchen. "Did you go with your folks?"

She preened a little. "No, I had a date. Why didn't you come?

Mama thought you'd go with Phil." She watched me closely to see my reaction.

I aimed for casual. "Not this year. I've been busy."

"So has he, apparently. You should have seen him and Stacey."

The name was familiar but I couldn't remember why. "Stacey?"

"Stacey Childers, the new dean of students. She's a head taller than he is, but she's a wicked dancer. During one dance everybody stopped to watch her and Phil."

Surely the pang I felt couldn't be jealousy. "Let's go get your backpack, Wonder," I said.

Gage pushed his chair back. "Do you want some hot chocolate, Monique?" He was already on his way to the cabinet to fetch her a cup.

Wonder spent so long folding and refolding her clothes that I told her, "Come as soon as you get packed," and went back downstairs alone.

As I descended the stairs, I heard Monique and Gage chatting companionably in the kitchen. What topic could they possibly have in common? I should have guessed. Gage was saying, "We were playing Uno today and Wonder said, 'I'm gonna make a subtle move.' Then she laid down a Draw Four card. How did a four-year-old learn the word 'subtle'? Much less what it means?"

Monique laughed. "She's no dummy."

Gage was. He should have stuck with the subject of Wonder. Instead, he asked, "Speaking of dummies, how did you ever get hooked up with somebody like the guy you dragged in here one afternoon?"

I paused to hear how she would reply.

Her voice got an edge. "You mean Junior? He is brilliant. He's gonna make a million dollars someday."

"He'll need it to pay lawyers to keep him out of jail."

"He isn't gonna need a lawyer, Mr. Smarty Pants, he's gonna *be* a lawyer. He's going to law school next fall."

"Where—Pen State, as in penitentiary? He looks like bad news to me."

"If my daddy drops dead, I'll call you to come fill in. Until then, I'll thank you to keep your nose out of my business." She flounced out and nearly ran into me. She had a bright spot of color on each cheek.

"I have something to show you," I said. "Come and see."

I led the way to the living room and flicked on the lights.

"Grandmother's snowflakes!" Her face was brighter than the chandelier.

"Would you like to have them? You haven't gotten anything from the house, and I remember how you used to like them."

"I'd love them!" She walked slowly to the fireplace and touched one gently with her forefinger. "But I'd be terrified I'd break one."

"You'd need to keep them away from Wonder for a few years, but she loves them, too. Eventually you can pass them on to her."

Monique gently touched each snowflake. "Our first family heirloom," she whispered.

After everybody left, I drove around hoping a FOR RENT sign had magically sprouted in front of one of the few houses in town I wouldn't mind having. I returned home with a heavy heart. Unless I moved in with one of my sisters, I saw only one option for the immediate future.

I called Coco. "Does Lena Thompson still need somebody to live with them? I haven't been able to find a place and Gage is about to evict me. Albert has found a donor to buy the house."

"Lena's fine. Alice comes in to cook and the children seem to like her. Gage told me about Albert, though, so I've been giving your situation some thought. Why don't you look for a room to rent in someone's house until you find something permanent? I can't invite you here—our spare rooms are full of junk—but I know several widows with vacant rooms. Why don't I ask if any of them could have you for a while? You could put your stuff in storage and take your time deciding what to do next."

"I cannot tell you what a relief that would be."

After I hung up, I roamed the rooms again as I had the night after King's will was read. Although I was sad, I was not wrenched by grief as I had been the first time. I was either numb or learning to let go.

By Monday Coco had three possibilities lined up. I didn't know the women, but Coco assured me that my rent each month would help any of them out.

The first showed me a small room with an adjoining bath. The room was so hot I could hardly breathe. When I suggested opening a window, she tossed her blue curls. "Oh, no, honey, it's painted shut. We don't want to waste heat, now, do we?"

When I opened the closet door I staggered back at the reek of mothballs. "I've been storing Charlie's clothes in there," she explained. "I'll box them up and put them under your bed. Poor Charlie, he's been gone fourteen years."

The second room was light and airy, but I would need to share a bathroom with the landlady's middle-aged son. "We'll have a lot of fun together," he told me. His leer made me shudder.

"I need more privacy," I said. I hoped I sounded tactful.

Coco had informed me that my third potential landlady was a stellar cook. Maybe so, but she informed me, "You'll need to take your meals out. I cannot share a kitchen. However, as you see, we are right convenient to the diner." I looked out the window of her vacant room onto an excellent view of Danny's Diner's Dumpster.

"Sorry. I need a place where I can fix my meals," I told her.

Teddy always said, "Pray specific prayers. How will you know otherwise that God has answered them?"

On my way back home, I sent up a desperate plea. "Dear

God, is it possible to find a light, airy room with privacy, an adjoining bath, and kitchen privileges?"

I called Coco. "Sorry, none of those will do. I don't think I'm that picky—"

"Stop! I had a brilliant idea while you were out: I called Darla Enderble. She's lonely since Donald died last winter, and her daughter lives out of state. She said if you didn't like any of the other places, to come look at her rooms this afternoon. I think she would like the company."

Donald Enderble had been a gentle, humorous man who taught biology at the college while I was growing up. His wife was a sweet woman who still worked half days in the college alumni office and sang with me in the college chapel choir. I had noticed she was growing thinner since Donald died, but I had never invited her to a meal. Why not?

Mentally kicking myself, I drove over to Darla's.

She lived in a gray Craftsman bungalow trimmed in white, set in a nest of rhododendron. I had not been inside the house, but had often admired it. She ushered me into a small front hall. "Coco told me about your predicament. I think I would enjoy having somebody here. You can have as much space as you want upstairs—there are three bedrooms and a big bathroom. You can have your run of the kitchen, too. Sometimes, maybe, we could have dinner together. Would that suit you?" Her voice was wistful.

"It sounds like an answer to prayer," I said. "Especially if you will let me cook some of those dinners."

Her eyes twinkled. "Honey, you can cook as often as you like. Donald used to cook a lot, and I've sort of gotten in the habit of not eating much since he . . ." She swallowed, then said in an obvious attempt to be cheerful, "Like I said, take your pick of the upstairs rooms. I hope they aren't too dusty. I've developed a touch of arthritis, so stairs have gotten difficult and I don't go up there much. I'll wait for you down here, if you don't mind."

The rooms were half the size of mine at home, but they were charming, with sloping ceilings and views of the mountains. I chose the one adjoining the bathroom, which had an enormous claw-foot tub. Over iced tea we closed the deal. "I'll need to move in next Monday or Tuesday," I told her.

"That's fine. I am spending Thanksgiving weekend with my daughter in Nashville and won't be back until Sunday evening, but here's your key in case you want to start moving in while I'm away. I look forward to having you here. I think we will get along splendidly."

My sisters were not pleased.

I called each of them to report that Gage had a buyer for the house and I would be moving out in a week, so if they wanted any of Mother's Christmas decorations or family photos, they needed to come get them. Susan said, "I'm not interested in Christmas decorations and I have all the family photos I want, thanks." She hung up before I could mention my new home.

Regan promised to stop by Sunday evening after Thanksgiving, although she had more Christmas decorations than Macy's. "We're expecting you for Thanksgiving dinner, as usual," she added. "Then we can drive over to Ginny Linn's. I want you to see the nice rooms you will have."

"Thanks for the dinner invitation," I said, "but I'm not moving in with Ginny Linn. I've rented a room at Darla Enderble's while I decide what to do next."

"I told you, Teensie, we *need* you. Ginny Linn cannot continue to live alone. Besides, instead of paying rent, you will get paid."

"All that may be true, but I'm still moving in with Darla."

"Then you can jolly well spend Thanksgiving with Darla." She slammed down the phone.

She must have called Susan immediately, because Susan

called back a few minutes later. I hoped she would open with an invitation to Thanksgiving dinner, since Wonder had already confided, "Nana bought a turkey so big I can't lift it." As soon as I answered, though, Susan said, "What's this nonsense about you moving in with Darla? I told you, I want you to come live with us. You don't need to live with a stranger."

"Darla isn't a stranger. I've known her all my life."

"But Monique has to study for the SAT every day between now and the test, and she starts school in January. She needs you to keep Wonder. If you move over this week, you can help me cook the turkey. I've never baked one before." I hadn't, either. Until that year, we had always eaten turkey with Regan except for the one year when King insisted we eat at our house. Alice had cooked that turkey.

It took all the willpower I had to overcome a lifetime of saying "yes" to Susan. "I'll be glad to help you figure out how to cook the turkey, but I am moving in with Darla. Living at her place will give me a breather while I decide what to do next."

"You might try thinking of somebody else for a change. Monique—"

"Monique can put Wonder in the college preschool until one o'clock each day. I'll keep her the rest of the afternoon until after the SAT."

"Monique can't afford the college preschool. It's expensive."

"You can afford it, especially with your faculty discount. Consider it an investment in your daughter's education."

"I cannot believe you are so selfish. We need you."

"Not really. Wonder will adore preschool. She'll be running the place within a few days. If it would help, though, I could keep her all day this coming Friday, since school's out."

"Of course it would help. We need all the help we can get until Monique takes that test."

"Then I'll keep Wonder on Friday. Do you still want my help with the turkey?"

"No, we'll manage. I think we'll have a quiet *family* Thanksgiving. You can come eat with us some other time." She hung up.

I stared at the receiver in disbelief. How could my sisters leave me to eat alone the first holiday after King's death? Did they not feel, as I did, that we ought to cling to the little bit of family we had left? Full of self-pity, I went to the piano and played a gentle Bach sinfonia. At first the measured melody made me sad, but gradually the peace of the music filled my soul. My life was not falling apart, it was falling into place—at least for Wonder's "foreseeable future." I would not permit Susan's or Regan's rejection to ruin that.

I spent the rest of Monday finishing my packing and storing things in my sitting room, and with a sense of moving into a new era, I drove to the clinic Tuesday morning to say I could work again. I hadn't worked since King's death except the one morning when Regan tried to steal my furniture. I hadn't felt comfortable leaving the house for long stretches since then, especially after the odd young man had come.

As I entered the clinic, Wonder's vegetable man was coming out. "Hello!" I greeted him. "I've been wanting to . . ."

He passed me and climbed into his truck without a word.

"All I wanted to do was thank you," I yelled after him as he roared away. I stared at his tailgate in chagrin. Could he possibly believe I'd had anything to do with his dismissal from the college? Had Albert's cheapskate decision ruined his business? Was there any way I could repay him for having saved Wonder?

Not if he wouldn't speak to me.

I waved to Grantha, the administrative assistant—who was twenty but looked twelve—and presented myself to Mimi Starnes. "I'm ready to work again if you can use me," I told her.

"If I can use you?" Mimi tucked a strand of graying hair

behind her ear. "Honey, I could use you full-time to do home visits. You are so good at that."

Many of the people we saw needed long-term follow-up care. I enjoyed visiting homebound elderly patients, patients recuperating from accidents, and inexperienced mothers with new babies. I enjoyed chatting while I took temps and blood pressure, changed bandages, or taught new mothers how to bathe and feed infants. I sometimes suspected our chats did more good than the nursing.

"I could do full-time—" I began.

Mimi shook her head. "I can't pay you more than I'm currently paying." I knew that was true. Coco, who tended to know things like that, had confided that Mimi herself worked for little more than she paid me, simply because she loved the people she served. Dr. Starnes's name was at the top of our list of people who deserved sainthood merit badges.

"How about if you pay me for four mornings, Tuesdays through Fridays, instead of two full days, and I work for free Wednesday and Friday afternoons if you need me? At least until I find a full-time job." Mornings were when most patients preferred to be visited. The elderly and new mothers often napped in the afternoon. Some needed afternoon visits, though, and a few preferred them. "There's one condition to afternoon hours. I'll need to take Wonder. I'm keeping her every afternoon for a while. Would that be a problem?"

Mimi considered. "Not often. I think most of the patients would love having Wonder come see them, and four mornings a week would be a godsend."

"If there's a patient Wonder shouldn't visit, I'll go there in the morning."

"Great. Can you work this Friday? I know it's Thanksgiving, and if you are going out of town . . ."

"I'm not." I planned to cook a chicken breast for my Thanksgiving dinner and sit down with Jane Austen's characters in

*Emma*. They wouldn't eat much, and their manners were always exquisite. And with the estate sale going on Friday and Saturday, I would be glad to get out of the house. "I'll have Wonder all day Friday, though."

"Bring her along. I think the patients will get a kick out of her."

I ended up eating Thanksgiving dinner with Coco, the judge, and Gage—a last-minute invitation, but one I was glad to accept. As we said our good-byes, Coco said, "I'll see you tomorrow. I keep the reception desk at the clinic on Fridays nowadays, and Mimi told me you're coming back." A list of Coco's volunteer activities since she had retired would stretch to Atlanta.

The morning after Thanksgiving when Wonder and I arrived at the clinic, the waiting room was empty. Coco greeted us from the desk. "Mimi wants you to come straight to her office. There's a man she wants you to visit."

"Who is it, do you know?"

Grantha came in to water the plants. "It's an old farmer who lives out in the country."

I left Wonder with Coco and moseyed to the doctor's office. She handed me a folder. "I need you to go out to Tobias Jones's farm this morning. He was in here earlier this week, and while I don't have his tests back, I suspect he has hepatitis. I understand he lives alone, so we need to make an assessment of whether he can stay at home or needs to be in a facility. Have you had the shots for hepatitis?" When I nodded, she added, "The only problem is since he's contagious, you can't take Wonder with you."

"She can stay in the truck. We've got books, coloring books, and crayons." I'd make sure not to be inside so long that she got chilled.

I returned to the waiting room to explain all that to Wonder, who was not pleased. Coco looked around the empty waiting room. "Since we're not busy this morning, let me ask Mimi if I can ride out with you. Wonder can entertain me while you're in the house."

Mimi agreed. On the way to the car, Wonder asked, "Who are we going to see?"

"A farmer, honey. Mr. Jones." To Coco I added, "Mimi thinks he's got hepatitis. I hope it's A, not B or C."

"What's the difference?" asked Wonder, skipping between us.

"I don't know, either," said Coco.

"You get A from raw seafood or contaminated food or water. It lasts a couple of months and the patient gets well. B and C are passed through contaminated blood from getting tattoos, sharing needles, or getting blood transfusions, and both linger for years. They can be fatal. All three of them drain your energy, though. I cared for a few hepatitis cases in Atlanta, and they hardly had the strength to walk down the hospital hall." I pictured an old man lying on his sofa for several days, too weak to fetch a glass of juice, and I walked faster.

Coco looked up at my truck and said, "An hour in that cab with Wonder could be a long time. Let's take my car. We won't be so cramped."

We certainly wouldn't. Instead of her Honda she had the judge's Cadillac. Before I could protest she had opened the back door. "Get in, Wonder." She added to me, "My car's in the shop."

I transferred Wonder's booster seat and activities bag to the Cadillac and buckled her in. "Dis car is so big we could put lotsa kids back here," she announced with pleasure.

Coco held out the keys to me. "You drive. You know where we're going."

"Not really. All I know is where Jones Farm Road is. It branches off the main road three miles from town, at the corner where that crazy mechanic has his shop." I weighed maneuvering the judge's precious vehicle over a mountain road versus riding shotgun while Coco drove. Judge Brantley called her "my NASCAR chauffeur." I took the keys.

We set out as merry as if we were going on an adventure.

The day was bright and sunny with only a few clouds overhead, and the trees were at that halfway stage when some still wore their fall finery while others were beginning to bare their souls for winter. As we turned off the highway, I lowered my window a crack and heard the piercing sweetness of a mockingbird.

"The road's paved and looks relatively straight," Coco noted as I swung around the corner onto Jones Farm Road. She spoke too soon. A mile beyond the turnoff, the ancient pavement ended at a small white sign: END OF COUNTY MAINTENANCE. A black mailbox stood beside the sign, painted with a yellow seven-pointed star and the word JONES.

"Do you know these people?" I asked Coco. I knew few people in the country except those who had been patients. Coco tended to know far more than I did.

"No, but from the yellow star on the mailbox, I'd guess he's Cherokee. That's the Cherokee symbol."

Beyond the mailbox a dirt-and-gravel road climbed a steep grade. It wasn't much wider than the Caddy, and ninety percent mud to ten percent gravel. Heavy autumn rains hadn't improved it, either. Ruts had become shallow mud holes that still held water to reflect the sky.

"Dis road doesn't hab any icing," Wonder complained as we jounced along.

"I'll have to get the car washed or Daddy will kill me," grumbled Coco. I suspected she was wishing we'd brought my truck.

I didn't have time for wishing. I was worrying about a wooden bridge up ahead. It was one lane wide, had no sides, and hovered inches above a swollen creek. I approached warily and crept across with my hands tight on the wheel, as if by physical force I could hold the car above the greedy stream. The boards thumped and rattled beneath us.

On the other side, the road snaked in hairpin curves up a

mountain. Keeping the car on the road required all my attention. The alternative on my side was a plunge into the tops of oaks, hickories, and poplars.

"How on earth does he drive on this?" Coco wondered aloud.

"He prob'ly has a truck. He's a farmer," called our backseat Wise Woman.

A few minutes later I saw a sheet of water that cascaded down the rocky face of the mountain and across the road. The flow was five feet wide and swift. I opened my door. "I'm going to check to make sure that's not washed out too deep to cross."

Coco eyed my khaki slacks, green sweater, and emerald flats. "You are going to ruin those clothes."

"Not the shoes. I'll go barefoot. I can't drive through there without knowing it's safe."

Wonder was already unfastening her seat belt. "I'm gonna check, too."

"Your feet look like dead fish," she announced when I stepped onto the road in bare feet.

She punctuated the walk with "Ow! Ow!" as her feet encountered sharp gravel. Granted, she was overdoing the dramatics, but I clutched my lower lip in my teeth to keep from crying out, too. At the edge of the rushing water Wonder waded in, splashing muddy water all over me.

I grabbed her arm and pulled her back. "Stay beside me. We are going to use our toes to test how deep every step is. Roll up your pants and do this." I rolled up my slacks, pointed my toes, and probed the bottom. "Don't step down unless you feel ground close under the water."

Wonder imitated me like a small wood stork. "Oooh! Dis water is *cold*!"

"It comes from a spring underground."

"No, Teensie, dat's where hell is. De water would be hot."

That was no time for a theological discussion. "The middle of the earth is hot. Close to the surface it is cold."

"Oh. I didn't know dat. Now I do." She pranced farther in.

I grabbed her wrist. "Come back here! Remember how I told you we have to walk? We don't know if the entire road has washed away under some of this. You could be swept down the mountainside. Go stand by that bush over there while I see how deep it is."

She huffed, but she went. Maybe she was remembering, as I was, another time when she was swept away.

I shuffled forward one cautious step at a time until I determined that the road was intact. Although the water scarcely came above my ankles, my feet ached with cold.

Back at the car I helped Wonder pull on her socks and shoes over damp, muddy feet. I elected to drive barefoot until we reached our destination. I started the car and moved slowly forward.

We made it through the runoff and up another rise, but as I started downhill again, a startled rabbit dashed across the road. Instinctively I jerked the wheel to avoid it, and the rear of the Cadillac slid into soft red mud. When I floored the accelerator, I felt the back rear tire sink deeper.

By the time I had pushed the car out—with the assistance of Wonder and a few cloth bags the judge kept in his trunk for grocery shopping—my clothes were dotted with mud. "You want to go on or back home?" Coco asked as she slid over to relinquish the steering wheel. "There seems to be a sort of turnaround ahead."

I gave it a longing look. "Nothing would suit me better than going back, but Mr. Jones may need us."

As I turned on the ignition, it occurred to me that the muddy road was a metaphor for my current life: rocky, full of pitfalls, with an uncertain destination.

# PART TWO

# The Log House

# Six

Ten tooth-shattering minutes later we rounded a bend to see a broad cove nestled among the mountains like a hidden treasure. Hardwood forests ringed it. Most of the land was laid out in neat fields. A brook ran through them, playing leapfrog with boulders in its path. Half a mile away, the long drive ended in a metal shed that sheltered a green tractor. Beside the shed, the stained logs of a two-story house glowed like cinnamon sticks against the forest rising behind it. The house had a tin roof the same dark green as an enormous cedar beside the wide porch. People had probably been rocking on that porch for the past hundred years. To the right of the house two long greenhouses reflected the morning sun.

Coco pointed to a field of pumpkins. "The poor thing must have gotten sick before he finished harvesting. He should have sold those before Thanksgiving. Who'd buy them now?"

As we drew closer, I saw that the house was newer than I'd thought, and it had a neglected quality out of keeping with the neatness of the fields. The shrubs around it were scraggly. Abandoned pieces of farm equipment lay around the yard as if someone had upended the shed and shaken it, then left pieces where they fell. To the left of the shed an unpainted split rail fence circled a wood barn weathered to a soft rose. Beyond the paddock I saw a brick chimney where a former house once sat.

A donkey the same gray as the rails rested his chin on a fence post. As I pulled to a stop near the cedar, it set up a bray to wake the dead.

Coco raised her painted brows. "A watch-donkey?"

"Only the advance scout." I nodded toward an enormous tan dog of uncertain parentage that had loped off the porch. As it neared our car, it sent up a volley of barks. A fat turkey waddled around the house, tail feathers spread. A hen crawled from under the porch and made her awkward way toward the car. She listed to one side like a drunken sailor.

Coco gave them the wary attention of one unaccustomed to animals. "Do you think they are welcoming us or warning us off?"

"Warning us off, I suspect. Doesn't look like this place would get many visitors."

"Maybe you shouldn't get out."

"Look!" exclaimed Wonder. "Dat chicken's only got one wing."

Busy giving my face a spit bath with a tissue, I took time out to look. Sure enough, a cluster of feathers sprouted where the other wing should be.

The dog was at my door, slobbering great silver strings. I dropped the mud-streaked tissue in my purse, tugged a comb through my tangled hair, and put on a dab of lipstick—which did little to improve my appearance. My slacks were filthy and soaked at the hem, I had smears of mud on my sweater, and my hands were grubby from pushing the car. Mr. Jones might have several visiting nurses during his illness, but he would never have a more bedraggled one.

"We'll wait in the car," Coco said.

"I won't wait in the car," Wonder objected. "I wants to see de sick farmer."

"You stay here today," I instructed. "He has a disease you could catch."

"Dat's okay, I don't catch real good." She opened her door. The dog began to sniff her legs.

"Don't get out!" Coco commanded.

Wonder giggled. "Stop dat, dog! You're tickling me." The dog wagged his tail.

"You are not to come with me and that is final," I told her. "Now pull back that lip. The way it's sticking out, it will soon be in Tennessee."

Curiosity got the best of her sulk. "Where is Tennessee?"

"You tell her, Coco." I gave the dog the back of my hand to sniff while I closed Wonder's door. He must have decided I wasn't coming to steal the family silver, because he permitted me to get my case from the trunk and start toward the house. He stuck close, though, and the turkey gobbled and the hen complained behind us as we walked along large flat stones set in gravel that served as a front walk.

I climbed four wooden steps, crossed the wide boards of the porch, and knocked. Nobody answered. "Mr. Jones? I've come from the clinic." Nobody replied. I tried the door. It opened an inch and stuck.

The dog took my slacks in his mouth and tugged. Rather than lose my pants, I followed him around to the back of the house. A dusty black pickup was parked under a homemade carport beside a back porch. Boot prints up the wooden steps looked recent. Boots slung carelessly aside bore clumps of mud and wisps of straw.

I knocked on the back door and repeated my call. When nobody answered, I tried the knob. The door swung open. I looked into a large, sun-washed room. "Mr. Jones? Are you here? I'm a nurse from the clinic."

Nobody answered.

I stepped inside. He could be upstairs, or maybe he wore a hearing aid he hadn't put in that morning.

Whoever he was, his house was charming. A large living and dining area ran across the whole front of the house, with a wide island between the dining room and the kitchen. Ten-foot-high ceilings, birch floors and cabinets, and white countertops made the room spacious and airy—too airy. It was colder than the porch outside. "Mr. Jones? Are you here?" The big dog pushed past me and headed down a short hall to the left of the kitchen.

"In here." The voice was listless and came from a room beyond the hall.

"I'm from the clinic. I'll be there as soon as I scrub my hands."

I looked around for a thermostat. I saw only a wood-burning stove in the front corner of the dining room. It was not lit.

The counters were littered with remnants of many small meals—a plate and glass here, a plate and cup there, a collection of glasses beside the sink. I had seen that sort of clutter often in the homes of people who lived alone and had suddenly been struck down by illness.

While I washed my hands I read a small plaque propped in the windowsill over the sink. Varnished pine, it was the kind sold by the hundreds in cheap tourist shops. It said:

*When the white man discovered this country,*
*Indians were running it.*
*No taxes, no debt, women did all the work.*
*White man thought he could improve on a system like this.*

OLD CHEROKEE SAYING

Apparently Mr. Jones had a sense of humor.

I pulled on disposable gloves and headed down the short hall. I passed a small half bath and entered a dim cave darkened by a holly that pressed against the windows. Pine paneling did little to brighten the room. I could hardly see the couch to my left, much less the man who lay there, but I could smell the sweetness of ketosis—one result of hepatitis. As my eyes adjusted I saw on the floor beside him a bottle of Tylenol and a half dozen beer cans. One can had turned over and puddled on the floor.

"Close your eyes. I'm going to turn on a light." I flicked the switch and the room leaped from the shadows—a home office complete with a desk, filing cabinet, computer desk, and a wide-screen TV. My patient huddled under a brown comforter on the couch beneath the mounted head of an eight-point stag. What should have been the whites of his eyes were a dull gold, but his hair was dark above them. Joy welled up in me when I saw his face. An unspoken prayer had been answered.

As soon as he saw me, he jerked the blanket over his head with a groan. "Go away. I don't need your help. I've got the flu." His voice was weak but gruff.

Before I could speak, a small shadow hurtled past me and flung itself against his shoulder. "My poor veg'table man! I'll make you better."

"Go back to the car," I commanded. "I told you to stay there."

Her jaw tightened in a mutinous frown. "He needs me."

I drew her to the window and knelt so we were the same height. "He has germs that can make you sick. Neither you nor the vegetable man wants that. You also could carry germs that could make him sicker. You don't want to do that, do you?"

I got a reluctant head shake.

"You must go back to the car."

"I gotta help him."

"I will help him. You can help most by obeying me so I can start helping him."

"Will you get sick?" Anxious eyes darted from me to him and back.

"No. I've had shots that keep me from getting sick. Now scoot!" I gave her a playful pat on her bottom.

"Good-bye, Mr. Veg'table Man," she sang out with a wave as she left. "Aunt Teensie is going to make you better."

He lifted one arm to wave. As soon as she scampered through the door, he dropped it with a sigh, as if that little bit of movement had worn him out. "Go away," he muttered. "I do not need your help. Let me die in peace."

I stepped nearer the couch. "You do need my help, Mr. Jones." Never in a hundred years would I have imagined that the vegetable man would be called Jones. He should have some grand name of many syllables meaning "He Who Strides Through Waters" or "Teller of Wondrous Tales."

Although he gave no sign he was listening, I bent over him and explained, "We haven't gotten your test results yet, but you probably have hepatitis, a disease of the liver. You must not take any more Tylenol or drink any more beer."

He murmured without opening his eyes. "I'm thirsty and my head aches."

"I know, but acetaminophen and alcohol aggravate the condition."

I set the Tylenol on the desk across the room. "You are going to need a lot of rest and fluids." And help—my help. I could thank him for saving Wonder.

"All I do is rest, and I stink," he growled. "I took a bath this morning and already I stink. Go away—please." He pulled the comforter over his head again, as if that would shield me from his odor.

"I'm not exactly at my best, either," I told him. "Our car got stuck in the mud on our way up here and Wonder and I had to push it out. I'm covered in mud."

I nearly added, "And hey—twice when we met I was dripping wet," but I didn't want him to remember me standing in the river in my underwear. That sort of thing does little for your professional image. I said instead, "Let's forget how we both look for the moment. You helped our family by saving Wonder. Now I get to help you. That smell is part of your disease. When the liver doesn't function, your body begins to excrete sugar. I'll bet your mouth tastes like you have been sucking a ten-penny nail."

The cover rippled as he gave a weak nod.

"That's iron in your system, another sign of hepatitis. You must have had it a while. Why didn't you come to the clinic sooner?"

"Thought it was flu. Needed to harvest . . ." The sentence trailed off into exhaustion.

"I want to take your vital signs. Can you give me an arm, please?"

He reluctantly stuck one out.

I recorded his blood pressure, pulse, and temperature (slightly elevated), then pinched the skin on the back of his hand.

"Ow!" Startled, he drew back his hand. Not before I saw that the ridge I had pinched remained in place after I released the pressure.

"Sorry, I was testing for dehydration. Have you drunk anything these past few days besides beer?"

He shrugged. "A little water."

"Have you eaten today?"

He shook his head.

"I'm going to fix you something in a minute. First, you need heat. Where is your thermostat?"

"No furnace. Stove."

I was afraid of that. "I've never built a fire in a stove, so help me out here."

Under his direction I filled the stove with kindling and logs, stuffed paper beneath them, adjusted the damper, and lit the paper. "It's burning," I called a few minutes later. "Rest a little while I fix you some lunch."

"Wonder . . ."

"She'll be all right outside for a while. I have a friend out there with her and they have your menagerie to keep them company. If they get cold, I left keys so they can start the car and warm up. You rest while I find you something to eat."

I hoped for canned chicken soup or yogurt. The best I could find was stale bread and two eggs. I scrambled the eggs and made toast, added a glass of water, and carried the meager meal to him. "Can you manage to sit up?"

With heroic effort he maneuvered himself up against the arm of the couch. When he tried to hold the fork, his hand wobbled so much the egg fell off the fork.

"Here." I took the fork and offered him a bite.

He turned his head away.

"Don't be ridiculous," I told him. "You will never get well if you don't eat."

He managed most of the egg and toast and drank the water like a desert survivor before his head fell back against his pillow. "Good."

"Where can I find clean bedding?" I asked.

"Upstairs." He closed his eyes again.

Tobias Jones obviously favored the utilitarian school of decor. The living room held only a black leather couch and a coffee table. No rugs to cosset toes on a cold morning. The scarred dining table near the stove was stacked with books and seed catalogs. The front door I had been unable to open was not locked; it was blocked by a stack of newspapers three feet high. I shut it again to keep in the heat.

The far end of the room had a lovely stone fireplace flanked by birch bookshelves, but in front of the books he kept a haphazard assortment of trifles: a jar of colorful buttons, a pile of keys, a few paper clips, a glass of change. One shelf held a collection of antique lamps. I wouldn't have taken Mr. Jones for a collector of anything but newspapers.

Above the fireplace hung a large framed cross-stitch sampler:

*May the warm winds of Heaven blow softly on this home*
*And the Great Spirit bless all who enter here.*
*May your moccasins make happy tracks in many snows*
*And may the rainbow always touch your shoulder.*

Over the words arched a multicolored rainbow. At each of the four corners was the same yellow seven-pointed star I had seen on the mailbox. At the bottom was the name of the embroiderer, LUCY JONES, and a date thirty years before. I had no idea how old Tobias Jones could be. Had Lucy been his wife? What had happened to her?

I was about to turn from the fireplace and head upstairs when my eye caught the picture of a boy on the mantelpiece, framed in oak. He looked about six and had obviously been groomed for the picture—black hair slicked back, face shiny clean. He faced the camera with eager eyes and an endearing snaggletooth grin that made me want to hug him. The picture didn't look old, nor did it look like Mr. Jones. The skin was fairer. I climbed the stairs wondering who the boy was, and where he was. I saw no sign of a child in that house.

The upstairs had four bedrooms and a large bathroom with washer and dryer on one side. "Practical," I murmured. In the marble house, laundry had to be carried downstairs and back up.

In the two back bedrooms twin beds were stripped to the mattresses and pine chests were filmed with dust. A brown comforter was folded at the end of each bed in one room, navy blue ones adorned the beds in the other. At the front of the house, the right bedroom had pink floral curtains and a matching comforter, but a family of dust bunnies had taken up residence under the double bed.

The other front bedroom was his, as spartan as the downstairs: a double mattress on a metal frame, one straight chair draped with clothes, and a scruffy pine chest. From piles of clothes on the floor, I deduced that the chest existed primarily to display a collection of framed snapshots of the boy as a chubby toddler hosing a car, a young Picasso painting at an easel, a child of maybe seven with dark hair flopping in his face and a wide grin as he steered a riding mower. Among them was one professional picture taken when the child was perhaps eleven, posed in front of a Christmas scene. His hair was slicked down and he had a forced smile and anxious eyes. Was he heading into the rebel years of adolescence or simply wishing his mother had let him wear comfortable jeans with his bangs falling in his face?

He was no business of mine.

I examined the piles of clothes to determine which were clean and which were not. The task wasn't easy. I pulled out a wrinkled sheet and pillowcase that I hoped were clean, dragged a couple of quilts down from the shelf of his closet, and grabbed a pillow from the bed. The pillow and brown comforter Mr. Jones had been using would need to be washed. Since I saw no sign of pajamas, I pulled out a set of what looked like clean underwear and a pair of socks to keep his feet warm.

Downstairs I tossed the bedding onto the couch and carried the clean clothes to him. "I'm going to make you a fresh bed in the living room."

He spoke without opening his eyes. "Like it here."

"Maybe so, but leather won't absorb odor and germs like the fabric on this couch does, and the stove will keep you warmer. I've brought you fresh clothes, too. Let me help you change."

"No!" He clutched his covers to him like a Victorian maiden.

"I'm a nurse, Mr. Jones, and you are sick. Do you need help with your clothes?"

"I can manage."

I laid the clothes on the comforter. He made no attempt to pick them up.

"I am going to make you a bed on the other couch," I repeated, "and tidy the kitchen. Put on your clean clothes and call me when you are done. I'll help you to the living room."

I made his bed, washed dishes, and wiped down countertops before I heard a weak rasp, "I'm dressed." I went in to find him sitting on the couch wearing the clean T-shirt—and the soiled comforter wrapped around his waist. Sweat beads stood on his forehead.

I looked at the comforter in amusement. "You really are silly, you know. Put an arm around my shoulders so I can help you walk."

"You're too little."

"I may be little, but I'm strong. Come on, now, let's get you back to bed."

It wrung my heart to feel how little strength he had. I kept remembering how solid his arm had been when I'd touched it only a few weeks before. I turned my back while he discarded his modesty blanket and got between the sheets, then I tucked the quilt around him.

"Feels good," he admitted.

"Rest. I'm going to carry your comforter and dirty clothes up to the washing machine."

While he dozed, I started a wash and went to straighten the den. On the desk I found a surprise: an exquisite chess set of turquoise and polished silver.

I put a quart of water on the coffee table with a glass of ice and fed the last of the firewood to the stove. I tried to be as quiet as I could, but even when the stove door clanged shut, he did not stir.

"Mr. Jones?" I touched his shoulder. His eyelids fluttered. "We need more firewood. Where do you keep it?"

"Under tarp beside porch." His words were so thick I could scarcely understand.

From a large stack of wood under a blue tarp I gathered as much as I figured he'd need until I could return. "Mr. Jones? I'm leaving now. I'll be back in a couple of hours. There's wood by the stove. Will you have energy enough to keep the fire going?" I got an infinitesimal nod. "You are going to need lots of clear liquids, so please drink all that water. As soon as I've taken Wonder home and picked up supplies, I'll come back to fix you some more food, bring in more wood, and give you an IV drip."

He shook his head. "Don't need . . ."

"You definitely do need. This is treatment ordered by the clinic."

His lids flew open over eyes like disks of obsidian. "No more treatment!"

I gathered up my things. "I'm going, for now. You rest. I'll be back later."

"Don't come back. I don't need . . ." His eyes closed. He was asleep.

I rounded the house and found Coco rocking on the front porch while Wonder talked to the donkey by the fence. "How is he?" Coco called as she stilled her rocker.

"Pretty sick," I called back. "I want to take you all home and pick up some things, then I'll come back for the afternoon. I'm going to ask Mimi if I can come every day for a while."

"You or somebody else." She made her way through the small machinery parts that littered the porch and down the wide wooden steps.

"I want to do it," I said when she reached the car. "He did our family a big favor."

"I was drowning in de ribber and he jumped right in and

pulled me out, dist like dat!" said Little Big Ears, prancing over from the fence.

I gave Coco a wry smile. "Now you know. I have been wondering how we could thank him. Now I've found a way."

Nobody said anything as we started down the mountain. I don't know what Wonder was thinking. I suspected Coco was planning excuses for having muddied her father's car. I was listing supplies I needed to take on my next trip up to the farm.

Suddenly Wonder exclaimed, "Dere's our stucking place!" Sure enough, we were at the place where our tire had gotten mired in mud.

"You mean the sticking place," I corrected her.

Her eyes met mine in the rearview mirror with the look children give adults who have managed to live so long in ignorance. "It's a sticking place if you stick a little, Teensie. If you get stuck and can't get out, it's a *stucking* place. If you're in a stucking place, you can't do nothing 'til you get unstuck."

"We ought to print that on T-shirts and sell them," murmured Coco with a grin.

Back in Unizilla, Coco returned the muddy car to her father while I drove Wonder home in my truck. She refused to get out at Susan's front door. "I need to go back to help."

"Mr. Jones is ill," I reminded her. "When he gets better, I'll take you to see him."

"Promise?"

"Cross my heart and hope to die."

"Don't you die before you keep dat promise."

I stopped by my house to change into jeans. Mimi required both staff and volunteers to dress professionally—either in scrubs or in slacks and a smock top—but I couldn't carry firewood and feed livestock in those clothes.

I found the marble house full of people examining my family's possessions with avid eyes but pursed lips, as if to say, "Is this really worth the asking price?" After I had strolled through the downstairs and read sticker prices, though, I hurried upstairs to call Gage. "The people running the estate sale are pricing things at half what our appraisers said they are worth."

"Dealers have to make a living," he informed me. "They will sell things at the appraised value if they can get that, but they seldom pay more than half the selling price."

"So the true value of any item is approximately half of what the appraisal says it is—unless you are a dealer or a buyer?"

"You got it. Maybe that's why the Bible says 'Do not lay up treasures for yourselves on earth.' Treasures aren't as valuable as people think."

I locked myself in my bathroom to change, then took time to check to be sure nothing had been disturbed in my sitting room. A dealer about to enter King's room saw me at the sitting room door and warned, "We aren't to go in there."

"It's okay," I told him. "I live here. This is my room." I took one of Teddy's Navajo throw pillows as I left. I also grabbed a jacket I used for yard work. Heaven only knew how many trips I'd have to make to the woodpile and out to the barn.

On my way downstairs, I discovered that furniture none of us wanted had more value to me than I had realized. As I watched dealers laughing and joking as they carried away great chunks of my childhood, I wanted to run after them crying, "Not that lamp! My mother used to read under it at night! Watch that table! King put his drink on it while he watched television!"

I managed to stay pleasant until the man I had seen earlier going into King's room came down behind me carrying Mother's sewing table. Mother had never sewed, but King had bought that table in an antiques shop on one of his trips to Savannah. When he lifted it from the car, her face had lit with the smile she reserved for him. She set it by their bedroom window next to a small rocker, and on the table she placed her Bible, her devotional book, and a small lamp painted with pansies. Every morning until she could no longer leave her bed, she sat in that chair for half an hour for what she called "my time of peace."

That was not simply a small table the dealer was carrying down. It had my mother's spirit embedded in its grain. To me, it was a shrine.

I stopped him at the bottom of the stairs. "How much do you plan to sell that sewing table for?"

He considered, "Fifty dollars, maybe?"

"Can I buy it from you before you leave? It was my mother's."

"Lady, if you want to sell a table and buy it back at twice the price, I'll sell you everything I've got on my truck." Then he gave me a second look. "Take it for nothing," he said gruffly. "I've got enough already." He even carried it up to my sitting room, and rested one hand on my shoulder briefly before he hurried back downstairs.

At the clinic, Mimi eyed my jeans with one raised eyebrow. "Casual Friday? I didn't get the memo."

"If you could have seen me after I'd pushed a car out of the mud and carried in firewood, you'd know why I changed. Mr. Jones lives three miles up a switchback road full of ruts, mud holes, and errant wildlife. He is very sick and he does live alone. I'm heading back out there this afternoon and before I leave I will have hauled in firewood for the night and fed a donkey, a turkey, a hen, and a dog, so don't raise your eyebrows at my clothes. This is Jones Farm chic."

She picked up a pink message slip on her desk. "The patient has asked us to drop the case. He called after you left and said he doesn't need our help, he can take care of himself."

"He most certainly cannot. The man is so dehydrated that I came by to ask if I can take an IV drip out for today and tomorrow. He is so weak he can't hold a fork and he heats with a stove that gobbles firewood. He also has livestock that have to be fed twice a day."

"Carrying firewood and feeding animals are not your job."

"No, that's payment for a debt. He did us a favor once. Did he say why he wants us to drop his case?"

Mimi clicked her pencil against the desk, a sure sign she was embarrassed. "No insurance. He paid cash for his office visit and tests, and he said that's all he can afford right now." She slammed the pencil down on her desk. "I wish people who voted 'no' on universal health care had to raise the funds to treat those who can't afford insurance. That's the only part of this job I hate."

I chewed on my lower lip while I considered my options. "How much will you charge him for this morning's visit? Since I'm working for free in the afternoons, you won't have to charge for this afternoon, will you? I'll pay for the IV."

"That must be some debt you owe him."

"It is. Wonder fell in the river one day and he happened to be nearby and pulled her out. The next week, Albert canceled his contract to sell produce to the college. I'm embarrassed to look him in the eye, the way my family has treated him. Feeding his donkey is the least I can do."

"You aren't responsible to pay Susan's family debts. Speaking of family, though, ask if he has family who can come help out until he is better."

"Good idea. May I take him an IV this afternoon if I pay for it?"

She stood. "You most certainly will not pay for it. What else do you need?"

I stopped by the grocery store for soft drinks, clear juices, and simple-to-fix items that I hoped would tempt him to eat when I was not there. With them stowed in my truck, I started up the mountain.

When I passed the place where we had gotten stuck—what had Wonder called it? The stucking place?—I wondered if I had been in a "stucking place" for years. I had thought of myself as being in a holding pattern, but if King had left me his house and as much money as I had expected, wouldn't I have stayed where I was for the rest of my life? That was a good definition of stuck. I would have nursed new patients and had different personalities to contend with, but what I had done for Teddy, Mother, and King, I would have continued doing for other people until I needed somebody to care for me. Was God going to use King's betrayal to get me unstuck?

Did getting unstuck have to be so painful?

As I rounded the last bend, I envisioned my life broadening in the same way the road opened into the cove. Coco was wise. Maybe she was right. Maybe I had a better future ahead than I expected.

I found my patient dozing on the couch. "Mr. Jones?" I shook him gently. "It's Teensie MacAllester. I've come back. How's our fire going? The room feels warm enough."

He opened jaundiced eyes. I thought he was glad to see me until he turned his face away and growled, "*My* fire is going fine, so go home. I told the doctor you weren't to come."

"Doctors don't take orders too well. She did say to tell you there's no charge for this afternoon. It's the other half of my morning visit. Would you like some juice? I've brought you a few groceries."

"I don't need groceries." He burrowed into his covers.

"Rest while I fetch a few things from my truck, and then I'll get you that juice. See you in a minute." As I left, I took the precaution of pocketing keys that hung near the door. I didn't want him locking me out.

When I returned, I found him leaning against the island

with a quilt wrapped around his waist. "What are you doing up?" I went to offer support to get him back to the couch.

He moved away from my hand. "I told you, I can take care of myself. I don't need help."

"You most certainly do, and I'm glad to have a chance to help. Consider it a small repayment for saving Wonder's life. I'm her aunt."

He glowered. "I know who you are, one of the MacAllesters." His tone made it clear that *that* was no compliment. "I know how your family shows gratitude, too. Your brother-in-law canceled my contract."

He looked ready to fall any second. I switched into Nurse-as-Dragon mode. "Look, I am grateful you saved Wonder and I'm sorry Albert canceled your contract, but at the moment I am mostly a nurse. I want you to get yourself back onto that couch by the time I count to five. One, two—"

He stood his ground. "You are one bossy lady."

"Don't you ever forget it. Three, four . . ." I had no idea what I'd do when I reached five, but I matched him glare for glare. With an exasperated huff, he hobbled back toward the couch. I felt like sending up a cheer.

I took Teddy's pillow from the things I'd brought in. "Let me swap your pillow for this one. The cover is washable, and under it is a plastic liner."

He touched the bright red, yellow, and blue cover. "Pretty. Where did you get it?"

"My aunt lived in Navajo country and brought this when she came back east."

I was surprised how thick his hair was as I lifted his head to exchange the pillows. I had never liked long hair on men, but it suited his strong brown face. Without thinking, I smoothed it over his quilt like I would have a woman patient's.

He swatted my hand away.

Embarrassment made me brusque. "Give me your arm. I'm going to start an IV drip on you. Once you get rehydrated, you will feel stronger."

He closed his eyes. "I don't need all this. I've got things to do." Even as he protested he was holding out an arm.

"You aren't going to be doing anything for a while. Is there anybody you could call to come take care of what needs to be done around here? A family member, or a friend?"

"My nephew, maybe. He lives over near Chatsworth."

"Good. You don't need any treatment, just rest and lots of fluids. The liver heals itself."

"How long?"

"A couple of months, maybe."

His eyes flew open. "*Months?* I can't be in bed that long."

"You don't have any choice. You'll gradually get stronger, but you'll be weak for a while. The more you stay in bed, the faster you'll heal. The more you get up and try to work, the longer you'll be sick. You might as well rest and enjoy it."

"Enjoy it?" The words ripped me with scorn.

"When my aunt used to get laid up with something, she'd say, 'I guess God is making me lie down in a green pasture. Might as well enjoy it.' That's from a Psalm in the Bible," I added.

"I know."

"I wasn't sure, you being Cherokee and all."

"This Cherokee is a Methodist." He frowned. "I don't like being waited on."

"Then these next few weeks will be good for your soul."

I brought in enough firewood to get him through the night. I made him a fruit cup and a slice of whole-grain bread lathered with honey for a midafternoon snack. I dried the clothes I had washed that morning and washed all the linens from his bed. I made a pot of homemade chicken noodle soup and a salad for his supper. I remade his bed upstairs.

At dusk, the donkey began to bray. My patient shoved back his covers. "I have to feed the animals."

"Stop! You are hooked up to a bag. Besides, you don't have strength to go out."

"I've done it until now. Has to be done."

I looked at him with astonishment. Where had he found the energy to walk to the barn all those days?

"Stay where you are. I'll do it if you tell me how. Donkey feeding was a class I skipped in nursing school."

Rain was falling as I headed to the barn, more mist than drops. A halogen security light had come on in the gloom. It lit hundreds of water diamonds on my jacket. I probably wore a diamond tiara. As soon as I opened the gate, the hen and turkey came waddling toward me, clucking and gobbling. The donkey trotted from the far fence and started nuzzling my front like an adolescent in the back seats of a movie theater.

"Stop that!" I slapped his muzzle.

He nuzzled some more.

"Stop it!" I backed away from him, tripped over a bucket, and fell flat on my fanny in something that felt suspiciously like damp donkey dung.

The donkey lowered his head and continued his exploration of my breasts.

"Stop that!" I smacked him so hard he galloped toward the fence in fright. I climbed to my feet and checked my backside. Yep. Donkey dung. I grabbed up some wisps of straw to wipe it off and only succeeded in smearing it.

Disgusted with myself and the donkey, I found food for the animals, gave them fresh water, and fended off the dog, who was now interested in my backside. The donkey, thank goodness, stayed by the fence until I left.

I stopped by my truck for rags and tried again, unsuccessfully, to wipe dung from my rear. I was no more successful in getting mud and straw off my once-white sneakers. Disgruntled, I went inside on sock feet to report, "Your donkey is a groper."

"Forgot to tell you," he said without opening his eyes. "Take a carrot in your shirt pocket."

"I'll bet you forgot on purpose."

He didn't deny it. Instead he sniffed. "You stink worse than I do."

"I sat in a donkey pat."

That earned a snort that I suspected was laughter.

Bone-tired and smelly, I was in no mood to be laughed at. "I'm going to borrow some newspapers to sit on going home, and you'd better hope I don't get dung all over my seat covers."

"You finally leaving?"

I began to disconnect his tubing. "Yep, I'm finally leaving. I don't relish driving that road of yours in the dark. You can send up fireworks when I'm gone, but expect me back tomorrow to give you one more bag of fluids."

"Don't bother."

"I don't want you dying after all the effort I've put in today. You have clean sheets on your bed, but I suggest you sleep down here to keep the fire stoked."

"Yes, ma'am." He closed his eyes.


I woke Saturday to a cold gray drizzle. Normally on a Saturday like that I made tea and toast and took them back to bed with a good book. King never minded, so long as I set out his cereal, juice, and coffee. That morning, as I pulled on warm corduroy pants, heavy socks, and a thick sweater, I wondered what made me want to splash up the muddy road to Jones Farm in that weather. Mimi had another nurse on call to make necessary home visits on weekends and Mr. Jones had made it clear he wasn't grateful for my help. So why was I going?

Because I was glad to thank him for saving Wonder.

But as I eased my truck up the switchbacks, I realized I was also looking forward to crossing swords with him again. After years of bland conversations with Phil, I found Mr. Jones stimulating. He was also a refreshing change from gushing new mothers and lonely people who clutched my hand to keep me from leaving.

Besides, I wanted to show him that some MacAllesters were nicer than Albert—who was, after all, a MacAllester only by marriage.

I had wondered whether he'd lock his door against my visit, even though he apparently was in the habit of leaving it unlocked. I was glad to feel the back doorknob turn in my hand. The house was cold again, but I found my patient asleep upstairs under the pink floral comforter. He looked cozy enough. I tiptoed back downstairs, relit the stove, carried in more firewood, and went out to feed the animals—remembering to take a carrot for the donkey. He eyed me warily but accepted the carrot as a peace offering.

As I trudged back through the gloomy drizzle, I thought of pioneer women for whom this had been a way of life. I thanked God that I could go home to central heating—and that Mr. Jones had indoor toilets.

I mopped the kitchen and cleaned the downstairs bathroom, then went out for more firewood. When I came into the house with my third load, I heard a weak call. "Who's there?"

"Just me," I called up the stairs. "I'll bring your breakfast in a few minutes."

He growled like a bear when I carried in a basin, a glass of water, and his toothbrush, and he insisted on washing his own face and brushing his teeth, but after that much exertion, he consented to let me feed him oatmeal. When he had finished, I asked, "Do you want me to give you a sponge bath?"

He recoiled. "I can take my own bath in the tub."

"Go on, then, while I change your sheets again."

Half an hour later he called, "I forgot to bring clothes." He barely cracked the door wide enough to let me pass them in. When he finally appeared, he was not only clean but had washed his hair. "I forgot to take my hair dryer to the bathroom," he muttered, heading to the chest and pulling a dryer from the top drawer.

I eyed the thick wet strands lying on his shoulders. "You don't have enough energy to dry all that."

"I'll go down by the stove, then, and let it dry."

"Don't be silly. You'll catch your death of cold." I moved a pile of folded clothes from the straight chair to the newly made bed. "Sit here. I'll dry it."

As it dried, his hair rippled coarse and strong beneath the brush. When a strand of it brushed across my hand, the feeling was so sensuous that I shivered.

Looking up from my work, I met his gaze in a mirror. Flushing with embarrassment, I circled him so my back was to the mirror. When I sneaked a peek down at his face, his eyes were closed.

When I was done, I asked, "Would you like to go downstairs?"

"Later. I'm limp as a cooked noodle." It was the first time he had admitted weakness.

"Rest, then. I'll hook you up to the IV and go downstairs to read. Looks like you've got plenty of books to choose from."

He waved me away. "Go home. I can do what needs doing."

"I want you to have one more day on the drip. I'll fetch it."

By the time I had connected him up, he was fast asleep.

I finished cleaning the downstairs, then browsed his shelves. Mr. Jones was an enigma: a farmer who read mysteries, biographies, histories, and theology. One whole shelf was devoted to Cherokee history and folklore. I pulled down *Trail of Tears: The Rise and Fall of the Cherokee Nation*, by John Ehle. Although I had grown up surrounded by Cherokee historical sites and, apparently, some Cherokee people, all I knew about their tribe I had learned from scant mentions in high school textbooks and one trip with Coco and Teddy to Cherokee, North Carolina, for the outdoor play *Unto These Hills*. I couldn't remember a thing about the play except Teddy muttering halfway through, "I don't think there's a Cherokee in the cast or the audience."

For the next hour, I read how the Cherokee and early whites in my mountains had both fought and adapted to one another. I had reached the place where Moravian missionaries were asking the Cherokee for land to begin a mission school when I heard my patient stirring. I marked my place and decided to ask if I could borrow the book.

While I was reading the rain had stopped. Rays of sunlight slanted across the living room floor as Mr. Jones made his laborious progress downstairs. I followed, carrying the drip pole. He sank onto the couch with a grateful grunt. Then his eyes scanned the room. "Looks like the Nunnehi—the Little People of the Cherokee—have been in to clean."

I waited for his thanks. Instead, he frowned. "What happened to my newspapers?"

"I carried them out to my truck. You were going to recycle them, right?"

"No, I am going to compost them. You can carry them back in. But first"—he glanced out the window—"I see the sun is finally out. How cold is it?"

"Nippy. Not too cold."

"I want to go out on the porch. Isn't sunlight good for jaundice?"

"It is. How did you know?"

"I looked up hepatitis on the Internet after you left. I must have gotten sick from some raw oysters I ate down near the Gulf."

"Could be. You can sit on the porch after lunch. Did you call your nephew?"

"Yeah. He'll be over later this afternoon. You can go now."

His easy dismissal got my back up. The man treated me as cavalierly as King used to! I took a deep breath to keep from snapping at him. "I have to wait until this drip is done, and I'd like to give your nephew some instructions."

"Suit yourself." He didn't speak again while I fixed lunch.

When we had eaten, he let me help him into a heavy jacket and support him and his pole while he walked onto the porch. When he was settled in a rocker in the sunshine with, in spite of his protests, a blanket around his legs, I asked, "Would you rather read or doze?"

"Doze. Can't hold a book." He laid his head back and closed his eyes.

While he rested, I went back upstairs and finished cleaning his bedroom, which included folding clothes I presumed were clean and putting ones I presumed were dirty in the washer. While the laundry chugged along, I dusted and swept the other bedrooms. By the time the wash was in the dryer, I felt as exhausted as my patient looked. I carried my book outside and collapsed into a rocker near his.

He made a touching picture dozing in the sun. One hand lay lightly on the back of the hen, which snuggled in his lap. The old dog lay at his feet, nose on his master's toe. The turkey squatted beside the rocker. The donkey stood at the fence with his chin hanging over, watching.

Too worn-out to read, I refreshed my spirit by admiring his view. The porch was warm, sheltered by the cedar from the wind. Mr. Jones's ring of mountains around the cove was as lovely as those I could see from my own porch, the pines a deep green against the silver-gray bark of deciduous trees. Most fields lay fallow awaiting spring planting, but I could picture them ripe with summer harvest. If somebody cleared away all those rusted machinery parts and took a little care of the front lawn and bushes, the cove could be beautiful.

*Not having a place of your own is no excuse to redecorate somebody else's yard*, I reminded myself. I picked up the book. Before I opened it I was startled to hear him ask, "What are you reading?" I hadn't known he was awake. His hand idly stroked the hen's feathers.

I held it up so he could read the title. "Could I borrow it and bring it back another day?"

"Why do you want to read it?"

"To further my education. I am woefully ignorant about Cherokee history."

He shrugged. "Suit yourself. You won't find it flattering."

"I still want to read it."

"Read it and weep." He settled back into his chair and closed his eyes.

Since he was still stroking the hen, I could tell he wasn't sleeping. "When did your family come back to Georgia?" I asked.

He spoke slowly without opening his eyes. "Never left. They hid in the hills. A number of Cherokee did, creeping out later to work for whites."

"Did this cove always belong to your people?"

"Cherokee didn't own land, we were stewards of it. Only white men insisted on owning land. My great-great-grandfather, who was a logger, bought the cove in 1910 from a white man. Our family has farmed it for four generations." He sounded tired.

"Rest," I said. "Let me read."

Half an hour later he was awake again, looking out over the barn. "The old house was there." He gestured toward the chimney. "Got struck by lightning when I was ten, and burned. Dad and I built this one."

I wondered where he had been when his house caught fire, what precious things his family had lost, where they lived while they rebuilt, but I had already asked too many personal questions. "You built a wonderful house, and it's beautiful up here, Mr. Jones."

"Tobias. You can't call somebody you have washed and fed 'Mr. Jones.'"

"Tobias, then." I felt as if he had given me a gift. I gave him one in return. "My name is Teensie."

"I know."

"Oh, yeah. Wonder called me Aunt Teensie."

He shrugged. "Everybody knows the MacAllesters." Again, he did not make it sound like a compliment. Still, I was embarrassed that he had known me when I had not known him. Had I passed him on the street a hundred times with a polite "hello" and never really looked at him?

I was trying to think of something to say to cover my mortification when he asked, "Why did your mother name you Teensie?"

"She didn't. My sister Regan did. Everybody in my family was tall, except me—"

"I know."

He seemed to know a lot more about me than I knew about him. "Well, Regan was six when I was born, and when she saw me for the first time, she exclaimed, 'She's mighty teensie, isn't she?' Apparently my folks thought that was cute, so the name stuck. I doubt if anybody in Unizilla except my sisters remembers that I was christened Deborah Ingram MacAllester."

"Deborah *Ingram* MacAllester?"

"Yes. It was my mother's maiden name."

I got a grunt that was distinctly uncomplimentary before he closed his eyes again.

I returned to my book.

"Deborah." He rolled the name on his tongue a minute later, as if tasting it. "That suits you. The first Deborah was a nurse."

"No, she was a judge of Israel."

Why had I said that? I was a pretty good Bible scholar, but I wasn't at his place to teach a Bible class.

"That was the second Deborah," he said. "The first Deborah was Rebekah's nurse, who went with her when she traveled to Canaan to marry Isaac."

I had never heard that. I suspected he was pulling my leg, and was irritated like I had been when I discovered he had "forgotten" to tell me to take a carrot to the donkey. "You made that up. The Bible doesn't give that nurse's name."

"Yes, it does. Genesis 35:8. Deborah, Rebekah's nurse, died and they buried her beneath a tree they named the Oak of Weeping."

"How could you possibly know that?"

"Sunday school Bible drills. I've got a whole box of ribbons around here somewhere."

The donkey brayed by the fence.

"Hush!" my companion called. "She doesn't need to know my sister won most of the ribbons."

The donkey brayed again. I laughed. I hadn't expected to spend my Saturday afternoon sitting on a sun-kissed porch discussing Cherokee history and the Bible with a sick man and a donkey. "Why do you keep him?" I asked. "You don't work him, do you? I saw your tractor."

He stroked his hen. "He's a friend. So is Tom"—his hand caressed the ugly head of the turkey—"and Homer"—the dog lifted its head and yawned—"and Lucky, here. Every man needs a few good friends."

"Lucky? You call a one-winged chicken 'Lucky'?"

"She's lucky to be alive, isn't she? If she'd hatched anywhere else, she could have been destroyed. I ate all the rest of Mama's chickens—got tired of fooling with them. Lucky has lived a long, happy life. She lays an occasional egg where I can find it, to show her gratitude."

I looked at him doubtfully. How could a man so rude have a whimsical menagerie? Especially a menagerie that couldn't seem to get close enough to him? Mr. Jones—Tobias—was something of an enigma. He must be one of those recluses who preferred the company of animals.

But how, then, to explain the fact that Wonder adored him?

The donkey brayed again. I sighed. "I must not have given him enough breakfast."

"Don't let him con you. If you weren't here, he'd come up on the porch and join the party."

I had no idea if he was serious, but I laughed again. The man might be exasperating, but he was not dull.

With a toot, a truck appeared across the cove. It was blinding blue with neon green lightning bolts along its sides. Homer loped off the porch, barking with delight.

"Damien," said Tobias unnecessarily. He added in disgust, "My sitter."

The young man who climbed down was tall and thin, not yet filled out to adulthood, and startlingly handsome. His hair, longer than his uncle's, was pulled back at his neck and tied with a cord. Two silver studs in one ear glinted in the sunlight. As he moved lithely toward us in jeans and an all-weather jacket, I searched his features for the square-faced boy of the pictures. I didn't find a match. "Hey, Tobe. Who's your lady friend?"

He stood at the bottom step, grinning from Tobias to me. I was tempted to tell him if I ever did contemplate the kind of weekend he was fantasizing, it would not be with a granite-faced curmudgeon who kept telling me to go home.

"She's no friend," his uncle told him. "She's a nurse. She's going to explain why you're here, then she's going back down the hill and leave me to your tender mercies." His expression was sour. I thought I knew why. No man likes to sit weak as a kitten in front of such a vibrant example of health.

I took Damien inside to show him the food and explain Tobias's disease. "You must not let him do a thing," I stressed. "He needs complete bed rest."

Damien turned dark red. "Can he . . . uh . . . can he get up to . . . uh . . ." He threw a pleading look at Tobias, who was making his tedious way indoors.

"I can go to the toilet," Tobias snapped. "I can also bathe myself."

"He's not to be feeding animals," I warned, "or carrying firewood or working in the fields. He is very sick. I will come back tomorrow with some serum to keep you safe."

Damien moved his feet uneasily. "Serum?"

"A hepatitis shot. You'll need two more later, and then you'll be protected for life. You don't want to catch what he's got, do you?"

"Uh, no, ma'am, I guess not, but I don't much like—"

A couple of Cherokee words from Tobias silenced him. Damien lowered his gaze, embarrassed. I wondered what Tobias had said. Probably something about warriors and bravery.

I fetched my purse and jacket. "I'll be off, then."

"Thank God for small favors," muttered Tobias.

I went home that night and drew a grizzly in a feathered headdress sitting on the porch of a cabin, a shotgun across his knees. But I smiled as I drew.


I went to Jones Farm early Sunday morning to give Damien his shot. I found him eating an enormous breakfast. "Our patient is still asleep."

"Good. Did he give you any trouble?"

"Oh, no." He sounded surprised.

"I'm glad. He can be difficult, I've found."

"Don't mind Uncle Tobe. He's a great guy, really. He just doesn't like women much since his wife took off."

"Where did she go?" I didn't mean to ask, but as Wonder would say, the words just popped out. "Not that it's any of my business."

He shrugged off my embarrassment. "She went off with a trucker eight years ago. She and my grandmother didn't get along, and Uncle Tobe said she found the mountains lonely. Since Grandma died, Uncle Tobe's pretty much kept to himself. He doesn't let on to people, but I guess Melinda's leaving hurt him real bad. Mama says he hasn't let anybody get close to him since. He used to be a lot of fun—laughing and playing with us kids—but since Melinda took off, he's become a regular old grizzly at times."

I nearly told Damien I'd drawn his uncle as a grizzly, but didn't.

I played a hunch. "Did he and his wife have children?"

"Brandon, three years younger than me. That's him on the mantel over there." He pointed to the boy in the oak frame. "He was seven when they left. I haven't seen him since." In his voice I heard regret for a lost cousin.

"Does Tobias see him?" The name felt unfamiliar on my lips.

"Not that I know of. It's a shame, really. He loved that kid. Now Brandon and Melinda travel with the trucker and she homeschools—or truckschools, I guess it would be called. I don't think they've gotten back up this way since they left."

I didn't pry any further. Tobias Jones's grief was his own.

After church on Sunday, I read Tobias's book. I was appalled to learn how the U.S. government had played a double game with the Cherokee. On the one hand, government agents persuaded the tribe to adopt European ways: live in houses, farm instead of hunt, send their children to school, and change their religion in order to get along with white settlers. However, once the Cherokee had built homes, educated their children, gotten baptized, developed a written language, codified their laws, and begun to publish a newspaper, the U.S. government broke all its treaties and forced them to relocate to a promised land in Oklahoma—failing to mention that the promised land was already inhabited by another tribe. Worse, nearly ten years before their removal, the state of Georgia started holding land lotteries to give away Cherokee land and threatened to secede from the Union if the government didn't "keep their promise" to relocate all the Cherokee—although that meant the federal government had to break a number of promises to the Cherokee.

No wonder Tobias had grunted in disgust when he heard my full name. All of Unizilla knew that my mother's family, the Ingrams, were the first white settlers in our area to benefit from the land lottery. They had a historical marker, as if injustice were a thing to be proud of.

I was glad when Wonder came after her nap to visit me. She distracted me from gloomy thoughts about my ancestors.

When we took a truckload of clothes and books over to Darla's, I was touched to find that in spite of her arthritis, Darla had made her way upstairs before she left for Nashville to carry the curtains, blankets, and quilted bedspread from my room downstairs to wash. She had also dusted, but left a note to apologize: *Sorry, but I could not carry the clean linens or the vacuum cleaner upstairs. See you Monday.*

While I vacuumed, Wonder arranged my dresser top and a bookshelf under my window. When she saw tree branches almost touching the window, she got excited. "De pwince can climb dat tree when he comes to find you."

"He'd better be a giant prince, then, or very athletic. The bottom branches are fifteen feet off the ground."

Soon after we got back to the marble house, Gage showed up and we played Junior Monopoly. Gage was good at that, too. Wonder won.

Monique showed up around five thirty, her hair teased into a wild black cloud. In a black cardigan, long black skirt, and chunky black boots, she looked to me like an impoverished immigrant arriving from Europe after weeks at sea without a comb. I didn't say so, of course, but while Wonder ran up to get some pictures she had drawn, Gage said, "Did the thrift store have a sale this week? I see you picked up a few things."

Monique's chin went into the air. "I will thank you not to criticize my clothes. What do you know about women's fashion?"

"Enough to know that isn't one of the more attractive ones."

She went to the door and yelled, "Wonder? Stop dawdling and get yourself down here. We need to go home."

After they'd gone, I asked Gage, "Why do you keep needling her? You bring out the worst in her."

"She brings out the worst in me, too." He busied himself putting away the game. I wondered if that was to keep from looking at me. He heaved a sigh that Wonder would have admired. "I guess it's that I keep remembering how cute she was at Wonder's age, deviling me to give her rides on the handlebars of my bike. Prettiest little girl I ever saw. It makes me crazy to see her messing herself up like that."

"Let up a little. She's not a child anymore."

He hauled himself to his feet. "You can say that again."

Regan and Holcomb arrived that evening wearing matching red sweaters and black pants. "We were having our Christmas picture taken," she explained.

He roamed the decimated downstairs rooms while I took Regan upstairs to look at the best Christmas ornaments, which I had saved in case she wanted any of them. She let her hand linger on the marble staircase. "Did Albert tell you he's going to call this the 'Harris MacAllester Center'?"

So much for the anonymous donor.

I wondered if Holcomb was compensating Regan and Susan for their shares of the house or whether both had been pressured to make tax-deductible donations. I didn't care, so long as I got my share.

I gestured to the ornaments and shoeboxes of pictures. "See if there's anything you want."

Regan gave the photos only a cursory look but examined the decorations with a scavenger's eye. "I want Mother's Lenox Nativity and— where are the Fräbel snowflakes?"

I was tempted to lie, but lies are boomerangs; they come back to hit you. "I gave them to Monique. She hadn't gotten anything else from the house."

Regan went from sunny to stormy in half a second. "She'll eventually get everything Susan took, and those snowflakes are family heirlooms. They ought to be handed down to future generations."

"Monique and Wonder *are* our future generation."

"But if I get pregnant—"

"—Monique will still be the oldest grandchild. You can leave all the things you took to your child." Resentment made me dance close to danger. "Besides, you left the snowflakes, along with a houseful of closets to be cleaned out. Any day this past month you could have been over here going through stuff and finding things you wanted."

Regan's eyes narrowed, a familiar sign that she'd be raging at me in a minute. "You had no right to give those things away without consulting Susan and me."

"Susan would have agreed to give them to Monique."

Regan's lips tightened at the truth of that. She snatched up the box holding Mother's Lenox Nativity. "Very well, then; I'll take this. You can throw out the rest, for all I care." She stomped toward the door.

"What would Jesus do?" I taunted.

She whirled. "What did you say?"

"You heard me."

Her eyes flickered with uncertainty. Regan and all her friends from her new church wore gold-and-silver bracelets with WWJD? engraved on them. I considered it risky to speculate what such an unpredictable man might do in any given situation, but Regan and I both knew the carpenter from Galilee would not have grabbed figures of his parents and himself because they were made of costly porcelain.

She thrust the box at me as if it had grown radioactive. "Did you want this?"

I was tempted to accept. Giving it away would probably be good for her soul. However, Mother had collected Nativities from all over the world and I'd already chosen a pottery one she had bought in Peru. "You take it. It will look better in your house."

"If you are sure . . ." She hovered in the door, looking down at the box.

"Take it. Mother would have liked for you to have it."

She gave me a rueful smile. "I'm glad you gave Monique the snowflakes."

Holcomb was prowling around downstairs. "When are you leaving the house?" he asked when I joined him.

"I start moving my furniture out tomorrow. Gage wants possession by Tuesday."

When he gave me a thoughtful glance, I braced myself for another plea to move in with Ginny Linn. He surprised me. "Do you want a crew over tomorrow morning to move you? And do you need a place to store some stuff? I've got space in one of my warehouses." He must have read my thoughts, because he added, "It's in the building where I store egg boxes. It doesn't smell of chickens. I promise."

"That would be great."

One objection occurred to me. "This isn't a sneaky way of getting great-grandmother's bedroom set, is it?" I asked Regan.

"No, it's all Holcomb's idea. He is a very nice man."

He was a very nice man. I accepted gratefully.


Monday morning was frigid. Holcomb's crew showed up at eight breathing dragon's breath. In addition to the truck and boxes they brought dollies. And Holcomb.

I was astonished that the head of a company would take time out to help his sister-in-law move, and I told him so. He shrugged it off. "You haven't had it easy lately. I thought I'd give you a hand. Now show the men what to take and let them do it. They're used to handling eggs. They know how to be gentle. All you have to do is make sure we're getting everything and aren't taking something that ought to be left."

I recognized two of the crew as the men who had come with Regan to steal my bedroom set. They looked embarrassed, but I didn't mention the incident. Neither did they until later in the day. As they staggered downstairs with my chest, I heard one mutter to the other, "We should have left it down here the first time."

Muriel watched them carry out my possessions with her vacant marble stare. "Does she go?" Holcomb asked. I saw two movers stiffen in apprehension.

I wanted to say, "Yes" to see their expressions, but they were working too hard to tease. "No, she stays. None of us wanted poor Muriel and neither did the dealers. Albert can decide whether to keep her or evict her."

Before noon the trucks were ready to leave. When I asked Holcomb how much I should pay the men, he told me not to worry about it. If he paid anyone, I never saw it, but they all left happy, so I figured he had. Before he left, I gave him a hug. "You are truly a prince among men."

As the truck pulled away, I stood in the big hall and looked at the snaggletooth rooms holding our unclaimed bits and pieces, the ones Gage would donate to some thrift shop. Jester whined at my ankles. "It's okay, boy," I lied. "We're going to be fine."

The truth was, the only home I'd ever had was an empty shell and I was a small boat adrift in an uncertain sea, without rudder or compass to set my course. I shivered as I met Muriel's blank stare. She looked as cold and naked as I felt. I gave her a pat. "Take care of the place, will you, love? I hope Albert will let you stay." My voice trembled.

I was saved from dissolving into tears by Gage pulling up to the curb. Mother had drilled into her daughters, "We do not cry in front of company."

I went out to meet him as he walked slowly up the front steps. "I came for Jester and your keys." He sounded apologetic. I appreciated that.

"Thanks. I'll retrieve Jester as soon as I can."

"He's no bother, are you, old boy? Come on. Into my truck."

Jester went so willingly that I had to swallow a lump in my throat. "I'll come get you as fast as I can get a place for us both," I promised, fondling his head before I closed the door. He licked my face.

"Would you like to lock up for the last time?" Gage asked. "Or are you going to cry? I don't do well with crying women."

"I'm not going to cry," I promised.

It was not easy, hearing the lock click for the last time, but by then I was numb.

When I climbed into Darla's low bed that night, I propped

myself on my pillows and thought what a pleasant house the bungalow was, like a dwarf cottage. If I were able to realize the cash Gage thought I could from the estate, found a modest-paying job, and lived frugally, how long could I stay with Darla? Five years? By then, would she be ready to give up her house? With my share of the marble house, could I buy the bungalow?

Who was I kidding?

As a single woman, I couldn't afford to waste years of my professional life waiting around to buy a charming little house. I needed to be storing nuts in the tree for retirement if I didn't want to wind up an old woman sleeping on a park bench with my belongings for a pillow. I couldn't count on Regan or Susan to take care of me.

I switched out the light and looked through bare branches at a pale full moon that looked like a disk of ice lit from behind. It bathed the earth in a light so white it could have been artificial and the mountains black paper cutouts against a navy paper sky. I remembered Coco saying those mountains had witnessed Cherokee women saying farewell to their native land. That hadn't meant much to me at the time.

Having read Tobias's book and been evicted from my own home, I could identify with the grief they must have felt. And since I had lost my home through the selfish cruelty of a white man who happened to be my father, I could also believe that what happened to the Cherokee was the result of selfish white settlers determined to have land and gold. I was sorry that ancestors I had been taught to revere had been among them.

# Seven

Tuesday morning at the clinic Mimi asked, "How's our hepatitis patient?"

"I haven't seen him since Sunday. His nephew is staying with him."

"Don't you have a couple of patients out that way to visit this morning? Why don't you run by and check on him?"

"Nobody runs by Jones Farm—it's a trek. I'll go up, though, if I have time."

I hoped my casual tone would camouflage the gladness I felt at having a reason to visit Tobias again. I needed to return his book, and hoped he'd be strong enough to discuss it.

Mimi had years of reading people's expressions. "You'll have time," she predicted.

I was halfway up the mountain before I realized I had forgotten to bring the book. I suspected a psychologist could make something of that, like I wanted a reason for yet another visit. However, if Damien had things under control, Tobias wouldn't need home visits anymore. I'd have to mail the book.

I was puzzled not to see Damien's truck beside the house. He must be in town buying groceries or on an errand for his uncle. I knocked at the back door and turned the knob. "Hello? It's me."

"Ah, Deborah."

Tobias was lying on the couch with the big tan dog beside him on the floor. The stove was warm, but the pile of wood beside it was low. Dishes littered the countertops again and the heavy jacket Tobias had worn Saturday lay on the floor. When I picked it up, it was chilly. "You haven't been outside, have you?" I asked.

He didn't answer.

I rounded the couch and stood over him. "Have you?"

He gave a weak shrug. "Just to feed the animals and bring in wood."

Homer woofed a greeting and his thick tail thumped the floor.

"Where's Damien?"

"He had to go back home for school."

"When did he leave?"

"Sunday night."

"*Sunday?* You've been by yourself since then?"

"He can't miss school. It's his senior year."

"It didn't occur to you to call the clinic and ask for help? Your tests came back. You definitely have hepatitis."

"I don't need help."

I gave a huff of exasperation. "What you mean is you don't think you can afford help. You can't afford *not* to have help, Tobias. This is not a light case of the flu you've got here. You need lots of rest and proper food so you can get your strength back. Have you had breakfast?"

"A little toast with coffee."

"See what I mean? You don't need caffeine. Rest while I fix you something."

With a frown for the incomprehensibility of male behavior, I set to work. I made a salad and heated a can of soup, and I made sure he ate them. I carried in firewood, vowing to keep my hiking boots in my truck for future visits. I washed all the dishes. I fed wood to the stove. I helped him upstairs to take a bath while I changed his bed, which reeked as much as he did. I settled him in the fresh bed with Homer on the floor beside him.

"I'll come back tomorrow afternoon to check on you," I promised when I was done.

"You don't need to do that."

"Somebody needs to. You simply must rest. And there is no charge for afternoon follow-up visits. Will it be all right if I bring Wonder? She ought to be safe if we all wash our hands thoroughly."

A smile flitted over his lips. "She'll have me up and about in no time."

For the next two weeks, I picked Wonder up each day after preschool, we stopped by Gage's yard to get Jester, and we all rode up to Jones Farm. After a few wary sniffs, Jester and Homer became friends.

Afraid our visits might be stopped, I warned Wonder on our way home the first afternoon, "If they ask you at home where we go, say you and I go to see my patients. If you mention the vegetable man, they might stop me bringing you." That silenced her.

I looked forward to those afternoons. Tobias was still adamant that I didn't need to be coming, but I enjoyed our verbal battles while I tried to convince him to do what he should and to let me do for him what he couldn't. I also marveled at how he and Wonder got along. He might buck my suggestions, but he meekly agreed when Wonder decided he ought to rest on the couch with his head at the far end, "so you can see me 'n' Teensie while we are working." He ate and drank anything she brought him without complaint. He let her wash his face and brush his hair. He even let her braid it into lumpy pigtails, although he gave a rueful grunt when she added red bows. After she was satisfied he was well tended each afternoon, she sat on a small stool beside the couch and he told her Cherokee stories. I listened while I tidied his house and cooked food for his dinner and lunch the next day.

One day in the supermarket Wonder saw strawberries. "Get dem for Tobias," she ordered. "Dey would be good for him."

When he saw them, his face lit in a rare smile. "My favorite fruit. Do you know where they came from?"

"A strawberry tree?" she asked while I washed them.

"No, strawberries grow on a plant with runners that trail along the ground, but the Cherokee have a story about why they were created. If you want to hear it, pull up your stool."

She dragged it near, a bowl of berries on her lap, while I washed dishes and listened, too.

"This story is about the first man and the first woman on the earth," he began.

"I already heard dat story in Sunday school. I didn't know it had strawberries in it."

"The Bible story doesn't. The Cherokee one does. One day the first man and woman had a quarrel."

"What is a craw-el? Is dat a baby?"

"No, it's a disagreement. A fuss. The woman got so mad, she decided to leave him. She walked away very fast. The man said, 'I don't need her around here,' but by nightfall he began to worry. What if something terrible had happened to her?"

"Like a bear eating her?"

"A bear eating her, or a fall off the mountain. He decided he would go tell her he was sorry and ask her to come home, for he did love her, although they quarreled."

Was he remembering his wife leaving? Did he regret not going after her? Feeling a rush of pity for him, I looked over and saw him watching me. Our eyes held for a moment. Did he know Damien had told me about his wife and son? I turned to put dishes away, sure he would resent any pity.

"Go on," Wonder commanded.

"The woman was far ahead of him, so although he walked as fast as he could, he couldn't catch her. When the sun went down and the earth grew cold, the man wanted to curl up in his blanket and sleep. Instead he walked all night long. The woman walked all night, too, so she was still far ahead. When the sun came up in the morning, it looked down and saw how far apart they were. How could the man ever catch her? The sun decided to make the woman slow down. It made huckleberries grow beside the trail, but the woman did not stop. The sun made blackberries grow beside the trail, but she still didn't stop."

" 'Cause she was still mad?"

"Yeah, she was still mad. She wasn't going to stop for huckleberries or blackberries. So the sun decided to make a field of strawberries in front of the woman. Nobody had ever seen strawberries before. The woman stepped on them and smelled something sweet. She looked down and saw beautiful red fruit at her feet. She picked one and ate it—"

"—and de debil came like a snake."

"Not in this story. When the woman tasted *this* fruit, she found it delicious. She said"—Tobias's voice became a high falsetto—" 'Oh, my husband would like some of these!' "

Wonder laughed and he laughed with her. His laugh had a rusty sound, like he didn't use it often.

"She gathered all the strawberries she could carry and she started home. She walked fast toward him and he walked fast toward her. When he saw her coming, he ran toward her and she ran toward him. She gave him the strawberries and they shared the delicious fruit, then they went home together. The Cherokee say that's why we have strawberries, and that strawberries are shaped like a heart because they brought the man and woman together. See?" He took a big one from the bowl and held it up.

"Dey do! Teensie! Come look. Dey look dist like a heart."

I joined them to examine the berry he held. "That's amazing. I've eaten strawberries all my life and never noticed they're shaped like the human heart."

"Do you want one?" Wonder asked. "Give her yours, Tobias. Den maybe you all won't fuss so much."

"We don't fuss," I protested.

"Only when Deborah is hard to get along with," Tobias said. He gave me a lazy smile as he handed me the berry.

Our hands brushed as I took it. Warmth flooded my body and I felt a redhead's flush on my cheeks. I was glad when Wonder commanded, "Wash it again before you eat it. You don't want to catch what he's got." I needed a reason to move away.

While I was washing the berry, Wonder wandered over to lean against the counter. "Tobias has a yellow box wit' strawberries painted on it," she confided.

"Have you been prying in drawers when I wasn't watching?" Still recovering from my reaction to that accidental touch, I was sharper than I intended to be.

"I wasn't prying," Wonder protested. "I was 'sploring up in de room wit' de pink curtains. Tobias doesn't care, do you, Tobias?"

"Not if you leave everything where you found it. I didn't know that box was still there. It isn't mine, it was my mother's. My father gave it to her."

"After dey had a fight?"

"Perhaps. I don't know. They did quarrel sometimes, but they always made up."

Wonder popped a strawberry into her mouth. "Dat's a good story, but de sun didn't really make strawberries. God did."

*     *     *

After that day, Tobias was still gentle and funny with Wonder but gruffer than ever with me. He ate the food I cooked and wore the clothes I washed, but he objected to what he called my "bossing" him, he frowned when he saw me carrying in firewood or going out to feed the animals, and one afternoon he snapped, "Go on home! I'm better. I don't need you coming up here every day."

I wondered if he had noticed my blush when he had given me the strawberry and feared I had designs on him.

I tried to dispel that notion by being as curt as he. "Don't worry—we'll only come for a week or so longer. By then you'll be strong enough to take care of yourself." I hoped he didn't hear regret in my voice.

That night I lay in bed trying to analyze what I felt about Tobias Jones. Why should I be so conscious of his touch or the ripple of his hair over my fingers? As a nurse, I often touched patients. I never blushed when their hands met mine. I had never blushed around Phil, either. Yet I certainly wasn't interested in Tobias as a man. He was a farmer, a Cherokee, and a patient. Any one of those would disqualify him as a candidate for romance—we had nothing in common.

He intrigued me. That was it. I was intrigued by how a man so gruff with me could be so gentle and funny with Wonder. I enjoyed his Cherokee stories. I loved watching Homer, Lucky, and Tom around him. I had come to respect his farming abilities when I'd walked with him out to his greenhouses one afternoon and heard him talk about what he would plant come spring. His nephew obviously liked and respected him. If Tobias was as pleasant to me as he was to Wonder, I might enjoy having him for a friend—a private friend, since my sisters weren't likely to invite him to dinner.

I also enjoyed the challenges of helping on the farm. My arms were growing stronger from carrying wood and buckets of mash. My knowledge of animals had increased when I had gone online and looked up treats for Bray, Lucky, and Tom. And I looked forward to leaving Unizilla each day to tackle that awful road to reach the peace of the secluded cove.

Maybe, I admitted since I was being honest with myself, my subconscious was also holding on to Tobias because as soon as he got well, I would have to begin looking for a full-time job outside of Unizilla. I didn't want him to remain sick any longer than necessary, but neither did I want to leave home.

I almost changed my mind about that the next afternoon when I came in with a load of firewood and heard Wonder telling Tobias a story for a change.

"De t'ird princess wasn't brilliant or beautiful, but she liked to help people, so she went to a big city and became a nurse."

I dropped the wood by the stove with a clatter. "Tobias doesn't want to hear that story."

"Yes, he does, Teensie. Ask him."

I frowned a query at Tobias.

"Yes, he does, Teensie," he mimicked in a mocking voice.

"It is a dull story with a disappointing ending. Wonder, get your coat on. It's time to feed the animals before we go home."

"Let her stay in this afternoon," said Tobias. "I want to hear her story."

"Heaven only knows what flourishes she will add to the plot."

I found it so humiliating to have Tobias hear the story of King's betrayal and my own rather barren life that I stomped out to the barn without remembering Bray's carrot. By the time I had convinced him that my pockets were empty, we were both out of sorts. I gave the animals food and water and hurried back to the house in time to hear Wonder concluding, ". . . moved into a room wit' a big tree, so her prince can climb up it and come in her window. Den dey will live happily ever after. De end."

"You added that ending out of your own fertile imagination," I told her angrily. Tobias would think I was a man-hungry spinster pathetically cloaking my fantasy life in fairy tales for the child.

Wonder pouted. "No, I didn't, Teensie. Dat's de real ending."

"No, it isn't. Intelligent princesses do not sit around waiting for princes to show up. They find something they enjoy doing and do it."

"Besides," said Tobias, "climbing to a princess can be dangerous. Almost impossible."

I gave him a sharp look to see if he was making fun of me. He lay on his side, scratching Homer's wide head.

I picked up Wonder's red parka. "Come on. It's time to get you home."

On our way down the road that afternoon, she said, "I made up a new story."

"I've had enough of your stories for one day, thank you very much."

"Dis is a different one. Listen! Once upon a time dere was a beautiful princess named Mama who had a little girl named Wonder. De princess met a Cherky who lived on a farm wit' a donkey, and a hen, and a turkey, and a dog, and dey fell in love and got married and lived happily ever after. Isn't dat a good story?"

"Don't tell it to your mother. We don't want people to know we go see Tobias, remember? She might tell your nana, and you couldn't go to the farm ever again. Besides, I don't think your mama would be happy on a farm miles from town."

"She might if she saw Bray and Lucky and Homer and Tom. Could we bring her to de farm? Den she and Tobias could fall in love."

I was surprised by a sudden spasm in my stomach, like a giant claw had clutched me. I took a deep breath to relax before I said, "Let's wait for Tobias to get well first, shall we?"

She heaved a huge sigh. "Okay, but on de way home, could we get more strawberries? Mama and Nana need dem real bad. Dey fuss all de time."

I went home and looked in my mirror. My own honest eyes stared back at me. "Teensie, are you falling for that man?" I demanded aloud. "If you are, get over it! He is nursing a broken heart for his first wife. Even if he weren't, you don't want to marry a farmer and live at the back of beyond. You need to get him back on his feet and hightail it to Atlanta as fast as you can."

The second Friday of December, rain stroked the world with ice-cold fingers. "Have you visited our hepatitis patient recently?" Mimi asked as I shook my umbrella in the clinic's front hall.

"Wonder and I have gone to see him some afternoons." I didn't say how often. Mimi might misinterpret my motives. Married people seem to think single ones do nothing but look for mates. "She does him a lot more good than I do. He's up and about a bit, but he still doesn't have strength to feed his animals and carry in firewood."

"And you've been doing that?" She didn't wait for me to answer. "I keep telling you that's not your job, but if you plan to go up there today, you'd better hit the road. The weatherman says the rain may turn to ice by midafternoon."

As I splashed up Jones Farm Road, icicle beards were already forming on granite outcroppings outside my window.

Only as I climbed the back steps did I realize this was the first time in two weeks I had been there without Wonder. Shyness wrapped me in a blanket of nerves. What if Tobias misinterpreted the meaning of my solo visit?

I was glad to find the house dim when I let myself in and to hear soft snores coming from upstairs. I stoked the stove and went for more firewood, which reminded me I had taken my boots out of the truck the night before to waterproof them and had forgotten to put them back in the truck. As I crossed the paddock to feed the animals, my hard-soled loafers slipped on the grass. Ice crystals stung my cheeks. Bray nuzzled me for his carrot, while Lucky and Tom lurched out of their warm nests to greet me. I gave them what they needed and hurried inside where it was warm. As I stepped inside, I welcomed the scent of burning logs.

I started a pot of potato soup and prepared a fresh bed on the couch. As I straightened up and dusted, I found myself humming. I hadn't hummed since King's death. In the den, I noticed a new game in progress on the chessboard. I studied the situation and moved the turquoise knight. One more move could put the silver king in check. As I went to the kitchen to mix up pancake batter I thought, *Log houses are pleasant. I might build a small one once I find a full-time job.*

I got so lost in a happy daydream of a little log cabin of my own nestled against a mountain, its yard bright with summer flowers, that I didn't realize Tobias was up until he called, "Why are you all here so early?" He walked heavily down the stairs, rumpled and yawning in a white T-shirt and jeans. Oh, he looked good!

"It's not that early. You're a sleepyhead," I informed him. "My watch says it's past ten."

I poured three pancakes on the griddle and hoped I sounded casual. "I came alone today. We may get an ice storm, so I thought I'd better do what needs doing here while I can still get down your road."

"I'll be fine. Go on home."

"Watch your manners, mister." I dropped blueberries onto the pancakes. "You're nicer when Wonder's around."

He sat down heavily on the couch. "Wonder doesn't come to do me favors."

I was puzzled. "You think I come to do you favors?"

"That's what you said the first day: you want to repay me for pulling Wonder from the river. Consider the debt more than paid. You can't possibly compensate me for losing the college contract or your family's taking my family's land, so go home. You don't have to keep coming."

I was so relieved that he hadn't thought I came for romantic reasons, I said flippantly, "Remember that dumb story? I'm the princess who likes to help people."

"I found that interesting. What do you get out of it?" He leaned back on the couch and spread both arms along the top. Damn, he could look sexy at times.

I busied myself finding syrup in his cabinet. "I don't do it to get something out of it. I like helping people."

"Nonsense. Nobody does something without a motive."

"Personal satisfaction, then. Come on to the table. Your breakfast is ready."

He slid into his chair. "So you like getting credit for being a helpful little elf?"

I managed not to slam his plate down in front of him, but my voice was sharp when I said, "This house was pleasant before you got up. Eat your breakfast and stop being rude."

He rested both elbows on the table and frowned at me. "Since Wonder's not here, I can speak frankly. I don't like being an object of charity, especially from somebody who stole my land. Do you think I don't know you've been sneaking food up here? Lucky hasn't laid an egg in ages, but I always have some— and salad makings, and bread, butter, and fruit. You've probably bought food for Homer, too. I was nearly out two weeks ago, and he's still eating."

"A little," I acknowledged. "If you like, I'll keep a running tab. You can pay me back when you get better. But you've said twice that I stole your land. For your information, sir, I don't own any land—unless you count one-third of my father's house, and since it sits on the campus, I technically don't own any *land* at all."

"Where did your dad get the money to buy that house?"

"Not that it's any of your business, but I think he and Mother sold some stocks she'd inherited from her father."

"Which he had inherited from his father, which he had inherited from his father. If you go back far enough, you'll discover one of those Ingrams got his money from gold he found on land that once belonged to the Cherokee."

I gaped. "You are holding a grudge against me for something that happened two hundred years ago?"

He shrugged. "We believe land is sacred. Your people saw it only as property."

"But you own land. You have a whole cove. And if you want to repay me for a few piddly groceries, you just do that. Or count them a partial repayment for your tribal lands. Meanwhile, eat your breakfast. I'm going up to change your bed."

"You don't have to do that. Go home. I don't need you here."

I slammed my palm down on the table. "Fine, Mr. Congeniality, I'll go! Call the clinic if you decide you aren't utterly self-sufficient and need a little help. They can send up another nurse." I grabbed my coat and left.

If I hadn't been in such a hurry, I might have noticed that a thin film of ice had formed on the steps since I went inside. Instead, *whoosh!* On the first step, my feet slid out from under me. *Bump, bump, bump!* My tailbone hit all three. Disgusted with myself, I checked for broken bones. Finding none, I climbed with difficulty to my feet. The world was still gloomy, but in the two hours I'd been inside, every twig and leaf had been encased in ice that reflected what little light escaped the clouds.

As angry as I was at him, Tobias still shouldn't be going up and down icy steps in his weakened condition. I couldn't leave without carrying in enough wood for a couple of days, and I'd better make sure the animals had enough food for twenty-four hours.

Maneuvering the slick walk in hard soles took care, and my tailbone throbbed as I limped like an old woman toward the barn. The donkey, hen, and turkey huddled together in the straw of the donkey's stall, warm but nervous. When Bray nuzzled me for another carrot, I pushed his head away. "Not now, fellow. I need to give you extra food and get down the hill."

Lucky waddled over to squat on my feet. I couldn't bend, so had to kneel to stroke her red feathers. They were soft and warm. Tom gave a low gobble in his throat and stretched out his head. I gave it a pat. I imagined the picture I'd sketch that night: me as Saint Francis talking to a donkey, stroking a hen, and petting a turkey. They were certainly better company than their master. I gave them a triple portion of food, then stayed in the barn for several minutes, reassuring them. When I crossed the paddock, frozen grass crackled like glass underfoot.

I loaded my arms with firewood and managed to dump it on the porch. I would not go inside that house again. I slithered back for another load. "Has the man never heard of furnaces?" I grumbled.

I was startled to hear my cell phone chirp in my jacket pocket. "Where on earth are you?" Susan demanded. "I've been calling you for an hour."

"I probably couldn't get a signal. I'm at a patient's house in the mountains."

"Well, Wonder is driving me crazy asking when you can come get her."

I checked my watch, puzzled. "It's nearly two hours before I have to pick her up."

"She didn't go to school. They canceled because an ice storm is predicted."

"Then can't Monique keep her? Surely she isn't going out to study in this weather."

"She took the test last Saturday."

"Why did nobody bother to mention that? I've been keeping Wonder all week as usual."

"Monique has a lot to do. She left early this morning to do Christmas shopping and she called to say she'll be staying with a girlfriend overnight." Susan might be brilliant, but she was incredibly naive about some things. "Meanwhile," she said in exasperation, "Wonder is making me absolutely nuts. Wait—she wants to talk."

A small voice came across the line. "I am disappointed in you, Teensie. You need to come get me so we can go see"—she lowered her voice to a loud whisper—"de veg'table man." She sounded as stern as her grandfather.

"Not today, honey. I'm up here already. I had to come early to do his chores before the road gets too icy." I arched my back, which was beginning to ache.

"If you come get me, I can cook him some lunch."

Lunch? The potato soup was still cooking. It would scorch unless I turned it off. I had to go back in his house whether I wanted to or not.

"I've made his lunch, and once I get down that hill, I'm not coming back." I had to swallow a lump in my throat at the finality of those words before I could finish explaining, "We're getting ice up here already."

"Nana says in a little while we'll have ice here, too. It will be on de trees, and de bushes, and de sidewalk, and—"

I cut short her recitation of everything she could see from her window. "Why don't you play with Nana this afternoon. I'll see you another day, okay?"

She heaved a Wonder-sigh. "Nana's not much on playing. If he tells you more Cherky stories, you remember dem good, you hear me?"

"My time now," Susan told her. She came back on the line. "Wait a minute, Teensie. Don't hang up." I heard her tell Wonder, "Go start a movie. I'll be with you in a minute." A second later, she asked me, "Who is this vegetable man? Isn't he that Indian Albert fired for hanging around Wonder?"

"He wasn't hanging around Wonder, he was telling her a Cherokee folktale, and Albert canceled his contract because he provided better vegetables to the college than Albert is willing to pay for."

"Albert's doing a good job at the college and you know it. Why are you at that man's place?"

"He's been sick and Mimi sent me up to check on him. And before you ask, yes, I have brought Wonder up here a few times. Now stop quizzing me. I'm not your daughter." She and I both knew if she quizzed her daughter like that, Monique wouldn't stand for it. "If you'll get off the phone, I can finish up here and get down a switchback road before it gets iced over. I'll call you later." I turned off my phone. I didn't want it dead if I needed it on the way home.

I opened the door and peered in. Tobias was dozing on the couch. I tiptoed to the stove and turned the soup down low. I might as well carry in the wood to save his strength. He looked peaceful sleeping. Nobody would suspect a grizzly lurked behind that face.

I was carrying in my third load when he spoke in a sleepy drawl. "I thought you weren't coming back." He startled me so much I dropped a log.

"I came in to turn off your soup and carry in a little wood. Then I'm on my way. You have enough soup to reheat for supper. You might want to make a tomato sandwich or a salad to go with it."

"I didn't have tomatoes. I suppose you bought me some?"

"A few. You can send me a check. The animals have extra food and there's enough firewood so you don't need to go out. I'll be—" The lights went out.

"A line must be down." He sounded unconcerned. I doubted if he had looked out a window all day.

"Do you have candles?" The house wasn't dark, but it was gloomy.

"There's lamps and matches on the bookshelf." What I had taken for a collection of antique lamps was in fact a practical necessity.

Lighting a lamp was another new experience. It took practice to twist the little knob gently enough to get the wick to exactly the right height so it burned, but not so high it smoked. I placed it on the coffee table beside him. "I don't like to leave you on this mountain with no electricity."

"I'll be fine."

"I could take you down to . . ." I stopped. I no longer had a big house with a spare room, and certainly neither of my sisters would take him in.

"Go home," he growled.

I went.


Every lump of mud on the rutted road was coated in ice and former mud holes were tiny frozen ponds. I should have driven with more caution once I started down the mountain, but anger made me reckless. At the first switchback, barely out of sight of the cove, my truck fishtailed. The back wheels slung back and forth on the narrow road while I fought the wheel to keep from plummeting off the steep edge to my right. *DearGodDear-GodDearGod!* With one last swing, my back wheels slid into the ditch on my left. I looked up over my hood, which pointed to the gloomy sky, and I breathed, *Thank you, thank you, thank you, thank you, thank you.* I could so easily have plunged down the mountainside.

The way I was shaking, I could hardly open my cell phone to call the mechanic at the corner. Could he pull me out before ice made the road too treacherous to drive?

I could not get a signal. The only thing I could think of to do was walk back along the road until I could connect to a tower.

I climbed down from my cab, my back screaming a protest. I stepped through a thin sheet of ice into a ditch of water up to my knees. Gasping from fright and pain, I clung to my front bumper and hauled myself up the muddy bank.

*You cannot afford to cry,* I told myself sternly. *Your cheeks will freeze.*

The world continued to ice over as I trudged that lonely mile. From time to time I tried my cell phone, but couldn't pick up even a roaming signal. Walking on the rocky verge in slick shoes required agility and determination, especially with soggy pants flopping against my ankles. I fell twice. As I hobbled along, my slacks began to stiffen. The chill under my thin soles made my feet ache. I could never remember being so miserable. The only thing that kept me going was the thought of Tobias's warm stove.

I kicked off my sodden shoes on the porch and stumbled inside on numb feet. As I leaned against the counter, basking in the warmth, Homer ambled in from the paneled den, tail wagging. I stroked his head, touched by his welcome, and saw the flicker of the lamp in there. Tobias must be resting on that couch for a change. I hobbled toward the stove and stood as close as I dared. When I had thawed, I went to put on the kettle for tea, grateful that Tobias cooked with gas.

Homer started for the den with little whimpers in his throat urging me to follow.

Tobias sat at the desk, his back to me, studying the chessboard. His strength was returning, for I saw muscles ripple across his back under his T-shirt as his hand hovered over one piece, then shifted to another.

As soon as I appeared in the doorway, he asked without looking around, "Did you move that knight?"

Now that I was warm, shock was setting in. I spoke through chattering teeth. "My truck went in the ditch." My voice was so soft, I don't think he heard me.

"I said, did you move that knight?" he repeated.

I walked up behind him and yelled, "Yes, I moved the knight and my truck went in the ditch!"

He looked over one shoulder with a frown. "Were you hurt?"

"Not much."

"Good." He turned back to the game. He reached for his rook, changed directions to hover over a bishop, then returned to the rook. With deliberation he took it down four squares. "Your move." He shoved back his chair and nearly ran me down.

I jumped aside, still behind him. "What am I going to do about the truck?"

"Call a wrecker." He picked up the phone, listened, and put it back down. "You'll have to use your cell. My line is dead."

"If I could get a signal on my cell phone, I wouldn't be here. Everything is dead. There's an ice storm outside, in case you haven't noticed." I discovered I was waving my arms exactly like King used to do. I clutched them around me instead.

He glanced toward the window. "Can't see a thing with that danged holly so close to the house. I told Melinda she was planting it too close, but she never listened to a thing I said." He nodded toward the board. "Make your next move, then I'll try my cell. Maybe I can get a wrecker."

"I don't think a wrecker could get up the hill by now. I'm sure I can't get down."

My legs were too weary to hold me any longer. I tottered to the couch and yelped in pain as I sank onto it. I had forgotten my sore tailbone.

"You *are* hurt!" Could that be concern in his voice? He gave me a penetrating look.

"Not from the wreck. Your back steps are iced over. I fell down and hit my tailbone on every one of them."

"Ouch! And you are soaking wet."

My teeth clattered like seeds in a gourd. "Good detecting, Sherlock. I climbed down from my truck into a ditch full of water. But my pants aren't wet—they are frozen. And my shoes are history, and—"

He interrupted. "Stop talking. You need to get out of those pants. Mine would probably be too big. . . ."

"I certainly hope so."

"My mother's robe is upstairs somewhere. Go put it on before you catch cold. But first, make your move." He scooted his chair away from the desk so I could reach the board.

I pulled myself painfully to my feet, stomped to the board, considered the turquoise king's position, and moved a bishop.

Tobias moved his rook out of danger.

I picked up the opposing queen, then realized what I was doing. I set her back. "I don't have time for this. I'll get pneumonia if I don't change. Any idea where that robe could be?"

"Mama's closet. I never wear it. Pink doesn't suit me."

The kettle was boiling, so I put tea in a pot to steep. Tobias didn't need much caffeine, but a cup wouldn't kill him and I was desperate for tea.

Climbing stairs was agonizing. When I reached the bedroom with floral curtains, I whimpered as I shed my slacks and pulled on a robe of soft pink velour. It was a size too large, but it brushed gently about my ankles. Tobias's mother must have been short. She was feminine, too. The robe retained a soft floral scent. Was that why Tobias had been unable to give it away? I stroked it with one hand, glad to think he had an ounce of sentiment in him.

A pair of deerskin moccasins lay on the closet floor. I rubbed my feet to bring back feeling, then slipped the moccasins on. They felt chilly and were too wide, but were as silky as water on my poor feet.

I rinsed out my slacks in the bathroom sink, although they'd probably always have traces of red mud stains. Normally I wore jeans to the farm, but that morning I hadn't dressed to go to the farm. "My biggest expense up here isn't groceries," I grumbled softly as I carried my slacks downstairs to drape over a chair near the stove. "It's the wear and tear on my wardrobe."

When I carried mugs of tea to the den, Tobias leaned back in his chair with a pleased smile. "Checkmate."

I was in no mood to congratulate him. "Don't gloat—I didn't lose. It wasn't my game." I sat gingerly on the couch. "Thanks for the robe." I held out one foot. "I put on some moccasins I found, too. Was that all right?"

"Mama won't mind. She's been dead five years. Good thing I never got around to throwing out her stuff." So much for sentiment.

"You do realize I am stuck up here until things thaw, if we haven't killed each other by then." I held my mug up to my face, closed my eyes, and inhaled the steam. I knew I should be horrified by that news, and I didn't want him to read in my eyes that I wasn't.

I heard his chair squeak. "Be my guest." When I opened my eyes, his back was to me and he was gathering all the chess pieces into the center of the board.

I carried our mugs back to the kitchen. When I went back to the den, he was lifting the chessboard. It wobbled in his hands.

I took it from him. "You aren't ready to leap tall buildings yet, Superman, and this thing is heavy. Where do you want it?"

"On the dining table. If you'll bring over several lamps, I'll light them. At the rate you lit the last one, the power would be back on before you finished."

"My pioneer days are long forgotten. Are you ready for lunch? Potato soup and a salad?"

"Sounds good." He seemed to have gotten over his snit that I'd bought groceries.

While I was fixing lunch I occasionally glanced his way. Several times I found him watching me, but as soon as I caught his eye, he concentrated on lighting lamps. By the time I brought lunch to the table, he had them all lit and set about the large room.

"How beautiful!" I exclaimed at the soft gold glow.

He nodded. "They are a lot of work to maintain, but they do give a nice light."

When I winced as I sat down to eat, he said, "You need a hot bath for that sore tailbone. I have a great bathtub."

I eyed him skeptically. "Since you have no lights, you probably don't have hot water."

"I use propane to cook and heat water. We can eat, bathe, read, and stay warm. What else do we need?"

I was too miserable to enjoy that "we." I could think of a lot of things I needed: central heat, my own bed, food somebody else had cooked, a caring friend to say, "Poor Teensie."

Did some of that show in my face? Tobias leaned on his elbows and said, "Poor Deborah. Leave the dishes. Go get that bath."

I was glad the room was a little dim. He probably couldn't see me blush.

I took a long, hot bath while he dozed on the couch. Up to

my neck in hot water in a locked bathroom, I indulged in a few minutes of fantasy. I imagined coming up to the log house with someone who looked a bit like Tobias but who was charming and attentive. Somebody who would light a fire and cuddle on the couch, sharing dreams. I had gotten to the part where we were about to go upstairs together when I heard a shout. "Have you drowned up there?"

I sighed. "I'll be right down," I yelled.

I put the robe back on and came downstairs rosy and warm. Tobias was setting up another chess game. I took my seat while mulling over a dilemma. I had no idea how good a player he was. Was he a man who could not stand to be beaten by a woman, or a man who admired a woman who could beat him? Should I play a fair game and take the chance he would hate me if he lost, or play poorly, permit him to win, and take the chance that he would despise that kind of deception? I despised deception, so I opted to play my best and let him deal with it.

To my surprise, we were pretty evenly matched. To my greater surprise, he was pleasant while playing. He didn't speak while I was thinking out my next move, he made a little humming sound while he thought out his own moves, and he congratulated me when I won. I enjoyed our game as much as I used to enjoy games with King.

"You are sick," I consoled him for losing.

"No, you're good." He didn't sound like that bothered him. "I am tired out, though. Never knew chessmen could be so heavy."

He rested again while I considered dinner possibilities. The two of us had finished off the soup. "I hope this ice doesn't last long," I told him. "We're almost out of food."

"Plenty in the freezer and more in the cellar."

"Where's the freezer?"

"Closet off the back porch. Don't leave the top up long. Don't want stuff to thaw if the power stays off a while."

"Nothing is going to thaw in this weather."

If I had noticed the closet, I'd have thought it was for yard tools. Instead it held a chest freezer full of neatly labeled packages. I chose beans, corn, and carrots. He didn't have a microwave to thaw meat even if we'd had power, and he needed vitamins more than protein.

"Did you freeze all that?" I asked when I returned.

"My sister." His voice was drowsy. "I give Lucy produce, she sends back some for my freezer."

Lucy? My eye went to the embroidery over the fireplace. "She did that sampler?"

"Yeah, when she was a kid. I think it was for our mother's birthday."

"If I gave my sisters produce, they would ask why I hadn't prepared it for the freezer before I brought it over."

That earned me the flicker of a smile. A minute later his chest was rising and falling in sleep.

I found the door to the cellar across from the downstairs bathroom. Feeling like Florence Nightingale, I carried a lamp down rough wooden stairs to find a hole maybe twelve feet square with dirt floor and walls. It was cold and smelled like red clay. Shelves on one side held jars of canned fruit, canned tomatoes, and applesauce. The other walls were lined with baskets of potatoes, cabbages, onions, brussels sprouts, carrots, and numerous spiders. I filled a small basket I found on the floor and carried it upstairs. I'd seen cornmeal in his pantry. I would make corn bread and vegetables for dinner. While we ate, I could stew a chicken from the freezer and make chicken vegetable soup for the next day.

The house was cozy and still. I found myself humming again as I cooked. When the food was ready, I knelt by the couch and shook Tobias gently. "Suppertime."

He turned over with a smile that melted my heart, but when

he opened his eyes, the smile vanished. Had he imagined for a moment that I was his long-departed wife?

He stretched and yawned. "Feels like all I do anymore is eat and sleep."

"God's healing touch," I said briskly to remove any vestiges of emotion I felt. "That's what one of my nursing instructors called sleep."

He grunted. "God has been conspicuously absent from this place lately."

I decided to ignore that.

After I had blessed the food, he asked, "How did somebody as small as you get born into the MacAllester family?"

"The normal way, I presume." Seduced by the intimacy of the lamp-lit room, I confided something I had never told a soul. "What used to worry me more as a child was why I had red hair when everybody else is dark. I crept downstairs one evening right after King had stopped in to say good night and I heard him ask Mother, 'Did we ever have a redheaded mailman?' Mother said, 'No, it was the butcher,' and they both laughed. I must have been about three. For ages after that I wondered why our bald butcher had given me his hair."

I was proud to have made Tobias chuckle. "When did you figure out what she meant?"

"Not 'til a few years later. Then I used to sneak looks at the butcher and wonder if he was my real father, but I found it impossible to imagine Mother with anybody but King."

A smile brushed his lips. "Poor Deborah, a cygnet among the ducklings."

"No, a duckling among the swans. They all grew up large and beautiful, while I—"

"Don't fish. I don't do compliments." But he was still smiling, even his eyes.

Still basking in having amused him, I said, "You tell good

stories. How did you come to tell Wonder the Milky Way one that afternoon?"

"She was in the cafeteria trying to get a glass of milk, but she couldn't reach the machine. I got it for her and teased that her milk mustache made her look like the Milky Way. She followed me onto the loading dock asking, 'What is the Milky Way?'"

"Did you pay for her milk?" Was that yet another debt we owed him?

"I offered to, but she said the family of the president doesn't have to pay."

"The heck they don't! When we were little, King wouldn't let us accept so much as a potato chip from a student, much less food from the cafeteria. Next thing we know, Wonder will be shoplifting in the bookstore."

"Next thing you know she will be president of the college. That is one smart little cookie. Why do you call your father 'King'?"

"It was his name."

"My father's name was Samson. I didn't call him that."

"Ah, but your father didn't have a Samson complex. As Mother used to tell the story, when Susan was two she wanted something one day and ran into his study calling, 'Daddy? Daddy!' He had a meeting going on and didn't pay her any attention, so she stamped her foot and said, 'King! I is talking to you.' That tickled everybody, including King. Susan, being brilliant, saw that he responded better to 'King' than he did to 'Daddy,' so she never called him 'Daddy' again. Regan and I followed her lead."

As I rose to carry dishes to the sink I asked on impulse, "Would you like me to build a fire in the fireplace? It might be cozy on this cold night."

"Do you know how to build a fire?"

"I was a Girl Scout for a while. I might remember what I learned that far back."

The angel of Girl Scouts must have hovered at my shoulder, because I soon had a decent fire blazing. Tobias lay watching the flames with Homer beside him on the floor. I sat in a rocker I dragged in from the porch, inhaling the mixed scents of burning oak and simmering chicken soup and watching shadows play on his strong face and blue-black hair. It was a moment to cherish. I couldn't remember the last time I'd felt so at peace with the world.

I fetched a sketchbook I always carried in my purse. A few minutes later Tobias asked in a lazy voice, "What are you drawing?"

My pad held four scenes: the log house with icicle icing and smoke curling from its chimney, Bray lying in the hay with Tom and Lucky snuggled up to him and icicles on the stable window, Homer snoozing by the fire with Tobias's hand on his head, and a little bluebird sitting on the railing of the log house looking at the mountains. Nothing incriminating. I passed it over.

"You are good!" His surprise was more complimentary than praise would have been.

"Thanks. Those are kinder than some. Much of what I draw is wicked and evil—my secret opinions of people."

"Who is the bluebird? You?"

"Why should you think that?" I stalled by the time-honored method of answering a question with a question.

"There's something about the tilt of her head." He laid the sketchbook on his chest and considered me through slitted lids. "Have you drawn me?"

I hesitated. "Yes, as an eagle pulling Wonder from the river."

"Not an ogre?"

Embarrassed, I admitted, "Once as a grizzly sitting on your porch with a shotgun, guarding your house."

"I guess that's better than a skunk."

We watched the fire twist into smoke and spiral up the

chimney. The silence was profound until a log flared and broke, sending sparks and smoke into the room. I got up to poke the fire and add another log.

"Do you know why the Smoky Mountains are smoky?" Tobias asked.

"Clouds," I said without turning around.

"Do you know why they have so many clouds?"

"No, why?" I went back to my rocker, as eager as Wonder for a story.

"Back when the Cherokee lived peaceably with all their neighbors, the mountains stood under clear blue skies, but when Selfishness came into the world, people wanted what belonged to others. They began to quarrel. One day two old chiefs met to settle a quarrel, but although they smoked the peace pipe together for seven days and nights, they continued to quarrel. The Great Spirit was displeased, for his children were not supposed to smoke the peace pipe until they made peace. So the Spirit turned those two old chiefs into flowers we call 'Indian Pipes'—"

"The gray ones?"

"That's them—the two old chiefs. They grow wherever friends or relatives quarrel. And the Great Spirit decreed that smoke would hang over these mountains until all people in the world learn to live in peace."

"What nice stories the Cherokee have. So many of them seem to encourage people to live at peace." I wished my own life could be like that.

Tobias echoed my thoughts. "Do we fuss as much as Wonder seems to think we do?"

"You're grumpy a lot. Maybe that's your sickness."

"What's your excuse?"

"I have a grumpy nature."

"I should have guessed." He chuckled, and I joined in.

I could not believe I was sharing a laugh with Tobias Jones in front of a lovely fire. I rocked in utter contentment.

Gradually, though, as I thought about his story, the sadness of the Great Spirit entered into me and filled me with regret. I sighed. "Those mountains will be smoky for my lifetime. I'll never live at peace with my sisters. We are too different."

Tobias thought that over. "Maybe it's not our differences that are the problem. Maybe it's thinking others ought to change the parts of them that are different so they can be like us. Radishes wanting carrots to be round and red, or potatoes wanting corn to creep along the ground. If radishes could let carrots be carrots and potatoes could appreciate the shade corn provides, the world would be a happier place."

His eyes were closed and his voice sounded far away, as if he were a disembodied spirit speaking to me through smoke. Was he remembering what had gone wrong with him and his wife? Had they been different and tried to make each other over? Was he wishing now that he had been more tolerant? Or that he had married a radish instead of a carrot? I found myself pitying him for his lonely life.

I didn't want him wallowing in grief, however. It wasn't good for his health. "Is there a Cherokee story about radishes and carrots?"

"Maybe. If so, I don't recall it."

"Did you learn the Cherokee stories from your mother and father?"

"No, I learned them from books. My folks never talked much about being Cherokee. They were like second-generation immigrants in their own country, wanting their children to put away the past and become fully American, but after—well, some years ago I started that collection of books about Cherokee

history and Cherokee folktales. Seems a shame for each generation not to pass along the wisdom of its elders to those coming
behind."

Had he been about to say, "After my son was born"?

Alone with Tobias in the womblike intimacy of the room, I
asked, "How long has it been since you saw your son?"

His hand froze in the process of stroking Homer. "How did
you know about my son?"

"Damien said your wife left several years ago and took your
son."

A log burst into new flame. In the sudden light, I saw his face
harden. "Damien talks too much."

"I'm sorry. I didn't mean—"

He pushed back his quilt. "I'm tired. I'm going to bed. Can
you put out the fire?"

Our evening was lost. "Of course."

"Good. Pick any bedroom you like."

"Do you need help up the stairs?"

"I've made it by myself all this time. I think I can make it
once more."

I sat staring into the fire, wishing life had a rewind button.
How could I have intruded on Tobias's private space and destroyed the fragile truce that had grown between us? How could
I have imagined anything *could* grow between us? It would have
been better for us both if I could have made it home.

Home! *Dear God, I should have called Darla!*

I carried my phone to the back porch, but couldn't get a signal. I decided to try upstairs. In Tobias's mother's room I leaned
close to the front window and watched my tiny screen. "Come
on, connect!" I whispered. Perhaps because the night was so
clear, perhaps because I was so high, or perhaps because prayers
are often answered promptly when they seek to alleviate somebody else's worry, I got a signal. Taking a leaf from Monique's

book, I told Darla I had been caught by the ice storm and was staying with a patient. "That's wise," she agreed.

That opinion was not shared by my family. My phone showed six messages from Regan. As soon as I called back, she demanded, "Where are you? I've been trying to reach you for hours. Susan says Wonder told her you and she have been taking care of some Indian man up in the mountains because he has nobody else to look after him."

"Wonder has a big mouth and I haven't answered my phone because I am in the mountains and can't get a signal except in an upstairs bedroom."

Too much information. Regan's voice skated closer to the edge of a screech than a princess usually gets. "Bedroom? Are you at his house?"

My silence answered for me.

"You be careful, honey! You don't have a lot of experience with men, much less Indians. What you are doing is not safe. Promise me to come straight home, you hear me?"

"I can't make that promise."

"Of course you can. It's for your own good. I care about you. You leave your Indian man to somebody else, okay?"

I had lived with my family's nasty prejudices all my life. I had usually managed to swallow my disgust, but at that moment rage choked me. "For the foreseeable future, I am stuck up here on his mountain with my truck in a ditch, so I'll be seeing a lot of *my Indian man*"—I gave the words heavy emphasis—"until the thaw."

Regan's voice was so loud I held the phone from my ear. "You can't stay up in the mountains alone with an Indian!"

"It's not as if I have any choice. I wouldn't leave a dog alone in this weather." I pocketed my phone.

I looked around to see Tobias standing in the door to his room. His face wore no expression whatsoever. I had no idea how much he had heard.

If only the floor would develop a hole and shoot me straight into the spidery cellar. Being eaten by spiders was minor punishment for what I had said. "I was talking to my sister," I stammered, "and—"

His voice was colder than the windowpane. "I got up to bank the stove. You can go do it, since you are still up."

"Bank it?" I had no idea what the meant.

"Never mind. We can build a new fire in the morning." He returned to his room and quietly shut the door. I'd have felt better if he had slammed it.

I piled both comforters on one of the beds in the room farthest from his and slept in Mrs. Jones's robe, but the mattress beneath me was so icy, I never got warm enough to sleep. I wouldn't have slept anyway. Guilt makes a rocky bedfellow. I kept replaying the disastrous end of our evening and wishing I'd said a hundred different things. Why had I brought up his son, a subject Tobias kept locked in a personal closet? How much did he hear of my conversation with Regan? Did he think I was as prejudiced as my sister? Did he think I had come back to spend the night on purpose hoping to seduce him? Or out of pity?

"Dear God," I groaned as the first sliver of pink lightened the sky, "why didn't I go to Belize?"

When I got up, a freezing house did nothing to improve my mood. I found Tobias downstairs building a new fire in the fireplace. A bucket of ashes sat beside him.

I opened my mouth to say, "Tobias, I'm sorry. Forgive me, please?" but before I could speak, he said without looking around, "Empty these ashes in the backyard and make oatmeal. I'll have the stove going in a minute." His voice was chillier than the room.

All my good intentions flew up the chimney. "I have put

up with your rudeness long enough. You'll eat what I fix." I snatched up the bucket and stomped outside, leaving the door open. What difference did it make, as cold as the house was?

"Empty ashes. Fix oatmeal. Who does he think he is?" I raged aloud, not caring if he could hear me. The day had only begun and already he had ruined it. It was such a beautiful day, too. The thermometer on the porch wall read twenty degrees, but sunshine turned ice-coated grass and branches into a glittering wonderland. Holly berries gleamed as red as the cardinal who sang from the tree's branch. Above the trees, the blue of the sky went on forever. The air was so sharp that each breath pierced my lungs. I wished I had my boots so I could go for a walk in the woods instead of staying indoors.

With regret I took one last breath of pine-scented air and returned to the house. I found Tobias on the couch with his head in his hands. I forgot my anger in immediate concern for my patient. "Are you all right?"

"Yeah, I'm okay." He lifted his head with obvious effort.

I repented of my tantrum. The man was sick. That was bad enough, without me opening a raw wound and making inexcusable statements about him. I would apologize for all of that eventually. Right now, he needed breakfast. "I've decided you're right," I told him. "Oatmeal would taste good on a day like this."

He didn't say a word until I set bowls on the table. As he poured milk on his cereal he said, "Your family is giving you trouble about staying here."

That answered one question. He had heard too much.

"They wouldn't know I was here except for Wonder. I think she told them because she's angry that I'm up here and she isn't. She wants you to tell her more 'Cherky' stories." I hoped that would bring a smile to his eyes. They remained as hard as ebony marbles. "Don't let it worry you," I added. "My sisters always give me trouble. They treat me like I am Wonder's age."

"They are right. You don't need to be here. I don't need you!" He said the last four words with such force that I felt his spit on my cheek.

Rigid with anger, I wiped it away with my napkin. "At the moment I don't have much choice."

We finished breakfast without speaking again. Bray pierced the silence. I sighed. "Time to feed the animals." I felt my slacks beside the stove. "Dang it, these aren't dry. You'd think being here all night—"

"The stove went out. You needed to bank it."

"I don't know how to bank a stove. We always had a furnace."

"Lucky you. I'll have a furnace, too, if I ever get rich."

"Which is my family's fault, right?"

He shrugged. "See if you can find anything else of Mama's to fit you."

I seethed all the way up the stairs. It wasn't my fault I was born into a comfortable family. It wasn't my fault that Albert had cut Tobias's income. It wasn't my fault that my ancestors had taken his family's land. Why did he expect *me* to suffer for all that?

I found jeans and a green wool pullover. Figuring I might as well take full advantage of his offer, I pulled sensible cotton underpants and a pair of thick socks from the dresser. When I had pinned the underpants so they'd stay up and gathered the large waist of the jeans with my belt, I glared at my reflection. "The best I can say for you is you are warm and dry." I rejected the moccasins for a pair of brown work shoes. "Jones Farm chic," I muttered as I tied them tight so they'd stay on.

Using a broom for support, I slid my way out to the barn. Unlike their master, the animals were overjoyed to see me. Lucky clucked, Tom gobbled, and Bray—well, brayed. My spirits rose as I petted them and was petted in return. I broke the ice on their water and fed them extra measures. I tossed handfuls of corn out in the paddock. "Come on, birds," I called. "Put on your skates. Breakfast is served." The red cardinal flew from the holly tree to the fence and sang praises for the day. I found myself singing as I returned to the house.

My song died inside. The room was dim with no lamps lit. Tobias lay on the couch, his eyes closed. I went upstairs and straightened the bedrooms. I couldn't do laundry without electricity. If the ice didn't thaw, I'd have to use my bed a second night anyway. I went back downstairs to find my patient awake and staring at the ceiling.

I pulled my rocker close to him. "Look, I don't know what you heard last night, but I want to apologize for anything I said to hurt you. I was furious with my sister for some things she said, and I turned her words back on her in an attempt at sarcasm— which failed. They are older than me, so they still see me as a child they need to protect. And yes, sometimes they can be bigoted and prejudiced and bossy, but they are my sisters, and I love them very much."

I was surprised to hear myself saying those words. I was more surprised to realize they were true.

"One of the purposes of family is to teach us we do not need to agree in order to love," Tobias murmured.

"Is that a Cherokee saying?"

"No, it's a Tobias saying." He hauled himself into a sitting position. "You drew me clearly. I have been a grizzly. It must be the sickness." He held his head in his hands. "Generally I am a nice guy."

"Then I will make allowances for how you feel."

"And I'll make allowances for the fact that you have a sore tailbone and are working hard to take care of me and my animals."

"Peace?"

"Peace. Is the ice melting yet?"

"Afraid not. You're stuck with me for another day."

"Then let's play chess. It's been a long time since I had a decent partner who wasn't a computer." We played one game in amicable silence. I won. After chicken soup for lunch, he napped again. I read, trying to remember the last time I'd had the leisure to read for hours at a stretch. When he woke, he asked, "Do you play poker?"

"Not well."

"Good, then I'll beat your socks off. The cards are in the top drawer of my desk."

When I fetched them, he asked, "What shall we play for?" His eyes burned into mine. Were my sisters right? Should I be afraid of this man?

My eyes fell on the jar on the bookshelf. "Buttons?"

He smiled. "That's what my sister and I always played for."

As I fetched the jar I noticed the empty space on his shelf. "I keep forgetting to return your book." Actually I'd been putting off bringing it back. I liked having a little piece of him in my room.

"Did you read it?"

"Yes, the weekend I took it home." I carried the buttons to the table and took my seat while he dealt.

"Did it make you want to beg forgiveness from me and every member of the Cherokee nation for the way white people treated mine?"

"What good would that do? It wouldn't change anything."

"Good. I don't want some soppy remorse scene while I'm beating you in poker."

"It did surprise me to learn that you all had a written language, a newspaper, schools, stores, and cultivated farms before you were sent to Oklahoma. I never knew that."

He glanced at me over his cards. "You've never visited the Vann House in Chatsworth? Or Major Ridge's home in Dalton? Those homes are as fine as any whites owned at the time."

"I've seen the historic markers, but I've never stopped."

That earned me a frown. "Why not?"

"Too busy, I guess." I would not admit that until I'd met him, Cherokee history seemed far removed from my own life. "I wondered how much of what I was reading was true. Did Major Ridge and the Vanns really have slaves?"

"Sure. The Cherokee enslaved enemies taken in battle long before we began to buy Africans. We were no more evil or virtuous than our white neighbors—just more gullible. We believed whites when they said our people could live side by side with them if we adopted their ways." He considered his cards, discarded two, and drew.

His husky voice was pleasant in the lamp-lit room. To hear more of it, I asked another question. "Were the Cherokee as educated as this author claims? He says that sons of the wealthiest Cherokee were sent to exclusive schools up north, and that they became teachers, lawyers, and businessmen. Surely *they* weren't made to walk all the way to Oklahoma."

He grunted. "Spoken like a true MacAllester. Being educated doesn't protect you from cruelty, Deborah. The Cherokee educated not only their sons but many of their daughters—one story says that Cherokee fathers complained to Major Ridge that his daughter was too educated for their sons and he told them, 'Then educate your sons.' However, an educated Indian was still an Indian in the eyes of white settlers."

I tried to picture my own family, our possessions on our backs, setting out to walk to Oklahoma. "I am truly sorry my mother's people were part of that."

He shifted in his chair, as if my apology disconcerted him, but if I thought he'd say, "It's okay, Deborah Ingram MacAllester, I forgive you," I could think again.

"You ought to be. It's a nasty blot on any family's history. However, it wasn't like the movies, you know. My people weren't sent to a desert, they were sent to eastern Oklahoma, which is similar to the land here. The government just failed to mention that it already was inhabited by the Osage. And, of course, when the new land turned out to have oil on it, the whites wanted it back. Still, before the great resettlement we were given time to pack our possessions and purchase wagons. A number of the wealthy ones took the train partway there."

"What about Cherokees who were married to white people? Could they stay? A number of Cherokees seem to have married whites."

"Both Cherokee men and women married whites more than any other Indian tribe. Full-blooded white men married to Cherokee wives were allowed to remain behind with their families and keep their land. That's how my mother's people stayed. Full-blooded white women had to go with Cherokee husbands."

I looked down at my cards so he couldn't see my eyes. I'd had a fleeting picture of myself having to go with Tobias to Oklahoma. Could I have stood to move? Would my family have let it happen? Could they have done anything to prevent it? Hoping he hadn't read any of that in my face, I said, "I was surprised that your chief at the time was only one-eighth Cherokee and didn't even speak your language well."

"John Ross was chosen because Major Ridge, who would have been the logical choice for chief, was getting old. He felt Ross would be a better chief. Ross was eloquent in English and knew Andrew Jackson personally—he was a scribe for him during the war against the Creek."

I laughed. "Cherokees and white Southerners have more in common than anybody admits. Both love stories and both revere their ancestors. You talk about Major Ridge and John Ross in the same way my mother used to speak of John and Mary Mac-Allester, who died before the Civil War—like they are people who live just over the mountain."

I don't think Tobias heard me. He was frowning at his hand. He drew another card, then continued, his voice bitter, "Ridge believed Ross could persuade Washington to honor its treaties. He did, too—the Supreme Court ruled in favor of the Cherokee. Unfortunately, Jackson was a politician, not a friend to the Cherokee. He joked, 'Since the Supreme Court made the decision, let them enforce it,' and he signed the order for resettlement. It insults my people to have his face on the twenty-dollar bill. What do you have?"

I thought he wanted me to check my wallet until I saw him looking at my cards. I laid them down. "Three of a kind."

He displayed his. "Full house."

I handed him buttons. "I still can't believe they sent away educated people who weren't but a quarter or an eighth Cherokee. I mean, John Ross . . ."

As he dealt again, he gave me a long, level look. "Would the removal be more palatable to you if we had been full-blooded savages wrapped in blankets and living in teepees?"

Honesty compelled me to admit, "I think it would. It still wouldn't be right to take the land, of course. . . ."

His voice hardened. "You didn't take it. Major Ridge—who, to my regret was of the Deer clan, as I am—and his son and nephew eventually signed away our land with no authority to do so. Ridge was the leading Cherokee of his day, but neither he nor the others were our chief." He checked his hand and drew a card before he continued. I was having trouble concentrating on both history and my hand.

"Ridge claimed he signed because the whites would slaughter us to get our land if we did not give it to them," Tobias went on. "That could have been true. However, he and his wealthy family went partway by train, got to Oklahoma early, and claimed some of the best land for themselves." He added in a low voice, "They were murdered before they got to enjoy it."

"Don't sound so satisfied. You send shivers up my spine."

"Show your cards." We laid down our cards again. Again he won.

"You've got all my buttons!" I complained.

"Good. I'm tired."

"Then rest. I'll feed the animals while supper cooks."

He lumbered to the couch and was asleep almost before he pulled the quilt to his chin.

After supper, he said, "I envy you reading. I wish I had the energy to hold a book." He gestured toward a history of World War II lying open and facedown on the coffee table. "I started that before I got sick, and haven't felt like reading since."

"Would you like me to read to you?"

"Would you do that?"

"Of course."

I read a couple of chapters aloud, feeling like a pioneer in the lamp-lit room. "You have a nice voice," he murmured when I finished. "Do you sing as well as hum?"

"Sometimes."

He gestured toward a mandolin that hung on the wall. When I fetched it down, he picked and sang, "She'll be comin' 'round the mountain when she comes." His voice was a clear, true baritone. I picked up the harmony and we finished together. After one song, though, he laid down the instrument. "I'm too weak to even play more. I used to play for hours."

"You will again." I picked up the mandolin. "Aren't these things tuned like a violin? I took violin lessons for a while, until we all agreed I wasn't playing for my own pleasure and certainly not for anybody else's. I think I remember the fingering." I began to play.

I sang mountain ballads until my fingers got sore. Sometimes he joined in. Mostly he listened. At nine, I put the instrument away. "I'll fix us a cup of hot chocolate, and then you need to go to bed."

"First let me teach you to bank the fire."

Following his instructions, I prepared the stove for the night while milk heated. When the hot chocolate was ready, I turned to find him behind me. "Here." I handed him a mug.

He set the mug on the counter and reached for me. "We make good music, Deborah."

I opened my mouth to agree, but he covered it with his own.

Unlike Phil's kiss, Tobias's was warm and mobile, full of yearning and desire. Of their own accord my arms wrapped themselves around his neck under that heavy fall of hair. My body pressed against his as if it belonged there. We stood entwined until the nurse's part of my brain reminded me *This is not professional behavior.*

I backed away. "We shouldn't be doing this."

"Why not? Oh!" He wiped his mouth with alarm in his eyes. "Am I giving you hepatitis?"

"No. I've had the shots, remember?" He looked like he was coming back for more.

I stepped farther down the kitchen. "You don't need excitement. You need to rest." If he kissed me again, I could not swear to be responsible for the consequences. My whole body was crying out for his, but the man was sick and my patient.

"What I *need*—" he began.

"Is to rest," I said firmly—as much to myself as to him. "Take the hot chocolate upstairs with you. I'll see you in the morning."

"Very well. In the morning."

It sounded like a promise.

I hummed as I brushed my hair and climbed between my icy sheets. Could he possibly feel for me what I felt for him? Did I want him to? Or was he simply a man who hadn't had a wife around for a long time?

*Slow down, Deborah*, I told myself. *The man has only kissed you once.*

But that kiss held a promise. "In the morning," he'd said.

I lay in the cold bed torn between hope and fear that Tobias would try to climb in with me. He didn't. Poor dear, he needed his sleep.

Sunday morning I woke to the silver music of melting ice. I lay in bed for a voluptuous moment reliving the kiss, but Bray was calling from the barn. I pulled on my now-dry slacks and went out to feed the animals. The grass was slushy underfoot.

I returned to the house shy and embarrassed. How would Tobias act when we met again?

Before I fixed breakfast, I went up to the empty front bedroom and called the mechanic down at the corner of Jones Farm Road. He promised to send somebody to pull my truck out, but said he couldn't get there until noon. "All sorts of folks went off the road in this storm. How long you been stuck up there with Tobias?" He sniggered.

"Mr. Jones is very ill," I told him sternly. He could not see how my face was flaming.

I had a voice mail from Susan, so I called her back. "You aren't still up on that mountain, are you?" she demanded when she heard my voice.

When I didn't reply, she asked, "When are you coming home?"

"I'm not sure. The mechanic is coming to pull my truck out of the ditch around noon. If it's drivable, I'll be home soon after that. Tell the choir director why I'm absent today, okay?"

"What shall I tell him, that you're spending the weekend alone with a man? I hope you've been using good sense."

"Mr. Jones is sick, Susan. And he's not a 'man,' he's a patient. I'll call you when I get home."

"That ought to dispel any notions of riotous living and dissipation." Tobias stood in the doorway. His face was stony as his voice rose to mimic mine. "'He's not a man; he's a patient.'"

"I didn't mean—"

"Your meaning was perfectly clear."

"I was talking to Susan. My sisters make me crazy sometimes."

"We both get crazy sometimes. Forget last night, okay? I didn't mean to do that. I forgot for a few minutes that climbing to a princess can be dangerous, almost impossible."

"I'm not a princess!"

"The hell you aren't. Are we having breakfast?"

We ate in silence so thick it was sullen. I tried to break it a couple of times, but Tobias responded in grunts to questions like, "Did you sleep well? Do you feel any stronger?"

When I asked, "How long do you think your power is going to be out?" he growled, "How should I know? The ice is melting, so you can go home. That's the only thing that matters. I'm used to living alone." He lay on the couch and pulled the quilt to his chin.

"Look, I didn't meant to insult you. I was reassuring Susan—"

"Drop it." In another moment he was snoring. I suspected he was faking and tiptoed over to look. He pulled the covers over his head.

I prepared enough food for two days. I stripped my bed and changed his, hoping the power would be restored in another day so I could wash the pile of laundry that was accumulating. I tidied the bathroom and the rest of the house. When I couldn't think of another thing to do, I dragged the porch rocker near the window and read. By then Tobias was genuinely asleep.

At eleven thirty I reheated some soup and shook him gently. "Come eat some soup. I have to leave soon."

"Good." I didn't know if he was glad about the soup or that I was leaving.

"I'll come back tomorrow to see if you have power," I told him as we ate. "If you don't, I'll leave you my phone. I'd leave it now except the battery is low and I don't have the charger."

"I don't need a phone and you don't need to come back."

"There's a huge pile of laundry—"

"I can wash clothes. I can fix meals. I can feed the animals—slowly. I'll be fine. I'm getting some energy back. I'll be well in no time."

"You need to give your body time to heal completely. You mustn't do too much."

"I won't do too much. I won't plow under the pumpkins. I won't repair the broken plow. I won't walk three miles down to the mailbox and back."

Guilt swept over me. He'd been confined to the house for three weeks. His box must be overflowing. "I forgot about your mail. Do you want me to bring it up to you the next time I come?"

"I told you, don't come. I'll get the mail when I feel like it. It's not urgent."

When I picked up my coat to leave, he reached for his. "Where do you think you're going?" I asked.

"To drive you down to your truck and wait for the mechanic."

"You'll wear yourself out."

"Then I will come home and rest. Come on. Don't wear me out standing here."

As we drove through the cove, he pointed to a pond over in the fields. "See that pond? My father kept cattle and built it to water them. When I was fourteen, my big sister bossed me one day. I picked her up and dumped her in that pond. She hadn't realized I'd gotten stronger than she was. I said, 'From now on, you respect me or that's what you'll get.' She never bossed me again."

"I don't have a pond and my sisters are giants. I couldn't lift them if I tried."

"It's the principle that matters, not the pond."

Neither of us said another word while we drove through the cove. I was surprised how forlorn I felt to be leaving the farm. I loved the view, the silence, and the quirky animals, and yes, in spite of myself, I was afraid I was beginning to love their owner. He was delightful when he wasn't awful.

"I had a good time yesterday," I said in a small voice. "I enjoyed the chess, and the poker, and reading and singing."

He gave me a small salute. "Glad to have been of service, ma'am."

"Don't be silly. You had a good time, too."

He looked out the windshield. "Yeah, I did. For a little while I forgot you were a lily white princess and I was an Indian farm boy."

"I'm not—"

He pulled up at my truck and peered out his window. "You really got yourself in a fix, didn't you?"

"Don't sound smug. It could have happened to anybody. I could have died."

"I doubt it. You're pretty indestructible."

"Look, I don't expect gratitude, but a few manners would be nice."

"I'm giving you a warm truck to sit in. What more do you need?"

I sighed. "Not one thing, Tobias. Not one blessed thing."

When the wrecker came into view, I collected my things. "Good-bye, then."

He put his truck in gear. "Good-bye, princess." The words clanged like a prison door.


The road down the hill was too slick for me to waste time thinking about Tobias Jones. Arriving at Darla's warm gray bungalow with lights shining from the windows, I felt I had traveled across a galaxy.

She greeted me with a hug. "I am glad you are home, dear." Tears made my eyes smart. I could not remember the last time anybody said they were glad I was home.

As I washed my hair and toweled it vigorously, I was annoyed to find myself singing "I'm Gonna Wash That Man Right out of My Hair." That man had never been in my hair. I could have smacked my sisters for their powers of suggestion. "It was all their fault," I muttered. "Without them, Tobias and I might have become friends."

My eyes met their mirrored reflection. Honesty made me admit I didn't want to be simply friends with Tobias, but any chances I'd had of being anything else had been frustrated by my own unruly tongue.

Warm and dry in my green plaid bathrobe and fleece-lined slippers, I plugged my phone into its charger and called Susan.

"Hello?" She sounded as if she'd been running.

"It's Teensie. I wanted you to know I'm back at Darla's safe and sound."

"I'm glad, but I can't talk right now. Wonder has created a crisis. Her preschool teacher taught them to dial 911 in case of emergency and Monique came home a little while ago pretty banged up. She fell on the ice yesterday afternoon and wound up with bruises all over her body. Wonder walked in on her in the shower, saw the bruises, and apparently thought that constituted an emergency, because she called 911 and told them her mama has been beaten up. Both the police and the EMTs just arrived. I need to go explain things to them and decide what to do about Wonder."

"Don't be hard on her. If your house had been burning, you'd have been glad she called."

I was talking to myself. Susan had already gone.

When I hung up, I noticed that I had been sketching on the back of an envelope: a small princess tossing two big cows into a pond, one with each hand. An eagle circled overhead, but he wasn't watching the princess. He was staring over the mountains.

As I added that sketch to the drawer where I kept my drawings, I remembered the ones I had done the night before. Had that been less than twenty-four hours? I had traveled across so much pain, it felt like weeks since I'd done those four little pictures.

I went to get the book from my purse so I could tear out the sketches and add them to the drawer, but the book wasn't there. Where had I put it?

I had handed it to Tobias. He must have set it on his coffee table.

I would pick it up when I went back. If I went back.

I sat at my window for more than an hour that evening watching the moon make its way up the branches outside my window. The moon didn't find the tree impossible to climb, but I doubted any princes were going to try.

# Eight

Regan and Holcomb always spent Sunday afternoons with his mother, so I didn't try to call my sister until Monday. She was in a rush. "I'm glad you're home, but I can't talk right now."

"Busy with decorating, or are you planning a party?"

Regan always spent December getting ready for Christmas. She alternately charmed and bullied a hoard of workers who transformed her home into a Christmas wonderland. She personally selected a twelve-foot tree for her front hall and supervised its decoration. She held three elaborate parties for all of Holcomb's employees, segregated according to professional rank. She still found time to wrap toys and assemble food baskets for her church's drive for impoverished families in the county, and she hosted Christmas dinner for our entire family—although, if Thanksgiving was any indication, the family Christmas dinner might get scratched.

"The decorating is done and the parties are planned," she said gaily. "Today I'm headed to see the doctor."

"Are you sick?" Most people didn't sound ecstatic to be visiting a doctor.

"No." My sophisticated sister actually giggled. "I think I'm pregnant! I've missed two periods already. Isn't that marvelous?"

"Marvelous." I hoped I sounded properly enthusiastic, although I couldn't help thinking that the child might well have been paid for with part of my inheritance.

I managed to be tactful. I didn't point out that her baby's parents would be retired before s/he finished college. At least Regan and Holcomb didn't have to worry about saving up for their old age.

Regan's voice was merry. "Get ready to babysit, baby sister. We're going to have another little person in the family!"

"I've got my babysitting shoes on. Call me when you know for sure."

"I sure will. Gotta go, hon."

She didn't ask a single question about my Indian man.

I didn't bother to dress that morning. An advantage of the Internet is that you can apply for work in your pajamas. I spent the next hour and a half checking out meager job opportunities for a nurse within commuting distance of Unizilla. I was bookmarking one to return to when my phone rang and the caller said without preamble, "Teensie, you gotta get over here."

I struggled to identify the caller. "Lynyetta? Is that you?"

Lynyetta Scarr was Regan's cook. She and I had gone through school together, so I usually went back to the kitchen to chat when I went to Regan's. I often told Lynyetta she ought to be cooking at a fancy restaurant in Atlanta, but she always laughed. "Can't you see me and Bucky living down there with his five hunting dogs and my three goats?"

"Yeah, it's me." She sounded exasperated that I didn't recognize her voice, even though she had never called me before. "You gotta get over here fast!"

"What's the matter? Is my sister pitching a hissy fit over sauce for roast duckling?"

"This is serious, Teensie! Regan come in from town with her eyes all swole up and red and her hair a mess. You know she never lets people see her like that. I axed what was the matter but she walked over to the cabinets and leaned her forehead against 'em like she was holding 'em up—or vicey-versa. 'I've got some baby back ribs for dinner,' I said, trying to make conversation. She went plumb crazy. Picked up a onion I was about to chop and pitched it across the kitchen. Then she started pitching all sorts of stuff. Punkin like to went crazy."

Punkin was Regan's Yorkshire terrier. I'd always considered him a poor excuse for a dog. He was easily excited and had a high-pitched bark that hurt the ears, and he was prone to bite when agitated. "Did he bite you? I can't treat a dog bite."

"Just my shoe. That ain't important. It's Regan. After she'd throwed everything she could reach, she went running into Holcomb's den and started pounding on the door to his gun cabinet yelling, 'I'm going to shoot myself! I want to die!' I'm glad Holcomb keeps it locked, ain't you? 'You stop that,' I told her, 'or you're gonna break that glass and cut yourself. You need to go upstairs and take something to calm you down.' She yelled back, 'I'll take something to calm me down, all right!' And she ran upstairs like the devil was behind her. I made her a cup of chamomile tea, thinking that might quiet her some, and when I got upstairs she was lying on her bed like Snow White. She'd took her hair down and brushed it and she was layin' there with her eyes closed and her hands folded on her stummick. I said, 'I brung you some tea,' and she said, in a real sleepy voice, 'I don't need tea. I need Teensie. Tell her I took a bottle of pills.'"

A chill started at my toes and crept up my body. "*What* pills?"

"I dunno. 'Pills' is all she said. I run straight to the next room and called you. How soon can you get over here?"

Not as soon as I could have if she had condensed her story. *Pleasegodpleasegodpleasegod!* "It'll take me twenty minutes, at least. Call 911. The paramedics are closer than I am, and they can take her to a hospital. Cover her with a blanket to keep her warm and take away her pillow so she can breathe better. Oh, and lock Punkin up. We don't want him biting a paramedic. And call Holcomb."

"Call 911, blanket, pillow, Punkin, and Holcomb." She named them like they were items in a recipe. "Okay, I got it. You hurry, you hear me?"

"I'll come as fast as I can."

I threw on my coat over my pajamas and, although mountain roads are not made for speed, I got there in fifteen minutes. My heart was pounding, my hands were sweaty, and I felt a deep sadness that my sister hadn't come to me with her troubles. *Poor Regan! Is there no baby? Did you want one that desperately?*

I was glad to see an ambulance and police cruiser parked in the drive next to a life-sized Santa, sleigh, and eight tiny reindeer. Police are always sent when suicide is suspected, because somebody who is willing to kill themselves may also be willing to kill anyone who tries to stop them.

I didn't slow down to admire the decorations that dotted Regan's lawn. I let myself in through the kitchen and confronted a furious Punkin yipping to the world, "Here we have all this excitement in the house and I am locked in the kitchen!"

"Bite me and you won't live to regret it," I promised.

Lynyetta sat at the kitchen table, equally indignant. "The police shut me in here like a dog. They won't let me be with her."

"It's nothing personal. That's standard procedure," I told her. "They have to be sure she doesn't harm you and you don't harm her. Did you call Holcomb?" I threw my coat over a chair and headed to the far door.

"Yeah. He's on his way. I wouldn't do nothing to hurt Regan, you know that. And she never did anything to me except fuss a little."

"I know that, but they don't." I was already out the door.

"I reckon they're pumping her stummick," she called after me. Now that the paramedics and I were there, Lynyetta was fueled by excitement.

I doubted the paramedics were pumping Regan's stomach. That was old-style poison treatment. They were probably wrapping her up to take her to the hospital, where she'd have to drink two cups full of activated charcoal to bind the poisons and eliminate them. Regan was not going to be a happy camper.

I ran a gamut of tree, holly, and mistletoe between the kitchen and the stairs and hurried along the upstairs hall, which was carpeted in gray plush too thick for speed. I heard Regan long before I reached her. "I don't need to go to the hospital! I want Teensie! Call my sister!" My heart felt like it would jump out of my chest from fear.

I had sometimes envied Regan her room. It was a decorator's vision in rose, forest green, and cream. The adjoining bath had yards of mirrors, thick rose towels, and a huge Jacuzzi under the window. Instead of a lavatory like the rest of us, Regan had a white porcelain bowl with a drain in the bottom that sat on her countertop. The bowl was painted with roses and banded in gold, and was one of the prettiest things I'd ever seen.

That afternoon nothing was pretty. My sister was writhing on her bed while two paramedics tried to get her on a gurney. Her hair was wild as a witch's and her face was damp with sweat and tears. "I want Teensie!" she screeched like a banshee.

"I'm here, Regan," I called from the doorway.

"Tell them to take their hands off me!" she shrieked. I was relieved to find her able to shriek

An officer stepped forward. "Ma'am, I'll have to ask you to wait downstairs in the kitchen."

"I'm a nurse," I told him. Only when I saw his skeptical look did I realize I was standing there in my pajamas. "She's calling for me." I pointed toward the bed to distract him from my flannel fashion statement. "I think I can calm her down."

The younger of the two paramedics threw me a grateful look. "Let her try, Wilson," he called to the officer. To me he said, "She won't tell us what she took."

I padded to the bed in my slippers and put a calming hand on Regan's shoulder. "Shhh," I told her like our mother used to when we were upset. "I'm here, Regan." I was gratified to feel her grow calm under my touch.

She looked up at me with frantic eyes. "I don't want to go to the hospital! I want you to take care of me!" She was so groggy I was surprised she still had fight in her, but Regan would wrestle Death to the finish line.

"I'm not allowed to treat you, honey. I'm family. These men will take good care of you." I smoothed damp hair from her forehead. "What did you take?"

She gave me a pleading look. "Some pills, but I don't really want to die."

"*What* did you take?" I repeated.

"Sleeping pills. I put the bottle in my hamper."

I retrieved the bottle and handed it to the paramedic.

"How many?" he asked.

"I dunno," she said. "However many were in there."

He read the label and shook his head at me. "They aren't strong. I don't think she could kill herself with the whole bottleful, but we'd better take her along."

"I don't want to go to the hospital!" Regan began to writhe again.

"Calm down," I told her, pressing her shoulder into the soft mattress. "They know what's best for you, but I'm sure they will let me ride with you if you'll be sweet."

"I'll be sweet." She collapsed like a doll stuffed with fluff. Her eyes closed.

I stroked her hair again. "Let them get you ready to go while I change, okay? I can't go to the hospital in my pajamas. I have my professional reputation to consider."

She gave me a weak smile like I'd made a joke. "Okay."

While med techs got her on the gurney, I went to her closet and grabbed the first things I touched—a pair of taupe silk pants and a matching knit pullover. The pullover had a fancy pattern of satin leaves running on a diagonal across the front. I took lacy pink underwear from her drawer and carried the bundle to the bathroom to change. The sweater hung past my backside. Its sleeves dangled several inches beyond my fingertips until I shoved them up. The slacks were so long I had to roll them three times. I also slipped my feet into a pair of taupe flats. They were four sizes too long.

Regan was already gone when I flapped out in her clothes. I found Holcomb in the hall, watching down the stairs as she was wheeled past the Christmas tree. He gave me a puzzled stare. "You look like a kid in her mother's clothes."

"I know, but I was in my pajamas. I couldn't go to the hospital like that."

He wasn't listening. He had gone to the hall window to watch Regan being put in the ambulance. "What could have made her do such a thing?" he demanded over his shoulder. "We were happy. We *are* happy, dammit!"


"I'll need you to drive," Holcomb said as we approached the drive. "I'm shaking too badly."

I glanced over to the ambulance. "I told Regan I'd ride with her."

"She's asleep. Come with me, please. She won't notice and I need you to drive." His hands shook so much he dropped the keys when he tried to give them to me.

I drove the Mercedes in bare feet. I couldn't drive in Regan's flats.

"Why would she do such a thing?" Holcomb asked again as soon as I'd started the engine. "Why, Teensie? Why?"

I decided to keep my suspicions to myself. "You will have to ask her, but I don't think she really meant to kill herself. She had Lynyetta call me as soon as she took the pills, and they aren't strong. I think she freaked out about something and wanted to get me over here fast."

He was puzzled. "You'd have come if she had just called, wouldn't you?"

"Yeah, but we both know Regan doesn't always think straight when she's having a conniption." That seemed to satisfy him.

Holcomb and Regan were well-known at the hospital since she was an auxiliary volunteer and he had donated the Harris Burn Unit. As soon as Regan's ambulance arrived at the emergency room, she went straight into an examination room. I avoided the eyes of people who had probably been waiting for hours.

While Holcomb went to the desk to take care of paperwork, I stepped back outside to make a few calls. The day was so chilly that I pulled my coat collar up and kept one hand in my pocket while I held my phone with the other. Between calls, I switched hands.

Susan's voice mail answered, as I had figured it would. She was teaching a class. "Call me as soon as you get this," I said in my message. "Regan's in the hospital, and I'm there with Holcomb." I called Albert's secretary and asked her to tell him he needed to pick up Wonder at preschool because I had been unavoidably detained. He wasn't going to be happy, but when was Albert ever happy? I called Mimi to tell her Regan had gone to the hospital and I wasn't sure when I could work again. She said to take all the time I needed.

I asked her to make sure somebody checked on Tobias that afternoon. I heard silence on the line. "Mimi? Did you hear me? I said . . ."

"I heard you," she said.

What I heard was her pencil clicking against the receiver. Why should she be embarrassed? "Listen," she said in a few seconds, "I need you to tell me something. Did you really spend the weekend up at Tobias Jones's farm?"

"How on earth did you hear that?"

"Never mind. Is it true?"

"Yes, but not like you're making it sound. I went up Friday like you suggested, to check on him and make sure he was set for the weekend. The road iced up before I got away, and my truck slid into a ditch, so I had to go back to the house and stay until the ice melted."

"Why didn't you walk downhill instead?"

"For heaven's sake, Mimi! It was freezing outside, three miles to the nearest house downhill, the road was icy, and I had on loafers. His house was less than a mile away, mostly across a flat cove. It was a no-brainer."

"How long were you there?"

"From Friday morning until noon on Sunday. What is this about?"

"Was anybody else in the house?"

"Nobody but his dog, but the man is sick. You know that. Nothing happened."

Well, nothing except a kiss I would cherish all my life, and it wasn't likely to happen again in Wonder's foreseeable future. I didn't tell Mimi that.

Her pencil kept clicking. "The reputation of this clinic depends on our staff keeping the highest professional standards. We both know that. So while you and I both also know that all you did up at that farm was take care of a patient, questions have been raised that I have to respond to. I need to ask you not to go up there again."

Tobias's prohibition I could have dealt with by simply appearing at the farm one day—if I got my courage up. Mimi's prohibition cut off my legs at the hips. I doubted I'd lose my license if I disobeyed her, but I would get a mark on my record that could keep me from nursing again. Before Florence Nightingale, nurses had a reputation something like that of prostitutes. We've been living it down ever since.

Miserable, I demanded, "Who's been raising questions? Tell me that. Not one soul knew where I was except my sisters."

Mimi didn't say a thing.

I thought it over. Susan had been upset, but she was too conscious of her own reputation—and Albert's—to smear mine in the community. That left . . .

"It was Regan, wasn't it? She called and told you I was getting too involved with a patient. Or did she say 'with an Indian man'?" I felt like running up and down the parking lot screaming.

Mimi said nothing.

"It's a lie!" I spoke so loud that a family going inside looked at me funny. I turned my back. "You know that. Regan is prejudiced and overprotective."

"And one of my largest donors." Mimi said that as if it answered all my questions. I guessed it did. "You don't have to worry about Mr. Jones," she added. "His sister called a few minutes ago and said she'll be staying with him until the New Year."

"That's good," I said. "All he really needs is somebody around to do his chores and fix meals."

"But, Teensie? I need your word that you won't go up there again."

I was furious. If Regan wasn't being treated as a suicide attempt in the emergency room, I'd have throttled her.

*    *    *

I went inside to find a doctor in blue scrubs talking to Holcomb. Most people don't get personal physician visits in an emergency room, but most people are not Holcomb Harris.

". . . refusing treatment," the doctor was saying. "We need to give her activated charcoal, but she won't take it."

"Oh, yes, she will," I said grimly. "Let me talk to her."

Making Regan swallow that nasty black stuff would be pure joy.

As we headed toward Regan's cubicle, the doctor told Holcomb, "As soon as a room is ready, we'll be sending her up to the psychiatric unit for three or four days."

I had expected that. Holcomb hadn't. "Psychiatric ward? My wife's not crazy."

The doctor spoke in a professional, soothing voice. "It's standard procedure after an attempted suicide. We want to make sure she's no danger to herself."

Holcomb laid a hand on my shoulder. "Teensie here is a nurse. She can come home with us and take care of Regan."

Sure. Just like that.

The doctor wasn't buying it, fortunately. "I'm afraid not. We want to observe her, perhaps put her on some meds to keep her calm, and decide on a post-discharge regimen of counseling."

"Regan is not going to be happy about this," Holcomb warned.

The doctor shrugged. "Psychiatric patients seldom are. We're used to that."

Holcomb rubbed a hand over his hair. "I don't think she meant to kill herself. You said that, Teensie, didn't you? She was just a little upset over something."

I saw pity flicker in the doctor's eye as he said, "We'll try to find out about that while she's here. She's in the third room over there. Go on in."

We joined Regan in her cubicle. A nurse stood at the head of the bed. She held a cup and wore an expression that I suspected was a lot like a zoo employee would wear after trying unsuccessfully to give medicine to a panther.

Holcomb bent over his wife like she was fine porcelain. "You scared me, baby, you know that?"

Regan's voice was low and drowsy, but she knew what she wanted. "Get me out of here. Take me home."

He looked at me. "What should I do?"

"Listen to the doctors," I advised. "They know what they're doing."

Hearing my voice, Regan struggled to focus on me. "Teensie? Are those *my clothes*?"

"Yeah, they are. I was in pajamas when Lynyetta called, and I came to your place without stopping to change. I had to have something to put on to come over here."

"You shouldn't have picked that outfit. It cost a fortune!"

"I was in a hurry. I grabbed the first things I found."

"Don't wash them when you take them off, you hear me? I'll take them to my dry cleaner. I don't want them ruined." She licked her lips. "I'm thirsty."

"Nurse!" Holcomb said, snapping his fingers toward a pink plastic pitcher by the sink. It was sweating, so it must have been full of ice and water.

"What Regan needs is this." I reached for the cup the nurse held. "Don't worry, I'm a nurse, too," I murmured when she started to protest.

"Here." I thrust the cup under Regan's perfect little nose. "Drink this."

Activated charcoal looks and smells like—well, charcoal. Regan took one whiff and waved it away. "Ugh! Nasty!"

I held it to her mouth again. "Yes, it is nasty, but you have to drink it to get rid of the poison."

"I'm not drinking that!" She shoved it so hard, some of it splashed on me.

"My sweater!" she moaned. "You've ruined it."

"*You* ruined it, if it is ruined. Now drink!"

"No!"

I took the cup away. "Fine, don't. If your hair falls out, or your skin develops a rash, or your fingernails get fungus, remember: you chose not to drink the charcoal. You've got poison in your system and it has to come out somewhere."

I heard the nurse behind me take a breath to tell Regan none of that would happen from the pills she took. I flapped a hand at the nurse to warn her to be quiet.

Regan pressed manicured nails to her flawless cheek, then moved her hand to stroke her lustrous hair. "All of that could happen?"

"Nobody knows what might happen. Maybe you'll get lucky. It's your decision."

"I have to drink it all?"

"You have to drink two cups. Hold your nose and do it."

I had thought watching her swallow the stuff would make me feel better for what she'd done to me. It didn't. The antidote for poison is one of the most unpleasant cures known to modern medicine. Holcomb could only stand to watch her drink one glass before he had to leave. By the time Regan had chugged the second glass, I felt as sorry for her as Holcomb did—which was almost as sorry as she felt for herself.

"Do I get to puke it up?" she gasped when she finished.

"No, it comes out the other end. You won't have any ill effects."

The nurse left the room and Regan lay back on her pillow to catch her breath. "I want out of here," she murmured when she could speak again.

"You'll have to stay three days or so," I told her. "That's standard procedure."

"Look, I got upset, okay? But I'm fine now."

"You need to stay, though. The psychiatrists know what they're doing." I have to admit I felt unholy glee at the expression on her face when she heard that.

Her voice rose with her temper. "Psychiatrists? I'm not crazy! Tell them that. Tell them you're a nurse and you'll take care of me at home. Holcomb will pay you."

"Nothing I could say would do a speck of good. You are going to the psychiatric ward, so you might as well accept it."

"Get me out of here!" She hurled her water pitcher at me.

Regan threw better groggy than she did wide awake. The pitcher hit me in the midriff and sent a cascade of ice water down my front. I yelled.

"My clothes!" she screeched. "Now look what you've done."

I grabbed a towel and swabbed my torso. "Stop blaming me for your actions. You're lucky the nurse wasn't here, or they'd keep you longer."

"What are they going to do to me?" Her voice held a trace of fear beneath the bluster.

"Give you some meds, counsel you, and set up a protocol for further treatment. Think of it as a short vacation."

"I don't want medicine and I don't need counseling."

"That's what all their patients say."

"It's true! I am not crazy."

"Their patients all say that, too. You tried to kill yourself."

She chewed her lower lip and sulked. "I didn't," she finally said. "I only took three pills. I flushed the rest. I told Lynyetta I'd taken a lot so she'd call you."

"Tell the psychiatrist that. Maybe he'll let you come home early."

Not likely. He would have heard that before, too. The difference was that in Regan's case, I was certain it was true. She hadn't wanted to die; she had wanted my attention.

"Think of this," I said. "If Holcomb checks you out before the staff is convinced you are fine, every time you come to volunteer, people will wonder about you. Do you want that? People looking at you and wondering if you are crazy?"

"No." She sounded uncertain, seeking a loophole.

"So go upstairs for three days, get some rest, read the magazines we bring you, and try to figure out what to tell your friends when you get out."

Her eyes widened in horror. "Will the hospital tell people who call that I'm on the loony ward?"

"No, they'll say you are in isolation and cannot have visitors. You'll have a few days to think up a good story for your friends about why you were kept in isolation."

Regan thought that over while I carried the sodden towels to the sink and squeezed them out. She said, her voice thick with tears, "The doctor said . . . he said I'm not pregnant. He said I'm going through menopause!" She burst into tears. "I'm too young for menopause!"

In that moment I saw her as a patient, not my overbearing sister. I laid a comforting hand on her feet. "Actually you aren't, and it's not the end of the world."

"God promised me a baby! That other woman was sixty when she had hers."

"Women aren't all the same. I'm sorry." I knew that would be little comfort.

"God promised me. He did!" She turned her face into her pillow and sobbed.

I spoke softly and calmly. "Maybe God will give you a child another way. You don't really want to go through childbirth, do you? It's messy, and it hurts. You can get a child in far less painful ways."

Her voice was muffled by her hands. "Holcomb would never adopt."

I squeezed her hand. "He might. When you get home, tell him how much you want a child. Ask him if he can love a child for your sake. He's crazy about you, you know."

She cried softly for a few minutes. "I was so sure!"

"I was sure King was going to leave me the house," I reminded her. "We don't always get things we are sure of."

She looked up, not so beautiful with her face damp and pink. "Were you this disappointed about the house?"

"Probably."

"You didn't try to kill yourself."

"No."

She reached out a hand and I took it. Hers was wet and sticky from tears. "You are stronger than I am. Will you stay with me a little while? I need you."

I felt tears sting my own eyes. Of course I would help her. That was what I did best. But when I opened my mouth to say so, I remembered the pond and a small woman hurling cows. "I'll come see you every day," I promised, "but I won't sleep over."


As Holcomb and I passed through the lobby going home, a family was coming in. The man and his four children all had shiny black eyes, short upper lips, two large front teeth, and small chins. Holcomb nodded toward them and said softly, "Bloodlines are funny things, aren't they? Look at that family of beavers. Anybody would know they are related. Have you ever thought about how many good bloodlines vanish without a trace?" We'd reached the sidewalk. Ever courteous, Holcomb took my elbow to escort me to his Mercedes. "King's and mine, for instance." He sounded downright morose.

"King's bloodline hasn't disappeared," I pointed out as I got in the passenger seat. "Susan, Regan, and I are still alive and well." While Holcomb came around the car, I sent up a prayer of gratitude that that was still true.

I hoped the conversation was over, but Holcomb continued as soon as he got behind the wheel. "The MacAllester name will die with you, though, and the whole family is nearly kaput. Teddy had no children and King had only you three girls and Monique."

"There's Wonder," I reminded him as he started the engine.

"Well, yes, but she's—" He must have seen my expression, because I was certain he changed what he was going to say. "King has no sons to carry on the MacAllester name, and one great-grandchild is a very thin generational line."

"Wonder is far too vibrant to be considered a thin line."

He heaved a sigh as deep as one of hers. "Well, our whole family will die out with me. My granddaddy had three sons. You'd think there would be six or seven of my generation around, but Daddy was the only one of them to have children who lived to adulthood, then Regan and I couldn't have kids, and my brother never had any before he died. It's like our whole family is under a curse or something. Mama's family—well, she has a few distant cousins, but she was an only child."

In my opinion, it was a good thing Ginny Linn's parents had had the good sense to realize that one of her was plenty.

Holcomb didn't expect a reply. He was only using me as a sounding board for his thoughts. "With Carleton dead and us not having kids—"

I must have jerked somewhere, because Holcomb gave me a keen look. "Was that what all this"—he gestured back toward the hospital—"was about? Regan wanting kids?"

Since he'd asked . . . "She does want a child. I talked to her early this morning and she was all excited because she thought she was pregnant."

He wavered between scorn and surprise. "Why didn't she tell me?"

"I think she wanted to be sure first. Instead, the doctor told her she's starting menopause. I think hearing that was what drove her over the edge." I gathered my courage and stepped in where I had no business being. "You might consider adopting once she gets out of here."

He shook his head. "Adopting wouldn't be fair to a child. I couldn't ever love it the way I would my own flesh and blood."

"Adoptive parents say that isn't so. Once you have a child, you love it."

"Maybe for some people. Not for me. I am ashamed of it, Teensie. I know that's not the way I ought to feel, but I'm not perfect. You know I'm crazy about Regan. I'd do anything for that woman that I could. I don't feel I ever could love a child who wasn't my own flesh and blood, though." He reached into his pocket for a cigar, gave it a mournful look, and rolled it between his hands, but he was considerate enough not to light it in a closed car.

"I've been looking into our genealogy," he said. "Did you know I have two ancestors who came over on the *Mayflower*? One branch of the family stretches all the way back to William the Conqueror."

I was tempted to boast, "One branch of mine stretches all the way back to Noah," but it was no time to be flip. He was dead serious. As Regan had said, listening to Holcomb on the subject of family was like reading a Dick Francis novel where people pored over racehorse stud books.


I drove Regan home from the hospital on one of our coldest days on record, but the way she huddled in her seat had nothing to do with the cold. "What's on the calendar this week?" I asked, trying to cheer her up. "A dinner party or two? Wrapping presents for a hundred needy children?"

"Holcomb rescheduled the company parties for a restaurant," she told me in a listless voice. "His secretary told people I've had the flu." That was the story she had settled on: a sudden attack of flu. Sometimes I thought she even believed it. "He said he'd think about adopting when I'm stronger, but he thinks we're too old for a baby. I'm old, Teensie! I'm going through menopause! In a year or two I'll look like a hag!"

"Mother didn't look like a hag even when she died," I reminded her.

"Mother didn't go through menopause until she was over fifty."

How did Regan know that and I didn't, when I was the nurse? Just one more evidence of how little my mother had confided in me.

For the next week I did home visits in the morning and, since Monique no longer needed me to keep Wonder daily, I went to Regan's every afternoon. Regan slept until noon and ate little of the tempting foods Lynyetta prepared. She snapped at all of us, cried on my shoulder, and raged at God. "He promised! He promised!" She and I watched old movies, worked out in their home gym, and swam in the heated pool. At least once an hour she searched her mirror for signs of aging.

I offered to drive her to her first session with a counselor that the hospital had recommended, but she informed me haughtily, "I canceled that. I do not need counseling. I need God to keep his promise to give me a child." She punished God by flat-out refusing to go to church.

I went to the college chapel on Sunday to sing in the choir. Coco clutched my arm at the door. "Did I hear correctly? Are you spending all your time at Regan's now that she's out of the hospital?"

"Just afternoons."

"You're falling right back into your old patterns, taking care of anybody in your family who crooks a finger. Regan had the flu, right?"

I nodded reluctantly. I hated lying to Coco.

"So she's not dying," Coco continued. "And she's got Lynyetta at her beck and call. She does not need you. Don't keep going over there." She gave me a little shake.

"It's only until she's a little stronger," I said. "She really does need me right now. She's weak and weepy and Lynyetta has work to do."

The truth was, I needed to go, since I couldn't be up at the farm with Tobias. I would get over him, I frequently promised myself, but I needed a little time.

When Regan still hadn't gotten back into her normal Christmas swing after a week at home, I began to worry. Granted she was sad that she wasn't pregnant, but she seemed more unhappy that she was menopausal. If something didn't change soon, my beautiful sister was going to talk herself into a major depression over getting old.

She constantly begged me to come live with them "until I feel better." That wasn't likely to happen. Aging is not a condition that improves. If she did finally accept her age, wouldn't she then start in on how much Ginny Linn needed me? Lacking any other plan for my life, I was afraid I'd succumb, so I returned to Darla's each evening to eat dinner and spend the night in my own small room.

I got little sleep. I lay in bed wishing I could go back up the mountain once more to check on Tobias. Was he getting stronger? Was his sister feeding him properly? Was he doing too much too soon? Did he ever lie in his bed, as I did, reliving our kiss?

*You fool, you are making too much of that*, I told myself

severely. *Regan is right. You don't have much experience with men. He simply hadn't had a woman around for a while and you were lonely. Both of you would have kissed anybody who was handy that night. It was a combination of cabin fever, lamplight, and music.*

I could tell myself that, but I couldn't make myself believe it.

Like some adolescent in the grip of calf love, I looked around when I went to town, wondering if I'd catch a glimpse of him in the grocery store or the bank. When our choir held its Christmas Season concert, I could have sworn I saw Tobias in the audience at the back, but the lights were so dim it could have been anybody tall and dark.

That night I forced myself to reread what Mr. Knightley says about young Harriet Smith in Jane Austen's *Emma*: she was "a good-tempered, soft-hearted girl not likely to be very, very determined against any young man who told her he loved her." In my current unsettled state, had I become that immature? I hoped not, but I pressed my hand to my lips to reenact the pressure of Tobias's kiss. I remembered the silent looks that had passed between us. I recalled how sweet he had been to Wonder, how he'd wanted to play chess and taught me to play poker, and how he'd said I had a pleasant voice. Oh, Tobias! In some fairy tales a princess marries a farm boy!

The next morning I was sensible again. *One kiss does not a future make*, I reminded myself. *You would be a fool to turn one brief incident between two lonely people into a teenage crush.* I remembered the finality of his last "Good-bye, princess," and made a fresh resolve to forget Tobias Jones.

The problem was, he had budded feelings in me that had lain dormant for years. I yearned for somebody to love. My body ached for a body to love.

I still painted birdhouses in the evenings. Thank heavens, with college on break, we had finished painting Main for a while, but Coco was on a kick building historic homes of North

Georgia. Each one was different and required concentration if I was to get the details right. After I painted the houses for little bird families, I filled my sketchbooks with a homeless bluebird exposed to storms, snow, and hail. My future looked as bleak as the weather.

"Come stay with us for the holidays," Regan begged.

I decided to accept. Mimi was closing the clinic. Darla was going to her daughter's again. Susan and Albert had made the unprecedented decision to take Monique and Wonder to Disney World for a few days over Christmas. Coco, the judge, and Gage had decided to take a cruise through the Panama Canal. After the autumn I'd had, I deserved a touch of luxury, too.

I went over the day before Christmas Eve and found Regan on the phone. "I couldn't! I just couldn't! Oh, honey, I know you do, but . . . Everybody else? You know I've been sick. No, I'm not contagious any longer. I won't have to wrap toys, will I? Just carry them in and wish everybody Merry Christmas?" She sighed. "I guess I could do a few. I'll have my sister do the driving."

She hung up and flopped on her couch. "Two of the women from church who were supposed to deliver Christmas baskets tomorrow have come down with the flu. They need me to deliver baskets in Unizilla." She glared at me. "And don't say this is God punishing me for lying that *I* had the flu."

I was pretty sure God would not punish Regan for lying by giving other women the flu, but giving her a reason to be out and about could be God's answer to *my* prayers. If she would leave the house, I didn't mind spending Christmas Eve driving her Lexus all over town with a backseat and trunk filled with baskets.

Our last stop was Lena Thompson's. As I pulled up in front

of her house, I remembered my conversation with Monique about her. I also remembered what the house used to look like. Lena lived in the neat brick ranch her father and mother had built soon after she was born. Jack Bates had been house-proud, and almost every hour he wasn't at the grocery store he had devoted to his house and yard.

Nobody had devoted time or energy to that house for a long time. The lawn Jack had worked so hard to cultivate was covered with last fall's leaves. A rusty tricycle lay on its side, ready to ambush a mower. A big oak had dropped dead limbs across the mess like decorations on an ugly cake. The green front door was peeling.

Regan carried a box of toys and I carried a basket of food to the front stoop, then I returned to the car. I might one day have to visit Lena in my capacity as a nurse, and I didn't want to confuse my roles. I saw Regan ring the bell, wait, then knock. On her second knock Lena opened the door. She wore a housecoat of faded red and her hair looked like it hadn't been combed for days. Regan stiffened; then I saw her relax and knew she had put on a gracious smile. Nobody I knew did gracious better than Regan.

She didn't hand Lena the stuff and run, either. She stepped inside the house and the door closed behind her. Ten minutes passed before she loped out to the car. She waited until I pulled away before she exhaled like somebody who has run a marathon.

"Phew! That was absolutely the smelliest place I have ever been in." She waved a hand in front of her face to dispel lingering odors. "It just reeks of bourbon."

"Were the children there?"

"Yes, and Alice, too. Did you know she was working there? She said hello, but the boy didn't take his eyes off the television the whole time I was there and the little girl hid behind her mother's dirty robe. The older girl was the only one to thank me for their presents. Her mother had the nerve to ask in a whisper if I had any cash because she needed to get 'a few things' at the grocery store. We both knew what she wanted to buy. But oh, Teensie! When I set down the box of toys, the older girl saw a Barbie doll in it. She picked it up and gave it to her little sister. Can you imagine?"

Such a selfless big sister had certainly never been my experience.

"The little one clasped that doll like it was the most precious thing in the world. Then the older girl pulled out a red sweater in her size, and you'd have thought I'd given her a whole Macy's." Regan leaned her head against the seat and I saw tears glint in her eyes. "This is what Christmas is about. I'm glad I didn't miss it."

I reached out and gave her hand a squeeze. "I'm glad you didn't, too."

# *Nine*

When I returned to the clinic the Tuesday after New Year's, Mimi said, "I'd like you to see old Mrs. Parker this morning." She hesitated, then said quickly, "Why don't you make a quick check on Tobias Jones as well?"

I gave her what I hoped was a casual nod. "If you like. He ought to be pretty well by now, so maybe we can close out the case."

Neither of us mentioned our prior conversation about Mr. Jones. I wondered if by any chance she had deduced that I cared for him. Mimi was a romantic under that practical exterior.

I decided to see Tobias first. That way I would have old Mrs. Parker as an excuse for leaving as soon as I'd made sure he was all right. *That*, I reminded myself as I turned in at Jones Farm Road, *is your reason for going.*

His road was better now that the ground had frozen solid. It was still rutted and rough, but not slick. The woods were stark and clean against a deep sky that looked freshly dusted by the high feathery branches of pines on long brown trunks. I found myself singing, "She'll be coming 'round the mountain" as I headed into the cove.

My treacherous heart gave a lurch when I saw Tobias leaning against the paddock fence, stroking Bray's ears. *Cool it, Teensie*, I told myself. *This is a professional visit*. But oh, he looked good.

In a heavy jacket and an old brown hat, he looked as rugged and enduring as the mountains. I hoped he realized that like them, he also could be worn down by too much exposure to rough elements.

Homer came barking a warning toward the truck, but he wagged his tail when he recognized me. As I climbed down, he slobbered all over my shoes. Tobias half lifted his hand in a wave like he was glad to see me, but then he dropped it like a railroad crossing bar. "I told the doctor you didn't need to come back," he yelled as I walked toward him. "I thought maybe you had finally listened."

"I pretty much go where I want to." I kept my tone light. "My days of doing what others tell me to are over."

I was glad the wind whipped hair across my face so he couldn't see how glad I was to see him. His face wore no expression whatsoever.

Far across the yard, Lucky and Tom started toward me with a babble of greetings. Tom slowed his mincing gait to Lucky's dragging one.

I waited until I joined Tobias at the fence before I spoke again. "Dr. Starnes said your sister was staying with you." My truck was the only vehicle I saw.

"She was for a while. Lucy got worried when my phone was out after the ice storm, so she came to check on me the afternoon you left. Being as bossy as you are, she decided to move in for a while. Her whole family came up during the Christmas holidays and stayed until the New Year and Damien's been coming back on weekends."

"That's good. I haven't been up lately because my sister Regan has been sick."

"I heard something about that. Is she better?"

"Yeah. She'll be fine."

We sounded like people at a cocktail party who scarcely know each other and can't wait to move on to somebody more interesting.

He started picking straw out of Bray's stubby mane. I scratched Bray's side. That old donkey wiggled and pranced like a coquette with a porch full of beaus.

I was looking for something else to talk about to prolong my visit when he asked, "Did you make any New Year's resolutions?"

I plucked a piece of straw from the mane on my side and my hand brushed his. I jumped at the shock that went through me. I quickly bent to scratch Bray's side and hoped Tobias thought my cheeks were pink from the wind. "Yeah, I resolved not to do everything my sisters want me to."

He moved his hand to scratch Bray's other side. "You didn't throw those sisters in a pond yet?"

"No, but I didn't move in with Regan, either, like she wanted me to—until the holidays, and I left right after Christmas. I have also refused to keep Wonder while Monique goes to college, though Susan is furious."

"A giant step for womankind."

"Probably not, but it's a start."

"How is Wonder?"

"Doing fine. She has learned how to dial 911." I told him the story and took it for a gift when he threw back his head and laughed with me.

"Did you make any resolutions?" I asked.

He propped a leg on the fence. "Yeah. I resolved to stay healthy. I need to be working."

"You'll be back to normal in a few weeks."

"I hope so. Are you still working full-time at the clinic?"

"I never did—just mornings." As soon as I'd said it, I wished it back.

He gave me a quizzical stare. "You and Wonder came up here afternoons."

I looked down at Bray so he couldn't read my eyes. "Yeah, well, she goes to preschool until one and she begged me to bring her up to take care of you."

"Plus you thought you had a debt to pay." His tone was flat.

"You were sick. You needed somebody around."

"Since I'm not sick anymore, I guess you'll need to find somebody else to help."

A silence fell between us. I felt like we were two people in a play for which I did not have a script. What should my next line be? Regan would have batted her lashes and said something like, "So we'll have to get together for other reasons."

I wasn't Regan. All I knew to do was give him a straight response.

"What I *need* is to find a full-time job. I applied at the hospital, but they don't have anything right now." The wind was sharp. I drew my collar tighter around my throat. "On days like this, I think about moving to Belize. It's warm and they speak English."

He looked around at his empty fields. "Nice, if you can afford it. I worked myself to death this year and I'll still barely break even."

"If you hadn't lost the college account, could you have made it?" I didn't notice I'd asked a very personal question. We had slipped into easy conversation like we had a few precious times before.

"Oh, yeah. I was doing fine until then, but I did lose the college account. And got hepatitis. Like I told you, God has been conspicuously absent from the cove lately."

He looked toward the house, and his face was sad. I wondered if he was thinking again about his wife and son. Had she left because farming was such an uncertain economic proposition? I found myself wanting to comfort him.

"My aunt used to say God is never absent—that when we think he is, he's working behind the scenes on a project we'll learn about later. I can hear her telling me when I was impatient for something to happen, 'God's timing is not our timing, but God's is perfect.' That's something we both probably need to remember at the moment."

"God's running late up here. I need an infusion of business now."

"Have you ever asked fancy restaurants down in Atlanta whether they might like some of your produce?"

"I've thought about it once or twice."

"You might be able to drive down before you are well enough to work. You're already looking better." He looked great. My whole body tingled being that close to him.

"I get around. Not as much as I'd like to, but my strength is coming back." He moved a few steps down the fence. "So, as you can see, I don't need any more nursing."

Lucky ducked under the fence and waddled up to cluck a greeting. I was glad to bend and stroke her so Tobias couldn't see hurt written on my face. Tom gobbled and got a pat on the head. "Your animals are a lot more hospitable than you are," I muttered.

He gave a grunt. "My animals didn't have to put up with you as much as I did."

We were crossing swords again, but instead of stimulating, I found it painful. "Your animals didn't mind accepting my help."

"That's why they are called dumb animals."

I couldn't think of a sharp retort. I settled for honest. "Look, no matter how much you disliked it, I did care about you getting well, okay? It's what I do."

He stared at the distant mountains like he wished he were up there. Alone. He breathed hard like a bull ready for the ring.

"What you do . . ." He clutched the top rail so hard his hands trembled.

"What I do . . . ?" I prodded.

His voice was so low I almost couldn't hear. "What you do is get under a man's skin until he can't think straight. You beat him at chess, then tell him it's okay because he's sick. You haul wood and feed animals in an ice storm, then show up in a pink fluffy robe looking like a child. You are—" When he looked at me, I thought for one dizzy second that he was going to pull me into his arms.

I couldn't remember how to breathe.

"You are a MacAllester and an Ingram!" His yell filled the cove. He gave the top rail a smack and strode off toward a distant apple tree.

I was so astonished, I forgot to scratch the donkey.

Bray gave a surprised *hee-haw?* at the interruption. Lucky and Tom waddled after Tobias, scolding all the way. Homer followed Tobias for a few steps, then stopped to give me a puzzled look over his shoulder. *Aren't you coming?*

I hesitated. Should I follow? Or should I get in my truck and go home? Tell Mimi somebody else needed to make future visits to Tobias Jones? I felt like I was balancing at the center of a seesaw: one step in either direction could irrevocably change my future.

I decided to go to him. By the time I got there, he had his arms propped on the lowest branch of the tree and was staring at the mountains.

"I know who I am, Tobias," I said softly. "What difference does that make?"

He glared down at me over one shoulder. "Do you remember the summer the college put a new roof on Main?"

"Yeah. I had just finished high school. Why?"

"I worked on that roof. Daddy was in construction and his crew got the bid. One day you came prancing by in a little green dress and expensive sandals looking like you'd stepped out of the shower a minute before, and you looked up at us on that sweltering roof and you called, 'Hey, up there, it's mighty hot. Do you all need lemonade?'"

"I don't remember that." Where was he going with that story?

"No reason you should. We were only sweaty roofers. Besides, the whole thing didn't last a minute. Daddy called down, 'Thanks, but we brought our own drinks,' and you called, 'Be careful, then. We don't want you to fall,' and you pranced off to whatever nice, cool thing you had to do. When you'd gone, Daddy spat and said, 'She's not bad, for one of them.' And I said, 'One of who?' He said, 'The MacAllesters and the Ingrams. Don't get mixed up with those families. They took our land and they took our pride. Don't you ever forget it. But I guess that one is the best of the bunch.'"

I circled the tree and looked over the branch at him. "Look, I can't help who I was born, and I don't intend to apologize for it. My family did good things for Unizilla, and my daddy did good things for the college. It sounds like your daddy did good things for the college, too—but what does that have to do with *us*?"

There. I'd said it. *Us.*

I held my breath. In any decent story he would declare, "Nothing at all," and he would duck under that branch and come to me.

Tobias shook both fists at heaven. "Oh, God, I don't need this!" It sounded like a prayer from Job. He rested his head on the trunk. "Go home!" he begged. "You don't belong here! These mountains are *mine*!"

That made me madder than anything my sisters had ever

done. Madder than King's betrayal, even. I propped one hand on my hip and yelled loud enough to be heard in Unizilla. "You don't have exclusive rights to these mountains! They are my mountains, too! You can sit up here ornery and alone all your born days, *but you can't have these mountains*!"

He stepped toward me then, his face dark with fury. "You sound exactly like your many-great-granddaddy talking to mine: 'You can't have these mountains!' I'll bet you still have the deed to Cherokee land your mother's people bought when Georgia first offered it for sale. Where is it—in a family scrapbook? Or in the bank with some of that famous *Ingram* gold?"

That cut like a scalpel. The deed was framed. It used to hang in King's study, with a tiny nugget of gold embedded in it. When I was Wonder's age I already knew to point it out to visitors, proud as we all were that it was the oldest such deed in our county. Albert would probably put it in the library in a glass case.

The pain my family had inflicted on Tobias's was too old, too deep for us to bridge.

Tobias must have seen the misery in my face. He clenched and unclenched his fists, breathing hard, until he had calmed down, then his voice was gentle. "I'm sorry, Deborah. That wasn't called for. None of what happened back then was your fault—or mine. But it does make a difference to us, here and now."

"I wish I could help. . . ."

"You can't help everything and everybody. Get that through your head. You did help me. You probably saved my life. But like you told your sister, you were the nurse and I was the patient. That's all we were. That's all we're ever going to be. You've done your job here, so please go. Since helping other people is what turns you on, go find somebody else to help. I've got work to do." With a salute he strode toward the barn.

I hadn't been on a seesaw at all. It was a waxed sliding board. In that instant, I plunged to the bottom.

\* \* \*

I would not let Tobias see me cry. That resolution got me inside my truck with a few shreds of dignity, although I stumbled twice on the way. I slammed the door hard. When I looked out my windshield, he was standing beside the fence watching me—probably making sure I left.

I rolled down the window. "Keep your precious cove, Mr. Jones," I yelled. "I don't need any more ingrates in my life." I turned the truck and roared down his drive.

I made it around the first bend before I started to bawl. Tears so blurred my vision that I had to stop. I would not pitch off the side of the mountain and have Tobias think I had killed myself over him.

"He's as ungrateful as my family," I raged. "No matter how much I do for them, they don't care once they don't need me. Alice was right. After today, I take care of number one. Tobias can jolly well take care of himself. But you will learn, Mr. Jones, that you can't do everything for yourself. Try as you will, you cannot live without the help of others. It won't be me helping you, though. No sirree. You will have to find somebody else. I'm done!"

I couldn't stop the tears that streamed down my face and soaked my blouse, though. I couldn't help remembering how strong and *right* he had looked standing against the mountains. I could scarcely endure the pain in my chest. Until that minute I had thought "broken heart" was a metaphor. I discovered it is having your heart drawn and quartered by invisible threads until the pain threatens your sanity.

I needed to get down the mountain. What if Tobias had an errand to run? I didn't want him to find me still on his road. But it took me a while to reach the bottom. I could hardly see to drive for my tears.

Yet somewhere in the back of my sorrow, I kept hearing one little phrase he had used. "It does make a difference to us." *Us*, he had said. *Us*. I held on to that word like a talisman. Maybe Tobias wasn't totally stuck in our past.


The highway was in sight when my phone chirped again.

"Where are you?" Mimi asked.

I swallowed and hoped my voice wasn't too clogged. "Heading to see Mrs. Parker. Mr. Jones is fine."

"Good. Save Mrs. Parker for tomorrow. Right now I need you to get over to Lena Thompson's. Her little girl called to say her mother is breathing funny, but the child doesn't know if it's an emergency. Go check on her, please."

As I turned onto the highway, I remembered Tobias's words: "Since helping others is what turns you on . . ."

*Helping* some *people, Mr. Jones. Only some.*

To Mimi I said, "I'm on my way."

Except for taking Regan by the house on Christmas Eve, I had never called on Lena Thompson. She and the children had come to the clinic, I was sure, but they had never needed a home visit before.

I tried the doorbell, heard nothing, then knocked. "Hello! It's Miss MacAllester from the clinic."

"Come in," yelled somebody over the sound of a television.

My eyes adjusted to the dimness of an unlit room furnished only with a couch and a television. The blinds were shut. The boy who had laughed at Phil and me aeons ago sprawled on the couch watching a game show. He exuded the rancid smell of dirty boy.

"Hello, Eric? I'm Miss MacAllester, a nurse from the clinic. I've come to see your mother."

He sat up. Uncombed dark bangs fell into eyes like black forest pools. He was a scrawny young adolescent dressed only in a faded navy T-shirt and khaki shorts, but he had inherited Lena's smoky good looks. His manners could use some improving.

"Kaitlin," he bellowed, "it's the nurse." To me he added, "Close the door. You're letting light on the screen." He lay back down to watch his show.

"Shouldn't you be in school?"

He gave a shrug that was more a guilty wiggle. "I'm not feeling too good."

"Shall I have a look at you later?"

He squirmed. "Nah, it's nothing. Mama's the one who needs help." He added under his breath, "Lotsa help."

Kaitlin hurried in from the hall, little Carrie at her heels. "I am so glad you've come. Come look at Mama. Hurry!" Her small face was pinched with worry, but at her best she would not have been pretty. Her nose was sharp, her chin pointed. Her hair was dark like her brother's, but lank and unkempt. Her eyes were the indeterminate dark of swamp water.

Carrie was lovely. Even unwashed, her hair hung in curls the color of molasses in sunshine and framed a pair of wide blue-gray eyes. A thumb plugged her mouth.

If the oldest and youngest children had inherited the family beauty, the middle child had inherited its burdens. Beneath a faded green sweatshirt, Kaitlin's thin shoulders sloped under an invisible yoke. I ached at the poignancy of that small back as I followed her down an unlit hall. "Sorry, the bulb's burnt out," she said. I wondered how long it had been gone.

"Where's Alice?" I asked. "I thought she worked here."

"She used to, but her mother got sick so she stopped coming."

"How long ago?"

"A couple of weeks."

"Does Judge Brantley know?"

"I didn't want to bother him. Alice might be back next week."

"Have you all been going to school?"

"Not recently. We haven't done laundry for a while."

I wondered if the school board counted that as a legitimate excuse.

Lena's room was a jumble of clothes, magazines, and cosmetics. The closet was full of liquor bottles. She lay on a mattress on the floor, her skin as gray as her dingy sheets. They molded a body that was little more than a skeleton. Dark hair lay over her face in lank strands. Her eyes were surrounded by circles like a heavy thumb had pressed in bruises. Her breathing was shallow. When I took her pulse, it was reedy and irregular.

"We need to get your mother to the hospital right away." I pulled my cell phone from my pocket. "I'm going to call an ambulance. Why don't you take your little sister in the living room until it gets here?"

"Okay. Come on, Carrie." Kaitlin put an arm around her sister's shoulders.

"I wants juice," Carrie said. As they went down the hall, I heard her ask, "Is Mommy gonna die?" I could not hear her sister's reply.

As I punched in the number, Lena groaned. I hurried to her bedside. "Don't . . . don't split up my kids. Don't . . . split up my kids." Her head rolled from side to side on the pillow.

"Hush," I told her. "I'm calling an ambulance. They'll get you to the hospital."

"Don't split up my kids!" Her eyes were wild.

"We won't." I hardly knew what I was saying. The 911 operator had answered.

As Lena was wheeled from her home, Kaitlin watched with worried eyes. Carrie sucked her thumb. Eric was too engrossed in the television to pay any attention.

"Let's get ready and go to the hospital," I said.

The surly look Eric shot me showed he recognized my cheerful voice for the hypocrisy it was. "I'm not going." He returned to watching his show.

Kaitlin ran to her room and came back brushing her hair. "I'm ready."

Carrie scurried toward the bathroom, pulling her shirt over her head. "Wants a baf."

"We don't have time for a bath," I called after her. "Let me wash your face and hands."

When I got to the bathroom, she had already flung off her clothes and was climbing over the side of a dirty tub. "We don't have time for a bath," I repeated, though she badly needed one.

Her rosebud mouth pouted. Fat tears rolled down her cheeks. "Wants to be pretty for Mama." Tears accelerated into sobs.

Kaitlin came to the bathroom and put an arm around Carrie. "You won't be pretty, baby, if your nose is red from crying."

Carrie blinked twice and her tears stopped as if by magic.

Getting another whiff of her, I said, "Okay, a quick bath—just a soap-up and rinse off."

When Carrie was clean, I wrapped her in a threadbare towel and carried her into the girls' bedroom. It held only a double mattress on the floor and two cardboard boxes of clothes, but the blankets were pulled up on the bed and the few toys were confined to one corner. I credited Kaitlin with doing the best she could. Judge Brantley made sure their bills were paid, but I doubted that he ever went farther inside than the living room. Had Lena sold off her father's furniture to buy alcohol? Why had Alice not reported how bad things were in that family? Probably because, as she often told me, she was a cook, not a maid.

Kaitlin searched for something her sister could wear and came up with a wrinkled pink dress and yellow socks. When Carrie was dressed, Kaitlin handed her scuffed brown shoes.

"I can't wear dose shoes," Carrie objected. "Dey hurts my toes."

"She's outgrown them," Kaitlin told me with an embarrassed flush. "I've been meaning to get her some more, but we haven't had anybody to carry us to the store." She fetched blue sandals from the closet and buckled them on her sister's feet.

"I'm hungry," Eric called from the living room.

I checked my watch. "It's not time yet for lunch."

Kaitlin ducked her head. "I haven't fixed breakfast yet. Mama was breathing funny, and—" Her voice wobbled. She swallowed hard. I had to swallow hard, too. A child her age should not have to carry the weight of an entire family.

After Lena reached the hospital it would be some time before the children could see her. "Let me fix you something before we go."

"I can fix it." Kaitlin pushed Carrie off her lap. "Come on, baby. Let's go fix breakfast."

Carrie picked up a naked Barbie doll that looked familiar. Could it possibly be the one Regan gave her for Christmas? If so, it had been loved to grubby. Holding the doll upside down in one hand, she stuck her other thumb in her mouth and padded after Kaitlin.

I went back to Lena's room. Nobody could straighten that chaos in the time it took to fix a small meal, so I settled for stripping the bed. I wandered to the kitchen with an armload of smelly linen to ask if they had a washing machine. I found Kaitlin cutting moldy crusts off white bread as if it were a familiar ritual. While I watched unobserved, she pulled a jar of grape jelly from the refrigerator and set it beside the bread. She spread one slice of bread with jelly, folded it in half, and handed it to Carrie. Carrie stood beside the table and ate while Kaitlin made four whole jelly sandwiches and set them on paper towels. After she mixed a package of cherry Kool-Aid with water she yelled, "Eric, breakfast is ready."

When Eric loped in, he took all four of the sandwiches and a glass of Kool-Aid back to the television. Kaitlin noticed me by the door. "Do you want some?"

The child only had two slices of bread left and she was offering me a sandwich?

"I've eaten, but thanks." I was tempted to gather them up in my truck and take them to Danny's Diner, but I didn't want to offend the small chef. "I was wondering if you all have a washing machine."

"Oh, yeah, we got one in there." She jerked her head toward the utility room. A pile of laundry on the floor was as tall as the washer. She must have noticed my dismay, because she came to the door to explain, "It hasn't worked for a while, but we're gonna get it fixed when we get ahead a little. Put them on the pile. Eric and I will carry them to the Laundromat later."

"You can't carry all that. It would fill my truck."

"We only take the most important stuff. We'll fix the washer next month if I can save up some." I wondered how long the clothes on the bottom had been ripening in anticipation.

"Judge Brantley would pay to get it fixed," I reminded her.

Kaitlin looked down at her bare feet and I saw shame flush her cheeks. "He already paid a man to fix it."

She stopped, her eyes downcast, but Eric didn't mind finishing. "Mama told the man there'd been a mistake," he called, "so he gave her the money back and she bought booze."

How often had that happened without the judge's guessing a thing?

In the next half hour Kaitlin casually introduced me to several items in the Thompson home that were waiting for the apocalypse. The dishwasher—broken—was used to store boxes of cereal and other frequently used items. "They're a lot easier to reach," said the four-foot-tall mistress of the household. Bags of garbage, some splitting at the seams, sat on the back porch "until Eric has time to carry them to the curb." A microwave on the counter, so old it must have dated from Lena's childhood, was full of canned goods. "Those ovens aren't healthy for you anyway, Mama says."

That would be the health-conscious mother who had been rushed to the hospital after ingesting what looked like a fatal combination of alcohol and prescription meds?

"Do you have anywhere you all can stay until your mother is better?" I asked.

"Not that I know of. I guess we ought to call Judge Brantley. He's our trusty. He oughta know Mama's sick."

Poor Judge Brantley. When he had promised Jack that he would serve as Lena's trustee, had he guessed he'd have to find housing for three children one day? What could he do with them?

With great foreboding I dialed the familiar number.

Coco sounded rushed. "You're lucky you caught me. I ran home from the hospital to get a few things, but don't worry—it wasn't as serious as we'd feared."

For a bewildered instant I thought she was talking about Lena. "Not as serious as we'd feared?"

"No, he has a broken arm and a slight concussion, and he can't remember a thing about it, but the doctor thinks he'll eventually regain his memory."

"Who?"

"Daddy. Didn't you know he'd had an accident this morning? He was pulling onto the highway and some speeder ran into him. They rushed him to the hospital by ambulance, but he's going to be all right. I thought that was why you were calling."

"No! I've been out all morning and hadn't heard. Thank goodness the judge is all right."

"Yes, we were fortunate. Why were you calling, then?"

"Lena Thompson went to the hospital a little while ago. I'm

at the house with the children right now, and we'll be coming pretty soon."

"Oh, my! I'll call Gage and tell him. He's with Daddy until I get back."

"See you there."

Kaitlin had overheard. Her face more pinched than ever, she asked, "The judge is in the hospital? Is he going to die?" Reflected in her eyes I saw a vision of all the important adults in her world disappearing one by one.

"Of course not. Miss Coco says he's going to be fine. He just had a little accident. Maybe we can go by and see him while we're at the hospital."

But we didn't leave. Carrie and Kaitlin were still eating their sandwiches and I was trying to make a dent in the chaos that was Lena's room when Gage called. "Lena died on her way to the hospital. Poor thing, she's finally at peace, but we need to think what to do about those children. Could Alice stay with them a while?"

I closed the bedroom door so I couldn't be overheard. "Alice hasn't been here for weeks. Her mother is sick."

Silence revealed his shock. "Nobody told us that." He paused to think. "I don't guess you could stay with them for a few days, could you?"

"Not here. The house is filthy, they have no food, the washing machine is broken, and the place stinks to high heaven of dirty clothes and bourbon. I'd take them over to Darla's with me, but she's still at her daughter's and I wouldn't want to invite guests into her house without her permission. Besides, she doesn't have a television, and Eric and TV seem joined at the hip. Not to mention that I don't know what I would do with them while I work. Could you take them?"

"No, I've got painters in this week. And Granddaddy's going to be in no shape to have kids in the house when he gets out of here tomorrow. Let me think about it. As far as I know, the children have no relatives, but I don't like to call social services."

"I agree. I doubt if any foster family would be willing to take three children of such different ages, and once the children entered the system, who knows how long it would take to get them out again?"

He heaved a sigh. "What a day this has been! Can you stay there a little while until I've finished the paperwork for Lena? I'll call you back and we can talk."

"I'll be here, but hurry. The air in this place is not fit for human consumption."

I gathered the children in the living room. Over Eric's protests I turned off the television and asked them all to sit on the couch. I knelt on the floor in front of them. "Gage Brantley called. I am so sorry, but your mother died on her way to the hospital."

"She died?" Kaitlin seemed more shocked than sad.

"I figured she would." Eric sounded no more concerned than if I had announced they were out of milk.

Carrie started to bellow. "Mama! I wants my mama! I wants my mama!" She sounded angry rather than heartbroken. When I tried to take her into my arms, she flailed and fought me.

Kaitlin slapped her hard. "Stop that!"

I was about to admonish her, but as soon as Carrie's yells stopped, Kaitlin pulled her onto her lap. "Don't worry, baby. I'll be your mama now." Carrie snuggled into her embrace as if it were a familiar retreat.

"Where is Mommy?" she asked me.

Kaitlin answered before I could. "Mama's an angel now. She's with Daddy, and Granddaddy Jack, and Buster—" She interrupted her litany to explain to me, "He was our dog."

"I wanna go be with Mommy and Buster and all the nangels." Carrie sat up in Kaitlin's arms, ready to leave.

Kaitlin clasped her tightly and rocked her. "You wouldn't have pretty clothes in heaven. All you'd have is one white robe."

"I doesn't want one white robe."

"Then you'll have to stay here with me."

"Okay."

I looked at Kaitlin in admiration. The child ought to be teaching a graduate course in psychology.

Carrie asked me around her thumb, "Are you a nangel?"

"No, I'm a nurse. I like your baby doll. What's her name?"

Carrie took her thumb out of her mouth long enough to say, "Wegan Alice."

"Regan Alice?" I wasn't sure I had heard correctly.

Kaitlin explained, "Miss Regan Harris brought her the doll for Christmas, so Carrie named it Regan, but she didn't want to hurt Alice's feelings, so—"

"She's Wegan *Alice*." Carrie held the doll up for my admiration.

"She's very pretty." Except for the matted hair, the doll looked a bit like Regan.

Kaitlin's gaze met mine over her sister's curls. "What do we do now?"

I was about to tell her that Gage was working on that when Carrie said, "I wants Miss Wegan. She's nice."

Was that worth a try? "I need to run out to my truck for something," I said.

"Are you leaving?" Worry wrinkles around Kaitlin's eyes deepened.

"No, no, honey, I'll be right back. In fact, I'll leave my keys here on the television while I'm outside, all right?"

I hurried to the far side of my truck and pulled out my phone. "Okay, Regan," I muttered as I pushed my speed dial button. "How far does your compassion stretch?"

\*     \*     \*

Regan listened to my pitch, then asked in a bewildered voice, "What? You want us to take in three foster kids?"

"Not foster kids—Lena Thompson's children. Lena died this morning and they mentioned you because you brought them Christmas baskets. Remember the girl who gave her little sister the Barbie doll? The doll is now named Regan Alice."

"That little one was a sweetheart."

"She's also an orphan. Could you just take them for a few days until Judge Brantley gets out of the hospital?"

"The judge is in the hospital? What's the matter with him?"

I went through that explanation again. "The problem is," I concluded, "he's these children's trustee and needs a place to put them until he is able to deal with them."

"I don't know. . . ."

"Come on, Regan. I'm sitting in my truck and I'm freezing out here. These children desperately need a safe, happy place to be for a few days. If I was still in the marble house I could take them, but I'm not. Won't you do it? Please?"

"I don't know how to help grieving children."

"I haven't seen a sign of grief in any of them. I think the older two are mostly relieved. They may grieve eventually, but I don't think they'll give you any trouble for a few days. Lynyetta can do most of the child care and you'd only have them until the judge can make other arrangements."

"Our house isn't set up for children."

"Ask Lynyetta to put away the breakables."

"I don't know a thing about teenage boys."

"Holcomb ought to—he was one once. Besides, this boy seems to do nothing but watch television. He'd adore the room I stayed in."

I held my breath while she thought it over. "Just for a few days?"

I could tell she was weakening. I pressed the advantage. "Only until the judge can find them a permanent home."

"Will you bring them, or do I need to come get them?"

I pumped air with one fist and tried not to sound too elated. "I don't have seat belts for them all in my truck. Why don't you send Lynyetta to get them?" Lynyetta drove a van Holcomb had bought her several years back.

"Okay. I'll tell her. How soon should she come?"

"Give me half an hour to tell them and get things organized here."

I found all three children still sitting in the living room. "I've been arranging a place for you to stay," I told them.

"We can stay here," Eric said without turning from the TV.

"You can't stay here alone, so for a few days you are going to stay with Miss Regan and Mr. Holcomb Harris. They will take care of you until the judge gets out of the hospital—"

"What's the matter with the judge?" That was the first interest the boy had shown in anything.

Feeling like a recording, I explained again, ending with, "So I need for you all to help me gather up your clothes to take to a new place for a few days."

The cardboard boxes that served for chests were pitifully empty. "Most of our clothes are dirty," Kaitlin explained. "Like I said, Eric and me haven't got around to washing this week."

"We can take dirty clothes. Miss Regan's cook will wash them." In the kitchen I found a supply of black plastic garbage bags—probably because they were something Lena couldn't sell. Kaitlin filled two of them with dirty clothes she pulled from the pile by the washer. I tried not to breathe the rank odors that came with them.

As we collected their pitifully few clean clothes in another bag, I asked Kaitlin, "Does Carrie go to preschool?"

"She goes to day care over to Miss Willowby's." Kaitlin's mind was on more important things. "Will robbers come steal our things while we're gone?"

If robbers came, they would most likely empty their own wallets in pity, but I didn't say that. Kaitlin was trying hard to take responsibility for what family she had left. "No, honey, we'll lock up tight, and I'll ask the sheriff to send somebody by every day or two to be sure things are okay."

"Just tell him Lena's place. He knows right where it is."

I followed Lynyetta and the children to Regan's, to introduce them and help them settle in. On the way I called Mimi to report.

I concluded, "If you don't have anybody for me to see when I'm done at Regan's, I'd like to drive over to the hospital and speak to the judge about the children."

"Go ahead. Sorry to saddle you with all this, but I'm glad it's you I sent over. I know how you like to help people. This certainly gives you a chance to strut your stuff."

I wondered if an angel with a warped sense of humor had been listening in on me back on Jones Farm Road.

Regan touched me with the gracious reception she gave those children. She smiled at Eric and Kaitlin and bent to give Carrie a hug. "You little darling!"

"You smell good," Carrie said, pressing her face into Regan's neck.

Regan gave Eric the suite I'd occupied, with the big television in the sitting room, and gestured toward a credenza. "If you know how to work that electronic game thingie over there, it's yours."

"I can work it, no problem." Eric was pushing buttons before we left.

Regan led the girls down the hall to a room with twin beds. The beds had pink ruffled bedspreads and Regan had unearthed dolls from somewhere to set on each bed. Carrie immediately climbed up to claim the yellow-haired doll. "Dis pretty baby is *mine*."

Kaitlin looked at the brown-haired doll like it was fine china she must not touch. "May we play with them?"

"You can have them," Regan told her.

Kaitlin picked up the doll and cradled it to her skinny chest.

"Isn't God amazing?" Regan asked softly as she and I went back downstairs, leaving Eric watching television and Lynyetta helping the girls unpack. "I found those dolls and the game thingie on sale last summer and bought them for this year's Christmas baskets, but I stuck them on the closet shelf in the girls' room and forgot about them. I found them when I was checking the closet a few minutes ago to be sure they had blankets. God must have known way back last summer that they would be needed."

For once I had no quarrel with her theology. I put my arm around her waist and gave her a squeeze. "Thank God you bought them and thank you for doing this."

"The little girl is a beauty, isn't she? But did you see that dress she has on? It's way too small. And why is she wearing sandals? It's freezing outside."

"She's outgrown her other shoes. She could use new clothes. They all could."

"What fun! I may enjoy having them. But it is only for a few days, right?"

"Only for a few days."

The judge looked small in his hospital bed but elegant in navy silk pajamas. He had a bandage on his head and his left arm in a splint. In spite of that, he was in good spirits. "Isn't this a fine howdy-do?" he greeted me. "One minute I'm setting out to fetch the mail and the next I'm hog-tied in this bed. Gage tells me my car is in pitiful shape, too. We'll have to decide whether to repair it or replace it. I'd sure hate to give up that car. But how have you been, Teensie? We haven't seen much of you lately."

"Regan was under the weather last month, so I spent time with her. She really did need my help," I added, mindful of his warning not to care for those who didn't.

*People like Tobias Jones.*

I pushed that thought back down where it belonged. "Did Gage tell you Lena Thompson died this morning?"

"Coco told me."

Coco spoke from the visitor's chair. "Gage is handling the paperwork and funeral arrangements, since Daddy is non compos mentis at the moment."

The judge bristled with indignation. "There's nothing the matter with my mind! It's only an hour or so of memory I've lost, and the doctor says I'll probably regain that."

"Where are the children?" asked Coco.

"I've taken them to Regan's. I hope that was all right? Gage and I couldn't come up with anything when we spoke."

"Regan's?" The judge's bushy eyebrows rose in surprise. "She agreed to this?"

"I wouldn't have taken them if she hadn't. I've promised her it's only for a few days, though, until you can make other arrangements. While you are lounging around in here waiting for your memory to come back, can you try and figure out where those children ought to go?"

"I'll put on my thinking cap," he promised.

As I prepared to leave, Coco stood up. "I'll walk Teensie downstairs. I think we both need a cup of coffee. See you in a little bit, Daddy."

In the coffee shop she gave me a shrewd look. "So why do you have a 'little girl lost' look in your eye?"

"I don't," I protested. "Or maybe it's because of Lena dying, and thinking about those poor children—"

"Don't give me that. You hardly know those children, and Lena's far better off now than she has been for years. So who's been nibbling your roses—Tobias Jones?"

I wished I already had a coffee cup to hide my blush behind. "Why should you think that? You don't even know the man."

Coco waited until the waitress brought our cups and moved away. "I know a lot more now than I did when we first went up there. I asked Daddy about him and he knew exactly who I meant: the Cherokee organic farmer. I remembered then that I've seen him around. He's real easy on the eyes. Then I ran into Wonder one day in the grocery store with her mother, and she whispered that you and she were going up every afternoon to take care of her 'veg'table man.' Are you getting involved with Tobias Jones?"

I concentrated on watching my spoon go round and round in my cup. "Don't be silly. He hates my family and everything we stand for."

"Why should he?"

A sigh started in the pit of my stomach, but it came out a wail. "Because my mother's people took his people's land." When she looked bewildered, I added, "You know, in the Georgia land lottery."

"That's been two hundred years."

"I know, but he's never gotten over it." In spite of myself I started to cry. I held the flimsy paper napkin to my eyes and it came apart in my fingers.

"Here." Coco handed me a tissue. "Looks to me like you have fallen for him."

"Hush! All I need is for a rumor to circulate in the county that Teensie MacAllester has romantic feelings for a patient. Besides, Tobias is the most ungrateful person I know—except King. The whole time I fed those animals and stoked his stove he kept telling me, 'Go home. I don't need you.' No way I have fallen for *him*." I blew my nose so hard that people at several tables looked our way.

Coco handed me another tissue. "He doesn't sound like a prince. He doesn't even sound like a gentleman."

That riled me. "He's more of a gentleman than you might think. He reads a lot, and plays chess. He also plays the mandolin and sings, and—" I caught myself rhapsodizing and finished lamely, "We talked a lot about Cherokee history."

The former history teacher raised one penciled brow. "What do you know about Cherokee history?"

"I read one of his books and we discussed it."

"And a good old time was had by all."

"Not often. He mostly slept or was grumpy and rude. I can chalk that up to his being sick, but believe me, I did not fall for him and he did not fall for me."

I thought I'd been pretty convincing—so why didn't Coco look convinced? "He doesn't sound at all like somebody Wonder would like."

"He's great with Wonder. He tells her Cherokee folktales and lets her fuss over him like he's her baby. He even let her braid his hair and put bows in it." I couldn't help smiling at that memory.

"And he keeps those animals who look more like pets than farm animals."

"They are. When he sat on the porch one afternoon, the hen settled in his lap like a feathered cat while the turkey and the dog rested beside him."

She gave me a puzzled frown. "If animals like him and children like him, he can't be an ogre. Maybe he pretends to be one to hide his feelings for you."

"He's not hiding a thing. It doesn't matter now, anyway, because as he pointed out this morning, he is well. He said—" I took a sip of coffee I didn't want, to swallow the lump in my throat. "He said that since helping people is what turns me on, it's time I find somebody else to help. So I did. Lena's kids."

"He doesn't sound like a prince," Coco repeated, "yet Wonder and animals adore him. A paradox. I can't deal with paradoxes after everything that's happened today. Waitress! We need two slices of chocolate pie over here, please."

I had gotten myself under control by the time the pie arrived. "The big problem is," I said, digging in with gusto, "Tobias made me wonder if I help people not because I like to help but because I want their gratitude."

Coco chewed pie while she thought that over. "I had a psych prof once who said the oldest child claims one corner of the family, then each child after that has to choose another corner. In a family where the brilliant and beautiful corners were taken before you were born, maybe you chose the helpful corner to get your share of your parents' attention."

"I didn't become a nurse to get their attention. My folks practically tossed me out of the family when I suggested it. I became a nurse because I actually enjoy helping people—or, at least, because I thought I did. Is it possible I care for people only out of a desperate need for gratitude? How pathetic is that?"

Coco considered me thoughtfully. "That question must be in your genes. Teddy told me once that the thorniest verse in the Bible for her was the one that says, 'If I give all I have to the poor and give my body to be burned, but have not love, it profits me nothing.' She said she was always wondering whether she helped people because she loved *them* or because she wanted recognition and praise."

I found it comforting to think I had anything of Teddy in my genes, even her struggles. "How long did it take her to get it right?"

Coco's reply certainly wasn't comforting. "She never did. She said answering that question is a lifelong process."

\* \* \*

Gage arranged a simple graveside service for Lena on the Friday morning after she died; then the judge, Coco, and Gage took the children to lunch. Regan asked me to walk with her back to their Mercedes while Holcomb had a cigar. On the way, she said, "You need to find another place for the children. They aren't working out at our house. The boy is sullen, rude, and utterly impossible. The older girl never opens her mouth and the little one wets her bed. Can you find someplace for them to go by Monday?"

I wasn't prepared for that. "Monday? Three days from now?"

"You said they'd only be with us a few days, and it's already been three—which is three more than plenty. Did you know that boy tried to ride my horse yesterday afternoon? Bareback! He said he'd seen somebody do it on television, so it couldn't be that hard. If he'd broken his neck, we could have been sued for everything we've got."

"I doubt you'd have been sued—who would do it?—but he could have broken his neck. Did you talk to him?"

"You bet I talked to him. I told him if I ever see him at that barn again, I will take my horsewhip to him. You know what he did? Curled that lip at me and said, 'I'd like to see you try.' He has to go, Teensie. The little one isn't bad, if she'd stop wetting the bed, but the other two have to go."

"We can't split them up. I promised their mother."

"Then find somebody to take all three by Monday. If they aren't out of our house first thing Monday morning, I'm calling a social worker to come get them."

# Ten

I arrived home to find Darla's front hall a chaos of suitcases, boxes, and overflowing paper bags. A teenage boy and girl were playing a computer game in the living room.

I moseyed toward voices in the kitchen. "Darla? I'm home."

Darla came to greet me, wiping her hands on a dish towel. "I'm so glad to see you. I meant to call yesterday and tell you my daughter and her children were coming back with me for a while." She lowered her voice to a whisper. "Her husband walked out on her and she's pretty upset. I thought a change of scenery might be good for everybody."

An emotional woman and more traumatized children—the perfect ending to a perfect morning. Darla took me by the arm and led me to the kitchen, where her daughter stood by the microwave. "Nancy has come home to visit for a while!" My landlady's voice was bright with false enthusiasm.

For her sake, I mustered enthusiasm as well. "Good to see you again, Nancy."

She looked awful. The pale, quiet girl who had been a year behind me in school had become a pale, drab woman with rimless glasses, graying hair, and the expression of a rabbit caught in the headlights of an approaching car. Her voice was cold with venom. "You are in my room."

Darla made a distressed little noise. "I told you, honey, Teensie rents that room."

"She can rent another room. I want to sleep in my room. I've never slept in another room in this house my entire life. I want my room!"

Watching a human deteriorate is a frightening experience. "You may have your room," I said quickly. "I'll move to one of the other rooms."

Darla followed me halfway up the stairs, concern in every crinkle of her soft skin. "The problem is," she whispered, "I don't know how long they will be here, and Nancy doesn't want to share with Mary. I can't ask you to share with a child, so I'll have to put the children together."

The solution was obvious, if unpalatable. "I'll go to Susan's. She has plenty of space."

Darla wrung her dish towel. "I don't want to put you out."

"You aren't putting me out—you're dealing with circumstances beyond your control. You'll all be more comfortable without me here. I'll go pack my things."

As I left my little room, though, I also left part of my heart behind. It is always hard to leave a place where you have been happy.

Susan gave me a room and fed me lunch, but warned that Monique was studying at the library and she and Albert were taking Wonder over to the mall for supper and a movie. "You'll have to fend for yourself for dinner. But we're delighted you're moving in. Monique's classes started yesterday and she's taking a heavy load, so Wonder needs watching again in the afternoons."

"I'll be glad to help when I can," I said cautiously, "but it's temporary. I'll be looking for a new place as soon as possible." She didn't hear a word I said.

I saved unpacking for later. I wanted to investigate what rentals might have come available since I last looked. Although I spent the entire afternoon with a Realtor, however, I found nothing. Disheartened, I stopped by Danny's Diner for comfort food: a cheeseburger with ketchup and a glass of milk.

Given the kind of day it had already been, I should have been prepared to find all four of Danny's booths occupied. Danny offered me a stool at the counter, but I said, "No, thanks." I did not relish balancing on a stool in the black wool suit I hadn't taken off since the funeral.

I had turned to leave when I heard a voice. "Deborah?"

Tobias beckoned to me from the farthest booth.

It was odd to see him in town, odder still to see him in a gray tweed sports coat and an ironed blue shirt. My heart gave a little lurch. As I headed his way, I winged a prayer of thanks for one bright moment in an awful day.

He pointed to the bench across his table. "You need a seat?"

"Yeah, thanks." My bubble of joy sank in a sea of weariness. I slid into the booth with the relief one feels at coming home.

Danny set a plate before Tobias. "You want the special, Miss MacAllester?"

I considered the plate—Salisbury steak smothered in gravy, mashed potatoes smothered in gravy, green beans surrounded by gravy, and a small bowl of canned applesauce. "No, thanks. I want a cheeseburger, ketchup only, fries, and a large milk— whole milk, not two percent."

"You got it." Danny bustled back to the counter.

Tobias picked up his fork and shoved his beans away from the potatoes. "I'd have thought a nurse would have better sense than to eat that much fat."

"I'd have thought an organic farmer would have better sense than to eat here in the first place."

"Touché." We watched gravy settle into the space he'd made.

"If you put a little gravy on your applesauce, everything will match," I suggested.

"Nah—it's good to have a little variety in your diet. What brings you to this elegant restaurant?"

Bantering with him had briefly lightened my weariness, but it settled back like a blanket. "Eviction."

"Eviction? What did you do—throw too many wild parties?"

I managed to dredge up a smile. "Danced naked on the piano. Or, if you prefer the boring version, my landlady's daughter and her children have come to stay and they need my room. Go ahead and eat before your dinner gets cold."

He grimaced. "Heat is about all it has to recommend it, so if you don't mind, I will. Lunch at the Varsity was a long time ago."

"The Varsity in Atlanta? I love that place. I used to eat there when I worked at the hospital."

"You are a surprising woman, Miss MacAllester. All that time you were cooking me healthy meals, were you secretly yearning for hot dogs and fries?"

"Nurses are human, Mr. Jones. We have our weak spots like everybody else. Now eat!"

"Yes, ma'am." He dug into his dinner.

I leaned back on my bench and thought how good it was to sit across from him and spar the way I couldn't with anybody else. *Oh, Tobias, if we had met in any place except Unizilla, could we have made sweet music?*

He must have sensed me studying him, for he lifted his head to ask, "Where are you sleeping—on the street? On a park bench? No, let me guess. You are with one of the sisters you did not throw in the pond."

"I still haven't found a pond. I'm working on it, though, and yes, I moved in with Susan this afternoon. I'll help out with Wonder when I'm not working or looking for a pond."

"Are those your pond-seeking clothes?"

"No, they are my funeral clothes. A woman I knew was buried today and I haven't taken time to change. Her funeral was right before my eviction, after which I went house hunting. It's been an exciting day all around." I heaved a deep sigh as I thought about trying to find those children a home.

He gave me a quick look across his plate before turning his attention to green beans. "You clean up pretty good."

I knew I was blushing, but couldn't do a thing to stop it. "Thanks. So do you. I'm glad to see you know how to dress for Danny's."

"I didn't dress for Danny's, I dressed to go to Atlanta to talk to some restaurants, like you suggested. Danny's was an afterthought when I realized I was too tired to drive home and cook."

I was about to ask if he was getting enough rest, but reminded myself he was no longer my patient. "Any luck in Atlanta?"

"Yes, as a matter of fact. Thanks to you, I now have three restaurants who will take my salad greens and one that said to come back when summer vegetables start coming in."

"Good for you!"

"Have you found a job?"

"Not yet. I may widen my search to Atlanta, since I now need to find a place to live as well."

"You'd leave Unizilla?" I thought I detected a trace of dismay in his voice, but could have imagined it. The next second he was saying matter-of-factly, "Of course you will, if you work someplace else. What happened to Belize?"

"It wasn't really an option. I enjoyed my years at the Atlanta hospital, so I thought I'd check around down there again." I hoped I sounded more enthusiastic than I felt. Having Tobias across from me, solid and real, made Atlanta seem as attractive as Siberia.

Danny set my cheeseburger before me, but I was no longer hungry. I nibbled the edges and fiddled with my fries.

Tobias's plate was clean. Danny asked, "Lemon icebox pie, Tobe?" Tobias nodded. Danny brought a piece with meringue two inches high.

Tobias ate half of it before he asked, "So who have you been helping this week?"

Before I knew it, I was pouring out the whole story. "Right after I saw you I went to the home of the woman who died. She was nearly comatose when I got there, so I called an ambulance, but she died before they got her to the hospital. She left three kids, whom I sent to my sister Regan's for a few days, but now Regan wants me to find another place for them by Monday or she's going to put them in foster care. It's really Judge Brantley's job, but he had a car accident and still hasn't completely gotten his memory back, so he has enough on his plate without worrying about three kids, but if the kids go into foster care, chances are real good they'll get split up, and I promised their mother before she died that I wouldn't split up the kids."

"Take a breath," Tobias advised. "That last sentence nearly did you in."

I set down my cheeseburger and stopped pretending to eat. "Don't make jokes. How can I find a place for three children when I can't even find a place for me?" I felt my eyes fill with tears. I concentrated on my fries until I could blink them away.

Tobias chewed pie with a thoughtful expression. "How old are the kids?"

"The boy is twelve."

He grew still. Was he remembering, as I was, the boy in the picture on his dresser?

"According to Regan, he's sullen and rude," I said, trying to create some distance between the reality of Eric and whatever Tobias imagined his own son to be.

"He's lost his mother. He has the right to be sullen and rude."

"I don't think he's missing her much yet. She was an alcoholic who has stayed drunk most of the time these past few years."

He paused midbite. "Are you talking about Lena Thompson's kids? I didn't know she'd died."

"Tuesday. You knew her?"

"Slightly. Her mother was a cousin of my mother's. She had a boy and two girls, right?"

"Right. I never knew Lena was half Cherokee."

"It wasn't a secret."

"I didn't know their family well." I took a bite of unwanted cheeseburger to hide my mortification at being so surprised. How had I lived my entire life surrounded by Cherokees and never recognized that fact?

Tobias finished his pie without speaking. I drank my milk. When he motioned for Danny to come over, I expected him to ask for his bill. Instead, he said, "Bring us two coffees, please. Deborah looks like she needs something hot inside her."

I took the steaming cup gratefully. I hadn't realized until then that I was cold.

"How old are Lena's girls?" he asked.

"Ten and four."

He spoke so slowly that he seemed to be thinking aloud. "I could take the older two kids, but I don't think I could handle a four-year-old and get anything done."

I was bewildered. "Why should you take any of them?"

"It's a Cherokee thing. Cherokee children belong to their mother." Only because I was supersensitive to his voice did I hear sadness there. "In the past, a mother's brothers were responsible for teaching and training her sons and caring for the children if she died. It was a good system, for it ensured that no child was left homeless. Since Lena had no brothers and her mother was my mother's cousin . . ." He shrugged as if taking on a family of orphaned children were a normal thing to do.

"You would take in three children you don't know?" It was such an unbelievably kind offer, I wondered if Tobias hoped Eric would replace his Brandon.

His answer surprised me. "If you still had your house, would you take them?"

"Well . . . probably. I thought for one crazy instant about taking them to Darla's."

One corner of his mouth lifted. "But then you got evicted for dancing naked on the piano."

I gave him a weak smile in return. "Yeah. Then I danced on the piano."

He studied me over his cup. "You don't have the franchise on helping others, you know."

I flushed. "Of course not, but you don't have time to look after children."

"I've got as much time as you have, and my schedule is more flexible. Besides, I've got a whole farm for them to roam around."

The magnitude of what he was offering made me speechless—until I realized he didn't want all three children.

"It's a generous gesture, Tobias, but I did promise Lena I'd keep them together."

"That could be a problem." He sipped coffee thoughtfully. "Is the little one home all day?"

"No, she goes to day care. Their granddaddy left a trust fund to help with their expenses and pay for some of their education."

"Let me think about that. Have some pie while I'm thinking?"

"Okay. That lemon pie looked good."

I accepted not because I wanted pie but because I didn't want to leave. This was a different Tobias than I'd known before. No, it was the same Tobias—a man of many facets who loved animals and children. He just didn't like my family. That thought made me miserable. I shoved it away. I'd have time to be miserable later. I would enjoy the little time I had with him even if all we did was discuss unfeasible ways of dealing with Lena's children.

He signaled Danny. "Two more pies and refills on coffee, please."

For the next few minutes, I got to enjoy Tobias's company but not his conversation. He ate his second piece of pie without a word. A couple of times he looked over at me and I thought he was going to speak. Then he looked back at his pie. When the plate was empty, he shoved it away. "Okay, I've figured out how I can take them all."

"Don't be ridiculous! I'll admit that the picture of those children running around the farm is irresistible. I can see them playing with your animals and digging in the dirt. But the thought of you trying to farm with the two older ones around is ludicrous. Add a four-year-old?" I shook my head. "There is no way you could do it."

"I can if you move up, too." He made the suggestion in an off-hand tone, like he was saying, "I think you'll need a to-go box."

I choked on my pie. "With you?" Had my eyes betrayed some yearning that led to his outrageous suggestion?

He held up his hands as if to ward off an attack. "Not with me, with the children. I've got three extra bedrooms and more food in the freezer than I can eat. We both like kids and are good with them. You can take them to the school bus and day care on your way to work, and one of us can fetch them in the afternoon."

"I can't move in with you." I wasn't being a prude—I was being realistic. It was next to impossible to sit across the table without giving away how I felt. How could I live with him? He would never suggest such a thing if he cared for me as I cared for him.

"I'm not asking you to move in with me," he said impatiently. Of course not. That hadn't crossed his mind. I blushed to the roots of my hair. "I'm asking you to help me care for three children," he continued, ignoring my blush. "At least for the rest of this school year. They don't need any more chaos in their lives right now. This summer, if it's not working out, the judge can make other arrangements."

When I continued to stare as if he had gone plumb out of his mind—which, in my opinion, he had—he settled back against his booth and pinned me with those black eyes. "You like to help people, right? These kids need help, right? And all of you need a place to live. I've got extra rooms and plenty of food. It looks to me like a no-brainer. These kids need help that you and I are uniquely positioned to give."

His arguments made excellent sense—without the human factor. The kindness of his offer overwhelmed me. I couldn't accept the offer, however. I *was* the human factor. It had been hard enough being around a weakened Tobias. I wasn't sure I had the moral fiber to stay in the same house with a healthy Tobias.

Since I couldn't explain why, I fell back on the most important question in my mother's Canon of Good Conduct: "What would people think?"

"Who needs to know?"

"Everybody. We'd have to sign on at the school as their guardians, and once Wonder got wind that you had other kids at the farm, she'd raise Cain to visit. Once she found out I was living there, she would go home and—as she would say—words would pop out of her mouth. Don't imagine we could keep it secret. People would know. My sisters would freak out."

"Frankly, my dear—and all that stuff." He reached over and took one of my cold fries. "Think, Deborah. This could be your pond."

Watching him eat my fries while I pretended to consider his

logical argument was almost more intimacy than I could bear. Could I stand to live with him on a strictly business footing? On the other hand, could I bear to turn down such an offer? Through my head flitted images of the cove in springtime, the log house by lamplight, Tobias across the dinner table with children between us.

As if reading my thoughts, he urged, "Think about the children."

I dragged my thoughts from myself and considered the children. It *would* be good for them to have a settled place where they could be together. Tobias would be good for Eric. Kaitlin and Carrie would be clean, well fed, and loved by adults. Kaitlin might enjoy helping me make the log house more homey. When I found myself considering what kind of curtains would look best in his living room, I knew I had rationalized myself into saying yes.

I tried to salvage some semblance of self-respect. "I insist on paying rent."

"Fine. I can use the money. So you'll do it?" His eyes bored into mine. Did he really expect me to accept, or was this a dare?

"It's an incredible possibility for those children. I guess we can try it."

"So, deal?" He stuck out a hand.

"Deal." Hoping God would not strike me dead as the greatest hypocrite on earth, I shook to seal the bargain.

Susan's voice rose to a crescendo. "You are doing what?"

I folded my pajamas and put them in my suitcase. "I am moving to Jones Farm this morning to take care of Lena's children until school is out."

"The children of the town drunk."

"That's not their fault, and they need someplace to go. Regan refuses to keep them any longer and the farm will be a great place for them. They'll have space to run around, good food, and a secure home."

It was Saturday morning and I had asked my elder sister up to my room after breakfast to break the news in private.

"I wanna go to de farm and run around." Wonder stood in my bedroom doorway, wearing a green fuzzy sleeper with feet. Her hair stood up like she'd stuck her finger in a socket. We'd thought she was watching cartoons. She must have heard Susan's raised voice and come to investigate. "I wanna live with de veg'table man. Get my suitcase, Nana—*please*." She belatedly remembered her manners.

"Go watch cartoons," Susan ordered. "We are having a grown-up conversation."

"I don't like cartoons. I wanna go with Teensie."

"You heard me! Go watch television!"

When Wonder had dragged herself at a snail's pace from the room, Susan closed the door and leaned against it. "I cannot believe I just said that. I am turning into one of those grandmothers who shout at children and use the television as an electronic babysitter. See how much we need you here? Anyway, you can't go live with that man. A hillbilly farmer with hair down to his butt?"

"He's not a hillbilly, he's a Cherokee, and his hair isn't any longer than Albert's was when you met him. It looks better than Albert's did, too."

"Stop talking about Albert. We are discussing your living with a strange man."

"I am not living with him, I am renting a room in his house. Judge Brantley is going to pay me to look after the children and he's paying Mr. Jones for their room and board."

"What could you possibly have in common with this Mr. Jones? Did he go to college?"

"I doubt it, but what does that matter?"

"What does it matter?" Susan stared at me in amazement. Education had been at the core of our family's values. When I didn't answer, she attacked from another front. "How old is this Mr. Jones?"

I was surprised to realize I didn't know. His face was unlined like a boy's and his hair unmarked by gray, but he could be anything from thirty to fifty. "He's old enough for Judge Brantley to give him responsibility for Lena's children, and I'm old enough to decide where I live and what job I take. This suits me for the time being, and Judge Brantley approves."

That might be a bit strong for the judge's response. When Tobias and I had showed up at his house Friday evening with our plan, Judge Brantley took us into his home office and greeted Tobias like a man he knew and respected, but he gave me a curious look that said, "What are you doing here with him?"

Tobias said, "Sir, I ran into Deborah at Danny's this evening and she says you need a place for Lena Thompson's children. Lena's mother was of my mother's clan, and as she has no brothers, I would like to stand as uncle for them and give them a home. I feel they have had enough turmoil."

The judge was as taken aback as I had been when Tobias first made the proposal. "That's kind, Tobias, but three children—don't you live alone?"

"Yes, sir, but I have plenty of space to house the children and food to feed them, and since Deborah, here, is also needing a place to stay, I have suggested that she move in to act as the children's caregiver. If you agree, the children can stay with me until the school year is over. At that time, you can evaluate our situation and, if you feel it necessary, make other arrangements."

The judge considered me gravely. "What do you think of this proposition, *Deborah*?" It wasn't his use of "proposition" that made me flush. He used it often to describe business agreements and seemed to have no notion of its more recent connota-tion. What brought color to my cheeks was his emphasis on a name he had never called me in my life. How much had he read into Tobias's casual use of it?

I strove to be casual, too. "It works for me, Judge, if you agree."

He gave me a piercing look. I suspected he wanted to ask the question King would have asked at once: "Now, Teensie, there will be no question of impropriety, will there?" The judge asked instead, "What will you all charge for this?"

Tobias and I spoke in unison. "Nothing."

"Oh, dear me, no. No, no, no. There is a trust fund set up for their care and education. I would insist on paying you, Tobias, for their room and board, and you, Teensie, to care for them."

I saw that Tobias was about to object, so I said quickly, "That would be fine. I will be paying Tobias the same rent I have been paying Darla."

"I see," said the judge. I wondered what he saw.

Within a few minutes we had agreed on satisfactory terms.

Susan found them far less satisfactory. "You cannot do this, Teensie. Single women do not rent a room in the house of a sin-gle man."

"As Monique would say, don't be prehistoric. Even if we didn't have three young chaperones, which we will, single women and single men live together all over the country—as housemates, not as lovers."

"Women like us don't move onto farms at the back of beyond with single men. Especially men of another race. We weren't raised like that."

"I don't know what race the Cherokee are, but I was raised to think my father would take care of my future. We both know how that turned out. I've looked at every place for rent in Unizilla and applied for several jobs, and Mr. Jones's offer is by far the most attractive I've found. His house is comfortable and those children need me."

"You are a nurse, not a nursemaid."

I couldn't argue with that. I'd said the same thing to Coco several months before. That, however, was before I met the children. Before I met Tobias . . .

I pulled myself up sharply. Tobias had no interest in me. My strongest reason—my only reason—for moving to his farm was to help those children.

If I told myself that over and over, I might come to believe it.

To Susan I replied, "I'll be more than a nursemaid. Lena's children have been through a lot of trauma—not simply her death, but all these years when she was drinking. They need not only TLC but somebody with medical training." I checked the room to make sure I hadn't left anything before I zipped my suitcase. "I think they need other children around, too, so if you agree, I'd like to take Wonder with me up to the farm this morning to settle in and get their rooms ready, then around one thirty, she can ride down with me when Mr. Jones and I go to pick up the children and take them to the farm. Wonder knows the animals and can introduce them to the children, and she is a great little icebreaker. She's also about the same age as Lena's younger daughter. They might become friends."

"What are you going to tell Regan when you pick them up? Will you tell her where you are taking them?"

"Why should I tell Regan anything? You'll be on the phone with her before I get to the farm." I hefted my case. Susan picked up one of my boxes. I hadn't unpacked a thing except what I had needed to sleep overnight.

"You don't need to carry that," I objected. "I'll come back for it."

"Oh, no, I'll help carry your things to the car. If you are determined to ruin your life, I might as well give you all the help

I can. And if you want to take Wonder, go ahead. Monique has plans for the day."

Monique was eating breakfast when we passed through the kitchen. She wore tatty jeans, an old sweatshirt, running shoes, and little makeup, and she had brushed her hair away from her face and tied a bandanna over it.

"Where are you going?" I asked as I put my suitcase down to pause for breath.

"A bunch of middle school kids are meeting at the church to paint their Sunday school room, and Gage asked me to come, too. He's their teacher. Can you believe that? Where are you going? I thought you had moved in."

Susan set her box on the table to ease the load. "She did move in and now she's moving out. Don't ask where she's going. I don't want anybody to know."

Monique gave me a conspiratorial smile. "So where are you going?"

"Up to Tobias Jones's farm, to help take care of Lena Thompson's kids for a while. Judge Brantley is paying us to look after them."

"Cool."

It was comforting that one member of my family didn't think I was crazy, even if it was the one who lived nearest the edge of crazy herself. Wonder didn't think I was crazy, either. When I invited her to ride along with me, she had her coat on by the time I finished explaining.

Tobias wasn't at the farm when we got there, but he'd left a note. *Gone to town for a few supplies. Back before lunchtime.*

He had done a good job of straightening the place, but my fingers itched to add a few homey touches. We could use more seating in the living room, too. Would he object if I brought some of my furniture up from storage? We could cross that ravine after we'd crossed several others.

"Bedrooms first," I told Wonder, who was playing with Homer. "We have a lot of beds to make."

"Dis is de girls' room," she announced, leading me to Tobias's mother's room. "Dey can sleep togedder in de big bed in case monsters come."

If I took the room I'd had before, diagonally across the house from Tobias's, that left Eric the other back bedroom. One of its twin beds was already made and had a science fiction paperback lying on it. Inside the front cover, Damien had scrawled his name. Would the boys become friends?

I was surprised to find all the rooms dusted and Tobias's mother's clothes gone from her closet and dresser. Tobias had been busy that morning. Wonder and I made the bed and lined dresser drawers with paper I'd bought for that purpose. "Dey will love dis room," Wonder told me, "but dey can't hab dis. It is precious." She carried the box decorated with strawberries from the dresser into Tobias's room. "I put it next to de picture of a boy," she called. "Who is dis boy?"

"That's Tobias's son, but don't mention him, okay? He went away with his mother and it makes Tobias sad to think about him."

"Maybe dat boy will come back in de foreseeable future."

She skipped back to help me make Eric's bed and get his room ready to be occupied, but looked at the brown comforter with a mournful expression. "Dat bed is ugly. It needs sumpin to make it pretty."

"Boys don't care if a bed is pretty," I told her, "so long as it's warm."

"Yes, dey do. Tobias has a pretty pillow on his bed. Come see." She grabbed my hand and led me to the door of Tobias's room. As many times as I had been in that room while he was sick, I hesitated to step over the threshold now that he was well.

I looked from the doorway and saw my Navajo pillow propped on his other pillows. I was trying to decide whether that was significant or not when Wonder said, "See, dere's where I put de box." She pointed toward the chest.

I saw not the strawberry box but four small sketches hanging over the chest. They had not been there before.

Tobias had framed the sketches I had made the night we sat by the fire. I could see why he'd want the pictures of his animals and the log house, but why should he frame the bluebird? *Not for romantic reasons*, I reminded my heart. *Four make a more symmetrical arrangement.*

I wanted out of his room before he got back. "I have another pillow like that," I told Wonder. "One day I'll bring it up here for Eric. Now let's make my bed."

I rooted out sheets from my boxes while Wonder prowled the room. "Did you already sleep here?" she inquired.

Startled, I asked, "What makes you ask that?"

"'Cause your robe and slippers are here." She held the closet door wide. The pink robe and moccasins I had worn on our ill-fated weekend were there to welcome me. "Those were Tobias's mother's," I told her, ducking my head to hide my blush. "Go to the other side of this bed so we can get it made before Tobias gets home."

He clumped in around noon, arms loaded with groceries. "Thought I ought to get a few snacks for the kids." From cloth totes he emptied out fruit, but he had also bought pudding, cookies, chips, ice cream, a bag of candy, and several bottles of sugared juice.

I cocked one eyebrow. "Organic snacks, I see."

He gave me a rueful smile. "Didn't want to turn them off their first week here. I doubt they are used to healthy food."

"We made de beds," Wonder informed him, "but we didn't have a pretty pillow for de boy's bed like you hab on yours."

Tobias stiffened. "You all went in my room?"

"I took de strawberry box. It was in de girls' room, and I was scared dey might break it."

I saw him relax. "I see. The pillow is Deborah's. I washed the cover and left the pillow upstairs to remember to give it to her. Put it on the boy's bed, if you like."

Wonder scampered up the stairs to comply.

He said to me, "I think we'll need house rules about going into other people's bedrooms."

"Absolutely."

As Tobias and I put away groceries, I made sure our hands did not touch.

He went upstairs to get ready, then we took both trucks to pick up the kids. Judge Brantley had promised to go to Regan's early to alert her and the children about what was going to happen. A rental Ford was in the drive when we arrived.

Knowing Regan's opinions about clothes, I hoped she wouldn't take one look at Tobias in his jeans, denim jacket, and work boots and send him around back. Instead, she opened the front door before we reached it and extended a hand to him. "Hello, Mr. Jones. Judge Brantley is here, and he's been telling me of your generous offer to look after those poor children. I hope you know what you are letting yourself in for. They have had little discipline, and the boy, especially, is a handful."

"I was once a boy myself, ma'am. I think we'll get along all right." He stepped past her into the hall.

"The judge is in the living room, first door on your left."

Not until she turned to close the door did Regan notice Wonder and me on her doorstep. "What are you doing here?" Apparently Susan hadn't called.

"Helping Tobias take the children up to the farm. He can't carry all of them at once in his truck."

"Tobias? You know this man?"

"Sure we do," piped up Wonder before I could cover her mouth. "He's my veg'table man." Regan gave me a disapproving look, but Wonder didn't notice. "I'm going wit' Teensie to show de kids Homer de dog, and de donkey, and de hen with one wing, and de big old turkey named Tom."

"Come on in, then. Would you take Wonder back to the kitchen, Teensie, where the girls are, and ask Lynyetta to send in a couple more cups and a new pot of coffee?" Regan was playing Gracious Hostess for the men's benefit. Normally she would not have asked; she would have told me to do it.

The girls were alone in the kitchen, sitting at the table with milk and cookies. "Where's Lynyetta?" I asked.

"Packing our clothes," said Kaitlin.

"Miss Wegan got us lotsa new clothes," Carrie added with obvious satisfaction.

Kaitlin's red corduroy pants and sweater put color in her pale cheeks, but Carrie's outfit—pink corduroy pants, pink sweater, and pink leather shoes—could be ruined by one visit to the barn. I hoped Regan hadn't completely outfitted the child in pink.

I started another pot of coffee and sat down with the children while it brewed. "Has the judge told you what is going to happen this afternoon?" I asked Kaitlin.

"Sort of. We're going to live on a farm with some people we don't know."

"I'm not going," Carrie informed me. "I like it here."

"You know the woman," I told Kaitlin. "It's me. I'm going to stay with you at the farm and look after you. Will that be all right?"

"Oh, yes." I was glad to see some of the tension go out of those sloped shoulders.

"And I'm gonna inter-duce you to a donkey and a chicken and a big old turkey name Tom," Wonder told them. "And Homer, de dog. You're gonna like dem a lot. And Tobias has a house made out of logs, and it has a fireplace, and a woodpile dis high"—she raised her hand as high as it would go—"and we made you a big bed with pink flowers on de bedspread."

"Who is Tobias?" Kaitlin asked.

"Mr. Jones." I wasn't sure what Tobias would want them to call him. "He owns the farm, and his mother and your mother were cousins, so he's not really a stranger, just a relative you haven't met yet."

"He grows healthy vegetables for people to eat," Wonder added.

Carrie reached for another cookie. "I doesn't like vegetables. I likes cookies."

The coffeemaker gave its last gurgle. I put the pot and a couple of cups and saucers on a tray and carried it to the living room.

"There's our coffee," Regan exclaimed with a too-bright smile.

While she refilled the judge's cup and poured some for me and Tobias, I asked the judge, "What's happening about your car?"

"Nothing yet. Gage had it towed to my yard and it's still sitting under a tree. I hear it's a mess, but I can't bear to go out to look at it yet. Can't bear to get rid of it, either, so I have a dilemma, because it would cost a fortune to repair it and I didn't carry insurance on it because it's so old."

"That's a dilemma all right." I felt sentimental about the old car, too. It had first carried me up to Jones Farm.

Regan handed Tobias his coffee. "By the time you finish this, we ought to have those children packed. If you don't mind, I'd like to speak to my sister for a minute." She nodded for me to follow her to the hall.

"In the den," she muttered when we were out of sight of the men. She had a familiar glitter in her eye.

The door was barely shut behind us when she stormed, "Am

I hearing the judge right? Are you seriously thinking of moving in with that man and those children?"

"I moved up there this morning. I'm surprised Susan hasn't told you by now."

"I'm surprised Susan didn't lock you in your room. Is he the Indian you shacked up with that weekend of the ice storm? I grant you, he's gorgeous—"

"We did not shack up. I got iced in and stayed at his house. He was very ill."

"So you say. But he's single, right? And Cherokee. And a farmer. Any one of those ought to ring alarm bells in your head. You can't move in with that man!"

"I can and I have. This morning."

"Do you realize you are ruining not only your reputation but mine and Holcomb's and Susan's and Albert's? The whole town will know about this by tomorrow. It's time you stopped thinking only of yourself and your raging hormones and started thinking about other people for a change."

"I do not have raging hormones and I am thinking about other people—those children. If you had kept them—"

"I can't handle them. Nobody can. The boy is impossible and the older girl is sneaky and sly. She keeps trying to do Lynyetta's jobs. What's worse, she lets her little sister climb into bed with her when I have told them again and again that they are to stay in their own beds. We weren't raised to sleep in each other's beds, and we weren't raised to move in with men in the mountains—Indian or otherwise."

She ran down like a balloon that has whizzed around a room under the force of its own air until it is spent. "Well?" she asked when I said nothing.

"Well, what?"

"Have you come to your senses? Are you going back to Susan's?"

"Absolutely not. Those children need me more than Susan does, and I need this job. Some of us don't have rich husbands. We have to work for a living. The judge is paying me to look after those children and that's what I intend to do."

"If you do, you are cutting yourself off from the family. You know that, don't you? Nobody in this family has ever lived with an illiterate Indian farmer."

"He's not illiterate. Not everybody needs a college degree. Besides, the main point here is that I'm moving up there to help those kids."

"If you do, I wash my hands of you."

"Fine, if that's the way you want to play it."

"You won't get invited to family dinners."

"I doubt I'll starve. He has a freezer full of food."

I was ready to leave the room, collect the children, and go when another thought occurred to her. "You aren't planning on taking Mary Bird MacAllester's bedroom furniture up there, are you?"

"What I take or don't take up there is none of your business. You've washed your hands of me, remember?"

"You know what you are? You are selfish, tacky, and common!" Having tarred me with a Southern lady's three worst brushes, she swept from the room.

I followed, hoping Tobias and the judge hadn't heard that exchange.

By the time Regan reached the living room her smile was in place and her voice under control. "I'll go check on Lynyetta and see how the packing is coming along." She gave Tobias an arch smile. "I'm certain Teensie will take care of *all* your needs."


Regan and Lynyetta came down with three bulging new duffel bags. Regan walked the children out to the trucks. I had expected to take the two small girls with me, but Wonder climbed up with Tobias and Eric. As Carrie got into the truck, Regan stroked her curls. "Isn't she a darling?"

Before we left, she came over to my window and said in a soft hiss, "You will live to regret this." Then she ceased playing the wicked stepmother in *Snow White*, turned into the Good Witch of the North from *The Wizard of Oz*. She waved good-bye to the children as if she were sorry to see them go.

"It's far," Kaitlin said uncertainly as we drove up three miles of mountain road.

"It's beautiful when we get there," I promised.

"I'm scared," whimpered Carrie, looking at all the trees. Poor little mite, she hadn't had but one tree in her yard.

"No need to be afraid," I assured her. "It is a very safe place."

"I'll take care of you, baby," said Kaitlin. She kept a protective arm around her sister all the way to the house.

At the farm, Wonder proudly showed the girls their room.

"It's nice." Kaitlin was polite but unenthusiastic.

Carrie pouted. "I wants my pretty room with the pretty bed."

"Dis has de prettiest bed in de whole house," Wonder told her sternly.

"Dis room is cold. I wants my warm house."

Eric slung his duffel bag on his bed without comment. In a minute he clattered downstairs, asking, "You got cable, man?"

"Sure do," I heard Tobias reply. "Plus Internet."

"That's good. I wouldn't want to stay in a place without cable and Internet."

I felt like shaking Eric. His mother's television had tinted people bubblegum pink, yet after a few days at Regan's, he—and Carrie—felt entitled to live like royalty?

I listened for Tobias's snappy comeback. Instead he said in a mild voice, "Then it's a good thing the cable company made it up this mountain. Pick any channel you like."

I heard Eric flop onto the couch, then yell, "Phe-eww! This couch stinks." I had noticed, too, that the odor of ketosis still clung to it.

I heard Tobias walk into the den. "I need to do something about that. Why don't you use the computer desk chair for now?"

"I'll show you de animals," Wonder offered the girls.

"Okay." Kaitlin still had a worried pucker in her forehead.

"I don't like animals," Carrie said. "Punkin almost bit me."

"Punkin bites everybody," I told her briskly. "Come on, let's go meet the animals on the farm. They don't bite."

On our way downstairs I took a quick peek into Tobias's bedroom to see my sketches. The bluebird had flown.

Wonder proudly conducted the outside tour. "Dis is de barn, where de animals live. Dis donkey is named Bray." She held out a carrot to Carrie. "Want to feed him?"

Carrie cringed. "He might bite me."

"You're a fraidy cat. He doesn't bite. Look!"

Bray nibbled the carrot from her hand.

Carrie backed away. "I doesn't like him. He has big teef!"

"Can I feed him?" Kaitlin reached for the carrot. When Bray took it from her, I saw that little girl smile for the first time.

She reached out a timid hand to stroke Lucky but shied away from giving Tom's head a pat. Carrie sidestepped both of them. Lucky thought she was playing a game, so she followed.

"Make her stop! Make her stop!" Carrie backed into a bucket and fell on her bottom in the dirt, roaring in distress. Lucky clucked up, full of sympathy.

Kaitlin helped Carrie up and dusted her off. As I had feared, her pink pants and pink parka had picked up some of Lucky's droppings. "We need to get you some jeans," I told her.

"I doesn't like jeans. I likes pretty clothes."

"Wanna climb a tree?" asked Wonder.

"I doesn't like to climb trees. I wants to go home to de pretty house."

Kaitlin gave me an apologetic shrug. "She's not used to being on a farm. She'll be okay in a day or two." She drew Carrie close to her side. "You'll be okay, baby."

Tobias and I had agreed that hamburgers would be a simple first meal. He was already broiling them when we got in. I found myself humming as I moved about the kitchen, helping him prepare our first family meal in our home. I asked the two little girls to set the table while Kaitlin and I made a salad. Kaitlin and Wonder set to work at once. Carrie stood beside the table, pouting.

Tobias asked Eric to go to the cellar to fetch a jar of applesauce. Eric looked down the steps and said, "I'm not going into that spider hole, man."

"I'll go," I said. I didn't want anything to ruin the evening.

After supper Eric returned to the television. Tobias asked me, "Want to flip for who does dishes and who takes Wonder home?"

"I doesn't want to go home. I wants to stay," Wonder protested. Her grammar had suffered from contact with Carrie's.

"You have to go home tonight," I told her. "You can stay another time, if your grandmother will let you." I ignored her pout to answer Tobias. "I can take her, but I can't take both of the other girls and I don't think we ought to split them up. Do you want to get them ready for bed?"

"I doesn't want to go to bed. I wants my mama." Carrie began to wail.

"Hush!" Kaitlin told her. When Carrie continued to wail, Kaitlin slapped her.

"Don't do that," I said sharply. "Carrie's sad tonight. She doesn't need to be hit."

Kaitlin had already pulled Carrie into her lap. Her parenting style seemed to be a slap followed by a cuddle. Was that what she had learned from Lena?

"How about some ice cream before bed?" Tobias asked the girls.

Carrie shook her head. "I'm not going to bed." She stuck out her lower lip.

I saw a flicker in Tobias's eyes. Could it be panic? "I think they can stay up until you get back," he said.

"Why don't you tell us a story before we call it a night?" I suggested.

"Tell us a Cherky story," Wonder commanded.

Tobias stroked his chin while he thought. "Have you ever heard about the Magic Lake of the Animals?"

"Nooo," said Wonder, her eyes wide.

"Not me," said Kaitlin.

"Tell us," commanded Carrie, clutching Regan Alice. The Barbie was now decently dressed in slacks, a top, and spike heels. Her hair was even brushed. Had the elegant Regan Harris been playing dolls?

Since we didn't have enough chairs in the living room, I sat with the girls on the couch while Tobias stood near the fire to tell his story.

"Once there was a young brave out wandering in the forest when he saw a bear cub limping from a hurt paw. He followed the cub as it struggled into the mountains. When it stopped for the night, he rested near it. The next morning it struggled up the high mountain that the Cherokee call Shakonige, the Blue Mountain. When the man reached the top, he saw that fog filled the valley below. It covered everything except the very top of the mountain."

"Dist like Unizilla sometimes," said Wonder. "Unizilla means 'cloud.'"

"Yes," Tobias agreed, "except the Cherokee word is *unitsila*. They are almost the same."

"What happened to the little bear?" In the flickering fire-light, Kaitlin's face looked more animated than usual. Even Carrie seemed to be listening as she sucked her thumb.

"He jumped off the mountaintop into the fog."

"Oh, no!" exclaimed Wonder.

"That's what the brave thought: 'Uh-oh. That bear is going to die!' But as soon as the bear disappeared, the fog became a great lake. While the brave watched, the cub swam out into the lake and back again. When he climbed back onto the mountain peak, his paw was healed. The brave continued to watch and saw a duck with a broken wing and a wolf with a bleeding jaw go into the water."

"And de wolf ate de duck!" said Wonder, clapping her hands in excitement.

"No, the wolf didn't eat the duck. They both came out of the water healed. As the brave watched, many hurt animals went into the lake and were healed, and when they came out of the water, the animals lived around that lake in peace. The brave said to the Great Spirit—"

"Dat's God," his small interpreter explained to the sisters.

"The brave said, 'I do not understand what has happened here.' The Great Spirit said, 'This is the Magic Lake of the Animals. Go back and tell the Cherokee that if they love me, if they live at peace with their brothers and sisters, and if they love animals, when they grow old and sick, they can come to this lake, too, and be healed.'"

"Is the lake real?" Kaitlin asked. "Have you been there?"

"No, I haven't. I guess I should have gone when I got sick last fall."

Wonder propped one hand on her hip. "You don't need a magic lake. You've got Deb'rah."

I felt a blush climb my neck.

"I think it's time for ice cream," said Tobias.

# Eleven

Wonder pouted all the way home, "Dose udder kids get to stay wif Tobias and I don't." I promised again that she could come spend a night soon if her grandmother agreed, but she was still pouting when we reached their house. Pout turned to fury when Susan informed her that Monique was out on a date.

"Did she go with dat man?"

"I don't know whom she's with. She didn't tell me."

"You shoulda made her tell! If I'da been here . . ."

I left them to battle it out.

There was no moon that night. On the outskirts of town my headlights picked up a woman walking down the edge of the highway. As soon as she saw my lights she darted into the bushes, but not before I had recognized her. I pulled to a stop and rolled down my window. "Monique?"

Nothing moved. "Monique? I know you are in there. What's the matter?"

I heard a rustle and she crept out. She looked up and down the empty road and ran to the truck. "Let's get out of here. If he finds me . . ."

She jerked open the passenger door and I saw that her chin was covered with blood. "Junior did this to you?"

"Yes." She spoke awkwardly through a split lip. One of her eyes was swollen shut, and she had a large pink place on one cheek that would be purple by the next day.

Headlights approached in the distance. She watched for a couple of seconds, then tumbled into the floor of the cab and shut the door. "That's him! Get us out of here!"

"Stay down," I warned as I pulled onto the road. "He's coming up behind us."

"Can you lose him? He said he'd kill me if I told anybody he did this to me."

"I think it's time we went to see your lawyer."

"I don't have a lawyer."

"You do now." I pulled out my cell phone. "Gage? Can Monique and I stop by? She needs a lawyer. And do me a favor, please—come out onto your porch and turn on the light. I want you to be visible when we arrive. Come to the passenger side to help Monique out as soon as I stop. It will take us about six or seven minutes."

"I'll be waiting for you."

"What did he say?" Monique asked in a quavering voice.

"He said he'll be waiting for us."

"That's all? He didn't ask what we wanted?"

"He's a lawyer. He's got it figured out. Don't get up. Junior's still following."

By taking back roads, I managed to return to town without having to stop and turn around. I didn't want Junior pulling in behind me and blocking my retreat. The big black SUV stayed behind me all the way to the college, but slowed as we approached the drive to the president's house. What would Junior do if I drove up Albert's driveway to take Monique home? I was too nervous to find out. I continued through the campus and uphill past the marble house, then down past Judge Brantley's. Gage stood on his porch with not only his porch light on but all the lights in his downstairs blazing. Jester was at his side. He hurried down to meet us.

"Don't get up," I repeated to Monique. "Junior pulled in behind me."

Monique reached for the door handle. "Maybe I ought to talk to him."

"Let Gage handle it."

Instead of opening my passenger door, Gage headed for the SUV. I heard his voice faintly through my window. "Can I help you, buddy?" I rolled the window down a crack so Monique and I both could hear better.

"I'm looking for Monique."

"You'll have to look for her somewhere else."

"I think she's in that truck."

"Sorry, you'd have to get a warrant to look in that truck, and at the moment you are trespassing on my property. I'm asking you to leave."

"Look, man, I think Miss MacAllester is holding Monique against her will." Junior yelled, "Monique? If you are in there and she has hurt you, jump out the door, honey. I won't let her hurt you anymore."

"Don't you go out there," I warned. "You and I both know who hurt you. The only way you are going to be safe is to put that man behind bars."

"I'm not going out there," she whispered scornfully. "Do you think I'm a fool?"

"Monique!" Junior bellowed. "Come on out of there, honey. You know I love you. There's never been anybody I loved but you."

Monique's hand moved toward the door handle as if on its own accord, but she clenched her fist and brought it to her chest.

"Please get off my property before the police get here." Gage had his cell phone in his hand and was pressing numbers.

"You can't come between a man and his woman."

"She is not your woman. She is her own woman." Gage spoke into the phone. "This is Gage Brantley. I have a trespasser. How soon can you get here? Oh, good!"

"There's a squad car two blocks away," he told Junior. "If you aren't gone before they arrive, I am pressing charges."

"You will regret this," Junior shouted. "You, too, Monique. Remember what I promised? I keep my promises, baby. Don't you forget." He burned rubber backing out of the drive and peeled off down the street.


Gage opened Monique's door. "He's gone. Why don't you all come inside?"

"Shouldn't we wait for the police?" I needed a minute to get my shaking body under control. I had been terrified Junior would hurt Gage and come after us.

"I didn't talk to the police. I called the weather number. You all come on in before he figures that out."

I took time to grab my medical kit while Gage hurried Monique into the house. When Gage saw the blood, his own face turned white. For a moment, I feared he was going gunning for Junior.

"Lips bleed a lot," I said to reassure him. "Let me clean her up." I spoke briskly, but my stomach churned with fury. Battered women always had that effect on me, and this was not only a battered woman but the closest thing I had to a child.

"Don't wash her until I get some pictures," Gage commanded. "Put Jester in the yard while I fetch my camera. I've got drop cloths and paint buckets all over the place."

Gage took several shots of Monique's face, breathing through his nose like a bull ready to charge.

"Do you have any other lacerations?" he asked her.

"No, but I've got a bad bruise where he grabbed me." She unbuttoned her blouse and dropped it from one shoulder. Prints of five fingers stood out clearly on her skin.

Gage snapped pictures of that, too, then showed us into his guest bathroom. It had been redone in black, white, and red. "Chic!" Monique told him.

I didn't take time to admire his new decor. I put the toilet seat down and motioned for her to sit. Gage leaned against the door while I gently cleaned her up.

"Let me get a few more shots now that we can see the whole damage," he said.

When I finished, Gage began to question her. "Why did he hit you?"

What I wondered was why he had hit her where it would show. Batterers don't usually do that.

Monique shoved her hair back from her face. "Okay," she said, trying to get her thoughts together, "here's what happened. It was our three-month anniversary of getting back together, so he'd bought some steaks to celebrate. I burned them because I'm not used to cooking steak. Benny and I couldn't afford it. Junior yelled at me for burning them and I apologized, but then I said that in the future he should cook them. He said, 'My women cook for me, I don't cook for them.' So I asked, 'How many women do you have?' He said that was none of my business and I said, 'It's my business if you are my business.' And he hauled off and hit me!" Her eyes widened in amazement. "He hit me!"

"How many times?" Gage asked. He was taping his questions and her answers.

"Only once, but real hard. His ring cut my lip."

"He hasn't hit you before?" I asked. "Like the weekend of the ice storm when you said you fell on the ice?"

"I did fall on the ice. I wasn't with Junior at the time."

"Did he threaten you if you told anyone he had hit you?" Gage asked.

"Not then he didn't. I said, 'I'm not putting up with this' and started for my coat. Before I got to the door, he grabbed my shoulder—that's when he left that big bruise—and he said I was not to tell anybody he'd hit me, especially not my parents. I was to say I had fallen and cut my lip. I jerked away from him and said, 'I'm not lying for you or anybody.' He grabbed me again and dragged me to his back bedroom. He locked me in!" She sounded as upset about that as about being hit.

"He has an outside lock on his bedroom doors?" Gage asked.

"On that one. He rents an old house outside of town and he keeps his hunting rifles in that room, so he put a Yale lock on the door. Anyway, he yelled through the door that I would stay there until I promised not to tell. I was still mad, so I didn't say a word. He yelled, 'Do you hear me, Monique? If you tell your parents I hit you, I will kill you. I swear it! The army taught me how to kill with my bare hands, and so help me God, if you tell your daddy about this, I'll kill you!'"

"Did you believe him?" Gage asked.

Monique trembled. "Oh, yeah, I believed him. I saw him kill a stray cat out at his place one day. It had climbed on his car and left paw prints, and when he saw them, he grabbed that cat and hurled it into a tree trunk hard enough to kill it."

"But you still stayed with him?" I asked, amazed.

She heaved a big sigh. "Yeah, I did. He said the cat had been killing birds on his property and he thought it carried diseases. And he was sweet to me. He said I brought out the best in him. He had never even gotten mad at me before." She touched her lip gingerly, as if to remind herself that things had changed. "I'm through with him now, though. No man can do this to me and expect me to stay. I watched some of my neighbors down in Savannah put up with their boyfriends and husbands beating them, and no matter what the guys promised, the beatings never stopped. Benny had to drive one woman to the hospital twice."

"How did you get away?" Gage asked.

"It wasn't easy. I tried to open a window, but they were painted shut. He didn't have a phone in that room, either. I thought about trying to shoot the door open, but I couldn't find bullets and besides, I don't know how to load a gun." She started to shake.

"So how did you get away?" I repeated. I wanted to know. I also wanted to redirect her thoughts toward the successful part of her evening.

"I heard him turn on the television to watch sports while he ate. He always does that, and he yells at whichever team he is supporting when they do dumb things. So I grabbed one of his rifles and I waited. As soon as he started yelling at some player, I used the rifle to break the window. Then I jumped out and ran."

"Why head out of town?" I asked. "Why didn't you try to get home?"

"And let my folks see me like this? And Wonder? No, thank you. I decided to go out to Regan's."

"That's fifteen miles!"

"I know. I hoped I could hitch a ride, but every time I saw headlights, I was terrified it was Junior, so I hid in the bushes until the car passed. I was beginning to think I'd have to walk all the way when you showed up."

"Thank God," I murmured.

"Amen," said Gage. "Are you finished with her for the time being, Teensie? We need to decide what we're—"

Jester barked.

"Into the hall," Gage commanded.

A car door slammed. Jester kept barking.

Before we had closed the door behind us, the bathroom window shattered.

The window was small and had frosted glass, so all the

shooter could have seen was the light. I guessed he could see we weren't in the other lit rooms and figured we had to be in there, but he shot high so nobody would get hurt.

Gage slammed the door behind us. "This time I *will* call the police."

As he punched in the number, Jester continued to bark. A second window exploded, then a third. Monique looked at Gage in dismay. "He's shooting up your whole house."

Gage was too busy talking to the operator to reply.

Within moments, we heard a siren, coming closer.

We heard one last shot, but nothing exploded. Feet pounded down the drive and tires screeched as a car left the driveway, then we heard only silence.

Monique whispered in terror, "I can't stay here. I've put you all in danger." She shook like a feather in the wind.

"That's one scary dude you've been hanging around with," Gage muttered. "If Jester hadn't barked . . ."

"Jester!" I dashed for the door.

Gage had the same thought at the same instant. We reached the back porch in a dead heat. Gage flipped on security lights in the backyard and I ran out.

I found Jester a few feet from the fence near the driveway. One side of his head was blown away.

I fell to my knees beside him, too desolate to cry. That dog had been a puppy when Teddy got him, he'd been my support through all those years with my parents, and he had died trying to protect me. Losing him, I had lost my best friend, both my parents again, and my last piece of Teddy.

Gage put a comforting arm around my shoulders, but when he spoke, it was in an icy voice I had never heard before. "I will get Junior Walters if it's the last case I try."

"Is Jester all right?" Monique called from the back porch.

"Stay back!" I cried.

Monique ran from the porch. She took one look and screamed to wake the dead.

A crowd began to gather on the sidewalk. Voices rose in hushed clamor.

"What on earth is going on? We heard something that sounded like shots."

"We did, too. Who is screaming out back?"

A cruiser pulled into the drive. Its lights flashed blue around the yard, bathing it in a cold, eerie glow. The siren wailed to a murmur and died.

I fetched a blanket from my truck to cover Jester's body.

The next few minutes were chaos. Neighbors milled around. Coco arrived. When she heard what had happened to Jester, she used words I hadn't known she knew. A neighbor who was a vet offered to take Jester to his freezer until we could decide what to do about burial. I asked him and another man to lift Jester into the back of my truck instead. If I could, I wanted to bury him on the mountain.

The mountain! I should have called Tobias to explain why I was late. He must think I had abandoned him and the kids. I moved to the relative privacy on the other side of my truck and pulled out my cell phone, but when I saw the blanket-covered mound in the truck bed, my grief was so sharp that I could scarcely punch in the number.

"Where the dickens are you?" Tobias's voice was harsh. "You said you'd come straight home." I flinched at the anger in his voice. Did he expect me to account for every second I was away from the children?

I had to clear my throat before I could speak. "Sorry, I would have called earlier, but on my way home I ran into Monique, and her boyfriend had hurt her. I drove her to Gage's and then Junior came over here shooting out windows—"

"Shooting? Are you hurt?"

"No, but—" I couldn't tell him about Jester on the phone. "Look, I can't talk right now. I'll be home as soon as I can. Did the girls go to bed?"

"Unwillingly, yes. Carrie cried for you."

"Carrie cries for everybody: her mother, Regan, me. Tomorrow if I put her to bed, she'll probably cry for you. I've got to go for now."

"Wait. You can't take Monique home after all this. What if the man follows her there? He could hurt them all."

I suspected he was thinking of Wonder, as I was. "What else can I do with her?"

"Bring her up here for the night. It's safe."

"Nothing is safe around that animal. I can't endanger the children—and you."

"The cove is well defended," he said in a grim voice. "Homer will let us know if anybody tries to come in at night, and I've got a security light and a good rifle. Bring her here. We can make long-term plans in the morning."

The tears I could not shed for Jester filled my eyes at his continuing kindness. "Are you working on a sainthood merit badge?" I hoped he couldn't hear how clogged my throat was.

"Come home," he said. Home. The word had a wonderful ring.


I told Gage what Tobias had suggested. Gage asked the police officer to escort Monique and me "to the place Miss MacAllester tells you." I appreciated his not mentioning the place, in case Junior or a friend of his was in that swelling crowd. I found myself looking at the darkness and picturing a gun aimed at Monique.

"I'll talk to you as soon as you get back," Gage promised the officer. "The women don't need to be here with all this mess. You can interview Monique tomorrow."

As we drove, Monique sobbed. "It was bad enough for Junior to hurt me. He had no call to hurt Jester."

"He had no call to hurt anybody." I brushed tears from my cheeks.

"He really could be sweet. I know you don't believe that, but he has never hit me before. Not in high school or after we got back together here. I think it was being in the army that turned him mean."

"Lots of people come out of the army and aren't mean."

She sighed. "I know, and I've told friends who got beaten up, 'If he could keep from hitting you when he was trying to impress you enough to get you to go out with him, he could keep from hitting you the rest of the time.' I know that's true, but I did like him. A lot."

She subsided to consider her own wisdom. After a few minutes of sniffling, she said, "I never saw Gage like he was tonight, did you? I mean, the way he was always playing games with you and Wonder, I thought he was a great big kid. This morning, the way he was cutting up with those middle school kids, he could have been their age. But he stood up to Junior and knew exactly what to do when we went inside: taking all those pictures before you cleaned me up and taping what I said. Will he put Junior in jail?"

"I certainly hope so. Rest, now. I need to concentrate on the road." I wasn't in any mood to discuss how wonderful Gage had been. I was grieving for my dog.

Before we reached the cove, I called Tobias again. I needed to warn him I was coming into the cove with an escort, in case he was at an upstairs window with a rifle.

"A police car is following me in," I informed him. "See you in a few minutes."

I hadn't known how tense I was until we reached the cove and I felt myself relax like a child in its mother's arms. Part of that was because the halogen security light that flooded the entire yard with a cold white glow would have revealed Junior if he had been there. Part of it was because of Homer on the drive. But mostly it was because Tobias was sitting on the front porch waiting for us. I slowed and waved to let our escort know we were okay. He blinked his lights, turned, and headed back to town.

Tobias came down to meet us. When I performed introductions, Monique stuck out her hand. "I never got to thank you for rescuing Wonder that day, and now Teensie is asking you to rescue me. As you can probably see, I'm a mess."

Halogen lights make even beautiful people ugly. Monique looked like something from a monster movie. Tobias didn't flinch. He waved her toward the door. "Come on in. It's cold out here and there's a fire inside."

Homer pressed himself against my legs, whimpering. Did he sense what I had in my truck? I fell to my knees on the gravel walk and buried my face in his neck, sobbing. Monique sniffled on the porch above us.

"What's the matter now?" Tobias asked from the front door.

"It's—it's—" I sobbed too hard to finish.

Monique was better able to cry and talk at the same time. "Her dog got killed."

"Jester?" Tobias sounded as if he thought he had heard wrong.

I nodded. Monique continued the story. "It was all my fault. My boyfriend came over to Gage's house shooting out the windows and Jester barked at him, so he shot the dog. Teensie's had that dog for years."

Tobias came back down the steps to rest his hand on my head. "I'm sorry, Deborah. I am really sorry." He stroked my hair while I wept. I knew it was no more than he would have done for one of the children, but I stayed where I was for several minutes, warmed by his touch.

When I stopped bawling, he offered me a hand up. I dropped his hand as soon as I rose. Sparring with him I could handle. Tenderness was too much.

I wiped away my tears and followed him inside.

The kitchen was spotless. I sniffed and swallowed the last of my tears, glad to have a mundane topic to discuss. "You put the girls to bed *and* did the dishes?"

"Eric and I did them after the girls went to bed."

Wanting us to get back to normal footing as soon as possible, I made a poor attempt at a laugh. "You got Eric to do dishes?"

"I told him it is an old Cherokee custom that men help their womenfolk. He apparently hadn't realized he was part Cherokee. Lena had never told him."

"He's lucky to have you for his new uncle. Is he still up?"

"No, he decided to go to bed, too. It's been a wearing day on everybody. You two look like you could use some sleep."

"Do you want to know what happened to me?" Monique held her chin at a brave tilt. She would tell him if necessary.

"That can wait. Go to bed and rest. Things will look different in the morning." He rested a hand briefly on her shoulder. "The Cherokee have a saying: 'The soul would have no rainbow if the eyes had no tears.'"

"We all ought to have rainbows after tonight, then." She looked around the downstairs. "Where do I sleep?"

"In with me," I told her. "Room at the left up the stairs. I'll be up in a little while." When Monique had climbed the stairs, I said softly, "Thank you so much for having her here."

"It's okay, but heaven help us when Wonder finds out you brought her mother here after you wouldn't let her stay. I'd better go out Monday and buy her a bed."

"Oh!" The words "go out" had reminded me of the sad burden in my truck. "I brought Jester back with me. May I bury him somewhere up here? I'll need you to help me get him out of the truck, though, and tell me where to find a shovel."

"You want to bury him tonight? It's cold enough. . . ."

"I don't want the children to see him. He—Junior shot off part of his head."

Tobias's face hardened. "I'll do it."

"No, I have to help. I have to say good-bye."

"Then run up and get Monique settled and come outside. I'll go dig the grave." He reached for his heavy jacket.

When I got outside, he was standing by my truck looking at Jester. Together we lifted the heavy dog out and carried him to a hole Tobias had dug at the side of the front yard. "The forsythia bush here comes out real pretty in the spring," Tobias promised.

I sat beside Jester for a few minutes, stroking him with one hand, silently saying good-bye. "Okay. I'm ready." Together we wrapped him in the blanket and lowered his body into the hole.

As Tobias finished shoveling dirt, he asked, "You want to say a few words?"

"I—I can't." I felt like my insides had turned to tears.

Tobias bowed his head. "Great God, you know what this sweet dog meant to Deborah. You know how he got her through some hard days. She's going to miss him. Please take him to that Magic Lake of the Animals somewhere in the sky. Heal all his wounds and take good care of him. We commit him into your care."

"Thank you," I whispered. "That was perfect."

I knelt beside the grave. "Good-bye, Jester." I stayed on my knees while Tobias tamped down the last shovelful of dirt and replaced the grass.

He offered me a hand to help me up again.

Trying to lighten the moment, I said, "I can remember when you were too weak to do that."

"I do, too." He put a comforting arm around me, as Gage had earlier. "You haven't asked me in ages how I feel."

"You aren't my patient anymore."

He looked down at me in the cold halogen light. "Which makes me what?"

I took a moment to steady my voice and consider my answer. I wanted to say "friend," but that might be presumptuous. "My landlord?"

"That works." He left his arm around me until we got inside. I didn't get chills up my spine, but I was glad of his support.

"I can't tell you how much it meant that you were with me out there," I said when we reached the house. "And that you'd take Monique in. I keep landing you with one problem after another, don't I?"

He heaved a sigh worthy of Wonder. "Let's say that having you around is never dull." Odd. That was exactly what I had said about him several moons before.

"I do have a question," I said, filling the kettle for tea I badly needed. "Why were you so angry that I didn't call to tell you I'd be late? Do I need to account for every minute I'm away from the house?"

"No, but you said you would come straight home. I didn't know if you'd stayed at Susan's or run off the road."

"You were worried? That's why you were mad?" I couldn't believe my ears.

"You ran off that road once before. Why wouldn't I worry?"

I felt like somebody had tied a balloon to my belt that lifted me an inch off the floor. "It never occurred to me you would. Nobody has worried about me for years. Poor Teddy couldn't worry, Mother never worried about anybody but King, and King—he never noticed if I was there or not unless he wanted something. Thank you, Tobias. Thank you for having Monique over to stay a while, thank you for helping me bury Jester, and thank you for worrying."

"If you had given me your cell number, I could have called you."

"I'll write it down right now."

He nodded toward the whistling kettle. "Do it tomorrow. Drink your tea while I finish in the bathroom, then go to bed. Don't forget to bank the stove."

Gage came up the next afternoon to report that Junior could not be found. "I think you need to stick pretty close up here until he gets picked up," he told Monique. "Once he's in the detention center, we'll try to get him held without bail. If not, you'll need to stay here until he comes to trial."

"How long would that be?" Monique asked. "I've got classes to attend."

"We'll see," was all he would say.

"There are a few other women on campus who might have stories about Junior if Monique speaks out," I told him. "Albert would know who they are."

"Good," Gage told me. "Granddaddy and I want to do everything in our power to ensure he goes to prison."

"One day he'll get out, though, won't he?" Monique was worried. "Won't he come after me then?"

"We'll deal with that when the day comes." I managed not to smile, but it sounded like Gage had long-term plans for Monique.

"Can I go home to get my car?" she asked. "I need to attend class, and I'll go crazy up here if I can't shop at the mall sometimes. Besides, Teensie's got all these kids to drive to school Monday, and she can't do that in her truck."

I hadn't thought about that problem.

"I don't want you in Unizilla," Gage told her. "Let me see what I can do about transportation for Teensie."

That evening he brought a friend up the mountain driving a used SUV. "The car now belongs to Lena's estate," he informed me. "I've put you and Tobias on the insurance as the designated drivers."

He also told Monique that he and Susan had arranged that he would stop by Susan's each evening to pick up Monique's class assignments, and he would deliver her completed work back to Susan so it could reach Monique's professors. Monique grumbled at being confined to the cove, but she agreed. "Until you catch Junior."

Although the next two weeks weren't easy in our oddly assorted household, I couldn't remember ever being so happy. I got used to getting up at dawn and cooking an enormous breakfast for the family before heading down the hill. I enjoyed helping the kids get ready for school and waiting with them at the school bus stop. I loved the sight of Monique running around in jeans with baggy sweatshirts, her hair in a ponytail. She didn't even put on much makeup when she took the girls shopping at a distant mall or went with Gage to a couple of movies.

Tobias's gentle firmness and Damien's presence on weekends cracked Eric's shell. A boy with a good mind and a delightful sense of humor began to emerge. Kaitlin began to lose her pinched, worried look and got some color in her cheeks. Only Carrie wasn't happy. She was scared of animals and insects, so she didn't want to go outdoors. She wasn't used to working, so she complained whenever I asked her to perform some small task. "Let her grumble," I told Tobias. "She'll settle in eventually."

One night Monique washed Kaitlin's hair and put it in French braids. The style suited her thin little face. "I've never had my hair fixed before," Kaitlin said shyly, admiring her new self in the mirror. The child's gratitude for little things tugged at my heart. "We get clean sheets every single week?" or "We get to put on clean underwear every day?" she would say. "I don't need *two* pairs of shoes," she protested when Monique took her shopping with my instructions, although the only pair Kaitlin had was fit for nothing but barnyard work. She came home with a glowing face. "We got Sunday shoes *and* pink-and-white running shoes!"

She was so helpful that sometimes I had to send her outdoors to play. She took charge of feeding a small flock of laying hens that Tobias brought home. She begged to wash dishes and help me cook. She wanted to mop the floors and clean the bathrooms. "I didn't know they had stuff you could use to get bathtubs clean," she said. I had to explain several times that she could do her laundry and Carrie's, but that each of the rest of us would do our own. (Eric wasn't thrilled about that, but Tobias was firm.)

Kaitlin remained fiercely maternal where Carrie was concerned. She gave Carrie her bath. She chose what Carrie would wear to school and dressed the child, though I kept telling her Carrie was old enough to dress herself. Kaitlin dished food onto Carrie's plate and taped her art on their bedroom door. She heard Carrie's prayers at night and listened to her prattle about what had happened during the day. Several times I had to rebuke Kaitlin for doing Carrie's jobs while Carrie played. I even had to chide her, "Go outside and play, Kaitlin. Your sister can amuse herself."

I was so busy during the daytime that I scarcely spoke to Tobias except to ask or tell him something about the children, but I reveled in those short conversations. In those days, we totally agreed on what was best for the children.

During the evenings after our boisterous brood went to bed and Monique slipped upstairs to take a long bath, he and I played chess. We said little during those times, content to enjoy the fire and the quiet. We won fairly equally. If I lay awake in the dark afterward, thinking of him sleeping only a wide hall away, I kept still enough in my bed not to bother Monique.

Those weeks are still recorded on several pages in my sketchbook. An eagle and a young heron muck out the barn. An eagle teaches a young heron to drive the tractor. A little brown wren scatters corn for hens. A plump baby pigeon backs away from three pink piglets in alarm, while Wonder—whom I always drew as Wonder—pours slop into their trough. She and Kaitlin named the piglets Huff, Puff, and Curlytail.

Yes, Wonder was with us for the two weeks Monique stayed. Tobias had been right about her insisting. He bought her a camp cot and I put it in my room, but before bedtime Wonder and Kaitlin dragged it down the hall to "de girls' room."

During one of our evening chess games, I asked Tobias, "Does it make you a little crazy having all these people in the house? It must seem overwhelming after living here so long alone."

His hand hesitated over a knight and moved to his bishop. "Houses are built to shelter people. This one is much happier now. Checkmate!"

I bent over the board. "You rascal! I didn't see that coming."

He gave me a smug smile.

I love the picture I drew of Eric's face the day he dashed into the kitchen one afternoon and yelled, "Come see, Deb'rah! Tobe bought a milk cow! He says she'll be mine, but I have to take care of her. He's going to teach me to milk and everything."

"You are spoiling those kids rotten," I pointed out that evening. "Chickens, pigs, a cow—I thought this was a vegetable farm."

"Animals are good for children. Besides, I figured we'd better get some food producers around here before the kids eat us out of house and home."

The biggest problem we had with Kaitlin and Eric was at

school. Both children were failing. Their attendance when they had lived with their mother had been worse than erratic, and their teachers were understandably frustrated because they had dozed in class, failed to study for tests, and seldom brought in homework.

"He didn't even bathe," Eric's teacher complained with a wrinkled nose.

"He bathes now," I pointed out. "Did you ever ask somebody to go by and check for neglect? Dirty clothes, erratic attendance, no homework—those are classic signs of neglect. Chances are good the kids didn't have pencils and paper at home."

"I figured it was a family of poor white trash where nobody cared," Eric's teacher admitted. Oh, the dangers of stereotyping, especially where children are concerned!

I started a strict regimen after school: change clothes, have a snack and one hour of free time, then do homework. Eric grumbled at first. Kaitlin was surprised I would sit with them in case they needed help. Gradually they both settled down. Between homework and supper they fed the animals, and after supper they helped with dishes and did one more hour of homework. The children were intelligent, I discovered, but far behind.

On Saturdays they did chores in the morning, had free time in the afternoon, and we did two hours of schoolwork before supper. Sundays they were free after church.

One rainy Saturday afternoon while Carrie napped, Tobias taught the older kids to play poker. The whole table laughed when I lost all my buttons.

That night I drew a flock of birds with happy faces fluttering around a button jar.

Eric watched less and less television. He was too busy. Kaitlin lost her worried look. Everybody was happy—except Carrie.

Carrie still hated getting dirty. She continued to balk at doing the small chores we assigned her. She was afraid of the animals. She cried when Homer tried to lick her face. She despised Wonder, who nagged her to climb trees and ride Bray.

That feeling was mutual. Wonder stormed one day, "Why don't you send dat crybaby someplace else so we can hab peace and quiet around here?"

Instead, the day finally came when a deputy apprehended Junior holding up a convenience store. That plus Monique's sworn statement was enough to persuade the magistrate to hold him without bail until trial. Monique could go home at last. Wonder lobbied to stay with us, but I reminded her that her mother needed her. "You need me, too. Who is gonna feed dose pigs? Dat Carrie sure won't do it. And don't you let Tobias tell any more Cherky stories without me."

The Cherokee stories had been a hit with all the children— and with Monique and me. Tobias told us how the deer got his antlers, why the bear had no tail, why the mink stinks, why the terrapin's shell is cracked, and why the turkey gobbles. When the children bickered, he told them the story about the Smoky Mountains.

Wonder and Carrie both loved the story about Forever Boy, a Peter Pan child who didn't want to grow up. As Tobias told it, "The Nunnehi, the Little People, came to the boy and said, 'Come live with us. You will never grow up and you can play tricks on grown-ups to make them laugh so they stay young at heart.' So Forever Boy went to live with the Little People. Now, when a Cherokee thinks he has a big fish on his line and pulls up a stick, he laughs and says, 'That's Forever Boy, playing a trick on me.'"

The little girls hid our shoes and changed tops on the salt and pepper shakers, then said with giggles, "It wasn't us. It was Forever Boy." That story was the only thing that brought them together.

On Monique and Wonder's last evening, we had strawberries and ice cream for dessert. "Tell about how strawberries got made," Wonder commanded.

Gage was up that evening to eat supper and take them back to town. When the story was ended, Monique leaned over and kissed him on the cheek. "Not all quarrels can be settled by strawberries. Some of them need lawyers." I would swear that he blushed.

Eric's favorite was the story about Nunnehi soldiers who protected the Cherokee village of Nikwasi when it was attacked by the Creek. "They were nearly defeated," Tobias said, "when suddenly the mound of Nikwasi opened up and little soldiers marched out by the thousands. They massacred all the enemies but one. He went back to tell his village, 'Never attack the village of Nikwasi because spirit people protect it.'"

"That was a bloody story," I said that night as we played chess. "I like the animal ones better."

Tobias shoved a pawn two spaces. "Life can be bloody. Eric already knows that. Maybe he needs to know there are protectors around, as well."

I smiled. "You are a good uncle."

He shrugged, but I could tell he was pleased. Old granite face wasn't as inscrutable as he liked to think he was.


In our third week I said to Tobias, "I don't think we are ever going to get the odor out of that couch in the den. I've got some furniture in storage. Would you like to bring some of it up here?"

"Your kind of furniture would look mighty odd in a log house."

"What do you know about my kind of furniture? Come look at it."

The following afternoon we all went down to Holcomb's warehouse. Tobias admitted, "This furniture would look great in the house. It is beautiful." He didn't bother to hide his surprise.

"Thanks. It was my aunt's—the one whose husband was an

artist in Santa Fe. I've always loved the furniture, both for its style and its memories."

"So how about if we put my black couch in the den where the kids can lounge around on it, and put all your stuff in the living room? And do you want to bring your piano?"

"Could we?" I had refused to admit to myself how much I missed it.

"There's plenty of room. Eric, do you think you, Deborah, and I can move all this?"

Eric eyed the piano doubtfully. "That thing looks heavy."

"It comes apart," I told him. "It's not as hard to move as an upright would be."

After we got the new furniture into the log house, Tobias and Eric took the old couch to the county dump while the girls and I arranged Teddy's furniture, her rugs, her husband's watercolors, and my piano in the log house living room. Afterward I took Kaitlin and Carrie to the mall and we chose drapes for the living room windows. After Tobias hung them, Eric looked at the living room and said, "This looks like something on TV." From him, that was high praise.

Tobias sat on Teddy's couch. "Okay, Deborah, how about a concert?"

"The piano will need tuning," I warned. "It's been moved twice."

"None of us will notice a thing. Play, woman!"

I thought about playing children's songs, but changed my mind. If classical music could lift me above my troubles, could it do the same for those children?

I played a Mozart sonata. I don't know how high they got lifted, but they all sat quietly until I was done. Kaitlin stood by the piano the whole time, and afterward, she gently touched one key. "Could you teach me?"

I went online that night and ordered beginners' books. I had recognized that expression in her eyes as she looked at the piano. I'd felt the same hunger as a child. I taught her each Saturday morning after that, and seldom had to remind her to practice.

She had stopped slapping Carrie by then, and the only time I saw her really cross was when Carrie banged on the piano. "Don't do that!" Kaitlin ordered.

Carrie pouted. "I wants to play, too." but when I tried to teach her the discipline of simple pieces, she soon lost interest.

One day in the drugstore, Carrie exclaimed, "Miss Wegan!" She pelted down the aisle. I hurried after her and saw her throw herself against Regan's legs. Regan picked up the child with a smile. "How are you doing, darling? Don't you look pretty!"

Carrie patted her cheek. "Can I come home wif you? I wants cookies and my pretty bed. Deb'rah won't give me cookies and I don't gots a pretty bed."

"You poor dear." Regan nuzzled her cheek and frowned at me.

"Deb'rah won't give you more than two cookies at a time." I corrected Carrie's version of the truth as I joined them. "And you have the prettiest bed in the house."

"It's not as pretty as Miss Wegan's bed. Can I come home wif you?" She patted Regan's cheek again.

"Why don't you let her come for a couple of nights?" Regan suggested.

"She doesn't have any clothes except what she's got on."

"I was going to the mall anyway. I could pick her up a few things." She rubbed her nose against Carrie's. "We could swim, and bake cookies—"

"—and blow bubbles and feed de horsie," said that treacherous child who refused to feed any animal on our farm.

"Take her, then," I said, "although what Kaitlin will say

when I come home without her, I cannot imagine." I would certainly not tell her that Carrie left with Regan without a backward look. I felt a little abandoned myself.

When I showed up at the school bus stop alone, Kaitlin's face wrinkled into its old worried expression. "Is Carrie all right?"

She didn't complain after I explained, but as she went around the farm that afternoon without Carrie by her side, she listed like poor Lucky with her missing wing.

That night Tobias stepped out on the front porch after the dishes were done and scanned the sky. He came back inside to ask, "Since Carrie's not here to go to bed early, is everybody else up for a little hike?"

"At this hour?" I objected. "It's already dark."

"The moon is full and will come up soon, so there will be plenty of light. We'll drive part of the way, then walk the rest. Come on. Coats, everybody. Maybe we'll see a miracle. You kids climb in the back of the truck."

"It's illegal for children to ride in the back of trucks," I reminded him.

"Don't take all the fun out of life. We aren't going more than a mile." Kaitlin and Eric were already climbing in with enthusiasm. "One rule, kids: anybody I see standing or kneeling rides in the cab. You understand? And hold on tight. The road gets steep."

Tobias headed across the fields to the stream, where a faint road led toward the mountain. "My great-great-great granddaddy used this road to get to Unizilla," he boasted. My heart warmed to see his happy face.

He never went above twenty miles an hour, and we could hear Eric and Kaitlin laughing as they bounced along. "Maybe I was envious," I admitted. "I never got to ride in the back of a truck. I never got to ride in a truck at all until King bought me one." I leaned my head against the back of my seat and watched a glorious moon slip over the eastern mountaintops.

We jounced up the narrow road until Tobias pulled to a stop. "We have to hike from here. The moon will make it easy to see our way, but it gets steep, so we'll need to go single file. Eric, you take the back and I'll take the front, okay? Ladies in between."

He led us beside the stream up a path that climbed steadily. As we walked he alerted me to rocks, ruts, and roots. Occasionally he put out a hand to pull me up a particularly difficult place. I hoped if he heard my heart thumping with happiness, he'd think it was simple exertion.

"Hey, man, this is hard," Eric complained when the trail got steeper. His voice in those days ranged from bass to soprano.

"Our people roamed these mountains for centuries," Tobias reminded him. "You can climb one small hill."

After that, I certainly didn't complain. Who knew what Tobias would say about *my* people?

A couple of times I put a hand behind me to help Kaitlin. She always said, "I can do it," and scrambled up on all fours. Her face was pink and happy in the moonlight. I blessed Tobias for having such a good idea on the night Carrie was gone.

I was glad, though, when he stopped and I could catch my breath. "Up there." He pointed to a large, flat rock. As we climbed onto the rock, I gasped in wonder.

"This is beautiful!" Kaitlin cried.

The dark forest was split by a narrow waterfall that looked like liquid silver in the moonlight. As it plunged from a great height, it filled the forest with its roar. When Tobias smiled down at me in the moonlight, the planes of his face were so sharp and lovely, they brought a lump to my throat. I would go home and draw him in moonlight with the waterfall behind him, and I would tuck it into a secret part of my wallet and carry it always.

"Watch now," he said, putting a hand on my shoulder. "In a few minutes, you ought to see something really special."

Kaitlin saw it first. "It's the ghost of a rainbow!"

Sure enough, the pale shadow of a rainbow lay across the surface of the falling water like a brooch on an apparition. Kaitlin sighed. "That's the prettiest thing I ever saw. Does it have a name?"

"It's a moonbow," Tobias explained, "a lunar rainbow. They are rare, for we see them only when the sky is dark and the moon is full and low. Sometimes you can see one in the sky if it is raining opposite the moon, and you can see them at certain waterfalls. My father showed me this one when I was a boy, as his father showed him. Rainbows are special to the Cherokee. There's a moonbow at Yosemite that I'd like to see one day. It's far more spectacular than this."

"This one is best," Kaitlin declared loyally. "It's ours. Why doesn't it have colors?" I had been wondering the same thing.

"It does, but because moonlight isn't bright, the colors don't show up to our eyes."

High above us an owl screeched. Small animals rustled in the underbrush. We human intruders stood silent. At last the moonbow faded and we turned to leave.

Eric looked once more at the waterfall. "This was worth the climb," he declared. Tobias and I shared a smile in the moonlight that I would take home and cherish.

He put out a hand for me as we started down. "Let's all hold hands. Going down is harder than coming up."

The moon was so bright by then that our trip down was like walking on a silver path through a magic forest. I was sure if Wonder had been there, she'd have said we were in a fairy tale. Tobias carefully warned me of boulders and logs and I passed the warnings back. I could have walked for miles with his hand holding mine.

When we got to the truck, Tobias grabbed me around the waist and hoisted me into the bed with a laugh. "Nobody ought to die without having ridden once in the back of a truck." I hadn't been that close to him since our kiss. I hoped he thought I was breathless from the hike.

"Sit with your backs to the cab going down," Tobias instructed. "The hill is steep."

"And hold on tight," Kaitlin warned me, snuggling close. "It's a rocky road."

Clutching the side of the truck as we swayed down the mountainside, laughing hilariously with the children as we bounced over rocks, was worth the bruises to my backside the next morning.

That night I lay awake longer than usual, thinking about Tobias and our strange relationship. Would the closeness of that evening linger into the morning? Had he reached out a hand to me as he would to one of the children? Or was I becoming as special to him as he was to me?

Apparently not. He was up and out of the house before I woke. I heard him down near the barn chopping wood. He didn't come in for breakfast until the children were already eating. "We need to get up earlier and work harder now that the days are getting longer," he told Eric. "I'll call you an hour earlier tomorrow." He scarcely seemed to notice I was at the table.

That afternoon when Kaitlin and I met Regan to exchange Carrie, Carrie cried because she had to come home. I could hardly bear the pain in Kaitlin's eyes

Regan called me that evening after the children were in bed. "I want to talk to you about that day-care place where Carrie goes. From what she says, they watch television all day. The child is four and can't say her ABCs or count past nine. I think she ought to go to the college preschool."

"You are probably right about her day-care home. I've been so busy trying to bring Kaitlin and Eric up to grade level, I haven't paid Carrie's education the attention I should have. I'm not sure Lena's trust fund would extend to the college preschool, though."

"It doesn't. I already talked to Judge Brantley. I've told him Holcomb and I will make up the difference. He said that's fine with him, if you agree."

Every fiber of my body wanted to scream, "Leave my child alone!" But how could I deny Carrie the same education I had urged Susan to provide for Wonder?

Carrie started preschool the following week, staying until three each afternoon so I could pick her up when I fetched Kaitlin from school.

Wonder called me the first afternoon. "Why did you put dat Carrie in my school? De teacher said I must play wif her because we are friends. We are *not* friends! I do not want dat Carrie at my school. She is a crybaby."

I sighed for the careless way adults lump children together. "It's the best preschool in town, and Carrie needs a good school. Help her make new friends, okay? She cries because she's lost her mother, like you lost your daddy. You can understand better than other children why she cries. Be nice."

"I will be nice but she is not my friend."

# Twelve

As spring budded the woodlands and crept up the cove, I was filled with restlessness. I wanted to run through a meadow and fling my arms wide like Maria in *The Sound of Music*. When I drove the children home one afternoon and saw Tobias riding his tractor, I found myself picturing what it would be like to ride in front of him with his arms around me. Some nights when I heard him up in the bathroom, I wished he'd stop by my room. Yearning to touch him, I went out of my way to avoid touching him, yet dwelled too often on the few times our bodies brushed.

To work off my frustration I took it on myself to clear the front yard of machinery parts and debris. I enlisted Carrie and Wonder and we made a pile behind the shed of the bits and pieces of machinery that lay strewn around the yard. When Eric asked if he could use "that junk behind the shed" for a school art project, Tobias said, "Sure. Saves me hauling it away."

We all went to the middle school art show one evening to see a four-foot-high sculpture Eric had created by cementing machinery bits together. He had named it "Recycled Farm." It had won a red ribbon.

"I never won a prize before," he exclaimed, his face shining with pride. He was even prouder when Tobias cemented the sculpture into place beside our front steps.

Tobias greeted spring by working harder. I never saw him except at meals. By the time I got down in the morning he was out doing chores. He ate breakfast rapidly, chatting with the children, and went straight to his tractor. I took the children to school and went to work, then picked them up after school and headed back up the mountain. Tobias set the older two to tending plants in the greenhouses and assigned Carrie to take over Kaitlin's job of scattering grain for the hens in addition to her own chores: feeding Homer and carrying table scraps to the pigs. He seldom spoke directly to me unless I had to ask him something about the kids. We didn't play chess anymore, for he went back out after supper to work until dark, and as soon as he came in he took a bath and headed to bed.

I knew there was a lot to do—it looked to me like more than one grown man and schoolchildren could handle—but he worried me. He was developing a strained look I didn't like. I wanted to remind him that he had been sick in the winter and still had not regained his full strength, but I didn't want to sound like his nurse.

One afternoon I asked whether there was anything I could do on the farm after I got home from work. "You have enough to do with work and caring for the house and the children," he said, his voice gruff. I felt as shut out of his life as I had been when he was sick. To give myself something to do in the evenings, I began to study flower catalogs. Together, Kaitlin and I planned where we would plant flower beds when the weather got warmer.

As days grew lighter, the rest of them worked later. Between farmwork and schoolwork, the children had little time for play. Tobias got up so early that he went to bed as soon as the children finished in the bathroom. I took over the house chores to give Kaitlin and Eric a little free time, and some days I felt like a drudge. Evenings after they were all in bed I played the piano softly. It was my only companion.

One Monday afternoon Gage and Tobias were at the table poring over sheets of paper when the children and I got home. The older two kids went to change out of their school clothes. I gave Carrie a snack and moseyed over to see what was so interesting.

"Pull up a chair and give us your wisdom," Gage invited. "I've been asking Tobias about Lena's house. A man is interested in buying it and fixing it up to sell. As a matter of interest, I met an inspector over there today, to see what needs to be done. It's a lot, but the question is, should we take what the buyer is offering and get it off our hands, or should we hire somebody to get it in shape and sell it for more profit? I find it harder to make this decision on behalf of the children than I would if it were my own place."

"What do you think?" I asked Tobias.

He was too busy scanning the inspector's report to look at me. "I think Damien, Eric, and I could do a lot of this work. Kaitlin could help some, too. I lean toward fixing it up ourselves." I noticed I was not included in the work crew.

I said nothing at the time, but while the older children were getting ready for bed, I hung up my dish towel and went to talk with him. He was in the den watching a basketball game until the bathroom was free. I took the other end of the couch and waited for a commercial.

Tobias shot me a quick look.

"Please don't take on that house," I said. "You can't add working on the house to everything else you have to do. You are already busy from dawn to dark, and the bulk of the spring planting hasn't begun. Besides, what do you know about fixing up a house?"

Eyes still on the television, he said, "My dad worked construction, and I worked some with him. I know how to do most of what needs done. The kids can help. I think it would be good for them to see the house restored from the place they knew to what it could be. It might help erase bad memories."

"Where would you find the time?"

"We could work weekends."

"You are already working weekends."

"I think we can get it done." His attention was glued to an attempt at a free throw.

"We'd never see you," I argued.

"Eric and Kaitlin would be working with me and Carrie doesn't care whether I'm here or not so long as she's got you or Kaitlin."

I chewed the inside of my lip to keep from bursting out, "I need to see you, too!"

"Besides," he added, "it's good for the children to keep busy." As a commercial came on, he changed channels to a *Law & Order* rerun.

"Could you mute that for a minute? Thank you. The children *are* busy. You've already got them feeding livestock, planting vegetables, mucking out the barn, and doing other chores, and they're working hard at school. They can't work all the time. They need time to play. We *all* need time to play. We could take them to the Chattanooga aquarium, or the new science museum over in Cartersville. You could take all of us to Cherokee sites around here. We could go on hikes, picnics—and every child needs time to think and dream."

"These children don't need time to think or dream. Their dreams could well be nightmares. I think they need to stay busy. We all need to stay busy." He checked to see if the commercials were over, saw they weren't, and flipped back to *Law & Order*.

I frowned at him. "You aren't a child psychologist."

"Neither are you. I understand what they need better than you. They need that house. We are Cherokee. The Cherokee do not sell land; we hold it in sacred trust."

I felt like he was drawing a circle around the rest of the family and leaving me out. "Those children are only a quarter Cherokee. I understand them as well as you do."

"You have never been a parent."

"That's not fair. You invited me to the farm because I'm good with children. Besides, you aren't exactly an expert, are you? How long has it been since you saw your son?" As soon as I'd said the words, I wished them back.

He wore his granite look. "You are here to look after the children, not run my life."

"I'm not running your life! I am thinking of the children. Cut them some slack. Cut yourself some slack. Take a little time to play. Don't work everybody so hard."

"People who work hard sleep better."

He was clenching his fist like a man strung far too tight. The nurse in me took over in spite of my good resolutions. "People who work too hard die. You are doing too much. You aren't back to your full strength yet. You've been sick. You don't need—"

He jumped to his feet. "Stop telling me what I need or don't need. You have no idea what I need!" He punched the power button, breathing hard. "I'm going to bank the stove. Good night."

I went to my room and drew exactly how I felt: a bluebird with an angry eagle dive-bombing her. By the time I finished, that poor little bird was so mangled that I could not bear to keep the drawing. I wadded it up and threw it away. Then I went to bed and sobbed into my pillow.

No matter how I replayed the fight, I could not come up with a dialogue in which Tobias would agree not to take on the house. He was going to fix it up no matter what I said. He and the children would exhaust themselves working on it—except for Carrie, who would pout and cry because Kaitlin wasn't around. The farm would suffer, his health would suffer, and I would not see enough of him to recognize him on the street.

"Oh, God, help!" I sobbed, stuffing my pillow in my mouth to stifle the cry.

In that dark, dark hour before dawn when misery cuts its sharpest teeth, I regretted my decision to move to Jones Farm. *I did exactly what I did with King*, I concluded. *I let a man talk me into doing what he needed without thinking it through.* Both times I should have gone to Atlanta—the first time to continue my career and the second time to begin folding memories of Tobias into a mental drawer. The strain of being close to him yet shut out of his life was more than I could bear. I wasn't good for him, either. He was exhausted, and all I did was increase his stress by nagging that he was working too hard. *Oh, Tobias! If only I could ease your burdens instead of adding to them.*

A germ of an idea grew into conviction in my chilly room. For Tobias's sake and my own sanity, I must leave the farm. The children would grieve, but they hadn't known me long. The older ones scarcely saw me anymore except on the way to and from school and at meals, and Kaitlin was all the mother Carrie needed. I would see if Alice could come cook and look after Carrie when Kaitlin was busy. They liked Alice.

*You can't abandon those children!* my heart cried. *They have already suffered enough. And you love them. Leaving them would be impossible.*

Maybe I could take them with me. I could rent us a little place somewhere and . . .

*You can't take them from Tobias. That's impossible, too. They love him and he loves them.*

"The whole situation is impossible," I complained. "Oh, God, help!"

Like many other supplicants, I didn't wait for an answer. At dawn, conviction became resolve. Sluggish and heavy, I got up as soon as I heard Tobias stirring. I hurried downstairs, wrapped in his mother's robe, and made coffee. He stopped at the foot of the stairs and looked at me in surprise.

"Come have a cup," I invited, holding out a mug. "We need to talk."

"We did talk." He jerked his jacket from its hook by the door. "I was a bear."

"I was a bear, too. Sit down, please. I have something else I need to say."

He dropped the jacket on the couch and joined me at the table.

"These children don't need to live with adults who are at loggerheads," I said as he pulled the sugar bowl toward him. He began to nod, but stopped when I added, "I think I need to leave."

"Leave?" His hand jerked. He spilled sugar on the table.

I rose for a sponge, glad for an excuse not to look at him.

"Yeah. Go to Atlanta, maybe." As I wiped up the spill, my sleeve brushed his arm. He drew away as if I had caressed him.

*Don't panic, Tobias. I'm not trying to seduce you. Not that I mightn't if I thought it would do a speck of good.*

"Judge Brantley could save money by hiring Alice Carter to come up afternoons and weekends," I continued. "She could look after Carrie and cook. She used to cook for Lena, and the children like her. I ought to get on with my life. I can't be a nanny forever."

There. I had presented a night's worth of anguish in a few concise sentences. Perhaps one day I would be proud of that. At the moment my entire being stood up and screamed a protest. *You are thinking of leaving Tobias?*

He stirred his coffee in deliberate circles. "You promised to stay until June."

"I—I can't." I looked across at him, willing him to understand.

"I thought you were a woman of your word." He shoved back his chair and strode out. He slammed the door behind him.

I snatched up his coat and ran after him. "You forgot—"

I ran smack into him on his way back in for it. His arms went tight around me for one heady instant, then he backed away, grabbed his coat, and headed for the woodpile. *It's only a reflex*, I told myself, but I could still feel his body against mine, and it left me weak and trembling. He chopped wood the whole time I fixed breakfast. He did not come in to eat.

"Run Tobias out a scrambled egg sandwich and a cup of coffee," I told Kaitlin when we were done.

"Is he mad at us?" She had a familiar shadow in her eyes.

"No, honey, he's mad at me."

While the children were upstairs collecting their things for school, he brought his dishes back. I said, "Don't be angry with me, Tobias. I'll talk to Judge Brantley this morning and see what he says."

"You want to go, go." He slapped his dishes on the countertop so hard he chipped the plate.

"Mind the crockery," I exclaimed without thinking.

He slammed the door behind him without another word.

On our way down the hill, Kaitlin said, "On Thursday we are having a program for parents at school. Can you all come?" Her face was pink with embarrassment. I hated the anxiety I saw in her eyes. Still, I would not promise what I could not deliver.

"One of us can go, I expect."

"I wish you could both come. I mean, I know you aren't really my parents, but I want you to see my projects and hear me recite. I'm saying a poem."

"I'll talk to Tobias," was all I could say.

When the children were all out of the car, I pulled into the grocery store parking lot, laid my head on the steering wheel, and bawled. I could not leave those children and I could not live with Tobias. What was I to do?

The first thing I had to do was get to work. Maybe routine and thinking about patients instead of myself would help. I had been too upset to pack a lunch, so I ran into the grocery store to pick up yogurt and fruit. At the front of the store was a big display of strawberries.

I stood in front of those strawberries and remembered Tobias's story. I picked up a berry and traced its shape with my finger. I could not break three children's hearts in order to save my own. I could not abandon Tobias, either, no matter what the cost. When I thought of leaving him, my heart felt like it was attached to him by a giant rubber band that would always pull me back no matter how far I stretched it.

"Strawberries just came in today from Florida, Teensie," the store manager told me as he bustled past. "Guaranteed to be sweet, like you."

I had to return to the farm.

I called Mimi to say I would not be in that morning. While I was in the store, I stocked up on groceries we needed and four cartons of strawberries.


As I climbed the mountain, I began to have second thoughts. What if Tobias didn't want me to change my mind? What if I had burned my bridges in the cove? By the time I saw the house I was as nervous as a bird surrounded by cats.

But when I saw Tobias by the fence scratching Bray, I knew I had made the right decision. He looked like he had that day in January, except he had swapped his heavy jacket for a denim one and wore no hat. His long hair blew in the wind. He looked like part of those mountains.

So was I.

I pulled up near the fence and climbed down. He gave me one quick look, then ignored me. I joined him and began to scratch Bray's other side.

"I thought you'd gone," he said in an expressionless voice.

"I came back."

He reached in his pocket and pulled out a wadded-up piece of paper. "I emptied wastebaskets after you left. I found this in yours."

I cloaked embarrassment in indignation. "You go through my trash?"

"Not usually. I recognized your drawing paper."

"You ought to. You stole my other drawings and framed them." I said it lightly, but watched carefully for his reaction. That was the first time I saw him blush.

"Maybe you'll be famous one day." He didn't mention the missing bluebird. Neither did I.

He smoothed out the wrinkles on the page he held. "This one is pretty gory. Was that how you felt last night?"

"I exaggerated a little." The wind whipped hair across my face. I brushed it away.

He shoved the paper back in his pocket. "My wife said I'm a dumb farm boy who doesn't have a clue how to treat a woman. She was right." He still hadn't looked at me.

I was appalled. "She said that?"

"She wrote it in the note when she left." He sounded desolate.

The thought of his wife and how much he had loved her made me desolate, too. "You want to talk about her?"

"Not particularly."

Since I was laying down my own pain for his, the brush-off hurt. "Talking to you can be like talking to a mountain, do you know that?"

He shrugged.

"Fine! Hunker down inside that wall you've built around your broken heart. Let the rest of us mill around outside."

His nostrils flared. "You don't know the first thing about my heart." He strode toward the apple tree and snapped off a dead limb. I stomped toward my truck. Might as well get those groceries inside.

Overhead, buzzards circled the cove.

As I drove up to the house, I cursed myself for a fool. Why had I bought those strawberries? Why had I come back? He didn't want me, except as a nanny to his foster children. He wanted Melinda.

I was putting cereal away when he came in. He stood in the doorway looking at me like he was memorizing my face. "I thought you were leaving."

"I told you, I came back."

"I meant just now. I heard the engine and thought you were driving away."

"I was driving closer to the house so I didn't have to carry groceries so far." I picked up one of the plastic boxes and shoved it toward him. "I got you these."

He picked it up and looked at it without a word.

I took the box from him and opened it. "I heard somewhere that the Cherokee exchange strawberries after a quarrel. So here."

He still didn't move.

I gave a huff of exasperation. "Here!" I took out a big strawberry, rinsed it, and held it toward him.

He hesitated so long, I thought he wasn't going to accept it. Instead, he leaned toward me and opened his mouth. I put it in. His lips closed, soft and warm, on my fingers. "Mmm. Good." Juice stained my fingers and ran down his chin. My whole body tingled.

"Sweet like me, the store manager said." I took a dish towel and dabbed his chin.

"The manager doesn't know you like I do." The words were teasing, but without a sting.

He chose a smaller berry, rinsed it, and held it toward me. I took the whole thing in one bite.

"Dainty Deborah." He ran a finger down my cheek. "Peace?"

"Peace. Do you want more, or shall we save the rest for the kids?"

"Save them for the kids—or our next fight." He set them on the island.

I unwrapped a stick of butter and put it on a plate to soften. We were back to normal: friends and comrades, giving Lena's children a safe home. In order to care for the children, of course we could live in the same house. I would just need to respect his boundaries and bank my personal fires. "I've realized that what you do about Lena's house is not my business. That's between you, Gage, and the children."

"I've been thinking you are probably right. It's too much for me to take on this summer. I'll talk to Gage about how much contractors would cost. I don't think we should sell. It would be a good rental property."

"And we both know how hard rental houses are to find in Unizilla," I agreed. "I'm sorry about the things I said about your son. You are a good parent, and you are doing a great job with these kids."

"I'm sorry I lashed out at you. I get a little crazy sometimes, thinking about Brandon—wondering where he is, if he's all right. It's a long time that he's been gone."

"Maybe you ought to contact him and see if he wants to come visit. He could even live here a while. He's getting pretty big to be riding around the country. He ought to settle down for high school."

I watched hope rise and fall in his face. "I don't even know where he is."

"You could find him if you tried. I'll bet he's on Facebook. All the kids are."

He looked at me while he absently picked up another strawberry and ate it.

"I also think it could help you to talk to somebody about Melinda." I managed to say her name without a tremor. "Your pastor, a friend, somebody. I think you are in what Wonder once called 'a stucking place'—a place where you can't do anything else until you get unstuck."

His brows drew together in a frown. "I'm not stuck on Melinda."

"I think you are, whether you know it or not."

He reached for my hand. "Come outside. It's time I told you about my marriage."

"You don't have to."

"Sounds like I do. Come on."

He led me to a simple bench in the front yard made from half a sawn log with crossed-log supports at either end. "My grandfather made this bench when my daddy was a boy, and planted that tree beside it." He pointed at the forty-foot maple shading the bench. "The tree grew while the bench stayed the same. There's probably a parable in there somewhere." He motioned for me to sit and lowered himself beside me.

He looked up at the buzzards, still circling the fields. "Great background for this particular story, buzzards looking for good pickings. Let's see, where to begin. . . . Okay, I met Melinda at the University of Georgia—and yes, this farm boy went to college."

"I didn't say a word."

"You were surprised, though. Don't deny it. I saw it in your eyes."

Drat my honest eyes.

"Daddy was getting old for construction and he'd gotten the notion he wanted to be a beef farmer. He'd fenced pastures, dug the pond, and bought a few cows, but he wasn't making any money, so he sent me to the university to learn how to make the place profitable. The problem was, I never took to cattle."

"You like animals."

"I don't like getting attached to animals I plan to send to a slaughterhouse. I have a hard time looking our three little pigs in the eye. So I majored in horticulture with a minor in biology. It seemed to me this cove had everything required for an organic farm—water, good soil, decent climate—but I knew Daddy would pitch a fit if I suggested plowing up his pastures, so I didn't tell him. I told him I was majoring in agriculture. He assumed that meant cattle."

"And Melinda?" He was straying from where we'd started to go.

"Ah, Melinda. I neglected to say that what I mostly majored in was baseball, with a minor in partying. We athletes were treated real good at parties. Melinda and I met at one and partied our way through two years. We got married right after graduation, to the disgust of both sets of parents. Hers didn't want a Cherokee son-in-law and mine didn't want a city girl on the farm. When Daddy found out I had spent four years in college and learned nothing about cattle, he told me I could take my degree elsewhere and see if I could support a wife. I got a job at a nursery near Atlanta and Melinda taught school. Brandon was born the next year. We bought five acres of farmland out in Rockdale County, put a mobile home on it, and I started a little truck farm. I did pretty well with it, working every free hour, and Brandon became a real little farmer. He rode on the tractor with me, discussed what to plant, and loved to watch our crops come up. Melinda, though—she wanted to travel. She'd go on the Internet to plan elaborate trips to see Houston, Las Vegas, or Seattle. I didn't want to see those places. If we'd had time and money to travel, I'd have wanted to see national parks."

He stopped, as if picturing some of the places he had not seen. "You could have seen both," I said, to keep him talking.

"Maybe, but I couldn't travel in the summer. It was my busiest season. Besides, Melinda wasn't interested in national parks. I learned one thing from our marriage: never marry somebody you meet at a place you don't enjoy being. That may not be who you are, but it could well be who they are. I partied in college, but I'm not a party person. Melinda loved parties, bars, and football games. One time in a fight she yelled that she hated baseball—she only pretended to like it to impress me, because I was Cherokee. She had thought that with that big casino up in North Carolina, all Cherokee were rich. Our marriage was a real letdown for her."

I was delighted to hear him say that with disgust, not distress.

"Things were real rocky even before Daddy died." He rubbed his hands on his thighs. "It's hard to believe that's ten years ago. He was a stubborn old cuss and we didn't always see eye to eye, but Samson Jones was worthy of respect."

"I wish I'd known him."

"I'm sure you saw him a few times. He and his crew built a couple of new buildings on campus while you were growing up. You wouldn't have noticed, though. He'd have looked to you like any other Indian."

"Or any other construction worker. I don't think I was prejudiced against Indians back then."

"And now?"

"Any opinions I have about Indians now are not prejudice, they are based on personal experience."

"My sister would tell you not to judge all Indians by me."

"I'll keep that in mind."

Tobias hadn't gotten around to Melinda's leaving, and any nurse knows you don't get rid of a boil until you drain it completely. "What happened after your daddy died?"

"Mama said if I wanted the cove, I needed to work it. She couldn't manage alone. If I didn't want it, she'd go live near Lucy and her husband, Pete, over near Chatsworth." He gave a short, unfunny laugh. "Melinda suggested that we sell the cove—she argued that with a good road, this would be a great location for a golf resort. She couldn't understand why Mama went ballistic. To Melinda, land represented money we could use to travel and build a house. She didn't want to move up here and farm. She complained that the mountains smothered her. She also complained I was trying to make Brandon a farmer— which was probably true. She and Mama bickered constantly. Melinda started going to town in the evenings. I worried she'd get drunk and run the truck off the road, so I tried going down with her, but she wanted to stay late and I had to get up early to feed cows." He exhaled unhappiness. "She was right. I was a farm boy and I didn't have a clue how to make her happy."

"Did she make you happy?"

"Not particularly. I wasn't sorry when she left, but it still rankles that she took Brandon without letting me tell him good-bye."

"She didn't!"

"Yep. She took off one morning while I was at the barn, so I couldn't see her putting her things in the car. I thought she had driven Brandon down to catch the school bus. Instead, when I got back to the house, I found her note."

I didn't try to keep indignation out of my voice. "You thought I'd left like that this morning, didn't you? That's why you checked my wastebasket—you wanted to see if I'd taken all my things."

His silence answered for him.

"I would never do that! It's not honest or kind."

"Melinda wasn't studying being honest or kind. Next thing I knew, I was served with divorce papers so she could marry a long-distance truck driver she had met in a bar up here. As far as I know, they've been seeing America ever since."

"You didn't ask for custody of Brandon?"

"I couldn't afford a lawyer. Melinda emptied our joint account before she left. In her note, she said I could keep two-thirds of whatever we got for the Rockdale property, but by the time it sold, she had gotten her divorce and hit the road. I've never had a permanent address or a phone number for her since. The few times I've needed to contact her, I've called her folks. They got in touch with her and had her call me."

I was too shocked to say a word. Tobias must have taken my silence for criticism.

"Okay, I could have hired a detective, or claimed my kid had been kidnapped. I didn't want to put Brandon through that. Besides, I thought a kid that little ought to be with his mother. I figured she'd send him back to me for summers, maybe, or holidays. At first she had him write me postcards from all the places they were seeing. She even wrote once, about the Rockdale property, and she said she was homeschooling Brandon and he was doing well. But after a couple of years his postcards slacked off and by the time he was eleven, all I got was a Christmas picture from Wal-Mart. I haven't heard from them since."

"Oh, Tobias." There was nothing more to say.

We sat and watched the buzzards in silence. They circled a couple more times, then flew away. "Off to happier hunting grounds," he said. "Just like Melinda."

My heart flew higher than the buzzards. Tobias didn't love Melinda. He probably never had, not the way he might love me if he got his stubborn prejudice and Melinda's cruel accusation out of the way.

He stood. "Well, that's the Myth of Melinda demystified and you know the unvarnished truth: I'm a dumb farm boy who is lousy with women."

"I know no such thing. One bad marriage doesn't prove that."

He dragged my drawing from his pocket. "Your subconscious clearly knows it." He flung it across the yard as he strode toward the nearest greenhouse.

Sometimes he made me furious, the big blockhead.

"That wasn't my subconscious, it was anger," I yelled after him. "If you had drawn a picture last night, you'd have had the bluebird pecking the eagle to death. Admit it. And don't litter our yard." I went to retrieve the drawing.

He called over one shoulder, "It's not littering on an organic farm, it's composting."

"Whatever you call it, I don't want you strewing paper scraps on the yard. Kaitlin and I have big plans for flowers out here come spring."

That stopped him. He came back a couple of steps and propped both hands on his hip. "Oh, you do, do you? Were you planning to tell me about them before you started digging holes in my ground?"

"It's not your ground, it's God's ground. The Cherokee are only stewards, remember? And you're not a real good one, leaving trash all over the place." I picked up a bolt the little girls and I had missed in the grass and hurled it at him. I wasn't worried I'd hit him—I was a dreadful pitcher—but I came close enough that he stepped aside.

He pivoted on one heel. "I don't have time for this. I've got work to do."

"That's right, walk away. Tell yourself it's all right, because you are lousy with women. Did it ever occur to you that if you can't judge all Indians from meeting one, you can't judge all women from marrying one? Has it ever entered your thick head that you married too young, without either of you knowing who you really were, and that maybe, just maybe, you might find somebody one day that you could *enjoy* spending your life with?"

He checked his steps but didn't turn around. "You got somebody in mind?"

I ran out of steam and courage simultaneously. "Maybe."

"It's highly unlikely. I'm no good at climbing, Deborah. Heights terrify me. So now you know." He stalked off toward the greenhouse.

I had a sudden conviction that the greenhouse was an enchanted place and if Tobias walked through that door he would come out a totally different creature. We would never have a chance at happiness. I had to stop him.

"Wait! I'm not through talking to you. Lena's kids need a permanent home. After something that happened this morning, I'm thinking we ought to adopt them, make it clear they have a home here forever."

Tobias might not be an expert on women, but he cared for those children. I had banked on it.

He came back to where I stood and looked down at me with a puzzled frown. "What happened this morning to make you think that?"

"Kaitlin got all red-faced and embarrassed on the way to the bus, asking if we could possibly come to her parents' night next week. And she said, 'I know you're not our parents,' but she clearly wished we were. Those kids need parents, not guardians."

His frown deepened. "Are you proposing joint custody?"

I gathered up every speck of courage I had. "Or just proposing."

He gave a short, unfunny laugh. "You know as well as I do that Ingrams and Cherokee don't marry, any more than eagles marry bluebirds. Besides, I'm a dumb farm boy who doesn't—"

"Don't you dare tell me you don't know how to treat women."

"I wasn't. I was going to say I don't have a thing to offer you."

That claim was so audacious that I laughed. "Don't be silly. You have a house, a cove, and all sorts of livestock. That's a heck of a lot more than a few shares of stock, a little money in the bank, and bits and pieces of furniture."

He folded his arms and glared down at me. "After what you've heard, why should you think I have a chance in a million of making you happy?"

The sun was in my eyes. I had to squint to make out his features.

"I have no idea if you could make me happy. I don't know if I could make you happy. I don't know why I said anything in the first place." I flapped my hands in despair. "Forget it. We can go on as we are." I gathered my tattered dignity and prepared to leave.

He caught my shoulder and his fingers dug to the bone. "No, we can't. We can't pretend this conversation never happened. We'd both go pussyfooting around here like strangers, embarrassed to death. Were you seriously suggesting that we get married?"

I winced under his grip. "Yes."

"Why?"

I was back on the seesaw, terrified that I'd say or do the wrong thing and tilt us in the wrong direction. The sun made my eyes water.

I think he took that for tears. He dropped his hand from my shoulder and took both my hands in his. He leaned down to peer into my eyes. "Deborah?"

Mesmerized by those black eyes, I stammered, "Because—because I thought it could be a good idea." I shut my eyes so he couldn't read anything in them.

"Why?" His word was urgent.

"For the children."

"Open your eyes and tell me. Why?"

I opened my eyes. Looking at him, I could not tell a lie. "Because I love you and I think you love me." I felt a hot flush rise from my neck to the roots of my hair.

The universe stopped while I waited for his reply.

He looked at me for a long minute, then he said softly, "Oh, lordy, I do. I most certainly do. Do you really love me back?"

I nodded, unable to speak.

He shouted to Bray, who was at the fence hoping to join the party, "She loves me! Did you hear that, Bray, old boy? She loves me!"

He lifted me at the waist and whirled me around with a whoop of joy that made me laugh out loud. "She loves me!" he shouted to the mountains as we whirled. "Deborah loves me!"

Bray declared his delight. Tom and Lucky made it a trio. Homer joined in from the porch to create a quartet. The piglets and cow joined the chorus.

And all the trees of the forest clapped their hands for joy.

"Put me down! I'm getting dizzy!" Still laughing, I pounded his chest with my hands.

Tobias set me on the ground and kissed me so hard I was breathless. Then he led me to the bench, his granddaddy's bench, and he got down on one knee. "Deborah Ingram MacAllester, will you marry me?" To himself, he added, "I can't believe I just said that."

I could hardly believe I was hearing the words. "I most certainly will. I thought you'd never ask."

He looked up at the sky. "Well, it didn't fall." He yelled into the clear blue ether, "Don't worry, Daddy. She is the best in the bunch."


Neither of us worked that day. Tobias built a fire, I made a pot of tea, and we sat on Teddy's couch to trace our history from two diffcrent perspectives.

He said, "You want to know when I first noticed you? It was when you took on that security guard. There he was, a big burly fellow pointing a gun at me, so antsy he could pull that trigger any second, and there you were—"

"—a drowned rat," I interrupted.

"No, a brave little mouse, ordering that guard, 'Put down the gun. My sister made a mistake.' I thought then, 'That is one heck of a woman.'"

I loved Tobias's praise, but had to confess, "It wasn't really a big deal, it was how we were raised. To King, people on campus were serfs. Our whole family treated them like that. It never occurred to me to be afraid of a campus security guard."

"Don't destroy my illusions. It seemed like a big deal from where I sat, on the business end of that gun. When you walked in weeks later, with me looking like a yellow dog and stinking to high heaven, I wanted to curl up and die. That was not the way I had pictured our next meeting."

"That wasn't our next meeting. At our next meeting you were a hero and I was standing up to my knees in the river wearing wet, transparent underpants."

He traced my face with one finger. "A memory I cherish. If our marriage ever gets dull, I'll throw you in the river."

I gave him a little sock on the arm, then pulled the arm around me. It felt so good to touch him whenever I pleased. "Why were you near our place that day?"

"There's a great fishing hole down river on the other side."

"As Wonder would say, I never knew dat." I rested my head on his shoulder. "How did you picture our ideal meeting?"

"Something along the lines of that night at Danny's Diner, when you came in pursued by dragons and I could rescue you—and figure out a way to keep you nearby."

"You mean you only took the children so I'd come along?"

"Oh, no, I did think having the kids up here was a great idea, but it felt like a gift from God that I could get you here in the bargain. I figured if you stayed long enough, I could impress you with my charm."

"Macho man. I'm still waiting."

"Oh, really?"

He bent his head and kissed me again, a kiss full of the same yearning I'd been damping down for months.

"When did you first love me?" I asked when we came up for air.

"You grew on me. I knew you only came up here because I was sick and you were a nurse, and because you thought you had a debt to pay, but you were so sweet, and never complained at all about the work you had to do, and you were incredibly good at taking care of me. Nobody ever took care of me before. My mother was a great lady, but she was not a nurturer. If she'd been alive when I got hepatitis, she'd have said, 'Okay, son, take an aspirin and get out on the tractor.'"

I laughed. "Sounds like you. Keeping you down was one of the hardest nursing jobs I ever had."

"One of the hardest jobs I ever had was keeping my hands off you when you came downstairs in Mama's bathrobe. And then you proceeded to beat me at chess, read to me, sing with me. . . ." He pulled me to him and kissed me again as he had that night. "I'd have slung you over my shoulder and taken you to bed that evening if I hadn't been too weak."

"You didn't do it once you got stronger."

"Heck, no. We had all those kids in the house. Besides, I kept telling myself it was silly to fantasize about you, because you were—"

"An Ingram and a MacAllester. I know."

"Partly. I'll admit it. But also because I was a farm boy and you were a princess."

"Lots of princesses marry farm boys. Ask Coco. May I ask you an odd question?"

"If you don't mind an odd answer."

"How old are you?"

"Does it matter?"

"Not unless I'm robbing a cradle—or you are in your dotage and remarkably well preserved."

"I'm two years younger than you. We went to high school together—and don't bother telling me you don't remember. Why should you? You were—"

"I know, a princess. I am so sick of that word I may never tell another fairy tale, but it's nice to know I'm a little older. Gives me an edge."

"Don't count on it. That night in Danny's you looked about twelve."

"The dragons were getting close. I was so glad to see you— and so afraid. When you had sent me away the Tuesday before, it broke my heart."

"It broke my heart, too, but I couldn't stand the idea that you were only nice to me because you thought you owed me something, and I was scared to death I'd let on how I felt. I almost blew it when you looked up at me and said, 'It's what I do.'"

"I so hoped you were going to kiss me after that tirade."

"Really? You loved me by then? I thought you only saw me as a patient, not a man."

I huffed. "I told Susan that *because* I loved you, silly. I didn't want her to catch on. I don't know when I started loving you, but after you kissed me, it was all I could do not to throw myself on you and beg for more."

"Like this?" He made up for lost time.

Memory by memory, we discussed the ways and times we had loved each other and tried not to show it. At last we made love on Teddy's couch beside the fire. I hadn't deferred passion too late—I had simply waited for the right man. I felt Teddy's blessing.

As we ate lunch, Tobias asked, "How soon can we get married?"

"Not next week. The children are on school break and have to work on catching up if they're going to pass."

"We could farm them out, to coin a pun. I'll bet Lucy and Pete would take them. They're both teachers, so they're off next week, too. They could even come over here to keep the animals and the kids, and help the kids with their schoolwork. "

"The children don't know them."

"They know Damien, and it's a good chance for them to learn more about being Cherokee. Pete teaches American history and is more active in Cherokee affairs than I am. Let me call Lucy and leave a message on her cell."

He was on the phone for a while. "Lucy was on her break," he reported, "and she is so excited somebody else is finally taking me off her hands—those are her words, not mine—that she wouldn't stop talking. She says they'll be delighted to come take care of the kids while we're on our honeymoon, that she's always wished she had a girl or two, and she feels she already knows you after everything Damien has told her. I told her we'll get married Saturday if we can get a license by then." He stopped. "Was that all right? Do you need more time to get a dress and plan all the fancy things women want in a wedding?"

I put out a hand and led him to the couch again. "The only thing I want in this wedding is you."

When I fetched the children, Kaitlin exclaimed, "You look so pretty, Deb'rah!"

"Thank you, honey. I feel pretty. Tobias and I have a surprise for you."

"Is it ice cweam?" asked Carrie hopefully.

"Better than ice cream," I promised.

She gave a happy little sigh. "Ice cweam and cookies?"

After the children had changed their clothes, Tobias said, "Let's sit in the living room. Deborah and I have something to say."

Kaitlin sidled up to me and whispered, "Is it a baby?"

"Stop guessing and sit down," I told her. I could tell I was fiery red.

She sat on the couch with Carrie tucked under one arm. I sat beside them. Tobias and Eric took the chairs. I couldn't help remembering the day King's will was read—how my family had gathered with a similar air of expectation and how my own expectations had been dashed. Five months later I had a new family and far greater expectations. I winged a prayer of thanks as Tobias cleared his throat.

"Deborah and I have an announcement. We are getting married."

Eric stared from Tobias to me and back again with a face as blank as any Tobias ever wore. Carrie continued to suck her thumb. Clouds of apprehension filled Kaitlin's eyes. "Do we have to leave?" It wasn't the apprehension that made me sad; it was the bravery with which she asked the question.

"Heavens, no," I told her. "We want you to stay with us forever. We want you to be our children."

Tobias looked at Eric. "If you are willing, we'd like to adopt you all."

Eric's face split in a grin. "That's cool."

Carrie cringed against Kaitlin. "Will it hurt?"

Tobias leaned over and laid a hand on her shoulder. "No, Carriebelle, it won't hurt a bit. We'll go to a judge and say we all want to be one family. The judge will ask each of you, 'Are you sure you want Tobias and Deborah to adopt you so you can be their children?' If you say, 'Yes,' then the judge will sign a paper, we'll go out for ice cream, and Deborah and I get to take care of you until you grow up."

Comforted, Carrie took her thumb out of her mouth long enough to say, "I'll tell dat judge I don't want to feed pigs."

Kaitlin looked at me over Carrie's head. "Can we call you Mama and Daddy?"

I smiled. "You sure can."

"You can call us anything except late for meals," Tobias teased.

Kaitlin laughed. I laughed, too—not at the joke, but because we were all so happy.

All but one. Carrie frowned at me. "You are not my mama."

"Our real mama is in heaven," Kaitlin reminded her, "and now I'm your mama. Deb'rah will be our stepmother, but not a bad one, like in the books." She looked to me for confirmation.

"I will be your adoptive mother," I said, correcting her. "Lena will always be your birth mother. And Tobias and I will go to the school parents' night this week."

When I got to my room that night, there was a gift on my bed. A small yellow box painted with strawberries.

We were married in Tobias's church on Saturday afternoon. Damien was Tobias's best man and Eric his groomsman. Monique and Kaitlin were my bridesmaids, Coco was my matron of honor, and Wonder and Carrie were the flower girls.

"Dat dumb Carrie didn't t'row any of her flowers," Wonder announced after the service.

"I'm saving dem." Carrie clutched her basket to her chest.

The flower girls were the best-dressed people at the wedding. When Monique had told Susan that Wonder and Carrie were to be flower girls, she had added that Wonder didn't need a new dress because we were all wearing Sunday clothes. Susan, of course, told Regan. Next thing I knew, Regan had sent Monique a Lord & Taylor's box holding two long yellow organdy dresses trimmed with lace. The morning of the wedding, she sent me a lovely bridal bouquet of white lilies and yellow roses and two small white baskets tied with yellow ribbons and full of yellow petals for the girls.

My bouquet was far grander than the simple white dress I wore. Tobias and the other men wore suits, and Eric was so proud of his first suit that you'd have thought he was the groom. Judge Brantley lent a touch of elegance to the affair. He walked me down the aisle in an ancient tuxedo.

"I will be honored to serve in King's stead," he had said when I asked him.

We had more people in the wedding party than in the congregation. Tobias's sister, Lucy, and her husband, Pete, sat on Tobias's side of the church and the only people on my side were Gage, Mimi with her husband, Larry, and Darla Enderble. I had invited both my sisters and their husbands, of course, but Susan had said, "You can throw away your life if you want to. I don't intend to support the process." Regan wrote, "Of course we aren't coming. You are dragging our family name through the mud. If it were possible to divorce a sister, I would start proceedings immediately."

"Trust Regan," I told Tobias when the flowers arrived, "to write a nasty note one minute and call her florist the next, remembering that yellow roses are my favorites."

At the small reception in the church fellowship hall, people mingled and seemed to be having a good time. Once Coco and Pete started discussing North Georgia history, I wondered if we'd ever separate them.

On the table with the wedding cake was Coco's present to Tobias and me: a birdhouse made of tiny logs. Once I had painted it, it would look just like the log house. "How did you remember what it looked like?" I marveled. As far as I knew she had been up there only once.

"I took pictures with my phone in the hours and hours Wonder and I waited for you," she replied. "It beat freezing to death."

After the cake, Wonder climbed on a chair and announced, "I have a story."

"Not now," I pleaded.

"I have to tell it now. Dis is a special story for today."

"Hear, hear," said Gage, tapping his glass with a knife.

Wonder raised her voice as the room grew quiet.

"Once upon a time dere was a princess named Deb'rah. She was not brilliant or beautiful, but she liked to help people."

I laughed with the rest, but caught my lower lip between my teeth. Who knew where this story might go in Wonder's agile hands?

"Her daddy, de king, promised he would give her his castle so she could help old people, but he broke his promise, so Princess Deb'rah was sad. She was also sad because no prince climbed her tree to kiss her. One day she heard dat a wicked veg'table man had captured a little princess named Wonder. He was going to kidnap her!"

I saw several people give Tobias a startled look. "Vivid imagination," I called.

Wonder basked in a second ripple of laughter as she picked up her story.

"Princess Deb'rah was brave. She said, 'I must save Princess Wonder!' So she ran out in de rain and found Princess Wonder and de veg'table man, but he wasn't really kidnapping Princess Wonder, he was dist telling her a Cherky story about de Milky Way. When Princess Deb'rah heard dat story, she liked it. She liked de veg'table man, too, for although he was not a prince, he was not a kidnapper. One day he saved Princess Wonder from drowning in de river and Princess Deb'rah saw he was kind and brave and grew healthy veg'tables."

"Absolutely," called Tobias.

Wonder grinned down at him without breaking her stride. "Princess Deb'rah liked healthy veg'tables so she fell in love with him, even if he wasn't a prince. When de veg'table man saw she was good and kind and liked to help people and dat she was Princess Wonder's aunt, he fell in love with her, too. Dey got married and lived happily ever after for de foreseeable future. Amen."

She took her bow to laughter and applause.

Coco leaned across Tobias to tell me, "Wonder clearly takes all the credit for your marriage."

"And I'm being married for my vegetables," Tobias added.

I could feel a soppy smile on my face and couldn't do a thing to stop it. "I'll give Wonder the credit and you can keep the vegetables. All I want is you."

As we prepared to leave the reception, Tobias's sister patted my cheek. "I've seen you once before, at a Christmas concert Tobe dragged me to back when he was so weak he could hardly walk. But now that he's strong again, don't let him walk all over you." Lucy was a plump woman, as short as I, with short dark hair and eyes that twinkled even when her face was solemn.

"Not a chance," I promised. "I shall rule him with a fist of iron."

She laughed. "You are exactly what he needs."

I wanted to thank her for all the food in the freezer and tell her how influential the story of the pond had been in my life. I wanted to say how much I loved the sampler above the fireplace and Damien coming over every weekend. I wanted to thank her again for taking the children. There wasn't time. Tobias was pointing to his watch. We had a plane to catch to a destination he refused to share. I reminded myself that Lucy and I would have years ahead in which to get acquainted. It was nice to have a sister I looked forward to getting to know.

She and Pete took the two older children as we'd planned,

but at the last minute, Carrie refused to go home with strangers. "We'll take her," Monique said in a resigned voice. "You've had Wonder often enough."

"Remember," I whispered as I gave Wonder a good-bye hug, "treat Carrie nice."

She heaved a huge sigh as she assumed the burden. "I will."

I couldn't believe it when Tobias handed me my ticket at the airport. "Belize?"

"I hear they speak English and it's warm."

While March winds and one last dusting of snow swept the Georgia mountains, we swam, snorkeled, and lay on sunny beaches. "I could get used to this," I said on our last night there.

"Don't," he replied. "We aren't likely to get another trip like this until all the children finish college. By then we may be too old to enjoy it."

If this were a fairy tale, the story would end with "and they lived happily ever after." In real life, a wedding is not the end but a new beginning and ever-after is not perpetual happiness.

We returned to the house Thursday night because Tobias wanted to go to the county seat Friday to see about beginning adoption procedures. We found that Lucy and Pete had taken our children home with them that afternoon.

*We've got a few things we'd like the kids to see over our way,* Pete had written in a note he left on the counter. *We'll bring them back Sunday afternoon.*

Lucy had added a postscript: *We think you deserve a little privacy in your own home.*

I called Monique to see if she could round up a couple of brawny classmates to help fetch the rest of my furniture Friday and move it up the hill while Tobias was gone. "I want to get everything out of Holcomb's warehouse ASAP, before Regan persuades him I am non compos mentis and should not have access to my own furniture. I'll rent a truck. I can't ask Holcomb for one when I don't want Regan to know I'm moving. Don't mention it to your mother, either, please."

"No problem. I can get two guys I know from the college and maybe Gage to drive the rental truck. Rental places don't let students drive their trucks. I need to tell you, though, that Carrie is with Regan. She pitched such a fit here the first night that Mama called Regan to come get her. I've checked on her a few times. She's doing fine."

Moving day started out well. The two students obviously admired Monique, though she bossed them. Gage watched them like a benevolent uncle as he helped with the heavy lifting. I toted boxes. In spite of my precautions, Regan showed up half an hour after we arrived. Somebody at the warehouse must have alerted her.

Carrie was with her, wearing a new pink dress, socks with pink lace, and the smug expression of a cat who has plundered the Christmas turkey.

When Regan saw the students placing Mary Bird's bed and chest on the truck, she burst into tears. "I'll give you a bedroom set for a wedding present! Come—choose any of the ones in my house! I beg you, don't take those heirlooms to that dinky log cabin. You'll ruin them!" She sobbed and dabbed her nose with a lacy handkerchief.

Carrie sobbed beside her. "Don't make Miss Wegan cwy, Deb'rah!"

I was not moved. Regan's tears, like Carrie's, turned off and on at will. "I am not making Miss Regan cry. Tell her we don't live in a log cabin, we have a log house with perfectly decent bedrooms and a beautiful view."

"It has pigs," Carrie complained. "I don't like pigs."

"Well, I like this bedroom furniture. It's mine and I intend to keep it."

I stood close to Regan and Carrie while the crew packed the rest of the truck. I didn't trust Regan as far as I could throw her. I discovered, though, that she didn't rattle me much since I had tossed her into Tobias's metaphorical pond.

As we were about to leave, I asked, "Do you want to come home now, Carrie? Kaitlin and Eric will be home Sunday."

I have to confess I was relieved when she grabbed Regan around the thighs and shouted, "No!"

"No, ma'am," prompted Regan.

"No, ma'am. I wants to go back wif Miss Wegan." At a glance from Regan, she added, "Please."

"Can't she stay through the weekend?" Regan pleaded.

I was delighted to have the weekend alone with Tobias. I gave Carrie a hug. "Fine. I'll get you Sunday afternoon, then. What time shall I pick her up?" I asked Regan.

"I'll bring her. I want to see what kind of environment she's living in."

"I'm not sure your car can get up our hill. The road washed out pretty bad this winter and we haven't gotten it graded and graveled since."

"Didn't you go up once in the judge's Cadillac? Coco told that story at some meeting or other. I'll bring Holcomb's car. A Mercedes can go anyplace a Caddy can."

Gage drove the big truck up the mountain road. I traveled with him and let Monique and her brawny admirers lead in my truck.

"Did your granddaddy ever get his car fixed after the accident?" I asked, feeling out of touch with what had been going on in Unizilla for the past several weeks.

"Nope, it's still sitting under a tree in his yard. The thing would cost more to repair than it's worth, but he loves that old car. He's had it since before Grandmama died, and I think the idea of getting rid of it puts him in touch with his own mortality. Or maybe he's a stubborn old cuss who sees no reason to buy anything new when he's already got something that might be fixed. In any case, he's sharing Aunt Coco's car at the moment, which is slowly driving her mad."

We rode in silence for a few minutes. Ahead of us Monique rode in the pickup between the two college students. Whatever she was telling them required a lot of animated hand motions.

"May I ask you a personal question?" I asked Gage.

"You want to know how often I floss my teeth?"

"No, I want to know your intentions regarding my niece."

"Ahhh. A *really* personal question." He stared at the truck ahead for a minute without speaking. "I don't mind admitting I have serious intentions regarding your niece. Is that all right with you?"

"Perfectly. If I were you, though, I'd show her a bit more dedicated attention."

"We've got time for that. She's got years of college. At the moment I am enjoying my elevation from Wonder's playmate to a knight in shining armor."

"Do you see the way she's been flirting with those guys she brought?"

"That doesn't mean anything."

"No, but if you'll accept advice from an old married lady, take off your armor."

"I beg your pardon?"

"It's princes Monique admires. Where do you think Wonder got her fascination with them? It's a family failing. Monique is waiting for a prince to sweep her off her feet, wake her up with a kiss, and waltz her off into happily-ever-after. She's been look-ing in the wrong places, but every man she has fallen for has had some princely qualities. Benny was smart, kind, and ambitious. Junior was arrogant, but he ruled other people and commanded attention. If you want Monique before she falls for some other pseudo prince, you'd better take off the knightly armor and stop sitting around on your horse. Think of the way Holcomb treats Regan, like fine porcelain. You've got all the best princely virtues—good looks, wisdom, intelligence, kindness—"

"Why, thankee, ma'am."

"—but they aren't enough. You need to overwhelm her with romance. Flowers. Music. Candy. Romantic dinners. Sweep her off her feet and into your arms before she begins to consider you simply a man in a tin can."

"I never thought I'd hear Teensie MacAllester suggest I take off my clothes for her niece." Still, he wore a thoughtful look as we pulled into the cove and saw one of the college guys lifting Monique from the truck. She had her head thrown back, laughing.

The crew was placing the last pieces of furniture when Tobias got home.

His face lit up when he saw the game table in the den with the marble chessboard on it. "Beautiful." He moved one pawn and moved it back.

"I hope you don't mind that I swapped my dining table for yours," I said. "Gage unearthed four leaves for that table when he was clearing out the house. I never knew there were leaves. At full length, it can seat twelve."

"I don't mind. It's pretty. My old table had served past its time."

"I've put our china, crystal, and silver in the matching hutch."

"Oooh-ee. We are getting fancy."

"Don't knock it. As Coco says, 'China and silver are not essential to daily life, but a little elegance does wonders to lift the spirits.'"

"I haven't experienced much elegance in my life, but I'm willing to give it a try."

His highest praise was for the high four-poster in our bedroom, bathed in afternoon light. "A bed worthy of a princess."

"And her prince. It was the wedding present of my many-times-great-grandmother, Mary Bird MacAllester. Sorry about the crates under it. I didn't know where else to put them and haven't come up with any way to hide them."

Tobias wasn't thinking about crates. "Mary Bird? Was she Cherokee?"

"I don't think so. All I know about her was that she and her husband, John, were married in 1805 in Morganton, North Carolina."

"She could have been Cherokee. We have a Bird clan, and a lot of Scotsmen married Cherokee women."

"Would that make us cousins?"

"If so, I'll never tell." We took time out for a kiss. As we stepped apart, he stubbed his toe against a crate. "What is all that?"

"Oil paintings Judge Brantley insisted I take to bulk up my list when we were distributing the furnishings. He thinks they could be worth something someday."

"How could we bear to sell them? They do so much for the decor. Have you refurnished the whole house?"

"No, only one more room." I led him to the bedroom I'd been using. "I've put Father and Mother's old furniture in here. Do you mind?"

"Not if you didn't put your father and mother in here, too. It's nice stuff."

"What shall we do with the old beds and chests?" At the moment they were filling up the hall.

"Tell the crew to take them by the Salvation Army. My table and chairs, too. That's where they came from in the first place. Melinda and I didn't bring anything up with us from the mobile home and Mother was never one to spend money on furniture. Wasn't I brilliant to marry a woman who came completely furnished?"

"Brilliant. You don't mind my taking up so much space?"

He rested both hands on my shoulders and pulled me close. "You can fill up the whole place as far as I'm concerned, so long as you don't take away my big-screen TV."

As I went downstairs, I heard a giggle from the den. I peeped in at the door and saw Monique in Gage's arms. I tiptoed away to unpack another box.

In that box I found my yellow bluebird house. Tobias took it out before supper and set it on a post where we could see it from our dining table. "The bluebird has come home," he murmured into my hair.

Damien brought the older children back on Sunday afternoon. They were full of news about what they had done that weekend.

Eric mostly remembered places. "We went to the Vann House and to Chieftains, the house where Major Ridge lived before he went to Oklahoma."

"Major Ridge was of our clan," Tobias told him.

"Wow! Major Ridge and the Vanns—those Cherokee were rich, man!" Eric was obviously impressed.

Kaitlin remembered activities. "I learned to cook Cherokee food," she boasted. "I can make fry bread and Cherokee bread pudding! And I bought Carrie a doll." She took a doll dressed like an Indian from her bag.

"That looks expensive," I said. "Where did you get the money?" We had given each child ten dollars for incidentals, but the doll had surely cost more than that.

"Lucy and Pete paid us for helping around the farm. I made ten more dollars."

"And spent every penny on Carrie?"

"Yeah, because she'll love the doll."

"She'll be home later today. Miss Regan's bringing her." I pictured our farm seen through Regan's eyes and wished I had time to paint the barn and wash the piglets.

Thanks to Teddy's furniture and new curtains, the inside of the house looked nice. Regan strolled through the downstairs like she was in a furniture store looking for something she might want to buy. She even climbed the stairs to look around. I followed without saying a word. As she left, she said, "It's not my style, but you've made a pretty place up here. Teddy's furniture looks better than it did at Mother's, and I doubt if Mary Bird MacAllester is rolling in her grave. I've seen a picture of the house they lived in. It wasn't as nice as this one."

"Tobias says she may have been Cherokee."

Regan gave me a long look. "Let's both forget you ever said that." She pressed her scented cheek to mine as she left, then gave Carrie a big hug. "I'll be seeing you, sweetie pie. Remember what we practiced, now."

"Yes, ma'am," Carrie said. "Thank you for a nice week."

"You are welcome, sweetie."

A tear rolled down Carrie's cheek. "I'm weally gonna miss you."

"I'm really gonna miss you, too." Regan stroked her hair.

Kaitlin stepped up. "I bought you a present, Carrie." She handed her the doll.

Carrie flung it away. "I doesn't want a Nindian doll." She looked at Regan and I could see her mentally backpedaling. "No, t'ank you!" she shouted, and ran for the stairs.

I couldn't bear the pain in Kaitlin's eyes, but there was nothing I could do to ease it. I walked Regan to the car. "'Yes, ma'am'?" I said mockingly. "'Please'? 'No, thank you'?"

She donned her sunglasses. "That child had no manners

whatsoever when she came to us. She never said 'ma'am,' 'sir,' 'please,' or 'thank you.' She ate with her fingers and sucked her thumb."

"We've been busy trying to get the other two through school while doing the spring planting. I haven't had time to play manners school."

Manners school had been Mother's way of teaching us what she felt we needed to know. It had gone on for years.

"We played manners school all week. I hope you will stick with it."

"I can try." As I waved good-bye to her, I decided Regan wasn't all bad.

That night at bedtime I gave Tobias a sketch I had drawn on our honeymoon. In a big nest, a bluebird happily cuddled against the breast of an eagle. Three little chicks slept nearby.

He went to the closet and with a touching sheepishness reached under sweaters on the shelf for the framed picture of the little bluebird. I watched happily while he hung her where she belonged.

# Thirteen

Before we could begin adoption procedures, we needed the children's birth certificates. "I've got their Social Security cards in a file," Judge Brantley told me, "but I've never had their birth certificates. I should have gotten them or a copy of them from Lena years ago, but I never did."

"Do you know where they could be?" Tobias asked Kaitlin and Eric.

Eric shrugged. Kaitlin said, "Mama kept lots of papers in her room. They might be in there."

As much as I dreaded it, we had to return to Lena's house.

Tobias had a dentist appointment, so he couldn't come. Gage, who had gone through the house with the inspector, said, "I cannot go back into that filthy place. There are few things you cannot ask your lawyer to do, but that is one of them."

I looked at Monique. "Will you go?"

She slewed her eyes at Gage. "Sure. The difficult things in life are always left to the women, aren't they?"

We arranged to meet at Lena's at ten on Monday morning, since Monique had no Monday morning classes and I had gone back to the clinic four days a week.

The odor of dirt and unwashed clothes swept over us like a wave when we opened the door. "Can we burn the place down and have it over with?" Monique suggested.

I handed her some disposable gloves. "Not until we find those birth certificates."

Inside, Monique looked at the bare dirty rooms in dismay. "Did she never clean? I cannot believe Gage ever dared compare me with this woman."

"I think he may have changed his mind."

She grew suddenly shy. "We've both changed our minds about a lot of things."

I led the way to Lena's room. "This is where Kaitlin thinks we might find the certificates."

Monique wrinkled her nose at the liquor bottles, clothes, and trash on the floor. "I hope they're in that dressing table, then."

It was a small piece with beautiful lines, the only furniture left in the house except the couch and the kitchen table. Its top was marred by liquid rings and scratches, but it looked like mahogany and I was willing to wager that the handles were brass. It was the sort of table where a woman might have sat to smile in her mirror as she sprayed herself with perfume.

"We could refinish this for Kaitlin." I touched the carved wood around the mirror. "I'll bet it was her grandmother's."

"Think about that later. I'm for doing what we came to do and getting out of here before we catch something." Monique jerked open one of the drawers that flanked a center kneehole. "Here're some papers." She pulled out a handful and started going through them. I found a similar stash in the other drawer.

The papers were everything from children's school papers to a personal notice torn from a magazine: *SWM desires attractive SWF interested in hiking, skiing, and romance.*

Monique held that up. "Do you reckon that's how she met

Carrie's dad? If so, you'll have the dickens of a time finding him to get permission to adopt her."

"We don't need to find him. Gage will advertise in papers around here for several weeks and if he doesn't show up to claim her, we're home free. Kaitlin and Eric's dad has already agreed to termination of his parental rights."

A few minutes later I held up papers joined by a paper clip. "Here are Kaitlin and Eric's birth certificates." The clip had joined the papers for so long it had left a permanent dent.

"And here's Carrie's." Monique's voice was odd. She stared at the paper she held with a pucker between her eyebrows.

"Is something the matter?"

"Look." She thrust it at me.

The child's name was Mary Carleton Thompson. Her father's name was listed as Carleton Harris.

"Uncle Carleton?" Monique looked around the squalid room. "He wouldn't have stayed in this filth for a second."

"Carrie wasn't conceived here," I reminded her. "Lena went to meet somebody a week or so before Carleton was killed. It could have been him, I guess. Lena could be beautiful when she fixed herself up, and Carleton always liked a pretty woman. I'm glad she wasn't in his car when he crashed."

Monique's imagination was as vivid as Wonder's. "Maybe she was, and ran away. Or maybe they'd had a fight that night and that's why he crashed. Maybe she stayed away after that because she was grieving or terrified—"

"Or roaring drunk," I interrupted.

"—or roaring drunk. Then she came home to discover she was pregnant. Or—I've got it! Maybe she read about Uncle Carleton's death in the paper! She probably put his name on Carrie's birth certificate hoping to get money from Holcomb, since Uncle Carleton wouldn't be around to protest."

"Regan and Holcomb would have insisted on a DNA test,"

I said. "Besides, if you take a good look around you, you might conclude that Lena never asked anybody for money beyond what her father left her. And as much as I hate to admit it, the child does have Carleton's eyes."

"I'll bet Lena really liked Uncle Carleton, then, and saw him as her ticket out of all this." Monique spread her hands to indicate the squalid little house. "I'll bet his death and the death of those dreams are what kept her drinking all those years."

"Could be. We'll never know."

"Let's ask Regan if Lena ever asked for money." She pulled out her cell phone.

"Wait!" A familiar feeling of dread descended over me like a blanket. "I want to talk with Gage before we bring Regan into this equation."

As soon as we entered Gage's office he stood and held his nose. "Let me guess. You've been at Lena's. You smell awful."

Monique rubbed her cheek on his jacket and purred, "Now you do, too."

He gave her a quick kiss and motioned us to chairs.

I handed him the birth certificate and spelled out the possibilities.

Gage took so long reading the certificate that I suspected he was considering all the legal ramifications before he spoke. "Either of your conclusions could be true. Carleton could have been the birth father or Lena could have seized the chance to use a dead man's name. In either case, Holcomb will have to be informed. I'm certain he will want a DNA test performed on Carrie to see if she's Carleton's child, and after that— Whew! The red tape will be endless. For four years Holcomb has functioned as sole owner of Harris Poultry. If Carrie is Carleton's daughter, she is also his legal heir and entitled to his half of the company— whether that is his half as of four years ago or as of now, I'm not certain. With the economic downturn, if Holcomb has to give her half of what the business was worth four years ago and half of the accruing profits . . ."

I was so nervous I was shredding a tissue in my lap. "I'm not worried about what Holcomb has to give her. I'm concerned about how this will affect our adopting Carrie."

"That ought not to be a problem. You'll have to have Holcomb's permission, of course, as her legal next of kin—" He saw the look Monique and I exchanged. "What?"

"We can't tell Regan," Monique told him. "She's crazy about Carrie. Heaven knows why—she's a brat, as far as I'm concerned—but Regan adores her and she adores Regan."

"And Regan's been wanting to adopt a child," I picked up the explanation. "Holcomb's objection was that he could not love a child who wasn't of his own bloodline."

"I know it's prehistoric, but if Holcomb gets wind of the fact that Carrie might be Uncle Carleton's daughter—" said Monique.

"—and especially if we do a DNA test that proves Carrie is Carleton's daughter," I interrupted, "I think Regan and Holcomb will insist on adopting her. I promised Lena on her deathbed I would not separate her children. Besides, losing Carrie would kill Kaitlin. I think she sees herself as Carrie's mother."

"Would Regan take both girls?"

"Not likely. She's only shown interest in Carrie. Besides, I don't want to split Eric off from the girls. We want them all."

Gage exhaled so hard it was a wonder he had any air left in him. "What a mess."

"Could we burn the birth certificate?" Monique suggested. "Nobody need know."

"I'm a lawyer, princess, and I've seen it. Besides, there's one on file with the state." He turned to me. "Could you and Tobias go on as you have been, serving as guardians for the children?"

"No, we've told them we are planning to adopt them. They

are already calling Tobias 'Daddy' and Eric calls me 'Mom.'
Kaitlin's working up to it."

"Holcomb's a nice guy. Let me take him to lunch and lay out
the whole shebang. Maybe if you offered to let Carrie visit them
a lot, he'd agree to let you adopt."

"We could waive her claim to any part of Harris Poultry."

"You can't do that. She is entitled to that money. But you
could come to some sort of agreement about that—an annual allowance put into a trust fund until she's grown. I'll tell him you
are willing to negotiate that on her behalf. Okay?"

I agreed. "We're willing to negotiate anything to keep her."


Regan was not willing to negotiate.

The evening the DNA test came back showing that Carrie
was, indeed, Carleton's daughter, Regan called me, her voice rip-
pling with excitement. "I can't believe it, can you? Carrie is actually part of our family!"

"She's been part of our family for months," I reminded her.

"I mean *our* family. Holcomb's family. His flesh and blood.
I'm not really surprised. From the beginning I knew Carrie had
better breeding than the other two. You can tell by looking at
her—"

"Come off it! The only thing you can tell by looking at her
is that she is a cute little girl who needs more exercise." I had
never held with stories like the princess and the pea, where
an aristocrat is identified under dirt and grime by heightened
sensibilities. It made me furious on Kaitlin and Eric's behalf to
hear Regan spouting that myth. "The only time I ever heard of
people's breeding being obvious by looking at them was a story
about a Japanese prison camp during World War Two where,
when other prisoners refused to clean filthy latrines, British aristocrats cleaned them without complaining."

"Phew!" I could tell Regan was wrinkling her perfect nose.

"Like I said, you can always tell real breeding."

"In any case, I am so excited by this news. It's an answer to prayer, isn't it? I told you God was going to give me a child, and now he has!"

My heart began to pound. It was Christmas morning again and Regan was eyeing my doll. "God hasn't given you this child. Tobias and I are planning to adopt her. If you want one of the children, you have to take them all."

"Don't be ridiculous. The other two are perfectly happy with you all."

"Kaitlin has cared for Carrie all her life. She mustn't be separated from her." As soon as I said it, I caught my breath, afraid Regan would offer to take both girls.

She had no intention of doing so. "It's not fair for you to get three children and me to get none."

"We aren't talking about dividing cookies here. These are children. Their mother's last request was, 'Don't split up my kids.'"

"Their mother was a drunk. She didn't know what she was saying. If she could make the choice today, I'm sure she would rather have Carrie come to us, with all the advantages we could offer, than have her grow up on a farm. Carrie is terrified of those pigs. Did you know that?"

"I know she pretends to be terrified to get out of feeding them. Little Carrie is a mastermind when it comes to creative ways of avoiding work."

"Carrie wasn't born to feed pigs. *You* may not understand that. . . ."

"My breeding is exactly the same as yours."

Regan sighed. "Yes, but you have departed from it. I'm sure you are happy in the life you have chosen, but don't stand in the way of Carrie having a better life than you." When I didn't reply, she added, "If we have to, we will take you to court on this."

"I'll see you there, then. We aren't going to let you have Carrie without a fight."

However, as I hung up I admitted we might have to do precisely that. Tobias and I didn't have the deep pockets Regan did.

We went to Gage's office the next morning after the children went to school. I took the precaution at Carrie's school of leaving a letter stating that *no one* was to pick up the child other than Tobias, me, Gage, or Monique. "You mean except Mr. or Mrs. Harris?" the receptionist asked. "I mean, since they pay part of her fees . . ."

"Especially not Mr. or Mrs. Harris—please," I added, to compensate for my fierce tone. "It's a family matter at the moment."

When we explained the situation to Gage, he looked troubled. "Going to court could be expensive. I'll do the best I can for you, of course—"

"I've got some money," I told him. "I can't think of a better use for my inheritance than to buy a child." I meant it for a joke. It fell flat.

"A custody battle could take all you have and then some, if Regan is determined."

"If necessary, we will take out a mortgage on the farm," offered Tobias.

I stared at him in amazement. "You would do that? What if we couldn't pay the mortgage? Crops could be bad, or you could get injured—you could lose the cove. There must be another way."

"We will do what it takes, so far as we are able," he insisted. Was it any wonder I loved that man?

Gage sighed. "It may take nothing short of a miracle."

"I'm not above praying for miracles. You work, I'll pray." I winged up a quick *Please, God!* while the men discussed strategy. I would get down to serious praying later.

"I think we ought to talk to Holcomb and Regan first," Gage suggested, "to see if something could be worked out. Maybe they'd agree to joint custody or frequent visitation rights."

"Sounds like a divorce," said Tobias. His voice was grim.

"It may be," I said. "If Regan takes that child, she is divorcing me."

We were interrupted by an uproar in the outer office.

"He's with a client!" Gage's secretary objected.

"I won't keep him a minute but I have to tell him about this. It's important."

The judge pushed his way into the office, an unhappy secretary behind him.

"Ah! *All* the people I wanted to see!" The old man rubbed his palms together in delight. "The most astonishing miracle has happened. I got my memory back."

"It's okay," Gage told his secretary. She departed as we congratulated the judge.

"That's not the miracle." He gave his pockets impatient little pats. "Where did I put that thing? Oh, here it is." He drew out an envelope. "I was putting a stamp on the electric bill this morning and all of a sudden I could see myself plain as day coming out of the post office the morning of the accident, carrying the mail. I noticed that one letter was important, but decided not to open it until I got home, so I laid it and the rest of the mail on the front seat and drove away. At the intersection a fool came shooting out of nowhere and—oh, my!" He clutched his head in both hands. "I wish I didn't remember that part. Anyway"—he shook his hands to dispel the bad memory—"the important thing was the mail. You see, there was a letter from Gage's friend. Here!" He thrust it at me.

I waved it away. "It's not mine. He is Gage's friend and it's addressed to you." Perhaps the judge had lost his mind when he found his memory.

"No, but it's *for* you." He sank into the vacant chair beside me. "I never believed King bought those dining room paintings simply because he liked them. Art wasn't something that interested him. So I invited a fellow Gage was at Yale with to come down from New York and have a look at them. His flight was my gift to you, to make up for the injustice I did you by not pressing King on the issue of his will. The fellow looks dumb as grass and has no social graces whatsoever—"

"Hey!" Gage protested.

"It's true and you know it, but he has an impressive string of credentials in the art world. He claims in that letter that the six paintings are all by artists in the Hudson River School and are of investment quality. As you will see, if you look at what he says"—the judge gestured with the letter, but didn't give it to me—"he would value one of them under twenty thousand but the rest are worth quite a bit more."

"More?" My word came out in a squeak.

"Oh, yes. He also said some watercolors in an upstairs room were worth two thousand each and likely to appreciate because the artist is coming back into vogue, so you ought to have hung on to them. It is unfortunate we didn't get this letter sooner. I don't know what happened to those."

"I have them." I was so numb my mouth hardly moved. "They were Teddy's." I remembered the man in the round spectacles praising one of them. "They are hanging in our living room," I added to Tobias. "The paintings are in those crates under our bed."

"Under our bed?" he repeated. "What if the place burns down before we get home?"

"You'd do well to get them insured right away," the judge suggested.

"Where was the letter all this time?" Gage asked his granddaddy.

"Under the front seat. As soon as my memory came back, I went out to the car to look for it." He pressed one hand to his heart. "I hadn't looked at my poor Caddy until now, and it gave me quite a turn. There was scarcely space for me left in there. I can't believe I survived."

"Tell me about it." From the sick look on Gage's face, I suspected he was thinking about the moment he'd seen the car after the accident.

"But the mail was still there—catalogs, a couple of bills I already paid overdue charges on, and this letter. Whitney—that's the art fellow's name—recommends that you sell the paintings one at a time through an auction house to avoid flooding the market. If you like, he will help you place them for a percentage of the selling price. I'd recommend you let him do that—in New York, preferably, so your sisters don't get wind of it."

He handed me the letter at last. "Keep this in a safe place and do not mention it to your sisters. Don't you say anything to Monique, either, Gage. If Susan and Regan learn about this, they'll be sure to raise a ruckus, though they have no legal grounds for complaint. You all signed a notarized statement accepting Gage's appraiser's valuation of all the contents of the house. Don't you find it interesting that all three appraisers set similar values on those paintings? None of them recognized them for what they are." He beamed like Santa looking over the world on Christmas morning.

I leaned over to Tobias and murmured, "Like Teddy said, God's timing is not our timing, but his is perfect."

He nodded. "Sometimes it is downright amazing."

"If Regan takes us to court, we'll fight her," I told Gage, "if it takes the sale of every one of those paintings to do it."

I smiled, remembering the gentle pressure Judge Brantley had applied to make me ask for them. If I hadn't given in, would he have told me about the art expert back then, before he'd received the appraisal report? No, he'd have tried another ruse. King always said the judge looked like a little lion but he was wily as a fox.

"I wish we didn't have to spend money on court fees," I said as Tobias maneuvered across the rough patch where water had swept across the road the first time I drove that way. "We need to be repairing this road and putting money into the farm."

"We'll do what we have to," he replied. "Children matter more than a road."

"I see no reason why we should tell the children anything yet, do you?"

"Not until we have to."

We rode in silence until he reached the place where my truck had slid into the ditch. He squeezed my hand. "I always thank God when I reach this stretch, both because you didn't go off the other side and because it gave me two unexpected days with you."

"Not that you jumped for joy at the time."

"Only in secret." He lifted his hand and stroked my cheek. "I frequently went up to my room and turned cartwheels."

"Pull over. Let's celebrate."

"Let's go home and celebrate. As long as you aren't working the next few hours, I see no reason why I should."

Hope rose in me later as I started to pick up the children. The day was warm and soft, a breeze dancing in the grass without chilling the air. The forsythia by Jester's grave blazed yellow as the sun. Such a day reminded me that the intention behind the universe is goodness, mercy, and peace. Who could worry on a day like that?

I had forgotten that the devil and his minions don't take good-weather vacations.

When I picked Carrie up at preschool, she cradled her pink backpack in her arms as she ran out to the truck. I started to toss the pack in the back like we always did but she cried, "No! Dat's special!" She held it on her lap all the way up the mountain.

The children changed their clothes and had their snack; then the older ones did their homework. Carrie vanished upstairs. When it was time to feed the animals, I sent Kaitlin upstairs looking for her. I heard Kaitlin demand, "What are you doing?"

That tone of voice warranted investigation on my part.

Carrie was putting all her clothes into her duffel bag, which she had dragged from under their bed. "I'm gonna live with Miss Wegan and be her little girl."

"No, you aren't, silly," said Kaitlin. "You are going to be adopted by Deb'rah and Daddy and live with all of us."

"Nunh-unh!" Carrie's voice grew shrill. "Miss Wegan is gonna 'dopt me. I'll be her little girl. She told me so and she gibbed me dis." Carrie held up one plump arm. She wore a bangle that looked like gold, set with tiny pink stones that looked like gems. She waved it in the sunlight for us to admire.

I took a breath to keep my voice casual. "When did she give you that?"

"Today. She brought ice cream cones to my class and she whispered to me dat we was having de party 'cause she's gonna 'dopt me and I'll be her little girl. She gibbed me de bwacelet and a kiss when she left." She touched her cheek. I saw a faint lipstick print I hadn't noticed before. I didn't know which I wanted to throttle first, Regan or the school staff.

"She's *not* gonna adopt you. Deb'rah's gonna adopt you, aren't you, Deb'rah?" Kaitlin raised indignant eyes to me.

"I certainly hope so, but there is one problem." Where was Tobias when I needed him? I looked out the window and saw him down at the barn, stirring slop for the pigs. That was Eric's job, but Eric had begged to be allowed to plow solo that afternoon. I saw him down in the far field, carefully making an almost straight furrow.

Fear spread over Kaitlin's face like creeping ice. "You don't want us anymore?"

"Of course we want you." I sank to the bed. "The problem is, Carrie had a different birth father from you and Eric. Hers was Mr. Holcomb's brother."

"How do you know?"

"Your mother put it on Carrie's birth certificate and a test showed it was true. That means Mr. Holcomb is her legal guardian, because he's her only living relative."

"We're her living relatives!" Hysteria made Kaitlin's voice shrill. "Eric and me." She pulled Carrie close.

"Of course you are." Why couldn't I remember how thin Kaitlin's skin was when it came to Carrie? "I meant that Mr. Holcomb is her only adult relative. That makes him her legal guardian."

"Carrie is my baby and precious to all of us. Miss Regan can't have her!" Kaitlin clutched Carrie so tight that Carrie squealed.

"Let me go!" She jerked away and clattered down the stairs. "I wanna go to Miss Wegan's!" she called back. "I like her better than you. She has lots of toys and she buys me better dolls and she *doesn't have no pigs*!"

"You silly child!" Before I knew what was happening, Kaitlin darted after her. I got downstairs as they reached the back door. By the time I got to the porch they were near the shed. Kaitlin grabbed Carrie's arm. Carrie started to scream. Kaitlin shouted over the screams, "If you live with her you won't have Eric, or Deb'rah, or Daddy, or me. You won't be my baby anymore."

"I don't care! I'll be Miss Wegan's baby."

Kaitlin gave Carrie's arm a fierce twist and ran toward the farmyard. Carrie streaked after her, uttering piercing shrieks.

I took off after them. I thought Kaitlin was headed to Bray in the paddock. I had sometimes seen her having a private cry there, her face buried in his rough side. Instead, she made for the pigpen at the far side of the paddock.

"No! No! No!" Carrie's legs churned like pistons as she raced after her sister. As I caught up to her she held up her arm, pink and scratched. "She took my bwacelet!"

Down at the pigpen, Tobias was pouring slop into the pigs' trough. The pigs' squeals mingled with Carrie's as they came running toward their next meal.

"Kaitlin, no!" I doubled my speed, but I reached the pigpen fence just in time to see a flash of gold splash into the slop.

"Shoo! Shoo!" I climbed over the fence and tried to reach the trough before the pigs. The ground was mud and filth. My shoes slipped and I fell on my palms and knees. By then the piglets were up to their snouts in dinner.

"What's going on?" Tobias demanded.

"My bwacelet! My pretty bwacelet! Kaitlin fed it to de pigs!" Love, even the love of a possession, triumphs over fear. Carrie threw one leg over the low fence, headed for the trough, and plunged her arm in slop up to the elbow while the three pigs nosed around her.

"Get away from there!" I jerked her up, terrified for her. "Those pigs could bite your arm off thinking it was supper."

Carrie fought to get free. "De pigs is gonna eat my bwacelet!" Tears streamed down her face.

Tobias vaulted the fence. "The pigs won't bite her and they won't eat the bracelet," he told us both. "They're intelligent critters." He took Carrie from me and cradled her against his shoulder as he had Wonder in the river, months before. "Hush, now, hush. You are okay."

"I wants my bwacelet." She hugged his neck, smearing his shirt with slop.

"I want that bracelet, too. I think it's gold." I braced myself against Curlytail and tried to shove him away from the trough. He shoved back, stronger than I was. Our little pink darlings had grown into fifty-pound porkers. Overbalanced, I fell into the trough.

Huff and Puff nudged me with their snouts, splashing slop on my face and hair. I wiped my face with filthy fingers—succeeding only in streaking it. When I got a look at Tobias's expression, I bellowed, "Don't you dare laugh!"

"It's tempting. You are a sight." He set Carrie down outside the fence and waded among the pigs, smacking them with his palm. "Hi! Get away from her. Get away." He offered me a hand and helped me out. The pigs jostled us for space to eat.

"You are one heck of a mess." Tobias rubbed my face and hair with the tail of his shirt. I swatted him away.

"Here!" Kaitlin climbed the fence holding a rake with wide tines. Two, three times she raked while the pigs snuffled around her and complained about their disrupted dinner. On her fourth pass the rake brought up a circlet of gold.

"Good job!" Tobias praised. "That was quick thinking." He gave her a hug.

She wiped the bracelet on her shirt and shoved it over Carrie's hand. "Sorry."

Carrie wrinkled her nose. "You stink, I stink, Tobias stinks, and Deb'rah stinks most of all. Phee-eew!" She sounded just like Regan.

"You little ingrate!" I raged. "We are all are filthy because of that bracelet. The least you could say is 'thank you.'"

She pressed her lips together and shook her head.

"I am furious with my sister," I told Tobias as he carried Carrie to the house.

"Who is your sister?" Kaitlin asked from a few paces behind us.

"Regan. If she hadn't given Carrie that bracelet—"

"I didn't know Miss Regan was your sister. Is she your little sister?"

"No, she's my big sister. I am the little sister in my family." I gently touched Carrie's cheek. "Big sisters can be hard on little ones sometimes, can't they?"

"Yes, ma'am," Carrie said with a sniffle. She gave Kaitlin a teary glare.

I commandeered the bathroom for the three of us and got us all bathed and shampooed. The girls ate supper early and I let Carrie watch a movie until her bedtime. Kaitlin pulled a book of Cherokee stories off Tobias's shelf. Nobody but Eric felt like doing homework that evening. Tobias worked with him on math.

After Carrie had gone to bed, I put my arms around Kaitlin's thin shoulders. "Carrie didn't mean it when she said she likes Regan better than you. She really didn't."

Kaitlin looked at me with fear-stricken eyes. She was learning, as I had, that caring for self-centered people can be a painful, thankless task, but that doesn't keep us from loving them. "You won't let them take her, will you?"

"I will do everything in my power to keep it from happening." She slept that night with both arms around Carrie.

I tried to call Regan after the girls went to bed, but she didn't answer—probably because she saw on her caller ID that it was me.

I called the preschool director at home. We'd been friends since first grade.

"I understand Regan came to Carrie's class today. I left a note saying not to let Regan anywhere near Carrie." I struggled to keep my voice reasonable and calm.

"Your note said not to let anybody take Carrie. Regan called around noon and said she was picking her up today, and when I told her about the note, she was real nice about it—said you all are having a little sisterly spat, so you are mad at her and not letting her see Carrie."

"Out of spite? Did she say that?"

"I think she did mention spite."

"It's a lot more than that. Tobias and I are planning to adopt Carrie and her siblings, but Regan has decided she wants to adopt Carrie—and only Carrie—instead. We object to splitting up the family, so the case will most likely end up in court."

"Whoa! I wish you'd told us all that. When she asked if she could bring an afternoon ice cream party to Carrie's class, I didn't think it would hurt anything."

"She managed to whisper to Carrie that she's going to adopt her and give her all the cookies and pretty dresses she wants, and she gave her a bracelet that I think is gold."

"I had no idea."

"It's not your fault. I should have fully explained the situation to you. For the foreseeable future, could you make sure Regan does not go to Carrie's class?"

"I'll try, but she is on the board of the college, remember. She pretty much goes where she wants to."

We were about to go upstairs to bed when Carrie came down, her duffel bag going *bump, bump, bump* behind her. "What are you doing?" Tobias asked.

"I'm going to Miss Wegan's." Her little mouth was firm with determination. The bracelet gleamed on her arm.

"It's a long walk, and pretty dark outside." He took her onto the front porch. "Do you think you can walk that far tonight?"

She backed up a step. "Could you take me, please?"

"Let's talk, okay?" He took her to the couch and held her on his lap. "Deborah and I know you have a lot of fun at Miss Regan's, and we don't ever want to stop you from going to visit. However, you, Kaitlin, and Eric are a family and you belong together. Kaitlin has loved you and taken care of you all your life, and if you were to leave her, she would be very sad. Do you understand that?"

"She can come to Miss Wegan's."

"No, Kaitlin is going to stay here. Miss Regan is sad because she never had a little girl, so she wants you to be her little girl, but Deborah and I think you would be happier here with Kaitlin and Eric as you grow up. Don't you?"

She thought it over. "No, sir. I t'ink I would be happier at Miss Wegan's. I don't get dirty dere and I don't have to work."

"Work teaches you things you will need to know when you grow up."

"Does Miss Wegan know how to feed pigs and wash dishes?" Tobias looked to me for an answer to that.

"No," I admitted. "She knows how to do other things."

"I wanna learn to do uvver t'ings, too."

He stood. "We can talk about this some more tomorrow. You can't go anywhere tonight, so let me carry you back to bed."

As I was brushing my hair, Tobias came to stand behind me, caressing my shoulder with one hand. I put my hand over his. I couldn't seem to get enough of touching him now that I had the right.

He spoke to my reflection in the mirror. "Don't bite my head off for saying this, but I am beginning to wonder if Regan wouldn't be better for Carrie than we would."

"Don't be silly. Regan would spoil her rotten. She'd let Carrie sit on a couch eating cookies and watching television all day."

To my astonishment, I heard him defend the witch. "I don't think she would. Carrie wants to be a princess, just as Regan is a princess, and princesses are beautiful. To be beautiful, you have to take care of your body."

He had a point there. Regan took better care of her body than I did, and I was the nurse who knew all the health reasons for doing so.

"Carrie by nature is self-centered," he went on, "and no matter how you raise a child, you can't change its nature. I'm afraid we'll spend our lives butting heads with her, trying to make her into a hardworking child who is kind and thoughtful of others, when she won't want to be hardworking, kind, and thoughtful of others. She'll fight us every inch of the way. But I suspect that self-centered people who want to be princes and princesses are the ones who benefit most from the kind of upbringing Regan would give her. The Regan you relate to is not the Regan other people see. I've heard other people talk about her. They adore her. She's beautiful, kind, hardworking on others' behalf, and generous."

"She *pretends* to be all those things because she learned from Mother that those are what a princess should be. It's only a veneer."

"My point exactly. Some people need veneers. Maybe we all do at times, but self-centered people need a permanent veneer. Veneers present an attractive appearance to the world. Regan couldn't make Carrie kind and loving any more than we could, but she would teach Carrie to *act* polite, kind, hardworking, generous, and gracious even when she doesn't feel like it, because that's the way a princess should act. She already did more for the child's manners in a week than we've done in months. Did you hear her say 'please' and 'yes, sir' tonight?"

I flung down my brush. "We can't give Carrie to Regan! It would break Kaitlin's heart. Besides, I don't think Carrie would be a better person for growing up with Regan, even if she would be a nicer one in public."

Tobias escorted me to bed and turned out the light. "Then we'll do the best we can and pray that Carrie turns out all right. Ultimately, that's all any parents can do."

\*　　\*　　\*

Breakfast was a stormy affair. Carrie wanted to take her duffel to preschool in case Miss Regan came to get her.

Eric—who had been clued in by Kaitlin—informed her, "You are part of our family whether you like it or not, so get over it."

Carrie whimpered. Kaitlin stormed at Eric, "Don't yell at my baby."

I asked Carrie to please leave the bracelet at home so she wouldn't lose it.

Carrie pitched a fit. I decided I didn't care if she lost it and let her wear it.

As Tobias and I stepped out on the porch for a good-bye kiss, he whispered, "Remind me again why we wanted to be parents?"

I was on my way to see a patient when I got a surprising call. "Hey. It's Regan. Don't hang up."

Her voice was so odd, I wouldn't have recognized it.

"Do you have a cold?"

"No, I've been crying all night. I look a mess."

"Am I supposed to ask why?"

"Because Holcomb is furious with me. I told him what I did yesterday, and he—I've never seen him so angry. He said I was cruel to you when I went to the school behind your back, and that the important thing is not what you want or he wants or what I want for Carrie, but what God wants, because that will be what's best for the child. He said if I really love Carrie, I will want what's best for her, too, and not just what I want. I was livid at first, but after thinking about it most of the night, I know he's right. Will you forgive me? I promise not to go back to the school without your permission. It was a dumb, selfish thing to do."

It took me a minute to respond. First I had to decide this was really my sister. Second, I had to admit that Regan's goodness might go deeper than her veneer.

"Holcomb is a wise man," I finally managed. "I wish we knew what's best for all the children. If it were only a matter of Carrie, I would at least consider letting you have her, but Kaitlin loves that child. She has practically raised her, and I can't watch Kaitlin endure more suffering than she's already been through. I think she'd die if we separated them."

"Well, sweetie, Holcomb says we aren't going to fight you for Carrie, because that would set all the children a horrible example. I know, though, that he would like to raise his brother's little girl, so I'm going to pray that God will show us a good way out of this mess. Will you pray, too?"

"So long as you aren't just telling God what you want to happen."

She sighed. "I wish I could, but Holcomb won't let me. Do me one favor, though. Please don't make Carrie feed the pigs."

"If you promise not to send her home with any more jewelry. I'll tell you someday about the mess we had yesterday when Kaitlin threw the bracelet in the pigs' trough and we all got filthy trying to retrieve it. You might get a laugh out of it. I might even get a laugh out of it by then. I've got to run right now, though. I'm going to see a patient."

I hung up thinking if we weren't careful, Regan and I might learn to like each other.

Before ten I got a call from Kaitlin's school. "Kaitlin's been feeling sick. She seldom complains, so I think you ought to come get her. She may have a bug."

*A bug named Carrie*, I thought as I arranged for another nurse to finish the rest of the day's visits.

Kaitlin ran to me and buried her face against my shoulder. "I want to go home, Mama. My stomach hurts."

I wrapped her in a big hug. That was the first time she'd

ever called me Mama, and it warmed me all over. I kept one arm around her as I led her to the SUV. She slid all the way over on the seat close to me and fastened the center seat belt around her. "Do you feel real sick?" I asked. "Like you are going to throw up?"

"No, I just need to be with you." She rode home with her head against my arm. "Is Carrie going away?" she asked in a small voice as we pulled into Jones Farm Road.

I sighed. "Not if we can help it, honey. Your daddy and I will fight my sister for her if we have to." I wouldn't put too much faith in Regan's recent conversion until she'd had a few days to think it over.

Kaitlin didn't say another word on our way home.

Tobias came from the greenhouse when he heard us drive in. "What's wrong?"

"Kaitlin's under the weather. Her eyes are feverish but her forehead isn't hot. I think she just needs a little tender loving care."

"You've come to the right place," he told her. "Deborah's good at TLC. She's a Friday's child, loving and giving." He lifted Kaitlin as easily as if she'd been Wonder.

"What do you mean?" she asked him.

"You don't know the old Mother Goose rhyme? 'Monday's child is fair of face, Tuesday's child is full of grace . . .'" He recited the whole thing while he carried her into the house.

"What are you?" she asked.

"I'm a Saturday's child. I work hard for a living."

"What am I?"

"Shall we see? I'll bet we could find out on the computer."

Sure enough he pulled up a program that could tell the day of the week you were born if you fed in your birth date. "You are a Friday's child, too," he told her, "like Deborah."

She gave me a weak smile over his shoulder, for she sat on his lap at the computer. "What are Carrie and Eric?"

I didn't believe in nursery rhyme horoscopes but was not surprised that Carrie was born on Monday. "Eric is a Thursday's child," Tobias told us. "He has far to go."

"Will he go off and leave us?" Kaitlin's eyes were shadowed with worry.

"Not in Wonder's foreseeable future," I promised her.

Tobias stood and let her slide to the ground. "When I used to get sick, my mother made me cinnamon toast and warm, milky tea. How does that sound?"

She gave him a faint smile. "Good."

When we were at the table with cinnamon toast and tea, she confided, "At school I kept thinking about the Forever Boy. I read that story last night, and there was part of the story you didn't tell us, Daddy. In the story in the book, the Forever Boy told the Nunnehi he couldn't go with them and stay young forever, because his uncle and his parents would miss him. But the Nunnehi said they would ask the Great Spirit to send a dream to his parents so they would know he was all right. Then the Forever Boy decided it would be all right if he went to live with the Little People."

"I guess I forgot that part," Tobias conceded.

"But wouldn't his family still miss him, even if they knew why he went and where he was? Carrie is like the Forever Boy. She wants to go live somewhere else, but I would always miss her very much, even if I knew why she went and where she was. That's what I was thinking about in school when my stomach got so tight and squirmy that I wanted to come home."

I smoothed damp hair away from Kaitlin's eyes. No child should have to wrestle with such enormous issues. "You can always come home if you need to, honey."

She nodded. "I know. I couldn't—before." That was the closest she ever came to criticizing Lena.

I rubbed her back. "Do you feel better now?"

"A little. But in the truck, when you said you all would fight your sister for Carrie, it made me think some more." She leaned forward on her sharp little elbows, her expression earnest. "If Mr. Holcomb's brother was Carrie's daddy, he's her uncle, right?"

"Right." We both nodded.

"And Miss Regan is your sister, so she's our aunt." She swallowed hard. "So if they adopted Carrie, she *wouldn't* be like the Forever Boy. She wouldn't go far away, and she'd *still* be in our family. And uncles are supposed to raise Cherokee children. That's why we came here in the first place, right?"

"Right." Tobias's voice was cautious. I wondered if he, too, was holding his breath as Kaitlin argued herself to an unbelievable conclusion.

"Carrie likes it better over there than here, so maybe"—she swallowed again and struggled to get the words out—"maybe we ought *not* fight them to keep her." She dropped her head on her folded arms. I couldn't tell if she was weeping or simply exhausted from the struggle.

"Oh, honey! You'd miss her terribly." I smoothed her bumpy braids.

She lifted her face to us and her eyes swam with tears. "Yes, but if we love her, I think"—she stopped to take a deep breath of courage—"I think we should let her go."

That's as far as logic could take her. She laid down her head and wept.

Tobias picked her up and carried her to the couch, where he held her on his lap. As she rested her head against his shoulder, he murmured, "You are the bravest person I know."

She shook her head. "I'm not brave at all. But Carrie . . . Carrie . . ." She turned in his arms and sobbed against his chest—not as if her heart would break, but as if it had already split in two. When her sobs lessened, I wiped her face with a damp cloth. Slowly she grew calm.

Poor little mite, she wasn't pretty at the best of times and at the moment her face was red and splotchy with tears, but a light shone from her eyes that I'd swear was holy.

"We'd see her sometimes," she said, as if trying to convince us. She had to gulp between phrases, but gradually her voice grew confident. "And next year she'll be at my school. And we can invite them over to eat, and they can invite us over to eat, and she can come for some weekends. Maybe we could even go on vacation together, the whole family, to somewhere like Disney World someday. That could be fun." She managed a tremulous smile.

For the rest of my life, my standard of courage would be Kaitlin's smile.

"Are you sure?" Tobias asked. "Do you want time to think it over?"

"No. Too much thinking makes me sick. I think we ought to just do it."

I cleared my throat. "Your idea about a trip to Disney World together sounds like fun. Shall we plan that for this summer?"


I have a sketchbook of drawings I made during our week at Disney World. We went as soon as school was out. Lucy and Pete came to keep the farm. I hated to impose on them, but Lucy reminded me, "I grew up here. It's coming home—except the house is prettier with your furniture in it and tidier now that you've stopped Tobe from leaving stuff all over the yard. The best thing you've done, though, is pave that road. Daddy always meant to, but he never got around to doing it."

We took Damien with us as his high school graduation present and to give Eric somebody to pal around with. We scarcely saw them the whole week. They were, in Eric's words, "too old to hang around with kids." Eric loves my sketch of a young heron and a young hawk riding the Rock 'n' Roller Coaster, beaks wide open and wings held high.

Kaitlin likes one of two eagles riding on the Astro Orbiter with three little fledglings. One of the eagles carries a big cigar. She told me earnestly, "I would never have imagined that Uncle Holcomb would enjoy Disney World so much. He's *fun*!"

Wonder's favorite is three little princesses in front of Cinderella's castle. Oh, yes, Wonder came along. On the strength of her Christmas visit, she was our Disney World docent. And while she said she was "disgusted" that Monique and Gage hadn't invited her on their honeymoon that week, she confided to me, "Actually, I'd radder go to Disney World than old Noo-ark City any day."

My own favorite sketch from our vacation is of two big princesses and three small princesses riding through It's a Small World. Regan and I discovered that spring that we do live in a small world, and we need everybody in it—even people who are different from us. She is no longer trying to make a cornstalk with silk out of me, and I no longer regret that she's not a potato. Slowly, through our children, we are learning what it means to be family.

On our last night at Disney World, Regan said, "This has been such fun, I think we ought to get the whole family together more often. Why don't we do Thanksgiving dinner at your place and I'll have everybody over for Christmas? The grown-ups can eat at Mother's table, and I'll set up a princess table for the little girls in the den. I'll even get three crowns."

"You'd better buy four," I told her.

She looked puzzled, then her eyes widened. "Really?"

I nodded. I had been hesitant to tell her our news, afraid she'd get weepy and jealous, but she wrapped me in a big embrace.

"When?"

"A couple of weeks before Christmas."

"Does Tobias know?"

"Oh, yes."

The night before we left for vacation, while we were getting ready for bed, I had handed him a sketch I had drawn that afternoon. It showed the big nest with the bluebird tucked against the eagle's breast, a fledgling heron and a small wren fast asleep beside them. The nest also held a small Christmas tree and, under the tree, one blue egg.

He studied it, then gave a choked cry of joy. "Are you sure?"

I caught his hand to my cheek. "I'm a nurse, remember? Of course I'm sure."

He pulled me close. "No more lonely bluebirds?"

"No more lonely bluebirds. This bluebird soars with the eagle."

"What will our baby be?"

"A Christmas miracle—a blend of Cherokee, Ingram, and MacAllester."

He kissed my hair, then drew me close. "Perhaps the day it is born, some of the smoke over the Great Smoky Mountains will disappear."

# Author's Thanks

One of the perks of being a writer is getting to learn new things. For this book, I was privileged to study Cherokee history. I especially thank Claudia Oakes, executive director of the Chieftains Museum in Rome, Georgia, for a private tour of that gracious former home of Cherokee leader Major Ridge, and for new insights into Georgia's history. I would encourage readers to visit Cherokee sites in North Georgia—visit and weep.

Ms. Oakes also steered me to *Trail of Tears: The Rise and Fall of the Cherokee Nation*, by John Ehle (New York: Anchor Books, 1988), which became my primary written source for this book.

Cherokee stories that Tobias Jones tells have been paraphrased from several sources, but especially *Long-Ago Stories of the Eastern Cherokee*, by Lloyd Arneach (Charleston: History Press, 2008) and *The Origin of the Milky Way and Other Living Stories of the Cherokee*, collected and edited by Barbara R. Duncan (Chapel Hill: University of North Carolina Press, 2008).

Nurses Lana Turner and Mary Duncan helped me with Teensie's medical procedures; Emi Sprinkle, licensed professional counselor, explained likely procedures following Regan's suicide attempt; and two generous women—Stacey Childers and Coco Ihle—each placed a winning bid to have her name in this book. In that way, they helped abused children and supported the Forensic Lab Project. Their namesake characters, however, are not based on the women but came from the ether whence all characters come.

As always, thanks to my agent, Nancy Yost, for continuing to believe in me, and most of all to the invisible presence behind this book, editor Ellen Edwards, who saw what I wanted to say when I failed to say it. Ellen, you bring out the best in me.

Photo by Byers Studio

**Patricia Sprinkle** is the author of three previous novels, *The Remember Box*, *Carley's Song*, and *Hold Up the Sky*, as well as bestselling mysteries and several nonfiction books. Sprinkle writes novels drawn from her own Southern roots, chronicling the lives of women in the contemporary South. In addition to writing, she is active in organizations that serve neglected, deprived, and abused children. Last fall she combined her interests of writing and children to teach creative writing to Dalit children in Kerala, India, for three weeks. She and her husband have two grown sons and live in Smyrna, Georgia, where she enjoys reading, gardening, and doing nothing. You can visit her at www.patriciasprinkle.com.

# Friday's Daughter

## PATRICIA SPRINKLE

This Conversation Guide is intended to enrich the
individual reading experience, as well as encourage us
to explore these topics together—because books,
and life, are meant for sharing.

# A CONVERSATION
# WITH PATRICIA SPRINKLE

*Q. What inspired you to write* Friday's Daughter?

A. The fact that many people permit themselves to get stuck in a life situation and presume that can never change. At the beginning of this book a number of characters are "stuck": Monique is stuck dating men who aren't good for her; Regan is stuck in a self-centered lifestyle; Teensie is stuck in a pattern of always putting family ahead of her own life and needs; her family and Tobias are stuck in prejudice that goes back two hundred years. The story explores what happens to everyone when Teensie is willing to get unstuck—which she discovers can be a painful but rewarding experience.

*Q. As a Northerner, I find* Friday's Daughter *very "Southern," but I can't quite identify why. Can you help me out?*

A. It takes place in Georgia, for one thing. It deals with a uniquely Southern Indian situation in which a highly civilized people were cast out of their land to permit white people to take it. It is rural rather than urban, and it has all the hallmarks of Southern literature in which family, faith, history, and place all become characters in the story.

*Q. There's a* King Lear *quality to the novel. How deliberate was that?*

A. When I began, I thought it would have more to do with *King Lear* than it actually does. Like *King Lear*, it deals with a king and his three daughters, the youngest of whom has demonstrated more love than the other two and gets less inheritance than she should have. However, *Lear* focuses on the tragedy of the king who disinherits his daughter, while this book focuses on the youngest daughter and how she survives and even thrives after that experience.

*Q. Many novels written for women dramatize sister relationships that are very close and loving. One of my favorite aspects of your novel is that Regan, Susan, and Teensie don't get along—their values and personalities clash at every turn. I enjoyed the tension among them, and their occasional efforts to overcome their differences. Why did you particularly want to explore this kind of sister relationship?*

A. I think it's more realistic. I have a sister, and there are many things we don't agree on, but as Tobias says in the story, God gives us family as a laboratory to learn to get along with and love people who are different from us, without making them just like us. This process doesn't end when we are adults—in many ways it begins then. That's what Teensie and her sisters discover as the older sisters have to deal with a maturing Teensie.

Q. *There are a number of lousy parents in this novel. King betrays Teensie by denying her the inheritance he promised. Susan fails to give Monique the kind of love she craves. Lena neglects and abandons her three children by falling into alcoholism and early death. Even Tobias allows his son to slip away without putting up much of a fight. Did you consciously set out to explore the consequences of bad parenting, or did that just creep into the novel?*

A. I hadn't realized that was a theme in the book until you brought it up, and I don't even think most of these are bad parents; they are, however, often self-absorbed, blind, and deaf. King, like many parents, felt that his work was more important than his children. Susan and Albert decided what was "best" for Monique without taking her personality into account. Tobias decided his son should be with his mother without ever asking Brandon what he wanted. Lena put her own sorrows and addiction ahead of her children's needs. Such choices are chronic in our society. We neither listen to children nor see them as little people who already have preferences, opinions, needs, and a set nature that will mature as they grow.

I feel that social neglect of children is reflected in everything from the architecture of our homes (huge master bedrooms, tiny children's rooms) and schools (no windows) to the way government allocates funds. Parents give children too many activities and too many possessions, but fail to see them and hear them as real and unique human beings. So, without meaning to, I guess I did climb on a soapbox in this story, and through Gage, Monique, Teensie, Tobias as he changes, and his sister, Lucy, and her husband, Pete, try to give a picture of better parenting.

Q. In our "me-driven" society, Teensie's need to help, and the significant self-sacrifices she makes to do so, might strike some people as old-fashioned and self-defeating, or—at the other extreme—as absolutely necessary to hold together the fabric of society. Is there a line between the two extremes, and where do you think it lies? Do you think we need to recalibrate where contemporary society places that line?

A. One blindness of the contemporary "me-driven" society is to think it is the first. Rome in the days of the emperors, England during the Regency period, France just before the Revolution, and America in the late nineteenth century are a few other examples of societies in which affluent people sought their own pleasures rather than the good of others. The social pendulum swings back and forth. We don't have to recalibrate society; it adjusts itself. Already some of the wealthiest in our society are beginning to discover that as they look for ways to share their wealth responsibly.

However, as a woman of faith, I think there are a few givens in the universe. One of those is that people were created both to help one another and to accept help from others. Genesis says, "It is not good for a human to be alone." What Teensie has not discovered when the book opens is how to distinguish between people who genuinely need help and those who simply enjoy being waited on. Just as it is not good for a child if the parent does everything for the child, so it is not good for King and Regan if Teensie waits on them. As Coco points out, our driving motivation for helping anyone ought to be what is truly best for the other person.

*Q. You give one of your main characters, Tobias, a Cherokee background and you weave several colorful Cherokee stories into the narrative. What role do you intend this background to play in the novel, and can you say a few words about the influence of Cherokee culture in this area of the South?*

A. So far, the Cherokee culture has little influence even in the parts of Georgia where the Cherokee once lived. Only recently has the "official" Trail of Tears been expanded to include sites where the Cherokee were rounded up in Georgia to begin their journey. Yet North Georgia once belonged to the Cherokee. I hope this novel will help make people aware of the rich heritage of the tribe and its rightful place in Southern history. As I try to illustrate, Cherokee folktales tend to urge people to live in peace and harmony with one another and with nature, which I think we all need to hear.

*Q. You have more energy that any woman I know, and you seem always willing to squeeze in some other project or take on some new job that needs to get done. What inspires you to keep going and doing? And how do you decide when it's time to say "no"?*

A. Until 1975 I was a woman who did far too much. Almost anytime somebody needed something done, I said "yes." In the next fourteen years, I felt God put me in a school of the spirit to learn how to focus my life not simply on important things to do, but on those things that were uniquely important for *me* to do. My nonfiction book *Women Who Do Too Much* was one fruit of that experience. For years I have prayerfully set annual and monthly goals in several categories— writing, personal life, family life, church and community life.

I take on only things that are consistent with those goals, and find it easy to say "no" to requests for help that aren't part of those goals. My focus changes, however, as seasons of my life change. For three years I worked on a master's degree while I wrote. At the moment I am often busy helping my father and our grandsons. I work as an advocate and supporter of children who are abused and neglected. And I write. That is, basically, all I do. I find that while I may sometimes be even busier than I was when I was trying to do everything that came my way, I am not as tired, because I am going with the flow of what God wants me to be doing. I have also learned to ask for help when I need it—and to recognize that I am not indispensable. A by-product of focusing my attention like a laser beam only on tasks I personally am called to do is that I have time when I can sit on my screened porch and do nothing without feeling guilty.

*Q. You've written in many different genres—articles, stories, essays, plays, full-length nonfiction books, and novels. Which do you number among your most satisfying accomplishments?*

A. The most satisfying for me are books, articles, or poems that touch other lives in a meaningful way. One of my most satisfying letters said, "Reading your MacLaren mysteries, I laughed my way through chemotherapy." To help people escape difficult situations for even a few short hours is very satisfying. I also love it when I can be a conduit through which some piece of truth reaches a reader. Often what touches them is a truth I didn't even know until I began to work with the piece. So the other satisfying part of writing has been what I have learned about myself and about life through the process of pulling characters from the ether and walking with them through a story.

*Q. Books about places to go and things to do before you die are currently popular. Are there places to go and things to do that you are nurturing right now, hoping that they'll eventually come to pass? Do some of them include more writing projects?*

A. As I finish this book, I am about to set out for India to teach creative writing for three weeks to middle school students who belong to the Dalit people, formerly called the Untouchables. My hope is that one or more of the students will feel a call to write, and will open their lives and imaginations in such a way that through their writing, Dalits can be seen as human beings who deserve respect and attention. This has been a dream of mine for many years, which ripened in the last months. Perhaps I will even get to see the Himalayas while I'm there. I may get a book out of the trip. If not, I still have a few in my head that won't let me alone. I stand on the threshold of a great adventure with no idea what the next year will bring.

# QUESTIONS FOR DISCUSSION

1. Teensie has spent many years caring for one ailing family member after another. Now she finds herself in middle age, having deferred her own life and professional development and without a family of her own. How common is her situation? These days, are middle-aged children giving up more of their own lives to care for their long-lived parents? Do you see Teensie's sacrifice as loving and giving or as ill-considered and self-defeating?

2. Teensie and her sisters, Regan and Susan, have very different values and personalities, and they clash constantly. What did you enjoy most about Patricia Sprinkle's depiction of their relationships? How realistic do you think it is? Do you think, as the author suggests, that it's possible for sisters to grow closer and more loving without changing the essential nature of who they are?

3. The three sisters inherit equal parts of their father's estate and immediately start claiming their shares and squabbling over who gets what. Do you have stories about how your own family, or families you know, acted when they inherited a portion of an estate?

4. What do you think of Teensie and Tobias's decision to assume guardianship of the three children and move in together to care for them, especially considering that each is secretly attracted to the other?

5. What would you do if you found yourself in Teensie's situation at the beginning of the book—middle-aged, unemployed, recently denied the full inheritance you were expecting, and about to lose your home? Which of her choices do you think are good ones and which are not so wise?

6. Discuss the men in this novel. Did you find them believable and realistic? Which of the male characters would you like to spend time with?

7. Who's your favorite character, and what do you like about him or her?

8. The author hints that Teensie's happy ending is part of God's plan, unfolding with his perfect timing. Is that how you see the end?

9. Teensie has spent her whole life as part of her small town's "aristocracy," but her father's death and her changed economic circumstances put that standing in jeopardy. Discuss how a person's social class can rise and fall and rise again, depending on that person's economic situation. In today's culture, what do you think determines one's social class?

10. Teensie and the children love listening to Tobias tell Cherokee stories, and their trip to see the "moonbow" is magical. What do you think makes this Cherokee lore so special to them?